WILLIAM HOPE HODGSON'S

NIGHT LANDS

Volume I, Eternal Love

WILLIAM HOPE HODGSON'S

NIGHT LANDS

Volume I, Eternal Love

Edited by
Andy W. Robertson

BETANCOURT
& COMPANY
Doylestown, Pennsylvania

William Hope Hodgson's
THE NIGHT LANDS
Volume I, Eternal Love
A publication of
Betancourt & Company, Publishers
P.O. Box 301
Holicong, PA 18928-0301

www.wildsidepress.com

FIRST EDITION

Table of Contents

Introduction

Andy W. Robertson

In composing this book, I have met with many whom, as *The Night Land* has it, "To know was to love." I can not possibly thank them all: but I will mention three.

The first is my friend and mentor, David Pringle, with whom I have worked on *Interzone* magazine for the past seventeen years. David's kindness, optimism, and cheerfulness enrich everyone who meets him.

The second is my co-editor Nigel Brown, an unfailing source of advice and support.

The third is one of the writers here, Nigel Atkinson.

It may seem odd that I select a single writer out of the many who have contributed to this project, but Nigel stands in a special place. In 1999 I started the Night Land website. At that time, my intention was simply to collect all the pictures, documents and essays that had ever been written concerning the Night Land in one place. The possibility of writing new fiction seemed distant, improbable.

But these doubts were ended when I received Nigel's first story, "An Exhalation of Butterflies," collected within these pages. It was this work that first set the whole tone of this anthology. Without him, the many stories that followed (and that are still appearing) would never have been written.

With this book, the first part of our *Night Lands* project is complete.

It is our intention to collect further books, and indeed to encourage a whole sub-genre of fiction centered around Hodgson's great strange work.

If you wish to participate, we may be contacted via the Night Lands website, which is at

http://home.clara.net/andywrobertson/nightmap.html

– Andy Robertson

What Visions I Saw. . . .

John C. Wright

In the life of every bookish person, there are a few favored books, read in the golden time of youth, that come to dwell in the imagination forever. The vividness of images, the strength of heroes, the beauty of heroines, the strangeness and wonder of the settings, are burned into the heart: every other tale read after is compared to these golden tales.

I had graduated college, and was past the age when the book of gold is found, and I was lamenting that I was, perhaps, too old and jaded to meet the wonders of youth again, when a friend recommended Hodgson's *Night Lands* to me. I had told him once of a fantasy I was writing, called Nigh-Forgotten Sun (the unfinished manuscript still exists), and my friend thought that I was consciously copying the theme of Hodgson's story: he was amazed that I had never heard of the book, since it was exactly suited to my own writing, both in style and theme.

So I read volume one of the Ballantine edition edited by Lin Carter. I found the golden time of youthful wonder was not past. What visions I saw!

At the time, poor as a church mouse (or, I should say,

rather, poor as a law student) I had no resources to find whether the second volume was still in print. In the days before the Internet, libraries and used bookstores did not maintain inventory lists where a poor student could find them.

And so this antique tale, when I had reached the point where the nameless narrator stands before the darkened ruins of the Lesser Redoubt, which he endured much toil, heartache, terror and incalculable dangers to reach, instead of finding his love, his spirit senses, somewhere hidden in the metal structure, dread and fell presences waiting to destroy him. His beloved, and all her people, her culture, her world, have been wiped out. At that cliffhanger I was left, and I did not know if any copy of the ending of the tale survived.

To me it seemed as if I had found an antique sea-chest in an attic, or washed ashore from the wrack of Atlantis, containing only one half of a manuscript, and that I had no hope of ever finding the finish of the tale.

How precious that dog-eared paperback was to me! In the opening paragraphs of the first chapter, the narrator is speaking casually to Mirdath the Beautiful, a maiden of the gentry of the English rural countryside. A more comfortable and bucolic setting cannot be imagined. Then, when he says, 'It is an elf night; the Towers of Slumber rise' she answers by speaking of the Moon-Garden, the City of Twilight, and the Bird with the Painted Head.

By that word she reveals that she is like him: a soul that is more than mortal, that has lived other lives in other cycles of reincarnation, dimly half-forgotten.

She and he are both travelers from moon-lit elfin lands or empires of cloudy nightmare, and they hail from places far beyond the little fields we know, older than human history: they have seen the light of other suns, other days. They dance to music we cannot hear. No one of their own time will understand them.

I cannot express how eerie this seemed to me, how pregnant with secret promise. What reader of fantastic fiction has not seemed, to himself at least, to be a changeling like this, someone who is more at home in stranger worlds than the mundane one around us? As a man who is out of tune with his own time (surely, dear reader, that is seen in the way I express my thought to you) I found delight to think that there might be, for me, too, a Mirdath the Beautiful awaiting.

Few books can match the strange promise of those hints: The Night Lands overmatches it. In chapter two our narrator, mad with grief and loss, recovers memories from uncounted millions of years in the remotest future, long after the sun is dead, and he gazes from the embrasures of the Last Redoubt of Man upon the wonders and horrors of the Night Land: he sees the dim fires burning in the Giant's Kilns; the single visible eye of the Southeastern Watcher shines from its hulking silhouette of its grim, huge head, unblinking; the Night-Hounds cry out, and the Silent Ones do not, and the doors of the House of Silence, in all eternity, have never closed.

Nothing I have ever read before or since contains such a mood of pure unearthliness. Wraiths and Dark Lords and devils from fantasy stories seem quaint and old-fashioned, and are more likely to invoke nostalgia rather than awe; aliens from science fiction stories share our laws of nature, and come from our universe. The inhuman presences and monsters of the Night Land, on the other hand, are cloaked in impenetrable mystery.

The stilted and archaic language, I find no fault with. Perhaps I am the only reader who does not. A language less formal and gravid might not serve to capture the dark, heavy, grim and gothic majesty of the piece. I know my friend Mr. Stoddard has made a brave attempt in this direction, but, for my taste, more might be lost than gained by modernizing the tongue.

Finally, after many years of wondering and waiting, I found the second volume. An archeologist finding the lost dialogs of Aristotle, the eighth book of Apollonius, or the missing ending to the epic of Lucretius could not know greater triumph than I did.

Here I met Mirdath the Beautiful, reincarnated as Naani, a daughter of the Lesser Redoubt. Many other readers find fault with her: let them. She is precious to me. I can think of no other character possessing her quirks, her cleverness, her playful heedlessness, her unparalleled bravery. She is self-sacrificing without being a martyr, shows both spirit and fortitude that would break any lesser lass, she is braver than a man and yet still humble and demure.

If I sound like a man infatuated, let this be a testament to the skill of Hodgson's writing. Keep your joyless Galadriel, your spiteful Titania, your lascivious Helen, your treacherous Guinevere and deadly Clytemnestra, your cunning Penelope, your absurd Xena: to match her for charm, perhaps you can hold up Nausicaa or Miranda as her equals; to match her for courage and endurance, who is there?

The love-story that C.S. Lewis so casually dismisses as a fatuous erotic interest, I thought was almost Promethean in its power. Here is a man who reaches across a billion years of time, and braves the unthinkable dangers of the Night, to save the woman who is his own true love, because he hears in his mind the whisper of her plea for help, as if in a dream. By the mysterious aetheric sympathy they share, from far-off, he hears her voice in the night, and he knows her. Based only on that whisper, and his hope, into the eternal darkness, like Orpheus, he goes. (The only other story that is even close in its scope and power is "At the Eschaton" by Charles Sheffield, appearing in the Far Futures anthology. With apologies to Sheffield, I found the short story more striking than the novel-version). Neither all the aeons of eternity, nor all the darkness and horror of the hopeless night, nor even death itself, can part the lovers.

The Victorianisms other readers find galling, I find as refreshing as an oasis in a wasteland of ash. The way sex is handled in *Stranger in a Strange Land* or even *Left Hand of Darkness* is the norm I was to meet, over and over again, unchanged, unchallenged, unquestioned, in every story I found in my childhood. The casual fornications James Bond and Captain Kirk were presented as normal, their penismanship as praiseworthy. Self-control, chastity, romance, marriage, family, even though they are the most normal things in the world (I am tempted to say, the only normal things in the world) were dismissed by all modern writers as psychopathologies of the Dark Ages.

Perhaps when Heinlein first wrote the idea of having a sloppy sex-life might seem boldly non-conformist, and shocking. Now it is the conformity, and the only way boldly to shock the new conformists is to suggest that some sort of self-discipline in the sexual appetites might be useful, wise and comely.

Self-control, temperance, prudence, and moderation are values much praised by ancient pagan philosophers, the iron-hearted Stoics of Greece and Rome. Odd as this sounds, the final theme that endears the Night Lands to me, is this very iron-heartedness: it is the kind of book a stoic might approve.

The universe is utterly hostile, utterly malevolent, incomprehensible, dark, brooding, malefic, and filled with dread. While there is reincarnation in this world, every indication in the text is that this is not a supernatural phenomenon, not a matter of religion, but of some yet-to-be-discovered science of etheric rays or spirit-vibrations.

In the Night Land, there are benevolent powers whose mysterious actions sometimes save a stranded wanderer. Hodgson might have added them to have something analogous to dolphins (which sailor's tall tales say aid drowning men), to contrast with his soul-destroying monsters, who circle the last redoubt of man as sharks follow a ship laden with bullocks.

But these are entities whose true purposes are unknown, who neither seek nor are given worship, and who appear only about as frequently as reports of UFO's or Abominable Snowmen appear among modern men. They are not Valkyries, waiting to draw fallen heroes up to feast in Valhalla; they are not Mercury, waiting to escort shades to Elysium; and they are not angels waiting to welcome the faithful to paradise. Ultimately, there is no comfort to be had from them. There is no comfort to be found anywhere in Hogdson's black and agnostic universe: save in the arms of love itself.

And, since this is a fairy tale, we are told the love can endure even if the eons change, even if the sun goes out, even if the beloved seems to die.

Like the real universe, the terror-haunted universe of the

Night Lands is both utterly hopeless, and utterly filled with hope: as inescapable as death itself, is love.

Years and years ago, I spent a dreamy summer inventing tales to set into Hodgson's background, imagining the culture, traditions, and lore, filling in bits of the history of the Last Redoubt, of the final race of man. I was certain that no one had ever read this book but me; I was sure such stories would never find a home. It seemed like providence, miraculous, that I came across Mr. Roberson's call for stories set in this background in a trade journal, after I had so long ago dismissed all hope of such a thing.

While my humble work falls appallingly short of Hodgson's genius, to honor the favorite story of one's young life, by writing a story of one's own, was a chance not often given to writers, for which my gratitude is endless. For honor him I ought: all the secret, youthful, golden places in my imagination are still touched by images and echoes from his work.

Still, I seem to behold the mighty Home of Man, surrounded by the sacred aura of its air-clog, windows and balconies ablaze, defying (though doomed to fall to them) the silent and motionless monstrosities crouching at its eaves; still the Silent Ones slide forward from the gray gloom, noiseless, draped in gauze.

In some place in my heart, the Masters of the Watch are always raising their weapons in salute to the brave and nameless traveler who stands at the valves of the gate leading out into the Night, with all lamps quenched, so that the horrors will not know a child of man creeps forth. Still the warm scent of the last kiss of Mirdath the Beautiful lingers on the bereaved lover's lips, though that kiss was kissed twenty-five million years ago; still he hears her voice across the nightland of a darkened world, calling . . .

Dream

Andy Robertson

"Red. White. Black. This is what I dreampt.

"I remember – nothing, but one thing. It is a dream that comes again and again. I remember her look – the essence of her expression, the message it carried – but I do not remember the shape of her face, what she looked like. I do not remember whether she was beautiful or not.

"But she was strong. I could tell that by the way her back twisted as her legs died, by the way she carried her arms and hands until they burned.

"We were high in some vast structure. Vast.

"We were there to kill her. The room was full of fire. White fire.

"I was wearing armor. Such a suit. I bore it like a second skin.

"And I remember we were – outraged at her. Traitress. Betraying Woman. Witch. She had bought the invaders in. Things like black trees of lightning, that moved faster than sight.

"We burned them, we cleaned the world – for the great building was our World, where we had lived forever – we burned every inch of it clean. Some of us died, fighting. I don't know exactly how we fought: it was our place to direct the fire, somehow. We didn't have weapons in our hands.

"When we died, we risked more than death, worse than death. And I don't know how that can be.

"All this battle is behind the dream, behind the vision, but not present. I did not see it, but the memory of it is there inside the dream.

"So much fighting.

"We were victorious. We came to the last room, the heart of the invasion, and she was there, among the Others.

"We poured in the fire, slaughtered our foes, and only she was left.

"Red? Her head was broken. I could see bone. She was blood all down her breast and flank. Her left arm was soaked.

"White? Her skin, and her hair. White as lightning. Whiter than the fires we directed.

"Black? Her eyes. Black like the Night, that lived outside. Blacker than the things that darted about her as we closed the barriers in upon them.

"And yet I cannot remember her face.

"And at last she fell. I would have been unaffected by any plea, any reasoning. But she stepped forward into the fire, and her legs died. She fell, and then I saw: she was trying to keep balance. Not to be forgiven. Not to survive. Just to go gracefully, not to sprawl, like some slut, but to kneel, submit, and die properly.

"To go *gracefully*.

"How could They have imitated that?

"The invaders could not have understood that. Never, never. And I saw She was still there, still human inside.

"But I could not save her. She fell down to her knees, hard, limp. She lost balance, and tried to support herself on one hand. But as it touched the fire, her flesh died. The hand she tried to support herself on died. And as her arm failed and buckled, she looked up. She looked right into my eyes.

"And that is what I see, again and again – that look. The message of that look. Not the shape of her face or the texture of her skin, but what that look communicated, what it meant. For in the middle of that fire, she was not compelled by fear or hope of mercy. She was outraged by the *awkwardness* of her actions, by the lack of grace she had been compelled to.

"Laugh at me. Say I am in love with a ghost. *But if she had looked at you.*

"I did something not permitted. I raised my hand and saluted her. I made a sign of high honor. And I saw her acknowledge me. I saw in her eyes that she saw my salute.

"And then she died, and fell down into the fire.

"That is all I truly remember. The rest, before and after, is the memory of a memory.

"What happened then? I was rebuked, and harshly, I think. But I don't truly know what happened next.

"I remember nothing more.

"But this is what I do remember.

"Her look. Red, White, Black."

The Siege of Humanity

Sean McLachlan

The laughter comes low, rolling through the steep ravines of the eastern mountains out of the Unknown Lands beyond, through the Valley of the Hounds. As it echoes off the rocks it seems to gather strength. It quickens like an ancient tide as it rolls over the low foothills, before rushing on swift mocking tones through the Night Land to pummel the steel slopes of the Last Redoubt.

I stand calmly upon the Watch Deck at the apex of the Great Pyramid, also known as the Last Redoubt of Mankind, that massive fortress of steel that humanity built so many centuries ago. I am one of the Watchmen, the last of Mankind's numberless armies, who stand vigil over the poor remnants of a vanishing race. We guard against the creatures of the Night Land, the fell beasts that slink and howl in the Outer Darkness. They are out there, beyond the protective glowing ring of the Earth Current, which casts prohibitive rays on half-hidden, inhuman forms and pale, lunar eyes.

We watch, and listen. We watch the strange fires of the Giants' Kilns, and the stranger hulks that gambol around them. We watch for the abhumans, those dimly seen minions of the Evil Powers that now stalk our world, those creatures who also watch and listen, hoping that we will flag in our vigil.

They have been more active of late, slinking furtively between the shadows and the sickly red light from their mysterious labors. At times they rise up in full view, and gesticulate in an arcane and threatening manner towards the Great Pyramid, across the many miles of sable shadows that stand between us.

It is not they who laugh, who have laughed these past thirty thousand years and more, although mock us they surely do from their freedom in the limitless blackness. No, it is a more awesome entity, an Evil Power. Some say it is the disembodied soul of one of the four Watchers: towering beings of stone that stand sentinel like four sphinxes on each side of the Great Pyramid, far beyond the moat of protective energy that is the Earth Current. Others say it is some other power, never seen by Man, which controls and masses the forces of the dark against us. I have listened to the laughter, I have listened long, and I have my own ideas as to its origin.

I am not the commander of these men. The title of Master of the Watch honors another. For although I am the most respected, and by long and bitter experience the most qualified, I am not to be trusted. I am old, far older than the old men of the Council who decide who will lead the Watch. I am older even than the Great Pyramid. I am as old as humanity itself. I am old enough to remember the ball of flame that shone in the sky and was called the Sun. I remember when night was just a passing horror, always to be replaced with day, its nocturnal terrors melting away in the first warm light of dawn.

I am old, and my ideas are not those of men who have known only night and watching and listening. I am old, and I remember when men would rather fight than hide. I am old, though this body I currently inhabit is aged only eight years and twenty, and I am not to be trusted.

The laughter subsides, followed by a faint rumbling. I squint eastwards, and see a small avalanche tumbling down one of the ravines. The laughter has caused it, as it always does. Each time that unseen thing bursts forth in derision, the mountains that separate us grow a little thinner.

I look up, a direction to which those who are not Reawakened from an earlier time do not look, for it has been many millions of years since anything has flown in the thin chill air of this sunless world. I look up, and remember.

I remember a brilliant sun in a pale primeval sky hammering down upon the wide bright spaces of the savanna. A river flowed there, blue and fresh and sparkling in the blaze of day. The waters teemed with fish, and its banks were crisscrossed by the narrow trails of gazelles that paced down to its edge to drink.

It was the dawn of civilization, when Man first ceased to stare out into the darkness beyond the campfires, but built walls to keep the night out. We retreated within them – our first guarded cities.

At a curve in the river stood the walled city of Uhrduk. It was peopled by men and women who caught the fish and hunted the gazelle, and increased the bounty of the river by channeling its waters to soak the rocky fields of the savanna so that they could bring forth rich crops of gourds and tubers and golden wheat. The river was a means of contact as well. To the north and south were towns distant and strange, from which men who spoke alien tongues plied barques laden with stores of myrrh and berberine in exchange for our rich surplus of food and useful things crafted by our skilled artisans. For Uhrduk was the greatest of the towns, our walls the highest, our people the most numerous, our goods the most prized. For greenstone axes and sharp obsidian darts did they come, and finely curved atlatls made from the leg bones of gazelles, and rich necklaces of shell, brought in by traders across the savanna from the Endless Water, and fashioned into the likeness of beasts and spirits by the craftsmen of Uhrduk.

But enemies we had then – the nomads. Those too uncivilized to know town or planting stick, those whose only roof was the rough hide of some slaughtered beast, who hated the towns for their luxury and wealth. Often they attacked the settlements along the river, laying waste to their fields, breaking through their walls of mudbrick, carrying off their goods and women. But they dared not touch Uhrduk. Our walls were of stone, and they stood to the height of two full-grown men. Stout they were, and no breach could be made in them. I had seen to that, for I, leader of the warriors of Uhrduk, had built them. The nomads feared and hated us, and dared not raid our lands without gathering in large numbers. But gather they did.

"It is time."

A young voice brings me out of the long-dead light and back into the darkness. I turn, and gaze upon he who has spoken.

It is one of the cadets, young and impulsive, but wiser than many of his elders. He swears loyalty to me rather than to the stolid and cautious man the Council has seen fit to make our commander. This youthful cadet follows me, for I have a strategy that offers more than watching and waiting. He follows me because he knows my many lives have given me the wisdom of a vast accumulation of years.

We take leave of the Watch Deck, leaving to the other Watchmen the duty of monitoring the Night Land, leaving them to their recording of the Laughter, and their speculations about the new, fifth, Watcher, that may or may not be approaching from the unknown South. What does it matter? New forces will gather and gather, eternally.

We enter the Watch Deck's single elevator, an oblong box of metal that plunges us from the thousandth floor deep into the innermost recesses of the Great Pyramid. The brilliant lights of the interior floors, each its own raucous and teeming city, flicker past unseen as we stand within the close-set casing.

I think upon the young man beside me. He is young, and eager for battle, though battle he has never known. He is like so many young men I have led, young men who had watched the enemy from stout walls and were not lacking in spirit when the time came for them to defend their home.

The sun shone bright then, upon the massive walls that ringed Constantinople. It, like Uhrduk, was a glorious city built upon a curve of water. But instead of flanking a primeval savanna, Constantinople was built upon the fabled peninsula that harbored the shimmering waters of the Golden Horn, where the Bosphorus met the Sea of Marmara. It was the easternmost bastion of Christendom facing the infidel horde of the Ottomans.

It was the year of Our Lord 1453, when years were marked in such a fashion, and I was the True Emperor of the Romans. Warm sunlight shone down upon the verdant Thracian fields of my Empire of Byzantium, and upon the red-tiled roofs of churches that housed columns of porphyry supporting arches bejeweled with luminous mosaics of golden tesserae. The Sun sent flares sparkling across the rippling waters that lapped the shores of both Europe and Asia, two hostile lands barely five bowshots apart.

The sun was brilliant then, but it was dimmer than when it blazed upon Uhrduk so many millennia before. But strong it still was, and strong it would remain for millions of years, as only one who has been Reawakened many times could know. The light above was dimming, but the brave knights of Constantinople could not know this, and their eyes were not cast upwards, but across that thin strait of water to the camp of the gathering enemy.

Many times the Sultan had hurled his men against our sheer walls, and many times we had thrown him back with bow and fire, lo these many centuries. Our walls were strong, stronger by far than long-lost Uhrduk's, but we fought alone against the infidel, with no Christian lord coming to our aid, and the Sultan was gathering a fearsome host.

We emerge from the elevator deep in the nether regions of the Great Pyramid, close to its base in one of the lower, more decayed and decadent levels. Millions live here, as is the case with all the thousand floors of the Last Redoubt, but their character is different from their cousins of the higher altitudes. Their walls are featureless, for even the smallest window is not allowed in the lower levels for fear it could be used as an entry way for some creature of the Night Land able to cross the Earth Current, although none had ever survived the attempt. The closeness of life in the lower floors has lent a dissipation, a listlessness and lack of vigilance to their character. This is perfect for our purposes.

The cadet leads me along a broad metal esplanade to a transport station. We board an autocar to take us to the rendezvous. We seat ourselves, and while the cadet works the controls, I watch the view as the autocar slowly picks up speed. Parks, stadia, residences, and avenues speed past.

The public lighting on this floor is dim, as if in sympathy for the waning willpower of its people. The dusky hues of shadowed proscenia and marbled courtyards bring my reveries back to another time, long after Uhrduk and Constantinople, to another city, now also dead and turned to dust, forgotten by all but me, but undreamed by any man who knew Uhrduk or Constantinople.

The Sun had dimmed much by that time. Its wan light flickered feebly over a featureless plain of cracked rock and fused glass. No life that Man would recognize as natural lived upon that plain, once blasted by an inferno of heat but now growing chill as the sustaining rays of the Sun gave way to an ever-deepening dusk.

At the curve of a dry valley that had once held a broad river stood Heliopolis, the largest of the declining cities of the Darkening Age. It was an ancient name, hoary even in the days when I ruled Byzantium, but it was an apt one. In those days of the dying light Man's faith had turned from the clay idols of Uhrduk and the dark-limned icons of Constantinople, and looked to the Sun itself for hope.

In Heliopolis there was no electric light. Instead, through a giant crystal lens suspended high above the city, and a clever arrangement of manifold mirrors, sunlight was magnified and reflected into every room of that vast metropolis. We, like the denizens of the Great Pyramid so many millions of years later, were harried on all sides by the evil forces of an unclean land. They were the Changed, the decayed remnant of humanity that still lived on the Darkening Plain. Though no clean human could survive for long on that blasted landscape, they seemed to thrive and grow in number. Constantly they assailed our walls, and the Sun died overhead, and though our prayers for its rebirth felt hollow in our hearts, none of us would be denied the privilege of sunlight.

The Master Lens refracted the crimson rays of the guttering Sun into a myriad of pale hues that bathed the city with a brilliant incandescence. Entire neighborhoods were soaked with deep violet or burning sapphire. In other spots, at the intersections of two or more faces, shimmering rainbows played endlessly over rooftops and alleyways, catching crystal sculptures and setting them ablaze in vivid sparkling color. The houses were daubed with bright paints mixed with mica, so the colors of the walls would blend with the shades descending from above and the mica would shine pure and bright with the tone of the neighborhood, rich and warm as rubies, cool and clean as tourmaline, pure and cold as diamonds.

At the city center, at the nexus of those varicolored lanes and pulsating buildings, at the point where all the planes of the Master Lens intersected, stood the Plaza of Rainbows. There the variegated rays clashed and broke and a thousand thousand brilliant colors played over flagstones of white marble, the distant death throes of the fading sun reflected in coursing hues that writhed and shimmered and blended into a controlled explosion of color, a blazing jewel half a kilometer wide, a final defiance against the fading of the light.

At its center was a simple circle of black upon which no color could play. This was the secret to our might: a device of ancient manufacture, another lens, not of pure crystal, but of an unknown material, its secret long since lost, with the smooth glasslike texture of obsidian but a hundred times more black. It absorbed the light and converted it to energy to power the machines that hummed and throbbed deep below the city. It was from here that our deadly weapons, the Incinerators, got their power, and to here that all our varied devices were tethered for life.

Beautiful was our city, fairer than the bright river and open savanna that surrounded Uhrduk, fairer even than the golden churches of Constantinople. But it was a city of sorrow. For although we commanded powerful weapons, we lay isolated from our brothers in the few scattered cities of Mankind. Alone we were, alone against the gathering forces of a decaying world.

The others are waiting for us at the terminus. The cadet slows the autocar to a halt and we are greeted by two dozen cadets and Watchmen. They salute me, and tell me all is in readiness. I study their faces. Set features. Hard, resolute eyes. They are ready to follow me – a leader who offers them something more than endless hiding and watching, a leader who offers them victory.

We make our way with haste through an abandoned square to the goal of our meeting, the Museum, a vast collection of artifacts and records from long-dead ages of Man. The Caretaker, an aged scholar who I have befriended, is waiting by the entrance to meet us. His white eyebrows rise and his black eyes glitter in recognition as he beholds me. The Caretaker is the only soul outside our inner circle to whom I have entrusted our plan. He has studied the ancient technologies of war for his entire life, taking especial interest of the period right after the final fall into Outer Darkness, when the craft of making weapons was at its most advanced. He has come to the inevitable conclusion that aeons of defensive inaction can only lead to folly for the defender. It was under his tutelage that I discovered our salvation, Man's means of victory over the dark forces of the Night Land.

The Caretaker leads us through the displays. We shoulder aside the few loiterers who stand gazing into the glass cases. My eyes do not rest on these soft citizens who while away their time studying trinkets of bygone eras, while the noose tightens around their necks. Nor do I look long at the displays. I know the artifact I seek. A sideways glance shows me some ancient playthings, a shelf of downy stuffed creatures and a half dozen miniature warriors made of tin, painted with the colors of long-forgotten battalions.

We turn a corner into an area dedicated to the simpler tools of an even more remote age. I walk with purpose, urging my followers along, eager to be at our work, indifferent to the labored breathing of the Caretaker hobbling by my side. I take no heed of the crude, primitive objects until a sight summons up a distant memory and stops me short. There, in a case to my right, is a simple axe of flint, preserved by the Earth from the halcyon days when the Sun shone bright and the only evil that existed was in the hearts of other men.

The nomads attacked Uhrduk at dawn, as the young Sun rose over the golden grass of the savanna. They came in numbers never before seen, throngs of ragged men who hurled themselves against our walls, seeking hand and toe holds to climb to the top. The men and women of Uhrduk threw stones and flint-tipped darts down on them. The attackers hurtled into the crowd below, their brains dashed out or throats transfixed by sharp spears. The nomads threw spears and stones back at us, but few of us fell. We were protected by a chest-high parapet of my own design, a little wall atop the large one, to protect the citizens of Uhrduk.

A group of nomads battered at the thick wooden gate with a log, but a score of picked warriors under my command threw swift javelins from atlatls. The javelins flew like birds and hissed like serpents, and soon the nomads were writhing in their death throes. Their simple battering ram thudded to the ground. In an instant it was picked up again, and again the air hissed with our far-flying darts of flint.

All along the wall, nomads tried to climb up, and although none made it, there were always more to take their place.

"Come," the Caretaker whispers. "This way."

He leads us through a small door into the restricted storage area of the Museum. We descend a spiral staircase and find ourselves on an old metal catwalk suspended high above a cavernous chamber so colossal its utmost reaches disappear at the limits of our vision.

Only a part of the Museum's collection is open to the populace. Beneath lies an echoing hall called the Chamber of Artifacts, containing a diverse array of machines of obscure use. Immense wheels attached to sealed chambers. Glass cylinders in which glowing shades coil and whip, giving off the smell of ozone and burned resin. Squat sealed vats that slosh and rumble and emit loud, urgent messages in forgotten languages.

I glance at these mysteries with only passing interest, for I know what I seek. And there, past a huge beast of pistons and tubes, whose innards of copper wire and black coils lie disemboweled on the floor, we come upon what we knew we would find. There, in the half-light of the Chamber of Artifacts, stands one of the Current Cannon. It is a massive weapon, a behemoth of metal and conduits. Six giant metal domes, each as high as a house, flank an immense central cylinder a hundred fathoms long and twenty wide. The cannon is set to one side, facing the eastern wall like some primeval beast turned to steel. At its snout is a platform swathed in wires. At one edge of the platform is a control console and a seat. In front, gleaming with oil, is a broad barrel of cold steel. It is set at a high angle, as if at attention, perfectly preserved by the ministrations of the Caretaker.

We rush along the catwalk, eager to get to our prize. The catwalk shudders under our hurrying feet, and we approach more cautiously. Once above the Current Cannon, we descend a clattering spiral staircase to the main floor. We approach the artifact slowly now, with reverence. I come upon it, and run my hand along the cool smooth steel. Then I turn to the Caretaker and order him to instruct my men on how to connect it with the power grid.

The Cannon is set between two partition walls. The back and top can be sealed off with a steel curtain that rises from the floor, curving overhead to form a roof. Thus the Cannon can be completely cut off from the Chamber of Artifacts. At the wall in front of the Cannon is a massive gun port, fully ten fathoms wide and as tall as a man, fused long ago when this weapon was abandoned. I order one team to revive the weapon, and another to cut through the soldering that has sealed the gun port all these long years. A third team sets to work reanimating the moveable back wall and roof.

As the men set about their tasks, I walk idly around the ancient machine. Before long, I reach the gun port, where the eastern wall of the Great Pyramid itself blocks me.

I press my palm against the smooth surface and gaze up at the inwardly sloping plates reaching far overhead. A chill runs through my spine as I think of the few paces of metal between me and the Night Land. An impressive wall, but I had defended impressive walls before, and against foes not a tenth as fearsome as the Evil Powers that were now arrayed against me. I press my cheek against the metal, then my entire body, and feel the cold of the outer darkness seep through the thick plating to numb my bones. For a moment, although I know it to be only fancy, I think I hear the Laughter resonating through the metal to mock me.

As the sun rose over Constantinople, the Turks prepared their immense cannon. It had been pulled into position the previous day by fifteen pair of oxen. The barrel was nearly thirty feet long and was said to launch stone balls weighing 1200 pounds. It had been built by a bastard Hungarian who first offered his services to me, naming an outrageous price that he knew my declining city could not afford. Now he worked for the Sultan, who had heaped him with riches taken from my lands.

A Turkish captain gave the signal. A soldier lit the cannon's fuse. Fire gouted from its wide mouth and a billowing cloud of saltpeter obscured our view of the beast. The air shook with a terrific thunder, followed immediately by a cracking sound at the point where the cannon ball smacked into the ancient masonry. The wall trembled. The men defending it gasped and offered a hurried prayer to God and the Blessed Virgin, then broke into a cheer when they beheld the wall still standing, its surface slightly cracked. The smoke cleared and the cheer died. The Turks were reloading.

A shout awakens me from my reverie. The young cadet comes clattering along the catwalk yelling gleefully that he has found another Cannon a little farther on, and boxes of spare parts to meet all our needs. There comes an ominous groaning, and the catwalk sways, and we shout for him to take care. The supports give way. The aged platform hurtles to the floor below. The cadet is dashed upon the cold gray metal, and lies still before us.

We gather around him in silence. After a long moment I pull my Diskos from my belt and hold it reversed over the young man's body. The others followed suit, gathering around in a circle and saluting our comrade with our Diskoi reversed, in the fashion of the Watchmen when one of our number has died.

Two of my men carry the cadet's body to a far corner and cover him with a sheet. I regret not being able to take him to the Country of Silence, on the lowest level of the Great Pyramid, as befits one our dead, but we have a more urgent mission at hand. We will have to come back for him after our moment of glory.

A rumble fills the air as the steel curtain rises from the floor. The odd collection of the Chamber of Artifacts disappears from view as half a meter of metal slides up the ends of the partition walls, then turns overhead, forming a roof. There is a sharp click and a shudder, and we are sealed from the rest of the Great Pyramid. We are alone with the Cannon and the Night Land.

I turn and contemplate my prize. Current Cannon have not been used for many years. They have awesome destructive power, focusing the Earth Current into a ray. The Earth Current is the bane of all the creatures of the Night Land, and cannons that use its power are the most effective weapon ever invented against them.

Foolish leaders banned them long ago, saying the weapons were wasteful of the Earth Current so necessary to our defense. But what good is the Earth Current if used only as fortification? What good is waiting for the Earth Current to wane and die? It is inevitable. Therefore, the Earth Current has already been wasted. It will not protect us forever. If it is no use to us a defense, then we must use it for attack, now, before we lose any more of its precious power.

I think back, to the time of the Darkening when we had other powerful weapons, the Incinerators, powered not by the Earth Current but by the waning rays of the Sun itself.

The Changed attacked Heliopolis without warning. They came in a mad rush from out of the cover of a nearby ridge. One moment, quiet, the next, the dim plain was alive with a sea of pustuled, glabrous creatures that screamed and gibbered as they sped towards the city. They carried clubs and other simple weapons, and some wore the ragged remnants of clothing, passed down by their unclean forefathers as a dim remembrance of the humanity they had lost by living out in that poisonous landscape. They swept up to the walls in a moment, but the guards were ready.

This was typical, and the recent years had been such that fully one quarter of the adult population manned the walls at any one time. In an instant, the guards switched on the Incinerators. Wide swaths were burned through their ranks, and the mutilated half-men screamed as the skin melted off their bones, or fell as burned hollow husks, lucky enough to take the full blast and die instantly, their bodies cored through and cindered.

It was just another attack, we thought. One of so many. We could fight it off. We always had. But then we heard a far-off mournful howl, the baleful keen of an unearthly hound, and our hearts turned to water, and we wondered.

A red light pulses on the communication console. The Watch Deck is calling down to us. Word has gotten to the top of the command quickly, as if they have been expecting trouble. But the partition is sturdy. It is meant as a second line of defense if the Evil Powers breach the outer casing. Now it has become a bulwark, our protection from interference by those weak leaders who insist on placating the Night Land and suffering it to exist, as if by doing nothing and staying still the hungry eyes of the dark will turn their gaze elsewhere and we will be saved.

The Watchmen and cadets are finished, and look to me for their orders. At my signal one of them pulls a lever and the gears of the gun port groan into motion. An entire section of the outer wall lifts. I stand at the Cannon with my men and we watch as the Night Land comes into view. Our chamber's lights have died: we peer into blackness until our eyes adjust to the Night. There is little to see beyond the brilliant ring of the Earth Current but the shadowy expanse of the dead plain and the pale glimmering of distant fires. The resonating hum of machinery clangs to a stop and we stand, listening to the silence of the Land.

"There is no laughter," one of the Watchmen says.

"It is listening," I reply. "For once, it is listening."

I personally connect the main line into the power grid and the cannon hums to life. The Caretaker had done his task well. Pale green dials illumine range and target data, while an electric thrill crackles through the room from the sheer vibrant power that shrills within the blue steel housing.

The alarm lights again, another call from the Watch Deck. They are sure to have noticed the new connection to the Earth Current. It will only be a matter of time before they divine its meaning. I am not certain my eyes tricked me when, at the moment I flip the switch, the Earth Current dims a little, if only for half a heartbeat. But the warning from the Watch Deck goes ignored. We are steeled to our purpose, and through with listening to the weak platitudes of our so-called leaders.

The gate and walls of Uhrduk were holding. Our citizens heaved and sweated atop the bare stone wall, hurling down stones at all who approached. Some died, pierced by the spears and darts of the nomads, but many were those who replaced them. The nomad's battering ram lay untouched on the ground, covered with corpses. No figure swathed in animal skins lived long enough to ascend to the parapet. Their broken bodies lay in a heap at the base of the wall.

Then, bursting from the riverside quarter, came a frightened wailing, and those too young or old to be atop the walls fled into the central square. The nomads had slipped in, swimming up a channel and into a cistern that watered the city and provided it with drink. It was but a short swim underwater from the river and one would be inside the walls. Once found, it was an obvious weak spot in the defense, but no one had seen it until this day.

The Current Cannon comes to life, revived from its millennial sleep. With a grinding crunch of gears it levels its barrel to the horizon. A readout glows with data, assessing risk, calculating vectors. Without any effort by us, it has instantly sensed the closest and most immediate threats. There, in the middle distance, clustered behind a heap of stones, are the crouched and twisted forms of a score of abhumans. We had not seen them – could not see them in the fuligin shadows of the Night Land – but they glow clear and plain on the screen. We see them clearly as they look up, directly at our gun port. They seem to notice us, although we are at such a distance that that surely must be impossible. They gesture to one another, and as we watch, more gather to stare through the darkness at our open window.

The Turks bombarded Constantinople for many days, and soon there were many breaches in the walls. We fought them off a dozen times, but every day they would attack again. Their numbers were far greater than ours, and we could hope for no reinforcements. Then, on 29th of May, they made their final assault. As the sun set low on the horizon, the Turks charged the entire length of the wall at the same time. Their battle cries rose like the wail of vengeful ghosts as they assaulted the many breaches in our defense.

I was at one of them, a huge rent in the masonry where the Turks' infernal cannon had reduced the wall to rubble. It had been repaired with broken stones and barrels, but it was a thin line of protection. The Turks came on in a mad rush, and soon the last knights of Rome were fighting for their lives.

We were pushed back. The breach still held, but our men were being forced back. A Turk faced me, a swarthy man in a pointed helm, a scimitar gripped in his right hand. He sent a vicious swing at my face, but I parried him at the last moment. I cut and thrust back at him with my sword, but he bobbed and wove and I could not hit him. Then he fought back, a savage hail of blows landed on my sword and shield. A dozen times I came a hairsbreadth from death. But then I saw my chance. For a brief instant his guard was lowered, and I gave a mighty swing and cut deep into his chest.

"Mother of God!" I thought as I wrenched my blade free. "These Turks fight like demons. What chance do we have now?"

"A pity," I mused as he fell at my feet. "This man died for nothing. They will win regardless."

I saw more pointed helms swarm over the smoking mountain of rubble. I charged, yelling out an oath to Our Savior, and plunged into their midst.

"The abhumans sense it. As if through some ancestral memory they have recognized this one weapon that can bring their destruction." It is one of the Watchmen who speaks, a brave man who has been with me for many years. His eyes gleam in the pale emerald glow of the screen, and in them I can see an emotion alien to the teeming metropolis of the Great Pyramid – hope. Here, before us, we have the means to fight back. Here, finally, we have a weapon.

I wonder how long the Earth Current will last once we begin to tap its force and send it hurtling across the plain. I am no fool. I know that the Council was telling the truth when they said the Cannon are wasteful of the Earth Current, but what choice have we? The Earth Current will die just as the Sun died thousands of years ago. Our only hope is that the Cannon can overwhelm all the creatures of the Outer Darkness before it runs out of energy. If it does not, we might still weaken them enough that we can send out our millions, armed and armored, and cut down the survivors with our Diskoi.

It is a desperate plan, but it is also our only plan. Humanity has little time. The Sun has guttered out. The world is cooling. The Earth Current will not sustain us for long. If humanity wants peace now is the time to fight for it, now, before this world finally dies. We do not have much time, a few centuries at most. Even I, who always Reawakens after death, do not have much time. This world will end, and I with it. I have lived more lives than any man, but when humanity dies out, I too will die.

Still the Changed assaulted Heliopolis, their diseased forms limping over the Darkening Plain as the sun bled high overhead. The people of Heliopolis worked the Incinerators in desperation, blasting smoking swaths through the onrushing crowd. The attackers carried crude ladders. They flung them against the steel palisade and scurried up. My soldiers were there to stop them, cutting off withered hands and smashing grotesque heads as they emerged over the wall.

For a while, it seemed, we held them back. They thronged in ever increasing numbers, but my men let not a single unclean creature set foot atop the wall. Then, over the struggling mass of humanity and its diseased cousins, came the lone high howl. As if it were a signal, the Changed slackened their assault. The howl broke through the air again, closer this time, and we spied a dark shape loping out of the distant shadows. It was a monstrous hound, as high as a house, with jet-black fur that made it look like a fragment of endless night as it sped across the plain.

The attackers parted to make room. Tall as our defenses were, the hound was nearly half the height of the wall, and in a single leap soared over us and landed in a broad lane inside.

My men gasped. A few were courageous and quick-thinking enough to shoot at the thing, but it barely seemed to notice. Without a pause, the hound ran away down the street.

Instantly I knew where it was headed, and choking with dread I summoned a unit of my men and sprinted after it. It was far ahead, but when it looked back and saw us pursuing it, it slackened a little, as if to taunt us.

It reached the Plaza of Rainbows, then turned to face us. We arrived, panting, a few moments later. We paused, unsure what to do. It made no move to run. Then it sat on its haunches, raised its snout towards the Master Lens far overhead, and let out a long, high-pitched howl.

We clamped our hands over our ears and wailed in pain. The arcane, bestial scream pierced our bodies. Many of my men fell to the ground, unconscious. In a panic I looked up to the lens. Thin cracks spread like spiders' webs across its surface. The howl continued, a perfect baleful pitch. Its sound encompassed everything, but in a moment it was joined by a slow, ominous cracking. I leapt into a doorway just as it shattered. Fragments of glass as wide as tables came crashing down. The men in the street were cut to pieces. I curled into a ball and hid as the glass burst on the flagstones and sent deadly flakes flying in all directions. My armor saved me, but wherever the smallest patch of skin showed through I was deeply lacerated.

It was all over in a moment, the din replaced with a still silence. I looked out of my hiding place. The street was covered in shards mixed with a bloody, unrecognizable pulp, all that remained of my men. In the center of the Plaza the hound surveyed the scene, unhurt. The glass directly above it had been pulverized by the full force of the howl. The beast's black fur was covered in a fine, scintillating dust. The hound shook itself, the glass powder tinkling softly as it settled on the marble flagstones. The Plaza, once a brilliant cascade of color, was stained a pale red in the light of the dying sun.

The hound looked directly at me. I scrambled to my feet and whipped out a pistol. It growled once, a low, mocking sound, then ran down a side street and was gone.

More abhumans are gathering, a vast mockery of humanity that fills the screen. They advance cautiously. Some walk on legs almost human, others undulate on foully pliable appendages, or scuttle like beetles on insectoid limbs. Slowly, almost imperceptibly, the gun barrel lowers as it adjusts its range.

Far on the horizon, on the ridge overlooking the Giant's Kilns, a crowd of huge, monstrous men has gathered to stare at the Great Pyramid. In an instant they jump and shake their fists in a barbaric cheer, and lumber forward, their long strides rapidly overtaking the abhumans. They soon pass their twisted brethren, and storm towards the Earth Current.

We hear the Master of the Watch calling to us on the intercom. We ignore him. He is weak, afraid to take on the horrors of the Night Land, too timid to fight in his own self-defense. I check my aim and fire.

I led a group of Uhrduk's warriors into the riverside quarter. We were few. Most of us had to remain at the wall to hold it against the assailants who still tried to scale up. We charged down an alley and straight into an advancing group of nomads. Those in front charged us with sharpened sticks and heavy clubs. Others emerged from houses on both sides, dropping their loot and snatching up weapons.

My men began to fall. We fought hard, but we were outnumbered. I swung my greenstone axe in wide arcs, breaking through the crowd and calling on my men to regroup, but there were none left alive to hear. Then a stone glanced my shoulder. I tumbled against a wall and tried to regain my balance. A nomad, a huge brute swathed in reeking animal hide, swung the leg bone of a bull at me and caught me on the forehead. I fell. Three more nomads leapt on me, beating me down with sticks. I tried to gain my feet. The world spun. I saw houses burning, and nomads dragging our goods and women down the street. Then there was a sharp pain on the back of my neck, and blackness.

We cheer as the Current Cannon sends out a blinding beam of energy, splitting the eternal darkness of the Night Land with a pure light. It hoves into the advancing horde, cutting through them as if they were shadows. More take their place, but I aim and fire again, and another hundred of man's enemies are disintegrated by the tremendous power of the Earth Current.

I swivel the cannon and fire on a crowd of giants, cutting through the first dozen. They fall in a jumbled heap of dismembered bodies and limbs. I shout for the sheer joy of it, the thrill of my voice drowning out the pounding on the door and the crackle of the cannon. I fire again, and again, slicing giants in half and cutting broad swathes through the abhumans.

No more hiding! No more slow death as I watch the defenses of my beloved city fall! Now I am taking the battle to the enemy. Now I am on the attack. One of the Watchmen shouts out a warning and points to the Earth Current encircling the Great Pyramid. It is noticeably dimmer, and seems to fade with each pulse of the cannon. I laugh at the man's fear, and fire again. What need have we for the Earth Current, if not as a weapon? What use is it as a defense, when it could lead to victory? The Cannon hums and blazes, and I exult in the knowledge that we may, for once, emerge victorious. I thrill to think that in my next life I may, finally, Reawake in a time of peace.

The men of Constantinople rallied and surged into the Turkish ranks. We stayed them. For one brief, brittle moment we stayed them. But it was not to last, a conceit to think it would last. They renewed their attack. We had fought without break the entire day, and now moved as if lead weights were tied to our limbs. Our hearts faltered as we looked upon so many dead comrades lying there broken on the jagged stones. Our strikes slackened, our parries became more ill timed. A sword struck me, and my cuirass was cleaved, and white heat burned deep in my shoulder, and I was on my knees. A struggle then, of many men around my person, while I swayed and the world became indistinct. Then a spear thrust, not too deep in my side, but enough, and I toppled backward. I did not feel my head hitting stone, and the battle raged onward topsy turvey for a time, growing dim at its edges, until a cold moment when all around were Turks, and one looked down upon me. But I was already dying.

Cheers echo through the room as I fire. The abhumans and giants are crowding just beyond the dimming barrier of the Earth Current. The beam of our cannon cuts through them. They gesture angrily, turning gnarled faces up at me, standing on heaps of their own dead. It is a slaughter. I am exultant. I keep firing. The cannon begins to glow with heat, the mechanism resonating with a high-pitched whine.

Then, as if a giant eye closed, everything goes dark. The Earth Current flickers and winks out. The cannon moans to silence. The Great Pyramid is plunged in darkness.

For a moment, silence, then the triumphant roar of the assembled creatures below. We hear the harsh rasp of their talons as they scrabble up the steep metal side of our home.

Our eyes are dazzled as the lights flare back on. The circle of Earth Current around the Great Pyramid bursts to life. For a brief second I see the hapless silhouettes of the creatures that were on its very surface when it relit. They were atomized in an instant. Most of the giants and abhumans fall back and rage helplessly, cut off from the Great Pyramid once again. But I see a full hundred have made it through and are now scaling the metal slope towards the gun port. It is nothing. Two sweeps of the Current Cannon and they will be gone.

I lower my aim, get a hulking giant in my sights, and push the firing mechanism. Nothing happens. The cannon is dead. My heart sinks and I know I have been betrayed. The cowards of the Council shut off the Earth Current for a moment, just long enough to disconnect the power coupling that leads to my cannon.

The cadets frantically work switches and wires, desperately trying to reconnect the Cannon, but I know it is useless. It has been shut off from the outside. The abhumans, led by the giant, are almost upon us. I draw my Diskos and order the others to do the same.

I staggered through the dim red roads of my once-brilliant city of Heliopolis. Everywhere lay the mangled remains of those who had been caught under the falling shards of the Master Lens. I approached the wall and saw innumerable creatures of the Darkening Plain swarming over them and into the streets. A tiny huddled group of survivors stumbled out of a building, and a mass of the Changed enveloped them, tearing them to pieces.

I pulled out my pistol and fired, burning a hole an inch

wide through the chest of one of them. The others looked up, then rushed at me in a mass. I fired again and again, standing in the middle of the dim bland street where rainbows once danced. I waited for them, not trying to hide, not trying to run, but shooting down a score of the hateful creatures until they tackled me and I knew no more.

I assemble the cadets and Watchmen in a ragged line facing the open gun port. There is no time to close it. At my signal they draw their Diskoi. A dozen spinning blades spark and hum. We stand. For a moment, nothing, Then we hear the scratching of a hundred claws gaining purchase on the metal wall, and the grunts and snarls of inhuman throats.

They come through the gun port in a rush, and we step forward as one man and swing at them. Tainted blood splashes on the metal floor as their first rank goes down, but more leap into the room and force us back.

I swing my weapon easily, decapitating the hunched creature in front of me and with a backhand blow cut off the arm of the beast beside it. I call on my men to rally, but slowly they inch back, outnumbered. Then a looming shadow blots out the opening, and a thick arm, muscles corded like steel cables, reaches inside and clutches one of my fellow Watchmen. The hand clenches. The man's armor creaks, then gives way. He is pulped like a vegetable.

The hand drops the broken bloody mass to the floor and sweeps in a wide arc back and forth. Men and abhumans alike are bowled over. I duck, then bring up my Diskos in time to cut off one of its fingers. The hand withdraws, and the giant pulls back away from the gun port, and a new crowd of abhumans rushes inside.

Our line is broken. Only a few men remain standing. The mêlée has descended into a chaotic mass of individual combats. I see my men pulled down by sheer numbers. A half dozen brutes surround me.

I thrust the spinning blade of my Diskos deep into one, its chest spouting blood, but another pounds on my armor with rocklike fists. I swing at it and it reels back, half its face cut away. Before I can regain my footing another picks me up in its burly arms and throws me to the floor.

I try to raise my Diskos, but one of the abhumans stomps on my chest. Winded, I am unable to resist as heavy hands pummel me. The scene fades, my eyesight dims, and the last I hear is the low, deep laughter coming over the hills from the east . . .

. . . and I Reawaken.

Black Irises

Lucy A.E. Ward

no female ever
Athani with her black irises
dwells at the edges, wide
pupils haunting the firefly trails of braves
seeking glory in the Outer Lands.

no female ever
Such dreams, kept invisible.
Devoured by tales of a lost past –
mammalian monoliths in a lost sea,
white desert bones bathed by the breath
of the Earth-Current, splinters of wooden ships
crewed alone by bare-breasted, scale-waisted
women.

no female ever
She had seen blood and broken bones
dragged back from the darkness,
deep scars, arcs of teethmarks,
yet still, a shadow beacon burned
unnaturally.

no female ever
no cure without medicine

her arm ached, longed
for the sharp sting
before freedom.

Only fear held her,
dreams of wide mouths,
claws matching scar scabbards
born by the knowing. Fear,
convenient law.
no female before

An Exhalation of Butterflies

Nigel Atkinson

"There are a billion stories in the Great Redoubt."

— *anon.*

The two hundred and fifteenth echelon of the underground country was, in Loomis' not-completely unbiased opinion, the most beautiful of all of the underground lands. He rested his hands on the balustrade and gazed down on the patchwork of farms and spinnies half a mile below. The scent of poppies and ripe corn rose to meet him. He leaned forward tentatively, then pulled back at once; heights were not his strong suit. Sniffing deeply, he became aware of the bakery halfway up the pillar that supported the Lepidoptery – there would be fresh mushroom and bilberry pasties this afternoon. He decided to investigate them later.

As he mustered his dignity, he became aware of someone standing next to him. It was an apprentice boy. Loomis did his best to ignore him, and looked towards the buildings that barnacled the rim of the nearest of the seventy-five lesser light wells. The well was five miles away, but it was just possible distinguish individual premises. Brightly colored refectories, and tailor shops, their windows trailing gaudy flags, and pallia dotted the higher parts of the wall. Lower down were the dormitories of the auxiliaries who worked the well's baffles and prisms.

Loomis' eyes turned to the waterfall of light pouring down the well. It seemed that the incandescent scintilla of the Earth Force rose like a fountain from the well. It was a common optical illusion. The intellect knew that the light was cascading down from the Earth Current-kindled luminary a hundred miles above, but sometimes the eye chose to disagree.

Loomis glanced to his side; the boy was still there.

He adopted his most imposing stance. "What do you want, lad?"

"How old are you, Master?" The boy asked. Loomis leaned on his pollen broom and brushed away the clump of Red Admirals that were dancing on his pollen stained brow. He attempted to pierce the boy with a flinty look. It seemed to have little effect. *The youth of today,* he thought, *in my day we had respect for our elders.*

"I'm exactly the right age I should be, Apprentice."

The boy persisted. "And what's that?"

"Old enough to give you a clout."

The boy was fearless. "And then will you tell me how old you are? They say you are a thousand years old – at least!"

The lad's ear was a tempting target. But Loomis didn't have the heart. In truth, he was quite amused by his determination. Not that he would admit that of course, curiosity was all right in its place, but too much of it always led to trouble. He could vouch for that. But, he still had some sense of duty left. The mysteries of the Lepidoptery were only part of what masters must teach the apprentices. Due deference and a respect for the natural order were also important, if less academically demanding.

Loomis nodded towards the clump of apprentices who were circling round Mistress Melrig at few dozen yards further along the gallery.

"I'm old enough to wonder why you aren't attending to your studies with the good mistress yonder," Loomis said.

The boy bit his lip and discovered something fascinating about his bare feet. He wriggled his toes in the thin layer of discarded scales that covered every surface in the gallery. Loomis wondered whether he was trying to taste the floor with his feet. Many a young apprentice tried that trick, after the mystery of where their charges tasting organs were had been revealed to them, but the boy seemed too old for that particular silliness.

Loomis estimated the he was about twelve years old, almost old enough to take his name. Almost as old as his son had been . . .

Putting the old wound aside, he turned his attention back to the boy. "Well?"

He shuffled his feet. "She's, y'know."

"Enlighten me."

"A bit, um, dull."

Loomis wrinkled his brow and peered over his nose pouches. He tended to agree with the apprentice's assessment of Mistress Melrig. As far as Loomis was concerned she was the worst fusspot in Wrangwysh Toft Lepidoptery, and quite possibly in the entire Great Redoubt. *She's probably boring her poor students half to death,* he thought. But, all that said, she was a sister of the guild, and it would not be seemly to allow such criticism to pass unscathed.

Loomis' hand was fast enough to pluck a butterfly from its darting, twisting, unpredictable path. So the boy never had a chance of avoiding the retribution that came to him in a blur of precise motion.

"Ow!" The lad exclaimed as he reached to comfort a painfully twisted ear lobe. "That hurt!"

"Consider yourself lucky. I'm in a benevolent mood, otherwise I'd have pulled your ear right off."

From the look on the boy's face, Loomis guessed that the lad's definition of benevolent was different to his.

"Did you think that was unfair?"

The boy look several seconds to answer, his freckled face

twisting as it echoed the battle going on in his mind. Eventually, he decided on discretion rather than continued defiance.

"No master, it was fair. I'm sorry."

"Good. Now come, sit with me yon arbor." Loomis said, gesturing towards a roughly cut wooded bench nestling in under a sheltering willow tree. Loomis wondered why he was bothering letting this fidgety, undisciplined, unnamed apprentice take up his valuable time. Not that he was exactly what you might call busy. Alone among the Elders of Wrangwysh Toft, he did not have to spend part of his time teaching. He was a peripatetic, in theory anyway. More often he was just ignored by the apprentices. Which suited him. On an impulse he handed his pollen broom to the lad, whose eyes formed amazed saucers almost as wide as his gaping mouth.

"Hold onto this for a minute," Loomis said gently.

"I'll be careful Master," the boy whispered. Loomis noticed that he had stopped fidgeting, so concerned was he with his burden. The broom was actually pretty durable. Loomis had used it for several decades without getting as much as a scratch on the iron-hard ebony of its ten-foot long shaft, nor causing any damage to its subtle gears and mechanisms. Nevertheless, it was very unusual for an apprentice to be trusted to hold a broom. So unusual in fact, that at least half of Mistress Melrig's class was now paying more attention to what was going on in the arbor than to their increasingly testy teacher. She hadn't noticed the reason for her charge's increasing inattention, and was dashing; as best a dumpy, not-very-young woman could, around the group, shouting and slapping at heads.

Loomis ignored the increasing mayhem. It was amusing, very amusing actually, but he had a job to do. He held his left hand out in front of his face; palm down and extended his eight inch long index finger. After a few seconds a black and orange butterfly landed on it. He presented his right palm to the insect. His fingers ran quickly though a complex series of shapes that were augmented by the patterns, some bright colored and others invisible to the human eye, tattooed on his palm. The butterfly froze. Loomis turned to the boy.

"Species?" He asked.

"That's a viceroy," the boy replied confidently, "*Basilarchia* archippus."

Loomis wrinkled his brow. "Are you sure? Looks like a monarch to me."

"Of course its isn't! Look there's a black streak on its hind wing. Crosses from top to bottom. Monarchs don't have one."

"Well, yes. But that was an easy one. How's your nose?"

The boy shrugged. Loomis thought that was a sensible answer. Olfactory skills were the hardest to acquire, and among the most important. No apprentice with a grain of sense would boast about his or her nasal skills. It was way too easy to come unstuck. Loomis decided it was worth a test. With great delicacy and precision, he ran his little finger down the paralyzed butterfly's abdomen. It came away carrying the merest trace of pollen, bound by a tiny amount of nectar. He sniffed it, then held his finger out. The lad leaned forward and inhaled deeply. His forehead tightened in concentration and his nasal pouches ballooned up as he sniffed deep and long.

Without intending to, Loomis found himself examining the boy's eyes for traces of red, his nose for signs of irritation. Every year it seemed that more apprentices were lost to the pollen allergy, like the bright-eyed boy who had been the joy of his life.

"A lantana of some sort, Master . . . I think."

Loomis smiled, the arbor was dotted with the flamboyant red and yellow spiked flowers. "Which one? Purple or orange?"

The boy sniffed again. "Orange?"

"Good guess, but wrong. Purple."

"How do you know that? They always smell the same to me."

"Me too." Loomis took a span to enjoy the mixture of surprise and bafflement playing out on the boy's face. He held his finger up. "Look. The pollen of the purple variety is slightly more yellow-red than that of the orange. Of course, if you had been attending to Mistress Melrig's botany lessons you might have known that already."

The boy looked suitably chastened. Loomis couldn't help but break into a smile, then a thin peal of laughter. The boy joined, in and soon most of the botany class were looking in puzzlement at them. Mistress Melrig had finally noticed the source of the disturbance, and was standing with hands on her ample hips, gazing balefully and wagging a finger at Loomis. He waved back cheerily. With a flick of her severely cut, straight white hair, she began to march towards him. Her class trotted eagerly after her.

"Oh no." Loomis groaned. But he was spared a showdown with Mistress Melrig. She had barely taken ten paces when the sound of a great gong echoed down the hourducts. Everyone froze in surprise. There was at least a third hour until the next scheduled sending, and they were not usually announced so clamorously. Something was up.

With a circular motion of his talking hand, Loomis dismissed the butterfly. Then he stood up and, after retrieving his pollen broom, headed for the balustrade.

Knotting his courage, he peered over the edge. On a roadway below a clump of startled hour criers were scurrying towards the nearest hourduct. Their black and white coats trailed long scarves, which twisted in the draught of their breakneck passage. The last one in line tripped over a trailing scarf, and tumbled headlong, much to the amusement of the watching gaggle of apprentices. He was quickly on his feet and chasing after his fellows while rubbing a bruised head. By the time the criers reached the hourduct, their minions were arriving and beginning the slow, difficult process of organizing themselves Fifty undercriers formed the van, behind each of them snaked a line of a twenty-five under-undercriers. Milling around behind them like competitors in a mad relay race were thousands of under-under-undercriers.

Loomis shook his head in mock dismay. The news criers were never the best regulated guild, and this urgent summons had wrought entertaining havoc among them.

"Master?"

"Yes, boy, what is it now?"

"Master, is it true that once the news passed throughout the Great Redoubt on the wings of the Earth Current? And there was no need for the criers, for all of humanity's uncounted billions could read it themselves."

"What an absurd notion!" Mistress Melrig snapped. "What on the black Earth have you been putting into the lad's empty head?"

Loomis shrugged. "Nothing I said." He felt an urgent need to change the subject. "Look now, the hour slip has arrived."

The chief news crier, a bony etiolated man called Redeheid, emerged from the hourduct clutching a sheet of yellow paper. His immediate underlings clustered close to him, their pens scribbling furiously as he recited the text to them. As soon as the cry was made, the criers spread out. In seconds they were surrounded by constellations of undercriers. The next order of magnitude of pens descended to paper. When they had the bulletin down they sprinted headlong away from the mêlée, each desperately seeking room for their own tiny solar systems of under-undercriers. Once again papers were inscribed, hopefully with the accuracy and precision that was the otherwise dubious guild's proudest boast. Finally, the lowest echelon of the crier's guild spread out in the four canonical directions, and all points in-between.

Loomis waited patiently. Before long an under-undercrier came scurrying past. The Lepidopterist's arm blurred out and snatched the paper from the man's hand. The under-undercrier stamped his foot and his face reddened with indignation, but there was little he could do to challenge someone of Loomis' high ranking. The lepidopterist carefully read the hour slip then returned it to the infuriated man, who promptly fled.

Mistress Melrig snorted at his departing back. "He might have at least told us what the substance of the hour slip was." She turned towards Loomis "Well?"

Loomis took up his lecturing pose, chin up, hands grasping his robe's collar.

"There is to be an exhalation."

A babble of excited apprentice's voices rose at this news. The last exhalation had been three hundred and fifty six years ago, and there wasn't expected to be another one for at least a hundred years. It would be like ten year's worth of the festival for the raising of the Wall of Safety, all rolled into one ecstatic day. And it would be a lot of work. *A devil of a lot of work*, Loomis thought, gloomily.

"When?" Mistress Melrig asked, pointedly.

"Five years from this day."

"You jest."

"No. Five years."

Sarcasm dripped from Mistress Melrig's lips. "By the Days of Light, our guild barely numbers five million. How can we be expected to raise an exhalation in five years? And why? Have the watchers been dismissed? Has the sun re-lit? Has Loomis found honest work?"

Loomis shrugged. He was stunned by the prospect. A mere five years – it was impossible. They would have to raise as many apprentices a possible, as soon as possible, aye and recruit millions of laborers. Then there was the co-ordination with thousands of other Guild Houses on hundreds of echelons and through the Great Pyramid. His head swum.

"So," Mistress Melrig insisted. "What's the big news?"

"There is to be a new Master Monstruwacan," he said simply.

Everyone's head turned upwards, as though, by dint of stunned curiosity, they could peer through the hundreds of echelons above, past the actinic detonation of the Earth Current-driven generators, onward through the thirteen hundred and twenty floors of the pyramid, to the Tower of Observation at the apex. Silence fell over apprentices and elders. They had not been a new Master Monstruwacan for time out of mind, at least the minds of the lesser mortals of the Great Redoubt. The more senior Monstruwacans would know, but they rarely descended below the surface. Except for exhalations.

Loomis' heart leapt with hope. He would ask one of them, they surely would know what had happened to his son.

All he had to do was wait five years.

Five years passed like the wind rustling through the lungs of the Great Redoubt. Five years of endless labor, convoluted planning and desperate racing against time. The Guild of Lepidopterists grew to seven million strong, but remained one of the smallest of the underground guilds. It was impossible to guess how many caterpillars were raised, pupated and frozen to wait for the great day. But in the first two years, the effort came close to ruining the Great Redoubt's fecund farmlands. Caterpillars were everywhere. On the fifty-seventh echelon every plant was gnawed down to a nub. Even where they were under more control, everything seemed to be covered with twitching, gliding blobs of color, voraciously seeking their first and last meal. Special precautions had to be taken to protect infants from suffocation, or poisoning by the many lethal varieties infesting the underlands.

Eventually, and to the great humiliation of the Lepidopterist's Guild, the Monstruwacan Council decreed a six-month hiatus to get the situation under control. Amid ridicule from the other guilds, the Lepidopterists regained their poise. The next great hatching was much better controlled, and the Monstruwacan Council again smiled on the butterfly farmers.

And so it went on, until hundreds of billions (some said upwards of a trillion) of pupae were stored in vast, cooled galleries on each of the Underground Country's three hundred and six echelons. A year before the exhalation, the Guild of Windmasters spread throughout the Great Redoubt, mapping the subtleties of wind flow through both Underground Country and the Great Redoubt. Loomis was far from being the only Greybeard who noted quietly that the two halves of the Great Redoubt, despite the claims of legend, did share the same set of lungs.

Finally, the great day dawned. As one of the elders of his guild, Loomis was offered the chance of watching the exhalation from the lowest tier. The offer was tempting; it was decades since he had stood amid the three hundred and six fields. There would be unbounded opulence on the lowest tier, the fields would be flowing with food and drink, and garlanded with million or so flowers, their scent as intoxicating as vintage Goldale wine. It would also be the best place to see the display; fully a half of the butterflies would be released from the lowest tier. But Loomis had chosen to stay in his home, its two hundred and fifteen fields seeming more comfortable. He also felt that he had a better chance to meet a Monstruwacan up there.

Loomis was one of the first people on his echelon to feel the exhalation beginning. He was standing on an ornate spiral stairway, midway up the North curve of the outer wall. Through his bare feet, he felt a subtle change in the normal vibrational timbre of the Redoubt's naked metal. The spectators chattering excitedly around him were unaware of the change at first, but then the amplitude began to mount. At first, there was only a single, pure tone, like a million voices in wordless, joyful unison. Then understated overtones manifested as harmonic variations on the ecstatic main theme. Loomis glanced towards the roof of the echelon. Six dozen great silk flags, each handled by a hundred hauliers, waited for the call to action. Loomis felt a pang of worry. He put it aside – whatever happened, his work was done.

He looked at the millions milling around below. They were clad in colorful garb, and garlanded with bright flowers. It was a happy chaos of color and joy, but Loomis was looking for something else. He opened his mind, then waited. As the butterfly armadas raced upwards, gentle breezes began to play through the echelon. From every metal branch, and bronchus and bronchiole of the underground country's lungs; from every hour tube; and from every balloon highway, soft, sweet-scented zephyrs played. His mind continued its search.

Then, someone touched Loomis' mind, with a clarity that made even his weak mental voice sing in harmony. He descended the stair, searching for the Monstruwacan.

As Loomis' reached the floor level of the echelon, the first butterflies erupted from the mile-wide central light well. They were too far away for him to distinguish individual insects, but he knew that the almost solid-looking column of flashing green, white and black was made up from uncountable four and five barred swallowtails. It had been deemed fitting that the first defiant challenge to the Night should come from the Aristeus named, as they were for an ancient, long dead sun god.

The column rose with majestic slowness, its homogeneity defying the chaotic flight patterns of its myriad members. High above, the great silk flags unfurled. As they measured their several hundred yard lengths, butterflies rose from ten thousand cages. Close by Loomis, legions of Birdwings, Pine Whites, and Pelidne Sulphurs formed arpeggios to the great chord ascending the central light well. All around the echelon, innumerable, minuscule specks of the Master Word were freed to ascend the lesser light wells. Their passing created a coruscation of winds, tousling the spectator's hair and whipping at the clothing. Ill-secured hats and scarves were grasped and thrown upwards never to return. Their owners cheered their losses until they were hoarse.

His professional pride satisfied, Loomis sought the Monstruwacan. He found him standing a few dozen yards to the North. He was an imposing figure: fully a head taller than the tallest normal man, and exuding an almost palpable air of authority. Despite the crush, there was a little empty zone around him, emphasizing how reluctant people were to approach him.

Loomis' mouth suddenly felt dry and his tongue tried to stick to his the roof of his mouth. He took a deep breath and stepped forward.

"Master," he said respectfully. "I would crave a word with you."

The Monstruwacan tilted his head and looked down on him. To Loomis, it seemed that a searchlight had been turned on his soul. He had met Monstruwacans before, but this one had a power and clarity rare even among his caste.

"Ah, a Lepidopterist. How may I help you, child?"

"It is of a child I ask, Master," Loomis said carefully. "My child. A boy rejected by my guild when he was cursed by the allergy sickness and since lost to me."

The Monstruwacan spread his hands. "Why would I know of this boy? Surely when he left your guild another took him in."

"No, Master. He rejected the blandishments of the other guilds, claiming to want to seek his destiny in the Great Pyramid . . . and perhaps beyond."

"Beyond? That is unlikely, its is very rare for –" He paused, as if recalling a long-forgotten memory, then considered the Lepidopterist carefully. "Is your name Loomis?"

"Yes, Master! How did you know?"

The Monstruwacan's brow furrowed and he contemplated the great ritual in silence for several minutes. Loomis, caught in a fever of hope and fear, dared not speak, lest he cause some fatal upset. In the rafters of the echelon, the last of the upsurging armies of butterflies were rising out of sight, disappearing through the many holes in the roof. Many would continue to climb the light wells, accruing new celebrants as they ascended the remaining two hundred and fourteen echelons of the Underground Country. Fifty echelons below the lowest floor of the pyramid, cunning nuances of light and scent would thin the relentlessly ascending butterfly nations by guiding many into long, Mobius-looped corridors, or tightly wound passages describing logarithmic spirals where they would wait their turn. After the majestic central column of life had passed from Humanity's Underground Kingdom in to the Great Pyramid, the waiting myriads would be gradually released to continue their journey.

"There was one," the Monstruwacan said eventually. "A boy bearing the signs of your calling on his face. He begged to be allowed to study for our guild. We refused. He was too old and it was unprecedented for someone from the Underground Country to seek such a boon. We encouraged him to return home and seek happiness among his people. He refused and defiantly set out to visit each of the thousand cities. For ten years, he wandered the Great Pyramid, staying a week in one city, a few hours in another. In due course, his peregrination was done, and he stood outside the Great Observatory at the apex of our world.

"His persistence greatly impressed the Council of Monstruwacans. You should be proud."

A lump grew in Loomis' throat, and tears pricked at the corners of his eyes.

"We expected him to ask again for admittance. We sought soft words to mitigate his disappointment. However, he surprised us again. He asked permission to brave the Land."

Loomis felt his heart lurch.

The Monstruwacan's face creased in sympathy. "He was of age, we had no grounds to deny his petition. Six weeks later your son – who was given the name Brere for his stout heart – set out in a party of forty-three brave, foolish young men. Millions watched as they crossed the Grey Downs without incident, skirted the Dark Palace, then fought valiantly in crossing the Road Where the Silent Ones walk."

Loomis felt a wave of peace encompass him. The Monstruwacan continued: "Then, as they approached the three Silver Fire Holes, a wave of blackness swept from the Thing that Nods and engulfed them. When it had passed, no trace of our valiant explorers was left behind."

An hour later, a group of sweepers found Loomis. He was kneeling in peaceful supplication, his face crusted with old tears. All around him were the bodies of millions of dead butterflies, the sad, inevitable fraction of the exhalation that had failed to achieve their destiny. Their broken, exhausted bodies were continuing to filter down, and were already two hand spans deep around the Lepidopterist.

High above, legions of butterflies swept through the thousand cities then burst out of the twelve hundred thousand embrasures of the Great Pyramid in a detonation of color and motion. Actinic beams kindled by the Earth current and guided by cunning prisms and mirrors illuminated the circling flocks.

The four hulking watchers quailed, if only briefly, at humanity's defiant exultation. The insects swept around the pyramid in ever-widening circles. After a little under an hour they began to die.

Night returned to the Earth.

Imago

Brett Davidson

In the declining hours of a certain day, Ael leaned over the balcony of her home and savored the evening glow which was like a sunset, but not a sunset. Her history teacher had told her of sunsets, but such things didn't happen in the Underground Fields and there had been no sun at all in the Night Land above for millions of years. Nonetheless, in the clock-created mornings and evenings leading up to the coming Exhalation, when the population of butterflies was being built up step by step, she often saw great clouds of shimmering crimson and gold wreathing the enormous hanging lanterns as they proceeded on their way along their ceiling tracks.

Her hands tightened about the rail as she was overcome for a moment by a feeling that was one part vertigo, one part claustrophobia and one part some nameless longing. She thought about those butterflies: they bore no resemblance to their larval stage, yet within the larva there was encoded the complete and inexorable directive of metamorphosis that lead to these shining creatures. How strange to be two lives, separated by a threshold of disintegration and renewal when human beings had but one, rounded as it were with death.

She looked down, and the world turned. She might have fallen, and toyed with the idea of leaping, because the spurt of fear that came with the almost-intention was a delicious thrill.

Because things must be balanced, she looked up and saw the crisscrossed ribs and vaults of the artificial sky. On the edge of sleep she often tried to imagine that roof of stone and the great metal mass of the Redoubt above her splitting open to reveal the free and empty sky. She imagined many things in fact; not only sunsets, but also islands and seas. She had never seen a sea, but lived in a village that climbed a stone-grey tree like metallic ivy. In the manner of most villages in the Fields, it was a cantilevered spiral that wound around one of the massive piers that supported the ceiling of her home cavern. The piers themselves, four hundred yards tall, were in an aperiodic arrangement which was supposed to give some sense of variation and surprise so that the structured scale of the cavern did not become oppressive, though it had that effect nonetheless. The accretions of ages had given individuality to the parts, but as the Eugenicists always seemed to be roving in search of genetic peculiarities to trim, so the Architects pruned their huge trees of stone and metal and consequently the lives of the people who lived within them.

The nearest lantern went into eclipse behind a pier and she retired indoors. "Genes, architecture and destiny," she murmured bitterly to herself. "If only something other than death might alter me." She did not fully understand it yet, but she had a very peculiar talent that could indeed change her as the butterflies were changed: she was a liar.

The lift ascended the central axis of the Great Redoubt at an interminable pace. Larger than a house, it had carried the class vertical miles from their home cavern and there were miles yet to go. Above the datum plane of the surface, the Pyramid and Observatory Tower of the Great Redoubt rose to a height of eight miles with over thirteen hundred cities layered within it like the pages of a book while below there were a hundred miles more of a hundred subterranean Fields. Ael's home was halfway below and her destination halfway above.

From time to time the Stress Master engineers stopped the lift at an airlock station and the attendant nurses on board checked the girls for signs of pressure sickness. For the periods of confinement as the atmosphere was carefully adjusted and the passengers were allowed to acclimatize, the lift car was equipped with entertainments, sleeping alcoves and facilities for ablutions, all of which were much used as boredom and vertigo took their toll. Ael herself spent much of the time sitting and reading the venerable poems of Aesworpth.

The Exhalation of butterflies had been in preparation for years and more and more resources were being poured into the breeding of vast flights of insects to be released all at once. As a consequence, the children and adolescents of the Underground Fields were both the subjects of neglect and a nuisance and to mitigate this dual condition, they were sent on trips to various parts of the Great Redoubt that they might not otherwise have seen. On this trip, her class would be billeted in one of the middle cities of the pyramid and be taken on to see Watchmen who patrolled Outside and then an aerodrome that opened on to one of the external balconies.

Ael was not impressed, and unlikely to be. She knew all about the supposed purpose of the Exhalation already: her father was one of the respected lepidopterists of her level, he was training his son to succeed him and she raised hawkmoths herself as a hobby. She had also seen plenty of dead insects pinned in display cases and supposed that the sight of an inactive flying machine could only be as uninspiring as those dead butterflies. It was not as if she would be allowed to stand on the balcony of an aerodrome while one swooped and soared Outside, let alone be carried in one herself.

What she wanted most of all to sit in the Tower of Observation and what she wanted even more than most of all was to walk out of the Great Gate into the Night Land itself where she could have grand adventures and become a hero, just like the Watchmen and Aviators she read about. Right now though, she was sitting and waiting for neither of these things and she hated it. She looked around at her companions and one of them, her friend Feste, pulled a face at her. She ignored her.

Finally the lift shuddered to its last stop and the girls were ushered out. Sister Maia, the leader of the party, gave an earnest speech about the importance of good behavior and not running wild simply because they were away from their familiar surroundings and neighbors, though those that weren't completely disoriented were more concerned that they might seem gauche and ignorant. Then they were shown to their billets by worthy citizens of the city.

As it happened, Ael and Feste shared a room and as she tossed in her unfamiliar bed in a seemingly hopeless attempt to capture sleep, she saw her looking back, an expression of gleeful anticipation on her face.

"Think of who we're to see!," Feste whispered. "Watchmen, Aviators!"

"Monstruwacans and Seers," added Ael a little snobbishly.

Feste blew a raspberry. "What do they do but watch the Watchers, who watch them in turn?," she asked.

"Watch and see and watch and see!," Ael said in return and the two giggled over word games for a while. "See and do, see and be!"

On the first full day, the class visited one of the Halls of Honor with its army of statues and then they saw a Watch house and observed the Watchmen drill in a spacious hall with their flashing diskoi. The men were indeed impressive: tall and with an icy precision about them and smelling of sweat, oil and ozone. Several of the other girls surreptitiously took slip names from the laughing brutes and a few were even foolish enough to raise their veils and leave cards with their own slip node addresses.

The Watchmen's helms presented blank planes and slots at first, and when raised, it seemed to Ael that the faces beneath were but growths shaped by the metal. They all seemed dull as statues to her and she haughtily kept her veil over her face.

The aerodrome was at once a stranger and a more familiar place. Living halfway up a pier with a father and a brother who bred butterflies for a living, the concept of flight struck more of a resonance with her. There was a strange combined feeling of the familiar and the extraordinary in the fact that she understood flight in the context of the enclosed Fields and stood beside the machines that would fly in the open space of the Night Land. She stared at the huge doors of the launching catapults and tried to imagine them opening as an airship carried her though and out and away.

The airships were beautiful things, made of brightly painted resinous silk composites stretched over extravagantly looped frames of alloy and composites, which Sister Maia described as "a brilliant concerto of tensile structure." Ael just admired the shapes without considering how or why, though she guessed that she should when Maia continued, this time talking about "form following function" and "the intersection of truth and beauty," which seemed to be the sort of language someone with poetic ambitions like herself should use.

She held her hand up to the clear nose of one airship which flowed back in sweeping planes to blend with the underhung fuselage and high shoulders of the delta wing. The belly of the fuselage itself seemed to suggest in one long and gentle sinoid curve both the dynamics of flight and the flank of a human body as it tapered towards the forked tail fins. Inside that mechanical body, Maia was explaining, coils of power cells charged from the Earth Current drove scimitar-bladed contraprops that spun on rings around the fuselages between the wings and tails. Each of the blades, Ael noticed, was painted a different bright color; this was probably meant as a warning to prevent the hangar crews away when the engines were powered up, but she saw it as a gesture of joyful defiance against the outer darkness. With their wings raised and arched just so, their glittering heads, extravagantly painted props and their delicate legs, the airships looked like a species of beautiful monster, and nothing like dead, pinned butterflies after all. She was told that the manufactories of the Redoubt were quite capable of making larger and more formidable wasp-machines but the Aviators, with their own heroic ethos like the Watchmen, refused to fly such things. This she understood perfectly.

The Aviators were scarcely less remarkable than the machines. Indeed they seemed to be the one half of a peculiar dimorphic species mated with the airships that only by coincidence roosted in the tiers of the Great Redoubt alongside human beings. Everything about them was light and colorful, like the butterflies that her family bred. Their costumes were of the finest silks, brightly embroidered and badged and thickly quilted for warmth in the cold air of Outside. Their armor was a lighter version of the set used by Watchmen in case they crashed and had to make their way back home on foot; their helmets were sculpted like the heads of insects and even the diskoi that they carried were more refined. Everything about them spoke, sang of a poise and intelligence that far outshone the blunt massiveness of the soldiers, or so it seemed to her. They had *glamour* – and one was the most glamorous of all.

Ael couldn't stop watching this one very special Aviator who had an airship painted like one of her hawkmoths and wore a rakish motley. He didn't swagger or brag and he spoke little, but everything he did or said had a greater value because of this. The exact opposite of the bulky Watchmen, he had an overall slenderness and slightness of stature that was unusual even among the lean Aviators. Overall, this gave him an odd, almost sexless appearance, but she forgave him for his grace and the affinity of insects that made him both more like her and so thrillingly different. His attractiveness was something that seemed to come close and then lead her away. This man flew, and maybe he would take her with him.

Of course she knew that this was a fantasy, but unlike many who were prone to fantasies, they were almost good enough in themselves rather than being a deception. Well, almost, she admitted. Then again, one might come true.

Feste, who had been watching nearby, gave her a pinch. "You are wake-dreaming, Ael – and I know of what you dream of too," she teased.

"Oh, of what?"

"Oh, you know. Go on: dare," she said smirking.

"Dare what?"

Feste laughed. "I know, I know! How can you not dare now?" She danced away, at least having the decency to leave her the space to make her approach to the Aviator on her own.

Ael turned around and saw the man watching her. He may have been just out of earshot and perhaps would not have made much sense of their dialect in any case, but nonetheless her face burned with embarrassment. She could run away now, but she would have to face Feste's taunts if she did.

Very well, Ael decided. I'll talk, and be just like one of the others. She walked up to him. "Hail," she said.

"Ah, one from the Low Fields?," he asked. "Who are you?" None of the Aviators were old, but his voice was very young.

"A poet," she replied. Of course it was an exaggeration and she had only shown her poems to her friends, but she had to appear to be something other than just another rustic devotee of the Aviators.

"Is that who you are or what you do?," he asked, thankfully not put off at all, though he was obviously rather skeptical.

"I ask this of each thing: 'What is your nature?'," she countered, taking up his challenge and immediately thinking that she'd overplayed.

"This thing might not answer." He said smiling, to her relief. She liked his voice, she decided, it was sweet – and he had decided to play a game with her.

"Then neither will I," she said. "Tell me of flight instead. Tell me of your airship."

So he did, and as she listened and watched him, she tried to speak like a sophisticated dweller of the high pyramid, rather than a rustic who constantly repeated and rhymed. He at least found her attempts amusing. His eyes glittered like obsidian. One pupil was dilated more than the other, she noticed, which was odd.

He demonstrated the controls of the airship, pointing out the function of the various dials and showing her how the manual levers in the cockpit made the wings twist and altered the pitch of the prop blades. She told him about her moths. He knew about moths, and had bought a few as pets in the past.

"Ah, you may have bought one of mine," Ael said.

"Maybe I did."

"Why do you fly?," she asked, thinking that since they had already unknowingly known each other as it were, he would also be a direct enactment of her own myths and motives.

"Because I couldn't walk. I've always thought of the Great Redoubt as a giant half-buried in the earth, the Pyramid its head and helm and the Underground Fields its lungs and entrails. We are penned here by the Watchers and I wish that somehow this giant could free itself, stand shaking the clods of soil from its body and stride across the Land. In an airship I can stand as high as a Watcher and fly faster than anything that runs."

She laughed. "Cap-dweller, you think that all sense is in this weighty top! Your Pyramid seals in something much lighter that wants to emerge and change. Can you see such, so-named Aviator?"

"Maybe I do now."

Ael laughed again; even she saw this as clumsy, but it was an exception and mostly he was clever, light and witty. Silently she thanked Feste for her provocation and decided that she'd like to continue talking with him. Time was running short, though; the chaperones and Sisters would never violate a girl's dignity by calling her name aloud in mixed company, but they were making it clear by their stances and raised voices that the visit was over its allotted time already and the group should be gathering together to move on urgently. Sister Maia was pointedly looking around, practically standing on tip toes as she counted heads.

Ael was not going to leave without also leaving some trace or link. She had to know the name of this Aviator and give him her own. She gave a sly grin to the Aviator and trotted up to Feste, tugged at her sleeve and demanded one of her cards.

"Oh-ho," Feste chortled. "What are you saying now?"

"Ssh! Grant me a card, tell none!"

Feste's smirk became wider. "If I don't or if I do?"

"Do, or if you don't I'll . . ."

"You'll what?"

"Grant me a card, Feste!"

She snickered and brought a card out from where it was

concealed in her sleeve lining. "Done – and don't forget your following favors, Ael."

Ael snatched the card away before she could tease her more and quickly scribbled her own slipname over Feste's. Looking around to see that the chaperones weren't looking, she darted over to the hawkmoth airship, flicked the card through its open canopy with a wink at its bemused pilot and hurried back to the gathering class, but not before she was noticed.

"Ael of Salmakis," hissed Maia in her ear. "You have been tardy!"

"My contrition, Respected Sister," she said earnestly. "I was fascinated by the airships – such I liked and so I see that I will be an Engineer!"

The trip ended with an address by a tall elderly woman in purple, one of the ruling Monstruwacans, who told them of the sublime absurdity of the Exhalation. How essential it was, she said, that something so pointless and contrary to the rule of the Night Land be performed on such a grand scale. It was to show the Watchers, the Silent Ones and entropy itself that the warmth of the vanished sun still endured in the heart of the Great Redoubt. The honor of this speech was supposed to be the highlight of the trip, but as far as Ael was concerned, everything significant that was going to happen had already happened.

Returning home to the depths of the home Fields, she found her father, as ever, inspecting his latest batch of butterfly pupae. "*Morpho rhetenor,*" he said proudly. "Seven inch span. Iridescent blue. Lovely."

"More butterflies for the Exhalation?," she asked without interest. It was almost to spite him that she kept her moths.

He smirked. "Some, but only some. These are far too valuable. Because so many are going Out, there's a premium on this breed now. I'll make a nice profit on these selling them as pets to society ladies in the upper cities."

"Good for you."

"Good for us, dear."

"So say." She went to her room to wait for a message from the fascinating Aviator.

There was no message from the Aviator that day, nor the next and on the day after that, Ael was sick. She sat in bed, wrapped tightly in her quilt and looked out of her window to watch the hanging suns go about their peregrinations. She was old enough to know that such crushes were irrational self-deceit, but she didn't know if anyone was ever old enough not to suffer in this way.

Listlessly, she checked the boxes of soil where a batch of hawkmoths were pupating, but they showed no sign of emerging yet.

A day later she was at school, pleading that she had succumbed to a delayed effect of the pressure changes, which was believed. As an added boon, she was excused for a while from physical culture and drill classes, in which to her shame she had never excelled anyway.

There were other girls who had fallen ill, but returned to school with knowing, possessive smiles and full of sly chatter about the messages that they'd received from the Watchmen and Aviators. They recited litanies of their names: Tires, Ashelden, Russ, Orlan, Angeleve and so forth. Ael suspected that most of these names were made up, but her spiteful accusation of one girl only left her the loser in a scuffle.

Finally, when she was at home cursing her own stupidity in both failing to learn the Aviator's slipname herself and in ever having seen him in the first place, her table chimed. She rushed to access her homenode and found the critical, vital message there. She at last had a name too: Sartor, of clan Phaenes. The message read: "?"

The civilization of the Redoubt was constrained more by custom and meme than it was by force. "We're here because we're here," as a tautological drinking song had it, with the chorus, "I am who I am!" While Ael was of the Underground Country and most likely destined to remain there, this was largely so because this assumption was not questioned. Likewise, while she was chaperoned when in strange districts, she was not watched in places where she was expected to be as it was assumed that she was already mindful of everyone's eyes. Therefore, she realized, it logically followed that if she was not accompanied, it would be thought that she was in her rightful place. Engineering and concealing an escape was technically simple: she informed the Sisters that she had suffered another attack of pressure sickness and absented herself from classes at a time when she knew that her father and her brother were on an inspection tour of the butterfly hatcheries. Everyone assumed that she was in bed and no one should be able to prove otherwise.

Of course while her strategies for escape were easy in theory, her most rigid guardian was herself and this waywardness was not easy at all. To rise even one level above her own without supervision induced reflexive agoraphobia and she would not have done so if she did not have one specific destination in mind that was as clear and real to her as her home. It was that goal, Sartor, that she defined as her foundation of identity and she even kept repeating his name to herself under her breath as a reassurance: "Sartor ex Phaenes, Sartor ex Phaenes, Sartor . . ."

The lift came to one of its halts with a bang and a hiss. She bit her lip behind her traveling veil and tried to act as if she had been on this trip a thousand times before. No one could hurt her, custom was her armor.

Sartor could hurt her. She was breaking custom with him as her classmates only dreamed to do. He could slip his dagger right into her heart through only a couple of layers of silk. A vulgar simile occurred to her and she felt queasy.

He met her in formal costume at the final stop, the silver moth clasp of his flight at his throat. She trembled with guilt, thinking that he was beautiful but that she had deceived herself and had to be lead away almost in a daze to a commercial billet for solitary women. Those who watched saw a man in uniform and a woman in a veil following all the forms of propriety.

"Why have you done this?," he asked when they had been alone for a while.

Ael was confused. Hadn't he invited her, or had she suggested the invitation first? "Why have I, you?"

It was so strange, she never thought that it would be like this at all. When she had thought of adventure, and when she had planned this assignation, the fantasy of that adventure had been illuminated with the tension and thrill of secrecy and deceit. What she had not expected was the feeling that somehow something within her was tricking her into pretending that it was all so accidental. Almost every step had been planned, but it seemed as if she had taken every one of those steps on a random walk determined by the oracle of dice lightly tossed from her hand. Her secret self had loaded those dice however and this paradox made her dizzy.

"Why anyone?," she asked.

He shrugged. "Perhaps I am tired of being only myself."

His manner seemed as casual as an imp of the perverse whispering temptations. "It is of no consequence, it is not true," it seemed to say in the spaces between his words. "Earth has slipped into its final night and thus all is a dream. Let your fate fall where it will, because when you wake you will be someone else and it will not matter."

"I had a dream last night," she said. "I dreamt that I was a butterfly, and when I woke, I wondered if I was a butterfly dreaming that it was me."

Sartor laughed. "I have read that story too – there is no need to lie to me!"

So she decided to trust him, on deceit, a chance and a coincidence.

"Take me flying," she said.

"Maybe," he told her.

Descending once again, Ael sat through the acclimatization stops with a grim determination. It was something to which she was going to have to become accustomed. She was certain that her plan had worked and indeed, when she returned to school, she showed the symptoms of pressure sickness and the nurses almost sent her home again. Her father and brother, returning from their own tour, were at once too exhausted and excited to even think that she might be lying when she said that she had been at home in bed the whole time.

It was at this moment of success that she realized that she was not who she thought she was. There was someone named Ael in whom everyone believed, but she was just a costume and the creature that inhabited that costume was some sort of nameless ghost or imp. She had thought a day ago that this imp wore her, but now she began to think that she was that imp herself now. It was most strange, but it gave her imagination a certain freedom that she had aspired to as a poet, even if at this stage she could not find a true name for herself. 'Ael' would have to do for now, with or without quotation marks.

The outline of a plan came to her from underneath her conscious thoughts as she pondered on her odd condition. It was obscure but compulsive at first, and swiftly become concrete and she realized that it was but the logical extension of her first trip to the heights.

The next day in class, her Sisters were much impressed with the energy that she showed, though they were rather critical of the way in which she applied herself. They reminded her that she would be sitting guild examinations next year and she should decide soon about which courses of study she should take. As it was, she was far too uncentered. "I'm to be a librarian," she lied merrily. "I'll want to read all, especially books historical and cartographical, plus those biographical and mythological." They shook their heads, but delivered the texts that she requested nonetheless.

Later, she took her notes home and began to piece them together. She was sure, from what she had read, that the settlers who'd left the Great Redoubt ages ago had set off for the North with the intention of building their own arcology in the more clement lands that were supposed to exist there. There was even an estimate of how far the expedition might have penetrated, or at least of its absolute limit to its range, which was just within the range of a well-charged airship of current design.

The maps themselves were of good quality, within the border of the horizon as seen from the top of the Tower of Observation. They detailed all the visible threats of the Night Land, noting especially the vast Watchers and the dreadful House of Silence, but these were of no concern to her. Sartor's airship would fly above these things, or swoop by so fast that they'd have no hope of stopping it.

Before she slept, rising naked from her bath, she realized that she was frightened. The water lapped about her calves, cooling.

Of course the plan was vague, but it was simple. Complications were excuses not to do something. She could commit herself to the simple plan and adapt to contingencies as they went a long, or she could stop everything now. She would not make up excuses; the two of them *would* go on this expedition. The Lesser Redoubt had the overpowering reality of all things that existed just past the limit of sight.

She dressed herself and hurried to her room to continue her calculations where she saw that the hawkmoths were finally freeing themselves of their soil beds. Bodies bigger than her thumb pulsed as they pumped blood into their new wings and on the backs of their thoraxes, white patches that resembled skulls or masks stared up at her. They were *Archerontia atropos. Atropos,* meaning unturning. Yes, she would be changed and would fly just like them and never turn back. She opened her window so that they could escape.

For a few frustrating weeks, Ael and Sartor only spoke over the slip network. The days when she would be free from the Sisters' observation were yet to come and sickness no longer a tenable excuse. Fortunately her father was too preoccupied to log her calls. Indeed he now seemed to live in constant pursuit of eternal daylight under the wandering suns while she had long nights alone with the face and voice of

Sartor. She saw this partition of light and dark as a symbol of the separation between the worlds of herself and her father, and a sign of her unity with her beloved, though a mere sign was no substitute for his real presence.

What he had to say to her was a further disappointment: "The Watch is ending all flights. They'll announce it on the hour slips a decent interval after the Exhalation."

Ael was exasperated. This was not how it was supposed to be. She had not even told him of her plan yet. "What? Why? Didn't you say no?"

He shook his head, nodded. "Of course I said no," he said. "It didn't do any good. The decision was made high up by the Monstruwacans."

"Oh, and what had they to say?," she demanded.

"They said that the air is too thin. It has been thinning for millions of years and now they have decided that it is not worth the risk of flying."

"What nonsense, what so say! They could . . . they could do all. They could, I see, I think, they could find the Lesser Redoubt!"

"If it still exists . . ."

"How to know if there is no search? What of the heroic creed? Men go Out into the Night Land and are feted for nothing more than killing a few spider crabs. Even criminals go Out and return pardoned! We send butterflies Out! Criminals and butterflies, but not women!" She almost stamped her feet.

"And certainly not girls."

"I'm not a girl!"

"You are, Ael, and will be for a little while yet."

She would have slapped him if she could reach through the screen. "And what of you? What do you say that you will do?"

He shrugged. "I don't know. Train endlessly, maintain my machine, put on the appearance of a hero and try to impress young girls."

She laughed at him so that she might not spit, but he was just as bitter as she.

It was afterwards that her impish self realized that this

situation could be an advantage. No one had expected her to visit Sartor on her own and thus it had been easy. Now no one expected an expedition to the Lesser Redoubt and therefore the two of them could flee there without the encumbrance of lengthy plans and the eyes of escorts. Delight overcame her as her mind spun strategies. Her only regret was that she had to trick Sartor, but she knew that he would understand he would understand and forgive her sooner rather than later.

The days of festival preceding the Exhalation came at last and classes were terminated. Ael was supposed to be sequestered at school for the guild examinations that were sat by all who had not already been granted positions by inheritance, or for various reasons had renounced them. Ael threw the loaded dice in her head and took the lift to see Sartor.

"I've got a present for you," he said with a strange furtiveness when they were alone in the hangar.

"What is it? Say, show what you have!," she demanded, slipping once again into the embarrassing alliterative dialect of the Fields in her excitement. Maybe he had thought in parallel with her and they were going to fly away this very night!

He turned and took a bundle out from under the pilot's seat. It was another flight suit.

"Where did you get that?," she gaped, reaching out to touch it, but not daring to take it. So I was right, she thought. He shares my intentions after all!

"I made it. We make our own, I took an old one of mine and stitched and sewed a bit. I knew that you were about my size, I guessed how you might be shaped differently and I let the adjustment of the straps and fastenings make up for any mistakes that I'd made."

"For me?," she asked redundantly.

"Do you want to try it on? We can't fly together now, maybe we never could, but you could wear this and imagine what it was like." He shrugged. "I know it's absurd, but I really did think that we could have flown."

So now the gift was a substitute. The childish Ael would have accepted that; she would have cried and even fought, but she would have been bound by dull fact in the end. Ael the imp however though saw this as another opportunity to make new facts. The suit was only a substitute for a flight now, but already she guessed that if he was willing to make it for her, she could twist the substitution into the real thing. She took the bundle and let it fall open. Was she going to put it on here and now? She would have to take off her own clothes first, and she certainly wasn't going to do that. The idea seemed somehow too casual without some form of symmetry. "I'll wear if you unwear," she said.

He laughed. "Now why would I do that?," he asked.

"Something must be equal."

"How is that equal? You'll be my equal if you put it on."

She clutched the flight suit to her, already feeling naked. The mass of quilted fabric held close already felt like some double of his body, which was most disconcerting. "You've been disfigured, haven't you?," she blurted.

He was taken aback by that. "Have I?," he quipped. She was sure that he was hiding something.

"That's why you won't unwear," she went on.

"I undress every day."

"But not for me."

"That's because we're not married. It wouldn't be proper."

"Suppose we were married, hmm?," she suggested. "What say then?"

"We barely know each other," he pointed out. "I only met you a few weeks ago."

"How can you so say?," she cried. "I know as if we've known each other forever!"

"You're exaggerating. Young people always say that." He laughed nervously, possibly regretting his gift now.

"If not in this life, then another. I don't know, I don't care. It's forever now."

"Maybe," he admitted, possibly more in resignation than acceptance.

She'd won something, but she wasn't sure what and she

was now bound to put the thing on. "I won't let you see me," she said, insisting on some form of balance.

"I won't look, then." He ostentatiously folded his arms and stared at the hangar door, but Ael ducked behind the body of his airship anyway. Removing her own clothes was easy enough, but the flight suit was a complicated thing with its own peculiar ties with a set of specialized undergarments and she had to stop and partially disrobe a few times to be sure that she even had things on the right way around. Even then she was not sure whether she could get everything right and she dithered with several fastenings untied and buckles hanging loose, red-faced with frustration and ashamed to ask Sartor for assistance. In the end, she waddled out to face him, feeling as bloated as a caterpillar. Of course he laughed at her, making her angry.

"What a funny little pupa you have made, then. Will you be a moth or a butterfly when you emerge?"

"Who's to think I will emerge? Have you?," she said in pointed reminder of Sartor's persistence in refusing to even loosen a button in her presence.

He ignored this, or at least overtly. "I'll call you moth anyway, just in case. You want to fly in the night."

"And I will!"

He sighed. "Moth," he teased, grinning.

"No!"

"Moth!"

"Stop it!" She pinched him, or tried to and was thwarted by the thickness of his own flight suit.

He laughed again. "Really? Do you want me to?"

" . . . no." She let him finish for her, correcting her mistakes. At various points he slipped his hand underneath the outer layers and she squirmed, not sure whether he was being lecherous or practical, nor whether she should be affronted or thrilled.

Finally, as he was tightening the final set of cords behind her back, she wrapped her own arms around him and looked seriously into his face. He immediately realized her intent and froze. His eyes were black and shining, like ink. His lips parted as if he was about to say something. He's only a boy, she thought. He's afraid of me. They continued their embrace for a while until he finally permitted her to loosen the straps of his gauntlet and the cuff of his undergarment. She found underneath a delicate wrist, pale and softly downed. His veins were like pale blue traceries. She stroked his skin, touched her lips to it. He sighed and she kissed his neck, the muscle that ran from his ear to his collarbone and then struck like a serpent. "I have an idea," she whispered in his ear.

"What's that?"

"The Monstruwacans' banning is just so say, isn't it? So they say you can't fly, but they can't stop you, can they?"

"They can stop me easily."

"Only if they know."

"Oh."

She smiled, hoping that in acceding to this conspiracy, he'd become complicit in a more visceral collusion. If not, she'd use those words in a tragic poem about unrequited love. She kissed him again. "Mmm . . . What say you now then?"

"Where would I go? What could I bring back but a stone?"

That was nonsense. He knew that he wanted to go, stones or no stones. Anyway, she had a brilliant idea. "Where *we* could go," she corrected, "is the Lesser Redoubt."

"No, nobody knows –"

"True! Thus we'll heroes; you will be King and I will be Queen!" She bit him before he could disagree with her.

Ael had never invited Sartor to visit the Fields because it would only have seemed to drag him down and shatter his myth. Now, somehow, her own myth was broken. Standing in the portals of the home lift station for what was probably the last time, with the disembarking passengers spilling out around her, the golden light of the artificial suns struck her like a chill. She felt profoundly out of place, which was what she wanted to know, but not to feel.

Appearances of beauty and falsehood conflicted in her senses. Through the towering stone and metal forest of the subterranean Fields, a half dozen of the hanging lanterns sent crisscrossed shafts of light through the living clouds of butterflies and diamond-bright flares from the windows of the spiral towns festooning the piers. Across the green landscape of the floor, myriads of scarlet banners were dotted like poppies in a meadow. The breeze brushed her cheek and was filled with the scent of flowers, carrying with it the echoes of distant festivities. Somewhere Masquers would be enacting mystery plays and revelers would be uncorking bottles of new mead and millennial wine. It was at once too intensely real and unreal as if it was reflected in a mirror, with left exchanged for right and all sense of direction lost. From the Night Land a shadow of the future had fallen across her and indelibly stained her being. She raised her veil, but still felt that she could neither touch nor see any of this now without feeling that some fine, invisible film of darkness coated her skin and clouded her eye.

A hand touched her arm and she started.

"Where have you been?" It was Feste, whom she had arranged to meet. "Maia sees your absence, the other Sisters know, and now they're all seeking and so forth!"

Ael looked at her. "I cannot tell," she said.

"You can tell, you can tell me? Surely I am your friend?"

"I do not know exactly where I have been."

"Ael, you affect to speak like one of the Cap Dwellers," Feste said.

"No, not even one of them . . ."

"Changeling? Has your Aviator taken you Outside?," Feste inquired. "Or have you . . . taken him inside?"

Ael barely recognized her friend, and it was this lack of affect more than her anticipation of loss that distressed her more. "Goodbye," she said, and turned back to the station.

"No, come!," Feste cried.

"I only came to go," Ael replied, and left.

The preparations and festivities of the day of the Exhalation, always a time of excitement and confusion provided perfect cover. Ultimately, the object of the Redoubt's security was to prevent any unwelcome influence from entering, and at a time when a significant portion of its biomass was to be deliberately expelled, their escape was almost easy.

The aerodromes were the obvious vents for the Exhalation. Chemical lures were atomized and forced out through the hangars and launching ports by fans in such thick concentrations that she could almost smell them. Her ears popped as the Redoubt's ventilation system built up an overpressure and in the great ducts at the rear of the hangar, she could hear the faintest whisper of the rising flight of butterflies. Most of the aircraft had been wheeled out of the way to provide as clear a route as possible for the escaping insects, except of course for Sartor's, and had the hangar boss been there, he would have been enraged at this. He was not there however, and the aircraft had been moved out of the way according to his orders and his satisfaction; Sartor had simply moved it back to its launch position as soon as he had signed his report. The boss would have been even more furious to have seen a civilian such as Ael there, she knew. The penalties would have been severe; disgrace and imprisonment for the both of them no doubt, but they were escaping before they were imprisoned. Reverse causality, she thought, and giggled, intoxicated by the pheromones and her own adrenaline.

Sartor was crouched under the aircraft already, disconnecting the charging cables and unlocking the catapult cradle. Ael ran to him and he ushered her aboard. The machine smelled of ozone and lubricants and it creaked and flexed under their weight, though not as if it were frail, but as if it were the body of sensitive lover responding to caresses. Quickly he buckled himself into the pilot's seat, seemingly making himself a part of the machine, or making the machine an extension of himself. She squeezed into the space behind him, her legs spread awkwardly to either side, his elbows against her thighs and imagined that the safety restraints around her waist and shoulders were his hands multiplied.

"Are you ready?," he whispered, his thumb on the launch trigger. The instruments lit up and cast colored reflections across his polished helmet. Already the props where whirring into life and the whole machine vibrated about her, transmitting that vibration to her and making her anticipation tangible. The airlock doors opened, revealing the darkness of Outside like an enormous eye or a mouth ready to swallow them. Around them, the first butterflies began to appear, their wings lightly rustling against the canopy.

"Yes!" Goodbye, goodbye, she thought. I've sold my world, so goodbye to all that I am and never was!

He flicked the trigger and they were flung forward, out of the bay and into the Night Land. At first, the acceleration of the catapult pushed her hard back against the rear of the cockpit and then, as it released, she was thrown against her straps in the opposite direction. About her, the structure of the airship creaked as its wings stretched to catch the air. The dark ground rushed up towards them and then they gained lift and their plummet became a soar and a climb. They were flying, truly flying. She whooped for joy.

The Exhalation burst from the colossal arcology, a great shout of light and life against the dark and the cold. Lit by the glow of the its many lamps, the great golden swathes of butterflies poured from the vents in every side of its armored hulk with an odd, almost fluid effect, first forming an enveloping nimbus of light and then billowing into the air so that it appeared as if the Redoubt had caught fire and exploded. An outside observer, and there were many, would have seen some sort of emergent order in the Exhalation as it expanded; myriads of milliards of butterflies were gathering in rippling curtains and veils that blended and overlapped and swelled outwards in pulses of light that synchronized in a slow and beautiful rhythm. Underneath the Exhalation there rose a sound like an ocean; the cry of millions of unified and joyful voices. A visitor from aeons past might have recalled a thermonuclear explosion, learned that this was a burst of life rather than malignancy, and drowned willfully in those voices.

The cloud began to spread over the Night Land, warmed for a while by the heat of the Redoubt's lamps, but as it diffused further and further, the light became attenuated and cold and the butterflies beat their wings less energetically, they shone more dimly and then they began to fall. One mote, not a butterfly but a Death's Head hawkmoth, flew farther and did not weaken, tapping rich stores of the earth current held in its own power cells. It soared over the land, climbed, looped slowly around the Redoubt almost as high as the finial Tower of Observation and the Final Light at its peak and then winged its way into the darkness of the North.

The Monstruwacans in their tower tracked it for a while until it was lost to even their sight.

About her the machine thrummed and the rotors threshed tirelessly against the air, carrying them onwards. She hugged Sartor from behind, wishing that she could be in his arms, knowing that she was. Onward they flew and everything she saw was nothing that she's ever seen or imagined before.

The Night Land scrolled below like an animated map, but it was real. It was at once more hideous and beautiful than anything she could have imagined. Painted largely in tones of black, it was ornamented and textured with points and smudges of illumination. In some places there were great rents in the earth, their depths filled with writhing flames and pustulant lava while elsewhere, odd little points of light generated by living beings clustered and moved and flickered. Once they passed over an almost perfectly regular hexagonal grid of bright green stars, then they flew by a braided tracery of dim mauve that flowed like a thick liquid down a gentle slope, painting the eroded contours of the land to either side. Beyond that there was a complex pattern of jale and ulfire that sported in the labyrinthine foothills of a Watcher, barely on the edge of perception and soon lost in their wake as they fled over a great slope towards something even stranger, something that shone and glittered like a plain of metal: it was a sea.

The waters unfurled in surf, then rolled on and on seemingly forever. Waves sparkled with marbled bioluminescence, lapping against the edges of ice floes and making her drunk with wonder, hypnotizing her.

She realized that she'd fallen asleep when she was jarred awake. The waves were choppy now and in the distance a volcano emitted a column of ash and steam that leant over the sea, its heavy belly illuminated a deep and threatening ulfire and red. "What's wrong?!," she cried.

"Turbulence!"

"Can't we climb above it?"

"No, current's too low."

"I calculated!"

"There's not enough, not enough to climb if we want to get as far as . . ." He didn't finish his sentence and concentrated on his piloting. Wisely, she didn't distract him.

The airship was shaken some more and her stomach leapt, a sensation that she'd experienced for the first time only hours before when they launched on their flight. She hadn't liked it then and she liked it less now and vomited immediately. The liquid splashed over Sartor's shoulder and down his back, but he didn't notice or ignored it. "Sorry," she mumbled unheard, and retched again. Eventually her stomach was empty, but still she heaved and coughed. She didn't dare speak up and there was no point anyway, so she decided to endure her misery. It was just another lesson in heroism, after all. Heroes don't care about being sick.

The airship spun again, there was a roar and a noise too sudden to describe and she struck her head against the canopy.

When she woke, it was still quiet and still and she was cold. The stink of her own bile assaulted her nostrils, mixed with other body fluids. There was a metallic tang, like the taste of copper which she knew was blood. Almost every part of her hurt, but nothing seemed to be broken. She could hear the rumble of the volcano in the distance, the lap of waves on a shore, and her own rapid breathing, but nothing else. That nothing else was clamping itself about her like dread.

"Sartor?," she asked tremulously.

Sartor didn't answer.

"Sartor!" She put her hands on his shoulders and shook him. He was as limp as cloth, his head lolling. She let go. Her hands were wet.

"Sartor, please . . ." Coils of chilly realization twisted in her belly and she had to get free. Gingerly she began to free herself from the binding straps and achieved as she did, albeit temporarily and tenuously, a certain detachment by focusing on this simple immediate task. She found the release for the canopy and climbed out where, for what it was worth, she could survey the damage.

She was surrounded as far as she could see by water as the waves breaking on the shore stirred sparks and pulses of bioluminescence from tiny creatures that lived in the water. They had collided with the peak of an island not far from a long, straight shore that she could see to the North. Perhaps Sartor had tried to make a fall to dry earth and almost succeeded.

Almost was still a failure. She began to walk around the wreck. The nose of the airship seemed to have taken much of the initial force of the impact and it was simply a freak of physics which had left her and not Sartor in a relatively undamaged cell of the vehicle. The great shining wings were crumpled and torn, one twisted almost entirely from the body of the aircraft and pointed directly up into the sky while the other was raked back against the fuselage and the props were almost tied in a knot. Even if . . . there was no chance that she could fly anywhere from here now. None at all.

It's like a dead and crumpled butterfly, she thought, and I have crawled out of it, as if I metamorphosed inside it. She giggled and then stopped before the laugh became hysteria.

The wind was rising and even under her flight suit she shivered. Her head spun and she doubled over, retching and heaving once more. A little mucus splattered on the ground. At least there was no blood. None of hers, anyway, but she stamped on the implications of that thought. Heroes didn't have thoughts, they dealt with facts and she knew what the facts were. This situation had been thrust upon her like an unwanted garment, but she would wear it as best she could. Yes, that was right, she told herself, her thoughts turning in odd circuits again as she tried to ignore the fact of her renewed imprisonment on this tiny redoubt. I'll be a civilization of one, she thought. Clothes make the man, the situation makes me, I'll match my face to my mask . . .

There was a splash and something black and serpentine emerged from the sea. Its fore end rose and bobbed and a pale tongue flicked out like a tooth-edged sword. "Glut!," it said and advanced. Ael scrabbled back, but it had her scent and continued, still cutting at the air. "Glut! Glut!," it repeated. She broke and ran for the airship and rifled amongst the wreckage of the cockpit. There was an emergency kit, she knew. There were medicines, food – and there was a weapon.

She found a lightweight diskos with a helical blade, flicked the trigger integrated with the grip and it came to life with a high-pitched whine. In the blue glow of the spinning blade, the horror was larger and nearer than she had thought, and she was almost within range of its flicking sword-tongue. She stepped back and was stopped by one of the crumpled wings. The thing crept closer still and she was trapped. Its open mouth swallowed her scream.

"Glut!," it said again and the tongue flashed out. She dodged it by an inch and it skewered the wing, tangling itself in the torn fabric. Before it could withdraw, she clumsily swung the diskos down and severed the appendage almost by accident. Shredded flesh and hot ichor splattered her face. The beast gargled and shrieked, its breath foully wet. The weapon, with so much inertia bound up in the spinning blade, seemed to have a life of its own and she had difficulty controlling it, but she nonetheless succeeded in swinging it around again and again, hacking into the body of the creature. It began to writhe spasmodically, probably mortally wounded, but all the more dangerous for that. Twice she was almost crushed against the ground or the wrecked airship before she seized an opening and leapt free to run across the fuselage where she watched its agonies subside. It took a long time and she didn't dare return to hasten the process.

Eventually the beast ceased to move, but she remained at

the tail of the airship. Every part of her ached, from the crash and from the battle. She groaned in pain, and them allowed herself to cry. She wondered if in a future age some hero would come this way and find the wreck and the remains of Sartor and herself and wonder why the airship had fallen. She hoped that they would, she hoped that someone would do better than they had and make it further and achieve some great, truly heroic goal and then carry word of what he had found back to the safety of the Great Redoubt.

Something within her became as brightly active as the blade of the diskos. She looked up and out. From her new vantage, she could see all sides of the island now, and it wasn't an island. The glowing waves described not a circle but a loop: there was a thin neck or causeway linking the peak to the greater shore. She could surely cross it, if no more horrors emerged from the sea to attack her – but then if they did, perhaps she could kill them too. She knew that she would continue to live in the Night Land and if she could, she would make it back home.

No. She could not turn back to the Great Redoubt. The sea barred her way to the South as surely as the crash did past from present. Her only route was North, towards where she had supposed the Lesser Redoubt had been built. She would go on, continue her journey.

The decision made, or made for her, she began to consider her needs item by item. To live and travel, she would need more than her insulated flight suit and a lightweight diskos; she would need food and armor as well. She went back to the cockpit and located the emergency packs of nutrition tablets and the powder that foamed to distil pure water from the air. On impulse, wrenched a tooth from the tongue of the dead serpent and pocketed it as a trophy. Then she began to methodically strip the stained armor from Sartor's body and rifle his flight suit for any more aids to her survival.

She stopped when the body was wholly exposed to her. Certain intrinsic things were revealed that were now irrelevant in death. She paused for while, amused at the mysteries that were resolved and the realization of her own naïveté. "Oh why didn't you tell me?," she cried aloud. Sartor did not answer, seeming instead to grin at this last joke. She continued in her task and ignored her tears.

She put the armor on herself, discovering that the range of adjustment was enough to accommodate her own frame. She was careful to tighten every strap and spring and elastic cord and to check that its power cells were fully connected so that the complicated device was worn like her own skin. From now on it would be her own skin: the armor was her face to the Night Land and all that separated her from death. This butterfly would undergo another metamorphosis inside the shell on her long walk to her destination, or she would not make it at all. She would keep this armor forever and indeed she would become a hero, exactly like Sartor. Her fame would buy her a new life, or she would be Sartor's phantom, she would pretend to be Sartor, which would be easy enough. Yes, she would be the living Sartor in her own heart. She repeated the name over and over to make sure that it fitted.

She turned back to where the body of her love lay. She could bury it, but a scavenger would dig it up. No matter what she did, it would decay and be consumed and defiled. The Sartor that she had known would have wanted most of all, to remain at the controls of the machine, so she left it there, its bare hands and face exposed to the air and those deep black eyes open to the darkness. She kissed Sartor one last time on the lips, fixed her mask over her face, took her new name and diskos with her and walked away down the hill, across the causeway and towards the Lesser Redoubt.

Catharsis

Nigel Brown

At first I thought the makeshift construction was a phantasm, a trick of my eye seeking structure amongst the tumble of girders, the warped barrel of a Current Cannon, shards of crystalline walkways, shattered chamber walls – the detritus of a wrecked City. I trudged down the slope of the final ramp; the twilight image solidified into my destination.

"Grandfather!" I called out.

The words died in the silent air.

I scanned his refuge as I approached. The twisted conduits and ducts, with their channels forced open to yeild what provisions they would, proved that I was in the right place.

But there was no sign of the old man amongst the algae pans – now dried out and caked in brown scum – or a hint of his presence around the huge water pipe that rose out of this Level's floor in a great arc.

As I drew closer, the floor plates grew slippery under my feet. There must have been a leak from the pipe. My engineer's mind wondered how that would affect the reconstruction work. I shoved those thoughts aside: I wasn't here to survey the City. That work was done.

After a hundred thousand years, it was time to clear out these Levels of the Long Siege – the lowest half-mile of the Pyramid that had borne the greatest brunt of attacks from the Night Land.

I quickened my pace, but my heart began to thump for another reason: What if he wasn't here? What if I was too late?

The small shelter, a crude lean-to framed by broken spears and walled with ripped cloaks, stood under the curve of the pipe. It lay concealed within its deeper shadows.

The irony struck me hard. It was hidden as if he – of all those amongst the Peoples of the Redoubt – was the frightened one. But my grandfather knew no fear, in contrast to those many millions; yet none of them would call him brave.

"Grandfather?" I repeated. I didn't want to alarm him, especially after his last encounters with the Clearing Teams.

The shelter was still. Just being this close to it brought back my earliest memories of the time when I lived in a hovel like this. I was eight years old again, and walking alongside our family cart as my father and older brothers hauled it through the City's ruined heart; we would scavenge useful items to trade with the Other Peoples for a taste of their delicacies, or to replace the precious baubles our own Tribe had lost.

Maybe this was the remnant of our own family shelter.

I shook my head free of its memories . . . this was no time for nostalgia.

I gingerly approached the entrance flap. My stomach flipped as I lifted it and looked inside. A bundle of rags lay on the flaxen mat. It resolved itself into human shape. The diskos lay alongside it, discarded and dark.

I hurried forward, lifted his head, and turned it towards me – it was my grandfather.

His eyes opened. They focused on me. Locked onto my features.

"Gathar," he said.

He recognized me.

"You have your father's face," he said. "Those eyes I remember well, when he last pleaded for me to leave our Homeland."

I sighed. He was never one to mince words. The old resentments still ran deep.

"So you're not going to chase me away?" I said. "Frighten me off with your diskos?"

My grandfather's ancient features cracked in a wide smile. He still had all his teeth. They gleamed.

"I sent those maggot turds away so you would come."

He pulled away from he, stretched and stood up. As a small boy, I remembered him towering over me. He still did. Despite my adulthood, his spare frame reached to the top of the shelter; he was a good head taller than I was.

I noticed that he still wore the battered breastplate of our family's House – that traditional armor borne as a constant reminder to himself of our Tribal lore . . . and of our supposed folly.

"I thought . . ." I began.

He caught the meaning of my words, and smiled again. Then his mirth exploded in a deep belly roar. His foul breath washed over me, but I didn't mind. He was alive, and well.

"This place is our Homeland. It cannot cause me harm. We have lived here for countless generations. So it has been . . ." then his voice stumbled. His eyes flashed with sudden anger. "So it should be."

I merely gazed at him. My silent disapproval spurred him into action. He slung his robe and hood over his armor to cloak it in white – the color of peace – and strode out of the lean-to. I followed him outside, beyond the shadow of the pipe. The uneven floor left me stumbling after him; my grandfather seemed sure-footed as his sandals crunched over the wreckage of a million lives.

"Come," he said. "This is what I mean."

He led me past the dried out algae pans, then stopped when we reached the edge of the one furthest from the pipe. I looked down into the basin. A metal sheet lay in one corner. My grandfather bent down, grabbed it by its edge, and flung it away with a clatter. Some water still persisted beneath it.

"Look," he said. Kneeling, he scooped some of the green scum off the surface. He took a deep swallow of the stringy film.

"Breakfast."

I saw now how he had survived, even when the Clearing Teams had reported that there was nothing to eat in this urban desolation.

"This is no life," I said.

"This is the life of our people," he retorted. "Why should it be no different now? We fought amongst ourselves before we saw the truth – then we discovered a life beyond the Battle: the way of Peace."

"The Frightened Peoples" . . . (How I slipped so easily back into the old ways of speaking! – though I no longer believed it) . . . "The Others have now decreed that these Lower Levels must be sealed off. They are ready to do a better job of salvage than we ever could, and strengthen these parts against assault. Times change."

"No," he muttered. "You've changed. Our tribe chose to live this life free of the rest of the peoples. So it has been for thousands of years! Now you've all joined them; you are caught up in their world. You deny alternatives; you deny the possibility of inner peace."

I shook my head. When the Pyramid's Council of Cities had come to us, explaining that they were sealing the bottom half-mile of the Great Redoubt for greater security, my tribe had at first denied that it was anything to do with them. But common sense prevailed. We accepted their offers of relocation – dissipation of our people amongst the Upper Cities of the Redoubt.

So we were the dispossessed of that half-mile: refugees of terrible battles and horrors who now deserved more than a miserable existence amongst the ruins of our greatest battles, our glorious victories . . .

It had taken all this time – centuries – for the Redoubt to recover from the last battles that shattered our Levels. Now the Others were ready to pay us restitution with their hospitality.

"Crap," my Grandfather said. "It's crap. They've brainwashed you to accept their version of the world."

I sighed. "It's for the greater good. Only you hold out, but the reconstruction machines will arrive soon. Father asked me to see you before that happened."

Grandfather's face darkened. "That man's no longer my son."

"Yet you don't deny me," I replied.

"I will, if you insist on accepting this erroneous position."

I turned, and began to walk away. The Clearing Teams would be along before the next sleep-time. I wasn't prepared to witness his burial as the City was re-sculpted for the good of the Pyramid's many millions.

"Where are you going?"

I refused to answer. If he wouldn't agree that this was the right thing to do – that our own people's traditions were no defense against the horrors of the Land outside, then we would never have any common ground.

"Don't you see?" he shouted. "There's nothing out there. Nothing to fear! It was just us, fighting amongst ourselves! It's their own horrors that they see when they look out. Their own terror that keeps them pinned inside this Pyramid of Pygmies!"

His words percolated through my mind as I marched, triggering an idea.

I stopped, and turned back towards his refuge.

"Are you ready for this?" I asked.

My grandfather stood tall and proud in the inner porch of the Great Gate.

He stiffened at my words.

"I have submitted to the Preparation, although I refuse to accept its purpose."

The lesser gate cranked upwards as he spoke. Though I had spent many years in the Upper Levels, I still could not bear to gaze out onto the Night Land. I would hurry pass any embrasures with my eyes averted.

I kept my gaze on his face. I could not look beyond the door into where he would soon stride.

His early teachings – though I believed them wrong in my head – could not be so easily scored from my heart.

"Farewell, Grandfather," I said.

His features softened, and he placed his hand on my crown.

"I cannot blame you for the sins of your fellows, Gathar," he said. "You have merely been weak. It is up to me to prove you wrong. Thank you for giving me this opportunity to do so."

He turned, with an eager look in his doomed eyes, and passed through the Gate.

The Testament of Andros

being the second chapter of Hodgson's *THE NIGHT LAND,* rewritten

James Stoddard

Since Mirdath died and left me alone in this world, I, who once cherished her sweet companionship, have suffered an almost unbearable longing. I have tried to continue my studies, my riding, and my physical training, but it all seems empty now. Mostly, I have spent my hours sitting beside the hedge gap where we first met, remembering the moments when we were together.

In the last few months, however, a miraculous event has given me hope, for in my dreams I have been transported into the future, where I have witnessed strange and marvelous things. Though I do not know if anyone will ever read it, I must set the story down, if only to ease my yearning for my beloved. If anyone does read my account, they will certainly disbelieve it. I scarcely believe it myself. Sometimes I think grief has stolen my sanity. But if you read with an open mind, you will gaze with me into the very portals of eternity.

From the time the dreams began, they continued night after night, always opening exactly where they ended the night before. They did not seem like dreams to me, but rather as if I woke in the future. A gray mist invariably obscured my vision when I first arrived, but it soon faded, leaving me in a land of darkness, lit here and there with strange sights. For the sun had died and everlasting night lapped the world.

From the moment I entered the dream, I possessed a full knowledge of the Night Land, and a complete set of memories, as if I had lived there all my life. In my earliest vision I found myself an adventurous, if hesitant, sixteen year old named Andros, standing at one of the windows of the Last Redoubt, high up in the side of a four-sided pyramid of gray metal forged to protect the last millions of this world from the Forces besieging them. The structure rose to a height of almost eight miles and held one thousand three hundred and twenty floors, each containing a city. I do not know its location, except that it lay in a tremendous valley.

I stood upon the One Thousandth Plateau, looking through a queer spyglass to the northwest, studying the hideous, but completely familiar landscape I had observed all my life. The window, which was made of a transparent substance much thicker and more durable than stained glass, rested in a recess the inhabitants called an embrasure. Thousands of embrasures covered the walls, which were all made of shining gray metal. The spyglass was a rectangular box set upon a pole, with not one, but two lenses, one for each eye. Its range could be adjusted using a thin lever; it hummed slightly and thin points of golden light burned within it.

In my right hand I held a copy of *Ayleos' Mathematics*, a book with a yellow metal cover, for as Andros I had always loved the art of numbers, particularly geometry. There is such certainty in mathematics; the world may change, but a seven is always a seven, and when added to two will invariably make nine. As a child I assigned personalities to the first ten numerals: 1 was strong, 2 friendly, 3 wicked, 6 funny, and so on. I even devised rules to explain how their personalities produced the correct answers in addition, subtraction, multiplication, and division. I considered the contemplation of numbers glorious sport, particularly the number seven, who I thought of as a good friend. Any time I was presented with a difficult decision, I could escape to mathematics for a happy hour. Often, after doing so, I would return to my troubles and immediately see the solution. But perhaps an interest in geometry is not surprising for one raised in a pyramid.

Because of my mathematical interest, as I stared through the spyglass I could give the name and distance of every object in sight, as calculated from the pyramid's *Center Point* – a mysterious strip of polished metal said to possess neither measurable length nor breadth, installed within the Room of Mathematics where I conducted my daily studies. In the wide field of my glass, my eyes first fell upon the bright glare of the fire from the Red Pit shining upward against the underside of the vast chin of the Northwest Watcher – The Watching Thing of the Northwest: *That which hath Watched from the Beginning until the opening of the Gateway of Eternity.* So Aesworth, the ancient poet had written.

To my amazement I suddenly realized the bard was incorrect, for deep within my soul I saw, as dreams are seen, the sunlit splendor of the past. Thus, even as I, Andrew, dreamed of the future, the youth in the embrasure remembered his former existence, though it seemed to him a vision of the dawn of the world. I looked back upon my life as Andrew Eddins as if I pondered dreams my soul knew as true, but which appeared as a far vision, hallowed with peacefulness and light. Since I had often demonstrated a knowledge of antiquity that confounded and angered the men of learning, I cannot claim to have been completely unaware of the past before then, but from that moment my awareness of the lost ages grew tenfold.

The knowledge struck me with such ferocity that I cried out and fell to my knees, overcome by the power of the revelation. I knelt there, stunned by all I knew and guessed and felt, overwhelmed most of all by the memory of Mirdath. As I recalled the way she had sung to me in the days of sunlight, the longing for her reached me from across the ages, and for the first time I understood the emptiness that had haunted me even from my childhood.

"Are you ill, Andros?" a voice asked.

I looked up to see the ancient, friendly face of Cartesius, my mentor and friend, who had taken me under his protection after my parents died six years before.

"Respected Senior, why are you up so late?" I asked, avoiding his question as he helped me back to my feet. "It's past the fifth hour of sleep."

"I can sleep later. A waste of time, sleep. I haven't slept in . . ." he blinked in thought, "forty-two hours. There's too much to do. The Thing That Nods has changed the angle of its movement by the slightest degree. We can see a fraction more of its face, if it is a face at all; the scholars are in furious debate on the issue. The whole tower is astir with excitement. According to the Records, such an event last happened four thousand seven hundred and twenty-six years ago, when Olin was Master."

"That's wonderful."

"Precipitous times, indeed. Who knows the ramifications?" He grinned happily, his eyes lost in distant horizons. "We are gauging the rest of the land, to see if any reactions arise. So far, we show a twelve percent increase in movement around the Giants' Kilns, but nothing more. We are watching the points of the compass steadily, though I just sent most of my assistants to bed – for some, exhaustion overcomes passion. A pity they lack fortitude."

He paused, his eyes suddenly focusing upon me. "But you were distressed when I first approached, and now you are trying to divert me. What is it, Andros? How can I help?"

I sighed. "It's hard to explain. I've. . . . seen something."

"Something unusual, by your demeanor. A revelation?"

"Yes. I think so."

"Tell me all about it. Leave out no detail, no matter how small. We shall find the significance in the insignificant."

I smiled at his old turn of phrase. A brilliant man, Cartesius served as the Master Monstruwacan within the Tower of Observation located at the pinnacle of the pyramid, where he and his fellow Monstruwacans observed everything that occurred within the land, peering into the darkness to extend their knowledge, always gleaning new information even while thwarted by distance – the plain of the Night Land remaining always beyond their reach. Their main duty was to watch, measure, and record the movements of the monsters and beasts besieging the Great Pyramid, so that, should one merely sway its head in the darkness, they set down every detail in the Records. The name Monstruwacan itself, in the strange language of the people of the pyramid, literally meant *Scholar of Monsters.* Though snow-haired with antiquity, Cartesius stood straight and unbowed, his dark eyes bright. He wore a perpetual stare, as if peering through the Great Spyglass had fixed his expression.

He had noticed me in my youth, for I possessed that rare and strange talent my people call the Night Hearing, a gift so uncommon that only I, of all the pyramid's millions, exhibited it to any great degree. I could detect, with better accuracy than the recording Instruments, the invisible vibrations pulsing continually through the eternal darkness of the ether.

"I have seen the past," I finally said.

His hoary eyes grew bright; he gave a happy smile. "Tell me."

So I related all I knew. The words tumbled from me. Even as I spoke, I expected Cartesius to reprove me, for I told of grass and trees, oceans and wind, and most of all, of the glorious, golden sun – such things as the people of the pyramid called myths. Then I detailed the tale of Mirdath and Andrew and all that had happened to them.

It took more than an hour to tell it, and when, voice choking with emotion, I finished, tears glistened not just in my eyes, but in Cartesius's as well. "Do you think it's all nonsense?" I asked.

The Master Monstruwacan sat upon a gray stone bench, his hand upon his bearded chin, his eyes lost in the strange world I had described. He cleared his throat. "Certainly not. Nor do I think an Evil Influence has affected your mind. You have surely experienced something. How extraordinary if it is true! And how sad."

I gave a sigh of relief. Even though, through experiments and the refinement of mental arts, the people of the pyramid spoke comfortably of ideas closed to our present understanding, as we of this day harbor beliefs our forefathers would have considered lunacy, still I feared my story too bizarre to be taken seriously.

"This strange gift you have, Andros," Cartesius said, "you have always known much about the ancient Days of Light. How I have laughed to see you confound and anger our scholars. How they long to believe you, even when they cannot accept your tales."

"But this –" I said. "It seems so unbelievable! Can a man live again?"

"I don't know. I have never heard of such an occurrence, but life is filled with many strange and wonderful events. I am perpetually astounded that we exist at all. How can I say something is impossible simply because it has never happened before? Every action must have originally occurred for the first time. I therefore grant that though your experience is unlikely, it is within the realm of the possible. I believe you."

"Thank you." My voice almost broke in gratitude.

"You need time to understand the revelation. Once you absorb it, you must write down everything – the tiniest bit, the merest speck. You must draw the shape of every leaf, show the precise color of the sky – a thousand things. Fear nothing and tell all! That is the way of the observer. Then I will set the Monstruwacans scouring the ancient histories – a man could spend a lifetime studying all you have told me. If only I were young! It makes me long to leap to the annals, to brush the dust away, to blow back the debris and look for correlation." A fire rose in his eyes. "This is even more important than the movement of The Thing That Nods! I will go to the

Hall of Records at once. There is one volume, yes, I see it clearly in my mind. I will rouse all the Monstruwacans from bed – they've had at least an hour's sleep; it should be sufficient. We must discuss this. We must correlate. We . . . must . . . correlate!"

He leapt to his feet, eager as a hound, and sped a dozen steps before abruptly turning.

"Forgive me, Andros. I forget the human in the hunt for the unknown. Will you be well, my boy? I can stay if you like."

I managed a smile. "I just need time to think."

His eyes focused gravely upon me; I felt him studying me with the meticulous scrutiny usually reserved for his work.

"Yes," he finally said. "You do need time. You must weep and laugh, grow angry and mourn, to prevent the vision from overwhelming you. But you will prevail, Andros. I see it. You will prevail. Come to the Tower of Observation if you need me."

As he vanished from sight, the thought struck me that I would not be the one to correlate my story with the Records. I did not need to; I had seen the past and knew the truth, but I loved my wise, old friend for believing me. Then the revelation overcame me again, and I sat and wept, clutching my copy of *Ayleos' Mathematics,* consumed by my memories of Mirdath.

Presently, when I could no longer bear contemplating my former life, I turned from the haze and pain of my memories back to the embrasure and the inconceivable enigma of the Night Land, for none of the inhabitants ever wearied of looking upon its dreadful mysteries. The old and young, from infancy to death, watched the black monstrosities of that fearsome country, which only our last refuge of humanity held at bay. But now I saw the familiar things with new eyes, as if from the perspective of that ancient gentleman, Andrew Eddins, and it left me dumbstruck to discover my impressions of the world so changed.

To the right of the Red Pit and the Northwest Watcher lay a long, sinuous glare known as the Vale Of Red Fire. Slightly more than fifty-three miles separated the pyramid from the Watcher. The creature could be seen from such a distance both because of the height of the redoubt, and the Watcher's enormity, for it stood twenty-six hundred and seventeen feet tall, or almost a half a mile. Its form was so cragged it might have been mistaken for a mountain if not for its brooding mouth and hollow-eyed, unswerving gaze. It possessed neither noticeable arms or legs, and its whole body cascaded downward from its head in irregular terraces. Beyond the Watcher stretched the dreary leagues of blackness called the Unknown Lands, across which shone the cold light from the Plain of Blue Fire.

On the borders of the Unknown Lands ran a range of low volcanoes, which lit up, far away in the outer darkness, the Black Hills. There shone the Seven Lights, which neither twinkled nor faltered through eternity, and which even the Great Spyglass could not make clear, since they stood over one hundred and sixty miles away. Neither had any adventurer ever returned to tell of them, for if he had, a record would have existed within the Great Library, which held the histories of all who ever risked not only their lives, but their spirits, by venturing outside the pyramid. The accounts of the Last Redoubt did not deal with mere thousands of years, but with millions, dating back to what we called the early days of the earth, when the sun still gloomed dully in the twilight sky. Of all that occurred before that, only myths and legends remained.

To my right, to the north, the House of Silence stood upon a low hill about seventy-five miles away. Many lights gleamed within it, but no sound ever rose. It had remained unchanged through uncountable epochs – always the unwavering lanterns shining from beneath its sloping eaves and twisted windows, but never a whisper our listening devices could detect. Our people considered this House the greatest peril in all the Night Land. From my earliest childhood, perhaps because of my Night Hearing, I feared it more than any other aspect of that terrible country, for I often thought I felt the evil seeping from it, reaching toward the pyramid. It always seemed as if some fate awaited me concerning it, and a violent trembling would seize my entire body if I stared too long into the beckoning blackness of its enormous, arched doorway.

Beside the House of Silence wound the gray, shimmering Road Where The Silent Ones Walk. We knew almost nothing about the Road, which passed around the eastern and southern sides of the pyramid before finally vanishing to the west. Many scholars held that of all the structures surrounding the pyramid, only it had been built, long ages before, by human hands. On this point alone were written more than a thousand books, all contradicting one another, and so to no end, as is the way in such matters. It was the same with every other monstrous thing – whole libraries had been penned on every aspect of the Night Land, and millions of volumes had molded, forgotten, into dust.

I stepped out of the embrasure. Because of the lateness of the hour, the wide corridor banding the One Thousandth Plateau lay deserted, save for a watchman riding the moving road spanning the width of the passage. Seeing this familiar scene from Andrew's perspective, I hesitated, for I could not help but wonder what he would think of it all, especially the traveling roads we called *migrators*, which ran around the outer edge of each of the plateaus. The One Thousandth Plateau stood six miles and thirty fathoms above the plain of the Night Land, and stretched more than a mile across. Numerous doors and passages lined the corridor's inner wall, and though most of the pyramid was made of the same shining gray metal, through the ages various artists had painted colorful scenes along the passage, so that as I stepped onto the migrator, I rolled past many-hued depictions from the history of the One Thousandth City, along with portrayals of battles with the monsters of the Night Land. The ceiling, which hung twenty-six feet above me, had always provided ample space before, but now, remembering the blue dome of the ancient sky, I felt confined.

In a few minutes, I stepped off the migrator at the northeastern wall, where I gazed through another spyglass at the Watcher of the Northeast – called the Crowned Watcher because a blue, luminous ring hung in the air above its vast head, shedding a strange glow downward over the monster's dreadful folds. The light revealed its vast, wrinkled brow, but left all the lower face in shadow, save the ear, which belled out from the back of the head toward the redoubt. Past observers claimed to have seen it quiver, though no living person had ever witnessed it. The night hid its body, though ancient travelers' accounts claimed that it stood like an enormous idol, its shoulders tapering down in a severe angle, its distorted hands hanging to its sides, its lower body an amorphous mound of darkness.

Beyond the Northeast Watcher, close by the Road Where The Silent Ones Walk, lay the region called The Place Where The Silent Ones Are Not, so named because the Silent Ones were never seen there. The Giants' Sea bounded the Road upon the far side, and beyond the sea ran another, smaller road called The Road By The Quiet City, which passed beside the unwinking lights of a strange metropolis. No spyglass had ever revealed life there; neither had any of the lights ever faltered through all the ages. Its towers and domes rose, row upon row, into the sky; strange sculptures dotted its high roofs, and sweeping stairs wound between its structures, as if it had once been home to a great people.

Close beside the lights of The Quiet City lay the impenetrable void of The Valley Of The Hounds, home of the monstrous Night Hounds. Beyond that, obscuring all the east, hung a tangible, absolute darkness we called The Black Mist.

As I moved through the quiet Hours of Sleep toward the southeastern wall, I heard a far, dreadful sound, down in the lightless east, and, presently, again – a strange, terrible laughter, deep as low thunder among the mountains. Because this came at random intervals from the Unknown Lands beyond the Valley Of The Hounds, we named that distant, unseen region The Country Of The Great Laughter. Despite having heard it many times, it always left my heart quivering in despair at the terrors assailing earth's last millions.

Again, I was struck by the contrast between my life and my vision of the world before the sun failed. How strange a man

Andrew Eddins seemed to me, who could, on whim, ride a horse through forests and glades! How different and yet how similar the two of us were, he with his interest in biology, I with my fascination for mathematics, he loving an outdoors I had never seen. I knew my environment had made me more contemplative than he; I lacked his quick temper but shared his impulsive nature. He seemed the strangest of creatures, a great hulk of a man, so alien as to be almost beyond my understanding, and yet, at the same time, an aspect of myself.

I gazed at the translucent cover of one of the pyramid's millions of interior lights. Though I understood the simple principle of its mechanism, the part that was Andrew, who lived in a world of torches and candles, looked upon it with awe.

I sat down on a bench, overcome once more, thinking of that whole lost world. How unfair it seemed for my people to suffer constant imprisonment when humanity had once roamed the whole world. I put my hands over my eyes, as if to blot out the vision, but in the darkness I saw only a tall, green-eyed lady, wearing unfamiliar garments.

After all these ages, where are you? The thought came unbidden, and I looked up, suddenly struck by the notion that if I had returned to life, perhaps Mirdath might do so as well. The idea filled me with excitement, but dismayed me as well, for if she dwelled among the millions within the pyramid, I did not know how I would ever find her, since she would undoubtedly look much different than she had before.

The Laughter sounded again, waking me from my reverie. As it died away into the eastern darkness, I rose and went to the spyglass, knowing my memories of Andrew's world would lend the image a new significance. My glass focused upon the crater of the Giants' Pit, lying south of the Giants' Kilns. The giants tended these Kilns, which were enormous, bulging cylinders casting a red, sporadic light that threw wavering shadows across the mouth of the Pit, so the titans could be indistinctly seen, crawling along its rim, performing incomprehensible tasks. We neither knew what they did to the Kilns, nor why they did it.

To the back of the Giants' Pit, between it and the Valley Of

The Hounds stood a vast, black Headland. The light of the Kilns struck the brow of the Headland, revealing things constantly approaching the illumination, looking over the edge, and swiftly returning to the shadows. Throughout our recorded history, never had an hour passed without at least one of the creatures emerging. Because this had happened through countless ages, we marked the region on our maps and charts as The Headland From Which Strange Things Peer.

The Road Where The Silent Ones Walk ran directly before me. I searched it with the spyglass, for the sight of its sojourners always stirred my heart.

Presently, alone in all the miles of that night-gray road, I saw a quiet, cloaked figure moving in the field of my glass. As was the way of those beings, it was shrouded, and looked neither to right nor left. Legends said the Silent Ones would not harm a human, so long as one kept a fair distance from them, but I could not help but shudder as I watched him leave that part of the Road lit by the light from the Three Silver Fire Holes and pass into the shadows.

Far to the southeast, beyond the Fire Holes, fluttered The Thing That Nods. I gaped at it a time; it had indeed turned a fraction more of its face toward the pyramid, and though its features remained indecipherable, I looked upon it in fascination. No one knew what it was, or why it moved; like so much of the Night Land it remained a mystery.

To the right of The Thing That Nods, but nearer, rose the vast bulk of the Southeast Watcher – the Watching Thing of the Southeast. The Torches burned to either side of the squat monster, and though they were easily a half mile away from it, they cast enough light to illuminate the beetled head of the unsleeping brute. Its body hung behind it in a mound resembling the distorted form of an amphibian. It seemed to rest its weight on its deformed, splayed front legs.

The Road swept farther southeast, on to where it swayed just south of the Dark Palace, and then further south, passing around to the west beyond the mountainous bulk of The Watcher Of The South – the greatest monster in all the visible Night Lands. My spyglass showed it clearly: a living hill of watchfulness, brooding squat and tremendous, hunched over the pale radiance of the Glowing Dome, its mouth gaping open, its eyes staring vacantly ahead.

Much was written concerning this odd, vast Watcher, for it had grown out of the blackness of the Unknown Lands of the south a million years before and had drawn steadily closer through twenty thousands years, but so slowly no one could discern its movements in a single year. Yet it did move, and the Monstruwacans had noted its approach and recorded every foot of its progress.

It had come quite far on its journey to the Last Redoubt when a Glowing Dome rose out of the ground before it, halting its advance. From that time on, through countless ages, it stared over the pale glare of the Dome toward the pyramid.

Because of this, many scholars wrote essays suggesting that even as the Forces of Evil were unleashed upon the last age of mankind, so other Powers of Good, incomprehensible to the human mind, aligned themselves to battle the terrors. The Glowing Dome was not the only evidence of such, as I will later relate.

Of the coming of these monstrosities, we knew little, for the evil began before the histories of the Great Pyramid were written, before the sun had even completely faded. We believed the trouble arose in the legendary Days of the Darkening, when ancient science disturbed powers beyond the earthly plane and allowed the monsters and Ab-humans to pass an unseen barrier previously protecting mankind. Grotesque and horrible creatures materialized, or later, developed, to assault humanity, while those entities lacking the power to assume material form grew into Forces capable of influencing and destroying the human spirit. As civilization degenerated into lawlessness, the surviving millions banded together in the twilight of the world to build the Last Redoubt.

Later, through hundreds and thousands of years, mighty races of dreadful creatures, half man and half beast, appeared. They warred against the pyramid, but were driven back, time and again, with much slaughter on both sides. After many such attacks, the people tapped the energy flowing through the earth and erected a circle of power around the redoubt. After sealing the lowest half-mile of the pyramid, they found peace in what was the beginning of an eternity of quiet waiting for the time when the Earth Current would fail.

Through the centuries, the creatures glutted themselves upon any who dared to venture beyond the sanctuary to explore the Night Land. Of those who went, few returned, for eyes peered through the darkness, and Forces of Evil moved upon the face of the earth, keeping vigil with senses superior to those of human kind.

As the eternal night lengthened across the world, the powers of the evil ones grew, and new and greater monsters developed and bred out of space and other dimensions, attracted like infernal sharks by that lonely hill of humanity. Giants arose, fathered of bestial humans and mothered of monsters, and various other creatures appeared, bearing human semblance and cunning, so that some of the lesser brutes possessed machinery and underground chambers for warmth and air.

I listened to the sorrowful roar rising continuously over the Gray Dunes from the Country Of Wailing, which lay midway between the pyramid and the Watcher Of The South, then I took the migrator toward the southwestern side. As I rode the traveling roadway, I watched the panorama of the Night Land, a landscape vast as a nation, through the passing windows.

I stepped off the migrator and looked from a narrow embrasure far down into the Deep Valley, four miles to the bottom, where broiled the Pit Of The Red Smoke. The mouth of this pit extended one full mile across, and the smoke filled the Deep Valley at times, making it appear as a glowing red circle amid dull, ocher clouds. Since the smoke never rose much above the valley, it left a clear view across to the country beyond. There, along the farther edge of the Valley, the gray, quiet Towers, each nearly a mile high, shimmered wickedly.

Beyond these, to the southwest, loomed the enormous bulk of the Southwest Watcher, a creature shaped much like a gargoyle with shoulders held high as if in a perpetual shrug. The Eye Beam projected from the ground before it – a single ray of gray light shining on the monster's right eye. Because of the illumination, that eye had been scrutinized through thousands of years. Some believed it looked steadily through the light at the pyramid. Others, thinking the ray the work of those Powers of Good opposing the Evil Forces, argued that it blinded the Watcher, preventing it from seeing the redoubt clearly. Whatever the case, as I watched through the spyglass, it seemed the brute stared, unwinking, as if fully aware I spied upon it.

I have told of the five great Watchers surrounding the pyramid: the Watcher Of The Northwest, Northeast, Southwest, Southeast, and South, each keeping silent, immovable guard upon the pyramid. Despite their motionlessness, we knew them as mountains of living vigilance, filled with hideous, steadfast intelligence.

To the northwest of the Southwest Watcher, extending an unknown distance northward, lay a region called The Place Where The Silent Ones Kill, so named because ten thousand years before a group of adventuring humans left the Road Where The Silent Ones Walk and were immediately destroyed. Only one survived to tell the tale, though he died soon after, his heart frozen. Our scholars could never explain the account, but it was written in the Records along with the testimonies of those who examined the body.

Far beyond The Place Where The Silent Ones Kill, in the very mouth of the western night, glistened the Place Of The Ab-humans, where the Road Where The Silent Ones Walk was lost in a dull green, luminous mist. We knew nothing of that region, though it stirred the imaginations of our greatest thinkers. Some believed that it was a place of sanctuary, differing from the Last Redoubt as we of this day suppose that heaven differs from earth. Those who held that view thought the Road might lead there, if only the Ab-humans did not obstruct the way.

Finally, my observations came full circle, back to the Red Pit and the Northwest Watcher. Between all the Watchers, monsters, flames, and terrors, numberless fire-holes pocked the surface of the Night Land. From where I stood, they appeared as pin-points of light across the dark plain. As a boy

I had often tried to count them, but they were too numerous.

I have described something of that land, and of the besieging Watchers and terrors that waited for the hour when the failure of the Earth Current would leave us defenseless. I stood, quietly gazing, lost in wonder both at my own, dark world, and at the forgotten days of sunlight. Sometimes I glanced upward to the gray, metal mountain rising measureless into the gloom of the everlasting night, or downward to the sheer sweep of the grim, metal walls, more than six full miles to the plain below. All around the base of the pyramid, which was five and a quarter miles each way, ran the great circle of light generated by the Earth Current, bounding the edifice for a mile on every side and having the appearance of a transparent tube which we referred to, simply, as The Circle. None of the monsters could cross it, because it created what we called the Ether Barrier, an invisible wall of safety. It emitted a vibration that disrupted the brains of the monsters and lower man-brutes and produced an even more subtle resonance that protected us against those Forces capable of affecting our souls. A Force of Evil could only penetrate the pyramid if an inhabitant dabbled in matters that left him open to its dreadful influence.

I could never look at The Circle without thinking of my parents, who had helped maintain the pyramid's mechanisms. They and their fellow workers had been required to perform a full survey of The Circle once every six months. A young member of the team, either through foolishness or carelessness, stepped across The Circle and was attacked by a monster. When my mother and father rushed to his aid, the beast killed all three. I was ten years old at the time, and saw the entire episode through a small spyglass.

As I stood thinking of my parents and Mirdath, I realized that in both instances death had stolen my loved ones while I helplessly watched. Leaning against the embrasure, overtaken by the losses of two lifetimes, I stared out into the night.

A Mouse in the Walls of the Lesser Redoubt

Nigel Atkinson

PART ONE

The Fixed Giants huddled under the glowing blue veil. Literally mountainous, their sluggish sentience rarely demanded movement. Sometimes, when the burning blue mist thinned, they would slump down a little. Days and millennia passed, but they never relaxed their scrutiny of the mile-high metal pyramid a hundred miles to the East.

On one otherwise unremarkable day, they watched as a flood of fire washed down the pyramid, incinerating a dozen beasts that had ventured too close and sending hundreds more fleeing for their lives. Before the liquid fire died away, a small door opened at the base of the pyramid, and a group of children stepped into the Night.

The children wept as armor-clad men stepped back inside the Lesser Redoubt. The last man in line hesitated, silhouetted in the splinter of light. He raised his Discos in a bleak salute; it flared for an instant, then he was gone. The dark returned, and a chattering, cacophony rose from its emboldened inhabitants. Beasts crawled, slithered and crashed among the sea of rubble that surrounded the pyramid. Most of the children cried and hugged each other. Alone among them, a young girl twisted a motley-colored cloth in her hands, and waited patiently.

The pyramid stood at the top of a half-mile high hill. Three vertical beams of light marked its corners, and a ring of fused rock surrounded its base. This marked the limit of the ambitions of most of the creatures of the Night. Once in a while, a newly spawned beast, or one driven mad by frustration, would launch itself at the Redoubt. Infrequently, entire clans of beasts would attack the Redoubt, often using the bodies of their fallen kin to breach the Ring of Fire. At these times, malevolent liquid fireballs rolled down the pyramid's sides with deadly accuracy, killing most of the attackers. The few that made it to the apex found the Prefects with their Diskos spitting electric fire waiting for them. The defense had held for eight million years, and the defenders saw no reason to believe that it would ever fail.

At the Lesser Redoubt's apex, two men watched the tragedy below. The well-used machinery of defense was scattered around, and watchers were bent over telescopes, alert for danger. They stood on a narrow gantry welded to the inner skin of the metal pyramid and looked out through wide loopholes. The gantry was open to the elements and a thin chill wind was blowing.

"You do not have to do this, My Lord," the older of the two men said. He was huddled inside a thick cloak that was slowly gaining a speckling of flecks of air snow. The other man was wearing a heavy samite gown, interwoven with strands of gold and silver.

"It has been my duty to watch this thing for the last ten years, Lord Gallowglass," the other man said. "The burden has not yet fallen on another's shoulders."

"It will soon enough, My Lord."

"Maybe."

"You have passed the first three hundred and twenty-five tests, old friend, surely this last one cannot be so hard?"

"The enKernelling? I understand it is . . . hard. Will you guard the door for me?"

"Of course, My Lord. The Moramor and I will stand sentry."

"Good. Your love will help keep me safe – from whatever awaits me."

They fell silent, and looked out into the Night Land. To the North the sky was tinged with a dull red light, and a faint blue glow painted the Western horizon. The rest of the world was lost to darkness. The Master Monstruwacan-designate leaned forward and looked down at the broken land. In the eternal gloom it was difficult to make out details, but things were moving amid the rubble – and the children were gone.

"It is done," the Gallowglass said quietly. "You should go back inside."

"Yes," the Master-designate said reluctantly.

"No good will come of this!" Essa said, brandishing the Hour-Slip.

"Be still, wife. If the council has decided to elect that young fella Master what's-his-name, there's nothing you or I can do about it," Hugh Leverhede replied, secretly cursing the Hour Criers Guild. They were an unpredictable bunch at best, and one never knew when the next bunch of Hour-Slips would filter down from them. Sometimes months went past without any news. That suited Hugh: 'no news ain't bad news' was his motto, and the Crier's sudden burst of efficiency was unwelcome.

"Pass the honey, please."

Essa ignored him. "It says here that's he's only thirty-eight years old. Imagine that."

"I don't think I can, sweet pea" Hugh said, feeling a sudden arthritic twinge in his back. "Pass the honey, please."

"Don't you sweet pea me," Essa said as she gave the pot a shove in his general direction. "Oh preserve us!"

"Now what?" Hugh asked as he spooned black honey onto his mushroom bread.

"His wife just died, poor thing, and he's been left with a little baby daughter. Who's going to look after the little mite while he's off running the Redoubt?"

"I imagine that –"

"They say that he's the first Master Monstruwacan whose grandchildren didn't have grandchildren of their own. Makes you wonder they the elected someone so young."

"Not me it doesn't. In any case, he's only the Master-designate. He might fail the trials."

"Yes, I suppose so," Essa said, a little mollified at the prospect. "Don't you have to be off soon? I thought you had a long trip today."

"Aye, all the way down to the Earth Current generator. Seems they've got some corrosion in one of the turbines. Nothing my little friends can't fix."

"I swear you think more of those things than you do of me."

"Now don't be daft, wife. No Jackotrade colony could take the place of a warm woman on a cold night – better than a hot water bottle!"

"Hmm," she said with a smile. "Get away with you, you old rascal."

As he waited to be called, the Master-designate opened a small locket. Inside were two miniatures painted in vivid enamels on translucent bone china; one was of his baby daughter, Naani, and the other his wife. He touched her image. It was strange, only six months had passed since she went to the funeral plains, and he was already having trouble remembering what she looked like. He closed his hand around the locket and stood up.

Monstruwacan Lanyard entered the meditation chamber. "It is time, My Lord" he said.

The Master-designate nodded. It was only a short walk to the Kernel, which was housed inside a featureless, white-painted cube located at the exact center of the pyramid.

He sat cross-legged on a granite plinth. The walls of the spherical room were made from six-foot thick black glass and were, so far as he could see, featureless. He had read detailed accounts of the room's manufacture in the Vault of Ages. Written from the perspective of the Guilds involved, they were mostly heroic tales of success against the impossible odds thrown up by physics, mathematics, and chemistry. The Guild of Glassmen were especially unstinting in singing their own praises. He conceded that they had a point; the glass sphere was a masterpiece of fabrication. Although he knew, more or less, where the door had been, he could see no sign of its circular outline. It was as if it had been created to allow his entry, and ceased to exist when its job was done.

The room was lit by a soft, shadowless light that fell almost unnoticed from the walls. The annals of the Glassmen claimed that an intense, burning light had been focused on the sphere for a hundred years. The glass had swallowed every scintilla and, so convoluted and cunning was its microscopic structure, it would take many tens of millions of years before the last of the imprisoned light had seeped through.

With heart pounding, he closed his eyes and opened his mind.

He was breath and animal electricity, sinew and blood, mind and soul, a self-ordered maelstrom working in miraculous sympathy. But it was not enough. Though strong in both the Night Hearing and the Master-Word, he needed the Kernel's help for the task ahead. Its glass walls hid cunning designs; buried inside it lay the last great work of the Electromechanics Guild. Cautiously, he let his mind brush against the invisible filigree of superconducting wires and neural nets hidden in the glass. It was like touching a cloud of razor blades that coruscated with lightning.

Consciously, he stilled his self-awareness and joined with the machine. His perception expanded, searching for the Master-Word, that undeniable measure of all true humans. The Gallowglass and the Moramor were standing shoulder to shoulder outside the Kernel. Their purity of heart was unquestioned and evoked a thrilling race memory of the forefathers and foremothers. Lanyard and the other Monstruwacans also shone with the Master-Word, but to a lesser degree than the Lords of the Prefecture.

How ironic, he thought, that the Prefects, so strong in the essence of humanity, would not pass their seed to subsequent generations. Yet it had always been so – the Prefect's oath setting them apart and above the petty concerns of the world.

His mind went back to the ancient labors of his people. For five hundred years, the builders labored on the mighty metal pyramid and the delvings beneath. A hundred thousand men stood shoulder to shoulder, and repelled the beasts of the Night. Four times that many, men and women both, quarried stone and ore, smelted metal and forged girders, dug deep and secret tunnels, or wrested life from the frozen black soil. Generations lived and died as the second greatest structure in human history rose to defy the endless night. When their task was done, the surviving three hundred thousand souls stood in massed ranks around the pyramid, raised a defiant song, then retreated into their final home.

The bubble of his search expanded, rushing past the few pinpricks of humanity in the rest of the metal pyramid, out into the dark night, and downwards to the hidden homes of man. He brushed against hundreds, then thousands of people. The Master-Word lit them, to varying degrees; but it burned brightly in few. Consciously, he slowed the onward rush his awareness, the better to rejoice in their anthem, thin though it was. It was a thousand warm homecomings – laughing children, buttered toast, soft embraces – infinitely more than anything built of metal or stone, it was home.

He left comfort behind and voyaged into the dark.

At first there was nothing, then Night fell across his mind. It was worse than the literal cold and dark outside the Redoubt. It negated hope, and screamed with accusations. The cries of condemned children came to him.

For pity's sake, how you do this to us?

Because it is necessary for the survival of the human race.

Murderer!

Leaving the ghosts behind, his spirit swept onwards, across the ruined valley floor. There were no human songs here, just the acid pinpricks of the beasts of the Night. They were alien, and easily dismissed. In the silence his search ascended to a new plane. He found what he was looking for.

The Master-Word of Great Redoubt was distant, but strong:

Where are you, our lost brothers and sisters?

The lament of the five hundred million humans in the Great Redoubt flew across unknown, uncountable leagues, and strengthened his will. He knew it was Fool's Gold, but he took what strength he could then closed his heart to the great longing. Soon other voices began to nibble at the edges of his consciousness. He resisted for a short while, then opened himself to their angry chatter. It was like being drenched in foul-smelling icy water.

You know who we are.

Yes, you are the descendants of the walker tribes. Your ancestors strode beside the moving cities for aeons then, at the time of your greatest peril; we abandoned you to the night.

The shame! The shame!

You are not what I seek. We parted countless aeons past; so long ago that the disgrace of our betrayal is almost forgotten.

Not by us! Never by us!

Nor by me. The shame is eternal. Ultimately we must pay. But now you will let me pass.

Go then . . . for now. The reckoning will wait.

With an air of crushing disappointment, they subsided from his mind. He was astonished and mortified at their numbers and the vigor of their aberrant chorus, and their passing left a void like a ragged wound.

In his mind, his body took a step on the valley floor. He felt the broken stones underfoot, and the icy wind in his face. The sky was grey-black and featureless, like some giant hand had clapped a cap over the world. He knew that image was uncomfortably close to the truth. In the rarely visited western quadrant of the Vault of Ages there was a single column dedicated to the lost science of astronomy. Examining it was one secret tests faced by every Master-designate. The ancient knowledge was always perilous, but the astronomy column had mired more would-be Masters than the rest of the Vault's blandishments put together. Exotic worlds and living suns – millions of them – vibrant in the universe's staggering immensity. Worst of all were poignant tales of Earth's own moon, silver and beautiful, a friend when the sun hid.

Until it was destroyed in a desperate attempt to keep the worst that the universe had to offer at bay.

The records were unflinchingly detailed about the consequences of that rash act, almost as if the chroniclers had an urgent need to ensure that history did not repeat itself. He could not imagine any circumstances that would allow mankind the opportunity. If the fabled other planets had ever existed, they were lost forever now. When the moon exploded, debris had quickly spread into an implacable barrier around the Earth. Worse still, the massive gravitational shifts had slowly, but inexorably begun to de-spin the Earth.

Hunching his shoulders against the cold, the Master followed the path of his mind's eye. The going was hard. His imaginary hands and knees were lacerated in regular falls, and his back ached like he was carrying a great burden. The way took him by treacherous paths into dark valleys filled with things that chittered; he scrambled up razorlike desiccated rills, and along windswept spurs. Only from the highest peaks could he see his destination, but he could always sense it.

He strode towards the blue glow in the West that marked the Shine.

After a thirty-hour labor, Bergthora was so tired couldn't even hold her baby. The pain and effort, and several doses of Poppy juice had left her exhausted. The midwife held up the squalling red-faced boy while her husband dabbed her forehead with a cloth. The child looks so angry, she thought as she fell into a long, troubled sleep.

At the last moment the Master Monstruwacan hesitated. The spirits of the Night crowded close.

We will snare your soul as it takes wings. We will rend it to shreds and gobble it up.

He ignored their spiteful taunts. They were dangerous to be sure, but they were small things, with petty hatreds. Mankind had defied their gibbering bile for millions of years.

A perfect image of his wife formed in his mind's eye. Beautiful and dying, holding their newborn baby in her arms, vowing that their souls would meet again.

He knew who had put there. He pushed the memory away, and stepped into The Shine.

Hugh the Jackotrade Master opened his toolbox and began to slowly pick out the tools of his trade. A couple of Engineers were watching him from outside the turbine housing. He could hear them muttering, but he wasn't about to rush on their behalf. He had spent the last half an hour fending off questions from increasingly high-ranking Engineers. In the end he had to chase them away but a couple had remained to spy on him. He shuffled around behind the turbine housing, hoping they would leave him alone.

The turbine had been cantilevered away from the Earth Current ring, but he could still feel its low vibration through the shining steel casing. It was rumored that some Engineers slept under the ring, the better to sense its moods. It was undeniable that they had a close bond with their machines, so close that they were usually able to catch the subtle bite of corrosion long before it could cause serious damage. He needed to look closely before he could see the little pits mottling the shining blades. Although the damage was superficial, he was surprised at how extensive it was.

No wonder they're so irritable, you'd have expected them to catch this a lot earlier.

He picked up a blue bottle half-filled with a viscous fluid and held it up to the light. A column of Jackotrades unwound from the main mass, and started to crawl sluggishly up the glass towards the light. Tut-tutting at their lethargy, he put the bottle down and picked up a rubber squeeze bulb. He sprayed the nutrient cocktail onto the turbine blade, taking care to lay trails between each little cluster of corrosion. Then he picked up the blue bottle, uncorked it and poured its contents onto the blade. In an instant, the Jackotrades spread along the nutrient trails, blind instinct leading the little machines to the places where their repair skills were needed.

Hugh sat down and dug a mushroom and bilberry pasty and a bottle of watered-down wine out of his toolbox. He would wait an hour, before using the come-to-home tinctures. He fervently hoped that the Engineers would leave him in peace until then. But he doubted it.

The Earth was gone. He stood alone on an endless blue plain. The Fixed Giants sat at the corners of an enormous pentacle with him at its center. Their shapes embodied an idea of perfection crafted aeons before the sun died – pyramid, cube, octagon, dodecahedron, and icosahedron. He had no conception of their size, only that the dim glimpses seen by the naked eye were a fraction of their true magnitude. Their vastness extended beyond mundane dimensions. At first he thought they were featureless but as he looked again, he realized that each was built from elements of the others – cubes inside pyramids inside octahedra – endlessly concatenated – winding back to find their origin had moved – had never really existed – a perpetual dance marrying energy and form. His consciousness expanded, letting him glimpse the true nature of the Fixed Giants.

They had existed since the universe cracked open, and they expected to survive its entropic death agonies. He couldn't comprehend how that was possible, and was terrified, so they anchored him to his own scrap of consciousness.

It was a small kindness.

He looked at the square and found himself staring back from the octahedron. His viewpoint encompassed the universe. Everything was in motion: stars, galaxies, living things, atoms, fractions of atoms, always searching for a new equilibrium then darting on, never satisfied.

They took him back to the beginning.

The universe exploded to life, birthing quick-burning, short-lived stars that destroyed themselves in fiery conflagrations, spreading their essence across the galaxy. He rode a burning wind pregnant with newly created heavy elements. They were inconceivably rare, but they tugged at each other and slowly, over vast gulfs of time, accumulated. Near the young stars, thousands of metal-rich protoplanets jostled for elbowroom. Collisions were frequent, and violent. Soon the deceptive peace of the solar system's babyhood was banished as billion-year long bloodbath of planetary formation and destruction began.

Further out, the giant planets were accumulating mass in a more sedate fashion – a hydrogen atom here, a water molecule there – they had time on their side. Aloof from the fiery maelstrom, their evolution was less hurried, but perhaps more sure-footed.

His guides hurried him along.

"Let me see."

They ignored him.

Three billion years before his life began, he stood on the shore of a foul-smelling sea; the air was thick with volcanic dust and sheet lightning cracked perpetually across a rain-lashed sky. In the seething, sulfurous water simple molecules jockeyed for position, driven by the blind laws of chemical equilibrium and electrostatics. For aeons the random forces of nature threw up countless variations. A tiny fraction gained prominence for an instant then fell back into the seething equilibrium. Eventually, a molecule containing a five-ringed sugar, a phosphate group, and nitrogen-containing base bumped into a similar structure. The chain grew, and miraculous things began to happen. The new molecules of RNA shepherded amino acids together, weaving them into protective membranes. Soon, simple catalysts emerged. A mere half billion years later the first simple cells appeared, and a cosmic eye blink later humans cracked rocks together to make fire, and dreamed of the stars.

The dream quickly died. Twenty million years of stagnation followed.

Monstruwacan Lanyard walked around the Kernel, his hands clasped behind his back and his head bowed. A gaggle of Monstruwacans burst into the room. Lanyard noticed the subtle hand signals flicking between the Moramor and the three Prefects guarding the Kernel.

"How long has he been in there?" Monstruwacan Cambyses asked.

"Three days and four hours and sixteen minutes," Lanyard replied.

"This is a day past the normal time. How do we know he's alive in there?"

Lanyard shrugged. "The annals suggest that the Kernel will open automatically in the event of the death of the designate."

"Naturally, the annals can always be believed," Cambyses sneered. "Curse this waiting, I've half a mind to go in there and drag him out."

"That would be inadvisable, My Lord," a new voice said.

"Ah, Lord Gallowglass," Lanyard said, with a small smile at the back of the rapidly departing Cambyses. "Welcome back, I fear your wait is far from over."

"It will be over when it is over, My Lord."

"Your stoicism does you credit. Some of my fellow Monstruwacans are getting impatient. That is understandable. The Master-designate is somewhat of an unknown quantity. He has only been a member of our order for twenty-four years – hardly enough time to get to know him."

"I'm sure you – and your fellows – have complete confidence in your candidate, My Lord. Otherwise why would you have elected him to the highest office."

"Your are correct, Lord Gallowglass," Lanyard said smoothly.

He blinked – and found himself at the center of the Circuit of Assessment. However, there were subtle differences. The walls and floors were still dead white, and soft white lights hung from the domed alabaster ceiling. But there was no sign of the circle of testing stations, with their banks of white dials with flickering white needles. The talc-faced Testors in their white smocks were also absent. He felt a slight pang of relief at that, even thirty-three years on, he still had the occasional bad dream about his Day of Assessment, and the Testors were always prominent in them.

"Why have you brought me to this place?" he asked.

What is the nature of the human soul?

He laughed. "You would catechize me on the nature of existence? I feel inadequate to the task."

What is the nature of the human soul?

"Very well. The soul is immortal and emanates from a single universal principle to which it is destined to return at the end of life."

Always?

"There is a tradition that some soul-pairs are bound by love and will return to inhabit new bodies until, after aeons, the lovers unite."

Did you share such a love with your wife?

He hesitated a long time before answering. "No. Our love was true, but it was for a single lifetime."

Is this humility?

"Do not be absurd. Why have you created this place?"

A dislocation passed through him, and he was standing in the Vault of Ages. Four black pillars, their crowns lost in the gloom high above, surrounded him. Black writing, in a thousand ancient and forgotten languages, flowed over their ebony surfaces.

You know this place.

"The four pillars of Heresy. Examining them is the sixty-second trial of a Master-designate. A dull exercise, perhaps that is why you have added these florid touches?"

Tell us about your heresies.

He pointed to the pillars in turn. "Primus: man is a fallen spirit who has forgotten his own divinity. Secundus: on death the soul may pass into the bodies of animals, even plants. Tertius: Transmigrations of the soul are tiny incidents in the great drama of world annihilations and restorations that occur over enormous periods of time. Quartus: the restoration of humanity depends both on human ethics and the performance of meritorious acts by an avatar of godhead."

On an impulse, he leaned forward and touched Secundus. For a moment the writing flowed over his hand, then the pillar's dark animation died, and was replaced by pictograms and studded metal rings.

"Why the mummery? Is this test just a show with mirrors and smoke? If this is the great secret that you hold in your cold hearts, them I have to –"

Why did you touch Secundus?

Before he could answer another dislocation swept him away. He was standing outside the Lesser Redoubt. The Great Door hung from its hinges and the pyramid was dark and silent. The hundred foot thick iron walls were gnawed through by red-brown corrosion.

Another dislocation. He was standing on the ruined land at the base of Redoubt Hill – and his people were fighting for their lives. With suddenly preternatural vision, he saw every detail of their ordeal. The Prefects had formed a running phalanx, their Diskos ladling out generous helpings of death to the beasts of the Night. But their valor wasn't enough. His people's path was strewn with the bodies of the fallen, and hideous things were picking gleefully over them over. He glanced to the West where the blue glow from the Shine washed over high, unscalable cliffs. When he looked back, the Prefects had been broken. Hairy beast men shrieked with joy as they fell upon the humans.

Unable to watch anymore, he hid his face. The earth under him was slick and chilly, and buzzed incessantly. A thin, icy wind carried the dying screams to him. Shamed by his cowardly refusal to witness the end of his people, he steeled himself and looked up. The battle was over. The Earth was stained by a five-mile long trail of blood. Oddly, the beasts of the Night were running away from the carnage. Sick to his heart, he realized that he could sense their feelings – they were terrified.

He examined the knot of pain eating at his heart. What he felt wasn't the Master-Word. It was something else.

"Secundus?"

There was no reply but his words took wings like an Exhalation and filled the Night Land.

Among the ruin of his people, someone had survived. His vision blurred, and was reduced to peering myopically at the figure walking serenely through the ranks of monsters. He couldn't tell whether it was a man or a woman. Whoever it was, her or she had an air of connection to everything in the world. He had been terrified by his own glimpse into the hearts of the inhuman hordes, but this person was possessed of another order of consciousness entirely.

"Who is this?"

A human born within the last year – and a hope for the future of the world.

"A child of the Lesser Redoubt? What do you mean the hope of the world?"

The child represents a novel – and surprising – iteration of humanity, and is the final chance for your species to fulfill its potential.

"We have managed for twenty million years, we survived the stilling of Earth's rotation, the all of Night, and the death of the Sun –"

Irrelevant – your greatest achievement has been millions of years of stagnation – and your days are numbered. Your pitiful metal tent is failing. Even the Great Redoubt is doomed. Their decline is slower, but no less certain. Humanity has nearly run its course and the universe will hardly notice its passing.

"What can one child do?"

The child is not alone. Another has come into this world – you know where.

"The Great Redoubt. They outnumber us ten-thousand-fold."

Numbers are irrelevant. Chance is everything. If this special child survives to maturity, and if it meets its soul mate, their genes will cascade down future generations. Humanity will have a small chance to regain its lost vigor. One day your species might even realize its true place in the cosmos and, eventually gain the strength to reach out into the wider universe.

Laughter rose in Master-designate's breast. He folded his arms over his chest. "Well, what you ask of me is a simple matter. All I have to do is find this child – one among hundreds – ensure it grows up; then deliver it to the Great Redoubt, which had been lost to us for eight million years. Even if I knew where it was, there is the small matter of the countless leagues of the Night Land, with its untold horrors to –"

We will ensure the child's safety.

"You need this child as much as humanity does."

You are placing interpretations on reality based on your limited knowledge of the universe. The concept of need is redundant in our terms. Will you pay the price to save the child?

"What is the price?"

You must destroy the Lesser Redoubt and cast your people into the Night Land. The hammer and anvil of Darkness will decide who is worthy.

"Impossible. How can you expect me to commit such a crime?"

Signs will be made evident to you. The price must be paid.

The Master-designate sneered. "That is not good enough – I cannot be expected to make guesses –"

What single achievement would you want to stand as your monument?

The answer was so obvious that he spent several moments trying to find hidden meanings in their words. In the end he decided that the question must be without guile, or if there were any, it was beyond his comprehension.

"If I survive this test, I will seek what every Master Monstruwacan during the last eight million years has sought – the building of a working Master-Word machine."

Why?

"So we can regain contact with the hundreds of millions of humans in the Great Redoubt, so we can unite humanity and, ultimately, cast you and your kin from this planet."

A paltry ambition.

He stood on the frozen broken plain. The frigid wind scoured his face with sharp blue snowflakes that stuck to his skin and refused to melt, sucking the heat from him. The Fixed Giants looked on, impassive as mountains.

"What do you mean?" he shouted.

There was no reply.

The Master Monstruwacan climbed out of the Kernel and looked straight through the waiting Prefects. They saluted, but he did not notice. Nor did he notice the ranks of kneeling Monstruwacans. A man carrying a ruby-colored robe approached him. He said something, but his words were unintelligible. It was like an insect had learned to speak. He laughed at the idea of the man rubbing his legs together, frantically producing staccato stridulations. The man draped the robe across the new Master's shoulder and pushed his face close. There was something familiar about his eyes and the look of concern on his face.

"Lanyard?" the Master said, his comprehension returning, along with crushing disappointment. He was one of the insects.

"Yes, My Lord. You are alive, we were sick with worry."

"I was only in there a few minutes."

"My Lord, you were gone of the best part of a week."

The Master pushed Lanyard gently aside. Distantly he realized that his body was a mass of aches and pains, and he was desperately in need of sleep.

"I must take my rest now, Master Lanyard. When I rise I wish to speak to the Gallowglass."

"And the Monstruwacan Council, My Lord?"

"Maybe later. The Gallowglass first."

As he limped out of the room, escorted by a pair of Prefects, the new Lord of the Redoubt left behind the frenzied whispers of his fellow Monstruwacans.

The Guild of Ancestors was one of the smallest, and least prestigious of the Lesser Redoubt's two hundred and six Guilds and Orders. It had three dozen active members, and several of them were over a hundred years old. The air in their tiny Guild House was thick with dust and the savory tang of varnish and glue. The Master Monstruwacan and the Gallowglass had to stoop to avoid banging their heads on the low wood-beamed ceilings.

"Who is in charge here?" the Master asked.

A glance propagated down the ragged line of Guildmen in front of the Master, before settling on a bald man who took a reluctant step forward, gulped silently a couple of times, then puffed his chest out.

"I am Hobnil, Master of the esteemed Guild of Ancestors."

The Master bowed slightly, setting of a wave of bowing and scraping by the Guildmen. One of them surreptitiously handed Hobnil the sacred Almanac of their calling. He held it close to his chest like a shield.

"Thank you, gentlemen. I would ask you too leave now. I will to speak with Master Hobnil in private," the Master said.

The Guildmen reluctantly shuffled out of the room, with many a backward glance. Individually, they were weak in the Master-Word, but collectively the Master could hear their unspoken annoyance. Beside him the Gallowglass was bristling with suspicion.

"Ahem, Master?" Hobnil said, nervously.

"I have a job for your Guild," the Master said. "It will suit your unique talents –"

"We are eager to serve, My Lord!" Hobnil said, a little too quickly.

"This thing must be done in secret, and no word of it must pass beyond the confines of your Guild House"

Hobnil's face fell. "Yes, Master, I suppose we can do that – I mean – whatever you say, My Lord."

"Good. The Gallowglass will advise you on security measures."

Hobnil visibly blanched at this idea, and there was a clatter from behind the one of the room's closed doors.

"It seems that there is much for the Gallowglass to do," the Master said. Hobnil nodded his head dumbly. "You keep records of all children born in the Redoubt –"

It was not a question, but that did not stop Hobnil answering. "Yes, My Lord. Births, deaths, marriages, Guildings –" He saw the look on the Master's face and stopped talking.

"I want you to keep watch on all of the children born between one year ago and one year from today. I want a report on each child every six months. I want to know about their growth, their accomplishments, their friendships, their beliefs, their performance in the Circuit of Assessment – anything that speaks of their future lives."

"But, My Lord, we are not equipped to gather such information, my Guild's high reputation is based on the storage of genealogical knowledge, we are ill-equipped to act as, well –"

"Spies? You are correct, that is why I have today promulgated a decree granting you the extra funds needed to expand the size of your Guild six-fold."

Hobnil beamed at the news. "My Lord!"

"Of course, such an increase in status will not pass unnoticed, and will certainly lead to petty jealousies among some other Guilds. To avoid too much scrutiny of your secret work, the decree also requires you to apprentice girls. That innovation should be enough to deflect attention away from matters

I want hidden."

Hobnil tilted his head to one side, then to the other, as if he was trying to hear a faint, distant noise.

"I am sorry, My Lord," he said eventually. "I must have misheard – girls?"

"Your hearing is adequate, Master Hobnil. Most Guilds will eventually be expected to recruit female apprentices, but yours has the honor of being the first. The interest that this innovation causes should be enough of a smokescreen. In any case, the task will require women; there are many situations where a man would stand out like a sore thumb. The care of young children for example."

Master Hobnil nodded, his eyes focusing on mid-air.

"Good, now I will leave you in the capable hands of the Gallowglass," the Master said. "You should know that his Prefects have already taken up defensive stations around your Guild. This heightened security will help in the changes that are needed."

"Yes, My Lord." Hobnil said gloomily. "One more thing: you say you are interested in all of the children born during these years – I assume the edict does not include your own daughter, sweet little Naani?"

"Yes, it does. All of the children – no exceptions."

"Yes, My Lord."

Things were moving on the plain below the Redoubt. Summoned by bells, a dozen pairs of Prefects stood shoulder-to-shoulder, ready to repel any attackers. The Moramor watched wheeled things rolling towards the foot of Redoubt Hill, and the legions of beasts following in their wake. Grimly, he ordered reinforcements.

It was an hour before an attacker reached the apex of the pyramid. The Moramor dispatched the creature with a coruscating slash of his Diskos. Battle was joined. A week passed before the creatures of the Night ended their assault.

The Gallowglass stood to attention just inside the doorway. From there he had a good view of the Master Monstruwacan's Audience Chamber. It was an unusual room, even for the Lesser Redoubt. Decagonal in shape, its vaults dwarfed the people clustered on its floor and walls. On the two sloping walls adjacent to the door ten pairs of Prefects stood to attention. The four walls behind the Master's dais belonged to the Monstruwacan Council. The benches were full today, with most of the two hundred and twenty-six council members present. Many of them were lolling back in their seats however, and it seemed that a few were actually asleep. Of the many innovations introduced by the young Lord of the Redoubt, Petitions Day was among the least popular.

Though not the most hated, the Gallowglass thought, the Master's five-year-old decree requiring the acceptance of girls as apprentices, was still deeply resented by many. In his heart, the Gallowglass sympathized with the stick-in-the-muds who were holding out. Though women would never be introduced to the ranks of the Prefecture, the idea was deeply unsettling. He knew his duty, however, and had been quite ruthless in stamping out the few signs of outright resistance to the reforms.

The all-male Monstruwacans shifted uneasily in their seats (another unpopular innovation had decreed the removal of cushions), and glared balefully at the petitioners. The Gallowglass, who was naturally strong in the Night Hearing, suspected that their collective bile might be curdling milk all over the Redoubt.

The Master's Clerk stepped forward and handed an Hour-Slip to his Lord.

"This petition is highly unusual," the Master Monstruwacan said after a brief glance at the slip. "I am surprised that that they managed to pursue it as far as my office."

The Clerk kept a blank expression on his face, but, when his lord's attention turned away from him, he shuffled a step away from the steel dais. Silence fell in the chamber as the Master silently read the petition.

The Lord of the Lesser Redoubt put the slip down on his lap and stared at the ragged bunch of postulants. Most of the half dozen men and women suddenly found something fascinating about their own feet. All except one, a woman with curled red hair. She kept her head high, and looked around the room with the air of someone who was determined to take in its splendors, whatever the cost. The Gallowglass wondered whether she appreciated the danger her impudence placed her in. For sure, many council members would have ordered her cut down already. He reflected that she probably had quite an attractive face, but her features were buried under a checkerboard of roughly applied, brightly-colored face paints, making it impossible to guess her age. Her dress was clean, but ragged and festooned with bright colored ribbons.

He was surprised that the Master had allowed the petition to get this far, but perhaps less surprised than anyone else in the room. Just two weeks ago, he had stood beside the man outside the Circuit of Assessment, while the child Naani was tested. The Master's mental sigh of relief when the girl was found to be a true human was full of love and fear.

The Gallowglass looked at the woman: he knew her sort. In the records of the Prefecture there were histories reaching beyond the age of the Road Builders, to the shadowy origins of Mankind. The oldest texts were written in languages too antique to comprehend, but there were translations of translations of translations that recorded remarkably consistent ancient heresies. The cults described all had certain beliefs in common; a charismatic, conveniently absent leader who would come back one day to lead his followers to some ill-definite promised land, or who would rescue them from whatever evil was currently stalking them. Of course, you had to be a special person to benefit – someone who the god especially loved, usually because he had been propitiated with prayers and other offerings. The rest of humanity would be left to the tender mercies of the beasts.

He could put a name to this cult's special little god – Harlequin – the enigmatic, mischievous will-o-the-wisp who had reached the apogee of his popularity three million years ago, before being wiped out in a bloody pogrom by one of his predecessors. He made a mental note to have the Moramor investigate the extent of the cult's influence. Most likely the handful of fanatics standing in front of him comprised the entire gang, but it was best to be sure.

The Master seemed about to dismiss the petitioners when the woman stepped closer. Astonishment rippled around the room and several council members shouted out. She stopped, her right foot almost touching the broad gold band that surrounded the dais. On it were inscribed the names of the thirty-seven thousand six hundred and fifteen Master Monstruwacans who had ruled in the eight million years since the Lesser Redoubt was raised.

The Master Monstruwacan help his hand up to stop her taking the fatal step, "Child, your persistence does you credit. I will judge your petition."

The woman fell to her knees. "Noble Lord," she said, "we humbly beg you to consider our proposal –"

A tall, white-haired Monstruwacan rose to his feet waving his fossilized wax staff of office.

"Enough of this! My Lord, why waste time on these low rascals? Be rid of them and let us consider more pressing matters."

"Master Beekeeper," the Master Monstruwacan said in an icy voice, "you have another appointment perhaps?"

"My Lord, of course not."

"Then sit down, this will not take up much more of your precious time."

The Bee Master sat down, hiding his anger by burying his face in a little flowering lithops he carried in a tapered terracotta pot that hung from a chain around his neck. The Gallowglass wondered exactly what ill odor his nosegay guarded him against.

The Master nodded to the woman. "Please continue," he said.

"I speak on behalf of the doomed children, My Lord. Though they are ab-human, they are still innocents," she said.

"Yes, I have read your petition, child. What do you seek?" the Master said, shifting uncomfortably on his throne. It had been a long day. Unconsciously, he fingered the plain gold locket resting on his chest. "It is Law. On a child's fifth birthday, it is taken to the Circuit of Assessment. If it is found to be ab-human, it must leave the Redoubt or accept mercy. Would you allow the creatures of the Night a foothold among us?"

"No, My Lord. We do not question Law's necessity. But, we humbly beseech you to let us give them the boon of a little training in wilderness craft, and . . . the mercy of Harlequin's teachings."

"That they will get pie in the sky when they die?"

"That is an oversimplification," the woman said. She had to raise her voice to be heard over the Council's laughter.

"Or will they have to wait for Judgement Day? That should be interesting, hearing your little God explain himself." More laugher echoed around the chamber. The Master leaned forward. "He has twenty million years of mankind's suffering to answer for," he said.

The woman lowered her head, and shook it almost imperceptibly. The Gallowglass looked at her carefully. There was something familiar about her but, when he tried a mental probe, it slid away from the surface turmoil of her thoughts.

"You asked for them to be give wilderness training?" he said. "And where did you pick up such unusual skills? Surely you have not been outside the Redoubt? You know the punishments – especially for a woman."

"Yes, My Lord, and no, My Lord it has been time out of mind since our people sallied into the great darkness outside, but we have honed our skills in the monstrous caverns of the Country of Husbandry, far beyond the populated parts of the Redoubt."

"And what discoveries did you chance upon in the noisome dark?"

The woman raised her head and looked straight at the Master Monstruwacan.

"The Country of Husbandry is a place where men go as quietly as ghosts. The dreary souls, who come to take our dead on their last journey, are a tithe of the forgotten tribe who dwell there amid the silence. They have little ken of the rest of humanity, and less concern for our doings. Limitless, vast caverns are their domain and they guard their deepest places jealously –"

"Why? What is down there?" he demanded.

"I cannot say, My Lord. The followers of Harlequin only touch upon the fringes of the deep. We have no wish, or need to delve deeper. The places we know are harsh enough for the teaching of the skills. Harlequin teaches us that we should take only what suffices our needs, and give generously –"

The Master's patience evaporated. "So, in truth, you know little about the deep places of our world."

"No, Lord."

"You are dismissed."

"What about our petition?"

"Do not anger me further," the Master said. "Gallowglass!"

The Prefects sprang to life, spinning their Diskos in furious salute as the Gallowglass marched forward. With a hand signal, he stilled his men's electric fury and knelt before the Master.

"How may I serve, My Lord?"

"Rise, friend Gallowglass. I will have need of your council. First, please remove these people."

The Gallowglass made another hand signal, and two of his men advanced on the petitioners. In a trice the petitioners were hustled out of the room. The Master leaned back and looked at the ceiling high above. The minutes ticked by while everyone else waited for him to speak.

"Clerk," the Master said.

"Yes, My Lord," the Clerk said as he stepped forward.

"Stand there."

"Yes, My Lord."

"Gallowglass, I want you to investigate this cult," the Master said. He pointed at his Clerk. "This one is in league with them. Extract what you can from him. Then we will decide how to deal with that heretical rabble."

White-faced, the Clerk fell to his knees. Two Prefects moved swiftly and grabbed him, twisting his arms behind his back. They pulled him to his feet and started to drag him out of the hall.

"My Lord, I beg you," the Clerk shouted. "I care not what happens to me but, please, grant the petition."

"Even now, when you are condemned, you seek this boon from me?" The Master said, aparantly astonished.

"My life is as nothing, My Lord."

"Oh, very well," the Master said eventually.

Later in his private office, the Master Monstruwacan examined a diorama standing on an agate pedestal at the center of the room. Inside a six-foot tall cylindrical diamond Jackotrades had created an intricate representation of the Lesser Redoubt. Myriads of the tiny machines had carved subtle interference grooves and gratings that, when viewed from the correct angle, created the illusion of solid shapes and colors. At his eye-level, there was a miniature of the mile-high metal pyramid that was the only visible sign of the Redoubt. He looked closely, fancying that he could almost see tiny human figures at the apex. Under the pyramid, a long blue pipe fell ten miles into the Earth, and connected to a flat green disk, ten miles in diameter. This was where the bulk of the Redoubt's population lived. It was where their fields, manufactories and homes lay. At the center of the disk, a mottled green ball marked the Flying Wood, hanging over the Great Arbor. Blue tetrahedra, signifying Guild Houses dotted the circumference, while a single red octahedron identified the Vault of Ages. Under the Arbor, a bright yellow band was cut into the native rock. This was Earth-Current generator – the source of all energy within the Redoubt.

He walked around the diamond and his perspective changed. The model of the Redoubt was replaced by a series of smaller images: the Pyramid standing on Redoubt Hill, overlooking the black plains below; details of the Stress Master's engines in the central shaft and beyond – none of them interested him. He changed his position again; this time finding images of the fringes of his domain – the Country of Husbandry – and the dubious lands beyond.

As he examined these unknown regions an old quotation

came to mind – *here be dragons* – and a tear trickled down his face.

Filangeri the Stress Master herded the passengers onto the granite disk. He wasn't in a good mood. Normally he would have left such a task to a minion, but an Hour-Slip signed in the Master Monstruwacan's own hand had demanded his participation.

Transporting ab-human children to the fringes of the Country of Husbandry was tedious and distasteful to him. The boy appeared normal enough, except for his perpetual smile. The religious woman frowned as he instructed her in the proper protocols. The two Prefects escorting them simply ignored him.

Filangeri prodded a flake of something blue that was resting on the burnished control panel. The woman's face and arms were covered in multi-colored daubings, and he had no doubt where the guilt lay. Fastidiously, he moistened the end of a finger and picked up the flake. His passengers were looking strangely at him, probably wondering why he didn't leave such a minor imperfection for the Jackotrades to clean up. He ignored their stares; he didn't trust the little machines to do a thorough job.

He instructed the passengers to grab firm hold of the handrail that sprouted from the center of the disk. Typically, the Prefects declined, settling for grounding the butts of their weapons for balance.

"Please hold on tight," Filangeri said. "The ride is long and can make some people a little nauseous. We will start now."

He pushed a brass lever, and the granite cylinder they were standing on began to fall. At first the movement was slow but, once the embarkation room was clear, the pace picked up. The smooth walls of the pipe became blurred with speed as the platform plunged downwards. Filangeri fussed over his instruments – speed, vibration, air pressure, temperature, static electricity – all were within accepted limits. There was a chattering of hour printers as the cylinder flashed through a junction. Filangeri scanned the slips quickly. Everything seemed in order. Back at the central nexus, his minions seemed to be doing their jobs adequately.

But he couldn't help but worry. The adjustment of forces needed to maintain the equilibrium between ascending cylinders with descending ones, and the balancing of hundreds of tons of moving rock and miles of stretching, articulating metal, was a subtle skill only understood by a master like himself.

"How long?" The woman asked.

"We will soon reach the first airlock," Filangeri said without turning.

He tilted his head. There was a noise. It was nothing really, just an overtone in the pure note generated by the cylinder's fall. He tapped a dial, wondering if there was a problem with the vertebral reciprocating assembly.

"Stop that at once," the woman said.

Fuming, Filangeri spun round ready to replay her presumption with scalding invective. Then he saw what the real problem was. The boy had left the handrail and, quite incredibly, was standing at the edge of the disk poking a hand in the stream of air dashing through the finger-wide gap between the wall and cylinder. Filangeri was apoplectic.

"Stop that at once, boy!" he stammered.

The boy giggled. He knew no one would stop his little game until the ride was over.

The bodies were arranged in a neat row. Two Perfects and a corpulent man whose fine clothes had been ruined by the blood that had flowed from his cutthroat. The bodies were several days old and the younger Prefect, although standing stiffly to attention, was visibly fighting the urge to gag. The Moramor made a mental note to arrange for suitable training to rid him of this foible.

Small cloth dolls had been found resting beside each body. The Gallowglass twirled one of them in his fingers. They were colorful but crudely made from scraps and coarse thread.

"The Harlequin sect?" the Prefect asked.

"Start the hunt," the Gallowglass said.

The Gallowglass was uncomfortable. He was used to the sharp angles and smooth surfaces of the Prefecture. The Master Monstruwacan's home had shaded alcoves and curtains. A bowl of peppermint comfits stood on a sandalwood table.

Somehow, despite knowing that the Master had a child, he had not expected her presence to so influence his Lord's home. Bowls of petits pois scented the air and a set of wooden alphabet tiles had spilled from a low table onto the floor. Their five-year old owner sat on her father's lap, and was scowling.

"It's not fair!" she said

"No, it isn't my sweet," the Lord of the Lesser Redoubt said. "But I have business of state to deal with. Here's Tanna, go with her. It's getting late, I'll come by to tuck you in later."

Naani stuck her bottom lip out. "Don't want to be tucked in."

"Oh, now what a thing to say." The maid said, as she swept the child up in her arms. "Don't you worry, My Lord. This little one will be on her best behavior when next you see her."

"Don't chastise her too much; I did promise to play with her this evening."

The maid curtsied, and herded Naani out of the library. She glanced at the Gallowglass as she left, then looked away quickly.

"Gallowglass, please come in," the Master said.

He limped in and knelt on his right knee before his lord, placing his Diskos on the floor beside him. His armor was splattered with dirt and dry stains that might have been blood. There was tang of ozone in the air, a sure sign that he had been in battle, and his face was grim.

"Is the rebellion dealt with?" the Master asked.

"I would hardly call it a rebellion –"

"I did not ask for your analysis of the political situation,

Gallowglass. Have the heretics been put down?"

The Gallowglass shifted his position and rested a hand on the floor for a moment before answering.

"Yes, My Lord. Half of the sect members were taken alive, and are being put to the question as we speak."

"How many in total?"

"Seventy-six."

"Seventy-six? So few, yet they had the confidence to resist your investigations and, when you hunted them down, stand and fight? You are slipping, my friend."

The Gallowglass bowed his head. "I beg your forgiveness."

"Did you find the ab-human boy or the woman?"

"No, My Lord, nor any evidence of their accomplices. But for sure they must have been others, a small boy and a woman could not overcome two Prefects."

"Did you find any evidence to link the cult with the murders?"

The Gallowglass held up a small rag doll. "This token of their sect was found with the bodies. It is more than enough to condemn them all."

"Yes, I suppose it is," the Master said, imagining the fury of the Prefects when they discovered the killers of their comrades. Something in the Gallowglass' expression caught his eye.

"There is something else?"

"Yes, My Lord. Our investigations of the Stress-Masters Guild turned up an interesting Hour-Slip. It held order for Filangeri to escort the ab-human boy to the lower chambers – seemingly it was signed by you – the sigils upon the slip are almost indistinguishable from the real ones."

"That is impossible."

"Apparently not," the Gallowglass said dryly. "The Stress Masters deny that it has any record of the Hour-Slip passing through their hands. They offered to open their achieves to me, the better to prove their innocence. I declined. If they are capable of forging your sigils, hiding a paper trail would be of little difficulty."

"What do you want to do?"

"I would like to kick the doors of the Stress-Master's Guild in and tear the place apart until I found answers." The Gallowglass paused for a moment, perhaps waiting for his Lord to speak, before continuing. "But that is impossible. The Guilds hold their secrets tight under ancient laws. We must seek other sources of information."

"You have my full confidence, Gallowglass," the Master said, with a tone of dismissal in his voice.

Bergthora watched as the Master ran his hand over the sandstone wall.

"Is this room secure?" the Master asked.

"The walls are lined with Jackotrade-filled capillaries, My Lord," Bergthora said. "We are hidden from the mental sight of your fellow Monstruwacans. Are you afraid that they suspect something?"

"Not really, they always suspect something, lack of trust it is in their nature. With the murders –"

"Surely that is a matter for the Prefects? Aren't they who we should worry about?"

"I can deal with the Prefects. Their straightforwardness makes them easy to manipulate. I laid a false trail leading into the heart of the Stress-Master's Guild."

"That's clever."

"Thank you."

"I wasn't being sarcastic, My Lord. The Prefects could beat their heads against that immovable object for weeks and still be no wiser. The capacity of your mind is not in doubt – after all that is why you are the youngest Master in recorded history."

"No it isn't," he said under his breath, his face turned away from the woman.

"Did you say something?"

"I do not know whether I did the right thing."

"In trusting me?"

"In not having your son be cast out of the Redoubt as Law demands. He failed the Circuit of Assessment, so I doubt he is worthy. In any case, there is a better than one in sixty chance that he is not the child I seek."

Bergthora noticed that he had not answered her question about trust. "That calculation has always been true. Yet you let him live. Your intentions were noble," she said.

"You do not know anything about my plans, and do not talk to me about good intentions – you are his mother."

"And you are complicit in the murder of two Prefects and a Stress-Master, not to mention a conspiracy to hide his survival, and you just ordered the deaths of over seventy members of my faith."

"You would blackmail me?"

"Of course not, My Lord. I am forever in your debt. I merely point out that our paths are inextricably linked."

PART TWO

When Naani was six, something went wrong with the Earth-Current machines. At that age she didn't understand what was happening, but it was very exciting, with people running round fixing lamps and getting meals ready early, so she wasn't worried that her father had to leave to help fix things. He had sat her on his knee and explained why he had to go away, and had told her not to be scared when the electricity stopped.

"I will soon come back," he said. "Until the broken thing is fixed we will have to manage with candles and oil lamps. There is nothing to worry about."

"I'm not worried, daddy," she said.

The servants scurried round preparing candles and olive oil lamps. At the appointed hour, the power failed. Flickering flames filled rooms with soft, warm light and cast intriguing will-o-the-wisp shadows. She was disappointed when it was bedtime, but her maid left a small oil lamp burning on her dressing table. She watched the little flame dance for a long time.

Then it flickered and died, plunging the room into darkness.

This was darker than when she closed her eyes tightly, or even when she covered her closed eyes up with her hands. Everywhere she turned there was absolute blackness. She wasn't scared; it was exciting. Carefully she climbed out of bed and took a step – then reached back – the bed was still there – she couldn't see it, but it was there. Laughing, she spun around. She might not be able to see but she knew where everything was in her room – the dresser was just over there – wardrobe here – the stuffed felt mouse she slept with when she was a little girl just –

Where? She couldn't remember. She reached out for the bed and her hand closed on air. In an eye blink, the room went from mapped and safe, to dark and terrifying. She stretched her arms out, searching for a familiar surface, suddenly afraid of sharp corners and bruising edges. Then her whole world fell away apart from the little patch of carpet she was crouching on. She wanted to call for help, but was suddenly afraid – the Night Land pressed close and was full of things that wanted to steal her soul.

Seven years later, Naani still kept a nightlight burning, and knew exactly what direction her bedroom door was, and how many steps away. Soul-eating monsters rarely troubled her dreams, even through she knew now that they were real. Her father would protect her.

Mirdath! Mirdath! Mirdath!

"Who's there?" Naani said. She sat bolt upright in bed, her bed sheets crumpled in her hands. She listened intently but the room was silent. The nightlight glowed on her dressing table, casting soft shadows around the room. Throwing the sheets aside, she stood up, walked over to the nightlight and turned it up to its full intensity. She was alone, and realized she had been dreaming: a strange dream full of the Night Land's darkness – and a bright warrior. She tried to recall his face, but it was hopeless – after all, he was only a dream.

And what was he saying? Mirdath – who is she?

A wheel turned and a dowel clicked in the sandclock embedded in the wall above her bed; in another hour it would the household would be rising. She climbed into bed determined to sleep, and maybe catch another glimpse of her bright warrior.

The Gallowglass parried a low sweep, feinted to his right, and slashed at his opponent's head. But the Moramor saw the attack coming and countered with a textbook vertical block. Their Diskos crashed in firestorm of electric blue scintillations. Jarred and dazzled by the impact, both men were flung back a pace. Gasping for breath, and shaking their heads to scatter the plagues of insubstantial fireflies half-blinding them, they circled each other warily.

"Had enough yet?" The Gallowglass asked.

"Yes, I yeild," the Moramor said as he spun his weapon hand over hand. In a few turns the quarterstaff, whirling disk and steel-shod foot were a blur. A heartbeat behind, the Gallowglass had set his Diskos spinning in sympathy. After twenty minutes of quarterstaff play, they were both tired. The tiniest miscalculation now would be fatal.

Simultaneously, the two warriors released their holds. The Diskos cartwheeled together and detonated in lambent fury. The air cracked with thunder and the concussion blasted the combatants a dozen yards apart.

The Gallowglass lay on his back. His vision blurred and his ears ringing. Groggily, he hauled himself to his feet and hobbled over to where his opponent lay. The air stunk of sulfur and burned iron. The place where their whirling Diskos met was marked by a ring of shattered and fused metal, which extended across the floor and ceiling, and up both walls. A faint band of charcoal – all that remained of their wooden staffs – surrounded the debris.

The Moramor looked up at the Gallowglass. "I think we can call that a tie, old friend," he said. "Unless you want to essay the best of three bouts?"

The Master of the Prefecture and his second-in-command embraced each other laughing.

Soon after, Gallowglass and his Moramor were luxuriating in one of the Prefecture's steam rooms. They lay naked, face down on wooden benches, letting the near scalding heat burn their aches and pains away.

"We are getting old, my friend," the Gallowglass said. "Ten years ago we'd have had no need for soapy massages and steam rooms to cure our aching limbs."

"Aye, My Lord. No actual need – but that'd not have stopped us. There's nothing like a good sweltering to keep a man sitting on top of the world." He raised his voice. "Hey someone, some more water on the coals here!"

After a moment, a young man clad only in a white loin cloth trotted into the room, nodded briefly, then spilled a brass urn of water on the bed of burning coals, filling the room with thick clouds of steam.

"Will there be anything else, My Lords?" he asked.

"Not for now lad, you're dismissed," the Moramor said. He lay on his side, wafted the steam away and watched the attendant leave.

"What a strange phrase that was," the Gallowglass said.

"You want to wax philosophical now?" the Moramor said, gesturing at the wisps of steam still twirling in the wake of the attendant.

"Sitting-on-top of the world. Whatever can that mean?"

"You spend too much time closeted with the Master Monstruwacan. You should get out and do some carousing."

"I have other things on my mind, Moramor. You would do well to bend your mind to them to, and spend less time about the pleasures of the flesh."

The Moramor snorted derisively. "Since when did you become a puritan?"

The attendant came back and replenished the steamy atmosphere. When he was gone, the Gallowglass broke the silence.

"How old do you think he is?"

"That's better. Twenty, twenty-one."

"Years?"

"No, parsnips."

"And what is a year – a measure of three hundred and fifty days. And a day – twenty hours. And a hour –"

"I get the point. Well, no, I don't. Is there a point?"

"Years and days are said to be based on the cycles of the Earth and Sun. But the planet stopped turning and we lost the Sun millions of years ago. Why hold on to these anachronisms?"

"The excitement of possessing arcane, if completely useless knowledge unknown to the common people?"

"Ha, old friend. You do keep my feet on the floor. Seriously –"

"You want to talk about the murder?"

"Yes."

"Do you remember the last murders to trouble our world?"

"Of course – twelve years ago – two of our best lads and that fat oaf Filangeri. Do you think the deaths are tied together? The killing of the Bee Master was a far more rarefied affair than slaying by slashing throats. Whoever turned the Monstruwacan's own bees on him was skilled in the apiarist's art. It was probably one of the victim's minions out to revenge some slight or other. I don't see any connection with the other murders."

"Four murders in the last three thousand years. All of them on my watch."

"No one could possibly blame you. If anything –"

"Say it."

"They blame the Master Monstruwacan."

"He is our Lord, take care of your tongue."

"His reforms are pushing people too far –"

"We will ensure that the people do as they are told."

"Of course. Damn, but you're in a strange mood. I know a sovereign cure – call that young fella back and invite him to share your sleeping mat tonight. If you don't I might just myself."

"Do as you wish, old friend. I have much to think on."

The Master Monstruwacan threw the sheaf of Hour-Slips onto the table, they fanned out, and a few slid onto the floor. Bergthora bent down to pick them up. She leafed through them and waited for him to calm down. The last of the children had turned twelve this month, and the reports from the Guild of Ancestors were more detailed than ever. Of the original sixty-three children, all but two were still alive. In an age when one in twenty children failed the Circuit of Assessment, that was remarkable in itself. But it was only part of the truth.

Bergthora shuffled the Hour-Slips into a semblance of order and pushed them towards the Master. "The Guild of Ancestors know far too much," she said.

"No one pays any attention to them. The other Guilds hold them in contempt for having the highest number of apprentice girls on their books."

"Imposing so many girls on them was a shrewd move on your behalf, My Lord."

"Do not patronize me. You might share my bed and some of my secrets, but you are not indispensable.

Bergthora bowed her head. "I am sorry, My Lord."

Scowling, the Master picked up the Hour-Slips and leafed through them with increasing frustration. It was obvious to Bergthora that still had not found what he was looking for. She decided to change the subject.

"My daughter has been apprenticed to the Jackotrade Master's Guild," she said. "You would have enjoyed the look on her instructor's face. The poor man –"

"Do not mock," the Master said sharply. "Millions of years of tradition cannot easily be set aside. Without the Jackotrades, and the skills of their Masters, the Redoubt would have long ago crumbled to dust. I pondered long before inflicting women on them – they and the Prefects are the most important of the Guilds."

"And yet the Prefects contribute nothing to future generations."

The Master's fist slammed down on the table. "The Prefects

are the best of us."

"Each generation they take the best young men out of our gene pool –"

"It is hardly unknown for young Prefects to sow their wild oats –"

"And thanks be for that small mercy!"

A long uncomfortable silence fell. Bergthora was tempted to ask him boldly what he sought in the children's lives. But she was afraid to. In the years since he had saved her son's life, and had recruited her to his cause, the enigma of his motivations had, if anything, deepened.

"Your daughter – I'm sorry her name escapes me," the Master asked.

"Theodora, My Lord."

The Master nodded and pulled a scroll-bound sheaf of Hour-Slips out of his gown. Bergthora noted the seal of the Gallowglass on the binding. "Corrosion in the upper gantries, stem-bore in the wheat crop, a drunken brawl in the Shambles – the list of novel problems increases every day."

"On the other hand, these problems validate your decision to apprentice girls. Every boy capable of passing even the first Estimation was already being recruited. Where else could extra apprentices be found?"

"If you ask most Guildmen, they will suggest that recruiting girls is the root of all of our problems."

"That's absurd."

"Is it?"

He ignored her question. "I must go now, I want to spend some time in the Vault of Ages," he said, abruptly.

"Maybe you spend too much time in that perilous place, My Lord."

The Master didn't reply but pulled his cowl over his head, hiding his face, brushed the curtain aside and left the room. Bergthora wondered, for maybe the hundredth time, whether it was sensible to ally herself to such a powerful and enigmatic man.

The Vault of Ages was home to one thousand two hundred and sixty-three adamantine columns. Each a half-mile high, they held the ancient wisdom of Mankind. From base to top, every pillar was intricately carved in hand-high bands filled with tiny words and pictograms. In many cases the ancient languages had been lost for millions of years. In others, although the words were individually comprehensible, their context was lost. Thinly carved lines separated most of the bands and between every twenty there was a foot-high studded metal ring. The ring allowed two different mechanisms to climb the pillars. The Master Monstruwacan had never used a chairsuit, and never intended to. He didn't like heights and the idea of being whisked about at reckless speed, high above the ground, was terrifying. In any case, searching by hand and eye was slow and ineffective. It was also dangerous. The Monstruwacan's Annals were filled with cautionary tales of Masters who were seduced by the Fool's Gold of the Vault's lost learning.

The Search Engines were a wiser, if not very much more effective, option.

His hands had danced over the rings at the base of the pillar, spinning some this way and some that way, methodically moving unwanted sections aside to revealing hidden connections.

The Search Engine was about the size of a man crouched into a ball. A silver-grey cowling covered most of its subtle, intricate works. At its base pinions flared from toothed wheels. Two of them hugged the lowest studded ring. Sixteen others were arranged in banks of four around the engine's circumference. The Master inserted his signet ring in a small hole on the engine's cowling. Gears and sprockets whirled as his cachet was read. Then the engine shifted backwards and embraced the pillar where he had left his search instructions. Pinions engaged with inscribed rings, spinning, pushing and pulling them in an exact reversal of the actions the Master had programmed. The process took five minutes. Then the Search Engine whirled towards the darkness above.

He had limited the search to a week, reasoning that should be long enough to track down the most significant references to alterations in the shape and size of the Shine. The Watcher's Guild kept him informed about the continuous subtle physical changes to the home of the Fixed Giants. Recently he had begun to sense that something was brewing under the surface fluctuations. The Watcher's records had little information, so he turned to the greatest, and most frustrating, repository – the Vault of Ages. No one alive understood the indexing system used, or could guess how much knowledge was lost even to the Search Engines. Or if they could be trusted – for all he knew, they might have been designed to hide vast swathes of learning.

Casting his doubts aside, he started to program another Search Engine. This time the algorithm was a familiar one, and the work went quickly. Every month since he was elected twelve years ago, he had searched the Vault for references to the building of a Master-Word machine – the device that would allow telepathic communication with the humans of the Great Redoubt. And every month so far his hopes had been disappointed; they were vast numbers of references to the glorious powers of such a device, but nothing on how to construct one.

After programming some final, subtle adjustments to his search parameters, he sent the machine on its way up a nearby pillar. He was about to leave the Vault, when a thin stream of oil-like liquid climbing easily up a nearby pillar caught his attention. He watched fascinated as the Jackotrade colony went about its inscrutable business. The legions of tiny machines were ubiquitous throughout the Redoubt, tirelessly repairing the tiniest rents and tears in the Redoubt's fabric. He suspected that, in a real sense, they had been a much more important factor than any Monstruwacan, however elevated, in keeping mankind's last home whole over the aeons.

It was rare to see a colony so united in its purpose. He hoped it was a good omen.

The Garden of Contemplation was one of Naani's favorite places. She loved the soft wind blowing across the hot sands, and the abstract tinkling of the wind chimes. The limestone pavement that wound sinuously through the garden was cool under her bare feet. She stopped to look at a particularly striking design. Fifty feet across, the basis of the sand painting was a flower with five petals like curved blades. A kaleidoscope of stripes of colored sand flowed through the design, sometimes seeming to dive under the petals, and at other times to flow over them. As she turned her head, hidden patterns were revealed – cubes and pyramids, octahedra and other shapes she couldn't put a name too. It was as beautiful as it was enigmatic. No one outside of their Guild knew how the Sand Masters made their designs; the Garden was always closed and guarded by Prefects when they were working.

A breath of wind suddenly threw up a faint layer of fine sand over the flower picture. Naani smiled sadly – this was the way of the Garden – no matter how beautiful a design was, it was doomed to be etched away a grain of sand at a time.

Naani walked on. She was alone, with no chattering maids or Prefects with fearsome weapons. They were just outside the Garden's gate of course, but she enjoyed the illusion of solitude. Then she saw something strange. For a moment she thought she had caught a Sand Master at work, but she quickly realized it was just a boy. He was about her age, and was lying face-down in the center of a hexagonal design, kicking his legs and flapping his arms like he was swimming. The sand painting was almost obliterated.

"Prefects!" Naani shouted at the top of her voice.

The boy rolled over and looked at her, then spat on the sand and ran away.

"A pretty thing is she?" Essa asked.

"Who?" Hugh asked with a sinking feeling in his stomach.

"Your new apprentice. What's her name?"

"Theodora," Hugh grunted.

"Pretty is she?"

"I can't say I've noticed. Anyhow, she only fourteen."

"Well before we know it she'll be sixteen then eighteen, and she'll not be a child then."

Hugh raised his voice in exasperation. "I didn't ask to have a bloody girl apprenticed to me. Fact is, I bloody near begged for it not to happen."

"Hope you don't use that kind of language around your new apprentice. I heard she's noble-born. Wouldn't do to have word about your juicy language reaching such exalted ears."

"Noble born? Where do you hear such nonsense?"

"Well, that would be saying wouldn't it. Oh I know! Why don't you invite her around for evening meal? Then we can all get to know each better."

"Can't. She's busy studying for her first Estimation. Got her head in books and jars for the next couple of weeks. Wouldn't do to interrupt."

"Alright then, Pumpkin. We'll have her round after her little test then."

Hugh groaned, knowing he was beaten.

Caliban was a strange name, but he liked it. The too-clever-by-half tutor who mentioned it was vague when questioned about its origins, saying something about an ancient sorcerer and a flying island. It was obvious the man has no idea what he was talking about, but the boy enjoyed the taste of it in his mouth, so he took it as his secret name.

Honey ran down his chin and his hands were sticky. He licked the outside of the stolen comb, and then snapped it open. A bee was trapped in the wax. He watched fascinated as the insect struggled, its antenna thrashing wildly. It was a long time before the bee gave up the fight, and he watched every second intently. Then he dropped the comb. It fell a long way before he lost sight of it.

He was sitting in a bole of a leafy oak in the Flying Wood half a mile above the floor of the Great Arbor, and was feeling very pleased. His raid had been a complete success. He kicked over three hives and, while the Beekeepers ran frantically around like giant versions of their charges, helped himself to a box of harvested combs. Then he ran away as fast as his twelve-year old legs could carry him. He wasn't worried about pursuit – he knew plenty of short cuts and hidden bypasses – he just enjoyed running. The bees didn't worry him either; insects never attacked him, no matter what he did to them.

He was special.

His mother had told him he was special when he was a small child. She thought that he didn't know. He remembered her whispering when she thought he was asleep, whispering about how he was one of a special generation, and how he might be the one they were looking for. As he grew older his mother stopped coming to him at night, but he had never forgotten her secret hopes. As Bergthora Baumgard's son, he had a comfortable life with plenty of possessions and most of his whims indulged. But there was something missing. He knew he was supposed to be weak in the Night-Hearing, but he found that difficult to believe. Strangers found him hard to read, but he had no problems reading them, especially when they were thinking about him. As he grew older, his companions – he never through of them as friends – whispered stories about when they visited the Circuit of Assessment. He always found a way to change the subject, often with some over-the-top clowning. He had a vague memory of being terrified in a place with white walls filled with people with dusty white faces. The first time he broached the subject with his mother, she had thrown up instant mental walls and forbade him to mention it again. For several years he tried to wheedle something out of her. He once professed to share her secret faith in Harlequin in the hope of influencing her, but she was adamant in her refusal and angrily added her dead savior to the list of things Caliban was never, ever to mention.

He leaned back and rubbed his back against the bark. It felt good. On an impulse he ripped a young shoot up and hurled it towards the ground. It fell a long way before it was whisked away by the fold in the Air-Clog. Part of him admired the outrageous vision and skill that hung a substantial hill, covered in gnarled oak trees half a mile up in the arbor's sky. Another part wondered how easy it would be to cut the glass ropes that held the Flying Wood up. That would be a sight to see, he thought happily, even better than the look on that prissy girl's face in the Garden of Contemplation a couple of days ago.

One day I'll show her and everyone else.

He took a small stone war out of his jerkin and poured a silvery liquid into the palm of his hand. The liquid spread out slowly then contracted into a tight ball. Caliban rolled it around on his palm then closed his hand tightly. A delicious shudder passed through him as the Jackotrades soaked through his flesh and bone, and spread over the back of his hand in a silver sheen.

One day soon.

Hidden in the roof above the Great Arbor was a room containing a failed experiment. It was almost forgotten, except for an obscure reference in the Vault of Ages that the Master Monstruwacan stumbled on it a year ago, while hunting for information on the energy fields that the Fixed Giants seem to feed on. There appeared to be no relationship between the things in the Shine and the ancient experiment, but the Vault was full of obscure connections, so he decided to follow the tenuous lead. It took him six months to find the experiment's location, and another two to get past the locking mechanisms on the chamber's massive granite cap.

The experiment was located at the bottom of a shaft cut into the bedrock above the Great Arbor. The shaft was a hundred feet deep and lined with foot-thick ceramic bricks. The only way down was by a perilous set of ladder steps cut into the wall. The Master had faced the Fixed Giants in their lair, but the first descent almost unmanned him. After that, and the equally terrifying ascent, he arranged for the Prefects to set up a pulley system with ropes and other safety features. The Moramor arranged the work, and didn't ask any questions, even when the Master ordered that the system be designed to that a single man could operate it. Nor did he ask why when the Master ordered a round-the-clock guard on the chamber.

The main feature of the experiment was a palladium cube, six feet along each side. It shone like had been cast yesterday. Pipes and thick conduits snaked from the base of the cube, and disappeared into the chamber's walls. The cube was covered with finely incised writing in dozens of different languages. The Master was sure that the writing had nothing to do with the purpose of the machine – it was more like million year-old graffiti.

He took a final wax rubbing of the writings, then prepared for the long haul back up the shaft. After months of study he was still no nearer to understanding what the machine was designed to do. Reluctantly, he accepted that there were no answers here – it was yet another dead end.

PART THREE

The Master Monstruwacan knelt outside his daughter's bedroom, his head pressed against the door. Naani was tossing and turning relentlessly, but his mind was attuned to deeper currents. Since turning fourteen, Naani had showed signs that she was growing strong in the Master-Word. It wasn't uncommon for puberty to be accompanied by a sudden increase in mental abilities, but her new gifts were spasmodic and uncontrolled, and were strongest when she was asleep.

He opened his mind and was swept up in her dream.

Naani walked through the ruins of the Lesser Redoubt, taking care to avoid the bodies of men and beasts. They were so closely entangled it was impossible to tell where one race began and the other ended. Effortlessly, she made long climb to the apex of the pyramid and, when she reached the top, she stepped into sky. Buoyed by fleeing souls, she was wafted across an ancient sea. The ire of the Fixed Giants reverberated from the Shine, but she dismissed them with a glance, and headed Southwest. She skimmed the Great Gorge with its dark flanking forests, then plunged down an immense slope into a pool of darkness. She could see everything – and everything could see her. The luminous ring crowning the Northeast Watcher pulsed with every shades of blue, and its country-sized forehead crinkled extravagantly. The Silent Ones were wreathed in vagueness but watched her with keen interest.

Naani ignored all of them and swept towards the eight-mile metal high pyramid that dominated the surrounding works of darkness.

Beloved, where are you?

It is not yet time, my love.

When?

Be patient – fate will bring us together when the time is ripe.

Naani woke up for a moment, turned over and mumbled something unintelligible, then fell into a dreamless sleep.

The Master backed away from the door. He was soaked in sweat and his hands trembled, but he was ecstatic.

"My Lady! Where have you been?"

"We were worried –"

"You know your father doesn't like you wandering off –"

"Especially these days, did you hear that the one of the Long Galleries had collapsed, My Lady?"

"Terrible it was, terrible –"

"Dozens were hurt –"

Naani's maids surrounded her like bees around a honey jar. Their faces were red as acorns and they were breathless. That didn't stop them chattering incessantly. In all her fourteen years, Naani had never been saddled with three such fusspots.

"I wasn't anywhere near the Long Galleries," Naani said. "I was just talking with that young gentleman over there, oh where's he gone? Did you see him? He was quite handsome."

The maids gagged for a moment, then after a brief, whispered conference, Melina – Naani was fairly sure it was Melina – adopted her sternest expression.

"That will not do, My Lady. Your father was most explicit that you are to be chaperoned when out in society. Running off and gadding about with young gentlemen is . . . unacceptable. What do you know about him? Is he well bred? Are his prospects bright? Mmm?"

The other two maids chimed in with mmm's of their own, while fussing at Naani's dress and hair. Naani was tempted to ask Moll (or was it Mimii?) if the underfootman she was so friendly with after curfew had good prospects.

"I didn't ask the gentleman about his prospects, or his breeding. I think both were quite evident," she said.

That set off another chorus of twittering. As her maids guided her back to the official reception, she wondered again about the young man. There was something familiar about him, but she couldn't recall if they had met. He was about her age, and was charming, but evasive when she asked about his background.

All in all, he was quite the enigma.

Her maids chivvied back to the dull party, and she smiled automatically as they introduced her to a succession of dull young men.

"More jam, dear?" Essa asked.

"No thanks, ma. I'm full up," Theodora replied. "I've never tasted better scones than yours, but one can have too much of a good thing."

"I'll wrap some up for you to take to work," Essa said, with a determined nod. "You're working so hard these days, you must be sure to eat properly."

"I'm working hard too," Hugh mumbled.

"Did you say something, husband?"

"Never said a word," Hugh said with a sly wink at Theodora.

"Good. Don't you be letting him run roughshod over you, my dear. You've been his apprentice four years now, you probably know as much about those Jackotrades as he does."

"I wouldn't say that," Theodora said, biting her lip to avoid giggling at the look on Hugh's face. "Master Hugh is highly regarded within our Guild for his great experience –"

"Aye, he's getting on," Essa said with sad shake of her head. "No denying that."

Hugh pushed his chair back. "I am going now. You two can cackle away to your heart's content. Theodora – met me in a couple of hours at Guild House – we need to restock on savory tinctures."

"Yes, Master Hugh."

Later, when they were doing the washing up, Theodora asked Essa a question that had been on her mind for a long time.

"Tell me, why didn't you have children?"

Essa was up to her elbows in soapy water, and her apron was flecked with soapy bubbles. She smiled a small smile, and shrugged. "It was wasn't to be. We wanted a family, but like so many other folk these days, it just never happened." She pulled a spotless tureen out of the sink and scrutinized it carefully, her face brightening. "I'll tell you one thing, though."

"What's that, ma?"

"It wasn't for the want of trying."

Bergthora sat up in bed with her knees tucked under her chin. The bedroom was chilly, but that wasn't why she was trembling. Beside her, the Lord of the Redoubt snored softly in a dreamless sleep. As his confessor, she could understand that; for sixteen years he had carried a terrible burden, and it must have been a tremendous relief to finally let another person share the secret.

But why me? Why do I have to know this thing? Am the only person in the world who he truly trusts?

For a guilty moment, she wished she could wind back the day to before their walk in the farmlands that fringed the South of the underground lands.

"You aren't worried that people will see us?" Bergthora asked.

The Master Monstruwacan held her hand a little tighter and nodded towards the saffron groves. A dozen heads poked above the soil ramparts. "I think it is a little late to worry about that," he said. The heads disappeared one-by-one as the Prefects flanking the Master and Bergthora's path approached.

"Did you notice?" Bergthora asked. "The men and women work together."

"The farmers have never bothered with such niceties as dividing life's work up between the sexes, if a job needs doing someone does it."

"A good example."

"I did not ask you to accompany me so you tell me things I already know."

"No, My Lord. I am sorry. You want my report on the children. There is an seat over there, shall we rest?"

"If you wish."

The seat was rough-cut from a block of limestone and was sited on a little mound overlooking the nearby groves. The farm workers looked up as they passed by. With a sudden flash of insight, Bergthora realized that the Master wanted her to be seen with him. Scandalized rumors would spread through the Redoubt's markets and taverns, and maybe deflect attention away from other things.

"The Children," the Master said.

"Yes, My Lord." She took a tight-wound sheaf of Hour-Slips out of a fold in her bodice, and took out a single slip. "This month's summary. One child was lost, the girl Chami, who died from the coughing fits."

"At fourteen?"

"A though investigation was done. There is no reason to believe her death was anything but a natural tragedy."

The Master shook his head and smiled thinly.

"The fifty-nine surviving children are all in good physical health –"

She stopped talking as two men hauling a handcart full to the brim with cabbages and parsnips passed by, filling the air with a rich loamy smell. One of the men smiled and waved. Bergthora overheard the Master's mental command to the Prefects – *let them pass in peace.* She watched the cart roll away around a corner, and the Prefects fanning out to prevent a repeat of the interruption.

That they had allowed the men to get so close in the first place was surprising, and a little worrying. The Master shifted a little beside her, and she felt his impatience.

She consulted the Hour-Slips again. "On average, their mental and physical abilities are only a little more pronounced that the older and younger control cohorts. There are exceptions, of course. The boy Aldous shows tremendous intellectual promise, Arian has empathic gifts that suggest she will become a great healer . . . and your daughter appears strong in the Master-Word –"

"Such things are relative. None of us comes close to the strength of our ancestors."

"Her potential is undeniable –"

"Continue your report. We will discus individuals at another time."

"Yes, My Lord. As might be expected, the parents of the boys are staring to make representations to their familial Guilds, and the Prefects have shown interest in three of them."

"I will decide which Guilds the children will be apprenticed to – including the girls – and I will take steps to deflect the interest of the Prefecture."

"Yes, My Lord. One other thing –"

"Your son," the Master said through tight lips.

Bergthora stood up, suddenly angry. "Preserve us! Will you stop picking my mind? I have a right to privacy."

The Master's expression softened. "Do not be absurd. You concern for the boy is like a beacon; I have no need to step inside your head to see your worries."

"The Prefects hunt him."

"In the last week treacle was used to block the pipes of the Musician's Guild's Harmonium, a plague of cockroaches infested the Baker's district, and offensive graffiti about the Prefects has appeared in several different places. Silly and pointless acts, but a growing source of friction and a drain on the Prefecture's already stretched resources. This time if they find him, he will be flogged and put to hard labor for a year, and there is nothing even I can do to save him."

"There is no proof these were his acts. Your regime is hardly popular, many people are opposed to your reforms."

"The people of the Redoubt are not given to malicious acts of vandalism, your son is unique in that respect."

"I wouldn't count on that –" She stopped herself just in time from raising the unsolved murder of the Bee Master.

The Master shook his head angrily. "You try my patience, woman. The Prefects will catch they boy eventually, and quickly extract the truth."

"No they won't."

"Pain is a great incentive."

"I wouldn't rely on that. I saw him put his hand in a flame once – I think he knew I was watching. He held his hand in the flame for minute after minute. I swear I could smell his flesh crisping. He showed no sign of pain, only amusement."

The color drained from the Master's face. "Life's breath – what if he is the one?"

Bergthora sat down, and took his hand in hers. "Maybe it is time you told me what happened when you were enKernelled?"

The Master was silent for a long time. "Yes, you are right. But not here. Let us return home."

He told her everything over a meal of pomegranates in lavender jelly with caramelized grasshoppers. The sweetmeats were among her favorites but, as he told her of his bargain with the Fixed Giants of the Shine, she decided she would never eat them again. Such petty self-punishment was absurd, but she had to do something.

She lay awake for several hours, mulling the Master's revelations over. She pushed aside a lock of hair that had fallen across his face and wondered if he was, in fact, quite mad.

Don't be absurd. He is the sanest man in the world, how else could he have hidden this thing for so long? The questions I have to answer are all directed at me, not him – a fact he knows perfectly well.

She remembered staring at her half-eaten bowl of grasshoppers while he told her that everyone was going to die.

No, not everyone – there will be a survivor – could it be my son?

"I found a strange old tale in the Vault of Ages," he said after a long silence.

"You spend to much time there," she said automatically.

He ignored her. "In the Dawn Times, even before the Age of the Moving Cities, when humanity still had ambitions, they did a great and daring thing. Tens – hundreds – of thousands of people worked for decades to build a great machine, to launch and single man into the heavens on a pillar of fire."

"Why?"

"To see what's there, I suppose."

"What did he find?"

"I don't know."

"That's not much of a story – oh, I understand – you see it as a metaphor for the eight million years we have been bereft of the rest of humanity. That is a thin reason to take these great decisions."

He picked at the skin of a pomegranate slice with a small fork. "I have other reasons. Are you with me?"

"Yes, My Lord." Bergthora said a little too quickly, wondering what he would do if she had said 'no'.

The Search Engines climbed over each other exchanging

information in their mysterious language of cogs and ratchets, sprockets and pinions, hairsprings and worm drives. A dozen of them were rolling around together in front of the Master Monstruwacan, while thirty more were climbing the pillars of knowledge, looking for snippets of lore, or obscure connections.

He had stumbled on this new way of programming the Search Engines by accident. Twelve months ago, just after the murder of the Bee Master, he had found a hidden panel on one of the engines. Inside was a set of eight cog-toothed wheels. Intrigued by this new enigma, he thumbed the unmarked wheels up and down randomly. Nothing happened for several minutes, then something inside the machine clicked. The Engine rolled away from him and clambered over one of its companions. At first he assumed it was an accident, or maybe he had damaged the machine's gyroscopes, but then he realized that the two engines were moving with a unified purpose.

It took him two months to discover that this was how information could be passed from one Search Engine to another, and another four to develop the programming techniques needed to take advantage of his discovery. For a time he hoped to revolutionize the gleaning of knowledge. A year on from his discovery he was less optimistic. The new technique seemed to prevent Search Engines from duplicating each other's efforts, which was a useful breakthrough, but the higher levels of efficiency he suspected existed still eluded him.

Just like the answers he needed.

A tinkling of bells caught his attention. The clan of Search Engines had reached some sort of conclusion. In their arcane way they had chosen one of their number to approach him. He fancied that its wheels and gyroscopes were perhaps spinning a little smoother than the others. It had lived up to its potential. It wasn't the machine's fault that the answers it was ready to show him were almost certainly useless. Humans had created the machines, and humans had lost the secrets of how to use them effectively – assuming they had ever known. He wondered if, left to themselves for eight million years, they might have evolved into a higher form, capable of accessing and synthesizing the lost learning into something useful, and maybe revelatory. He realized he was saddened for the mechanism. It would fail, and he would reset its whirling mechanisms, taking away the atom of consummation it had accrued.

The Search Engine was rocking slightly from side-to-side. In pity, not expectation, he leaned forward and tapped a little brass button that was labeled 'execute' in an ancient language. The irony of seeking knowledge by calling for its death was not lost on him.

The Search Engines began their oracular gavotte, swarming up pillars; the fleetest among them quickly disappearing into the gloom high above. He looked upwards, wondering what complexities lay hidden in the design of the Vault. Eight years ago he had discovered that a small number of pillars were special: their jackets of words and pictures were veneers hiding vacuous natures. They held no knowledge worth having. At first he had been angered at this wasteful deception. But later, while recording the gross characteristics of the Vault, he began to notice patterns. Four of the seemingly useless pillars would be set at the corners of a square a mile to a side. Sharing each corner was a circle of six more, and centered on that a two-mile diameter octagon. He realized that other patterns were waiting to be found. He even knew what to look for. The missing patterns would complete a sequence enumerating the faces of the five perfect solids: pyramid, cube, octahedron, dodecahedron, and icosahedron.

It had taken him two and a half years, but he eventually tracked the eight and twenty sided patterns down. The dodecagons orbited the numeric core with their centers fixed on vertices drawn through the centers of the square, circle and octagon. The twenty-sided figures were the most enigmatic. They grazed the outermost angles of the dodecagons, but were truncated by the rock walls of the vault.

The significance of their stunting escaped and worried him.

Naani turned the rose in her hand; it was perfectly symmetrical and had the most vivid red color she had ever seen. She inhaled its sweet scent and glanced at the boy standing beside her. He was still an enigma. This was the second time in a week she had slipped her maids to keep a secret meeting with him. The Prefects would have been alerted by now and would be looking for her. It wouldn't take them very long to find her, and she could expect a long scolding, and probably a slippering, when she was taken home. At that moment, she didn't care.

"It's beautiful," she said, twirling the rose.

"I suppose so," Caliban said.

"Where did you get it?"

"Read my mind."

"You know I can't."

Caliban grinned, and leaned over the balustrade. They were on the fifteenth tier of the Arborists' galleries, level with the bottom of the Flying Wood and a quarter mile above the floor of the Great Arbor. Suddenly, Caliban spat over the edge.

"Oh, that's disgusting!" Naani said.

Caliban pantomimed outrage. "Oh, golly! I've broken the law! Call the Prefects!"

"Well, it's wrong and –"

"Disgusting?"

"Yes."

Caliban nodded at the rose. "Funny, you don't seem to mind breaking the law when it's about something pretty. Oh, didn't you know? Having stolen properly is against the law." He wagged a finger. "Ignorance of the law is no excuse."

"Where did you steal it?" Naani asked.

"From the Shrine of Anamnesis in the Garden of the Dead."

Naani let the flower fall from her fingers. It tumbled into space and wafted slowly towards the Arbor floor. She stepped back; her hand left compulsively gripping the balustrade. "Get away from me! I never want to see you again."

Caliban reached forward, grabbed her dress and pulled her

close. "No, let's wait. The Prefects will be here soon. They might even catch me. It's not very likely – they aren't too bright. But if they did, you could watch them flog me. Would you like that?"

Naani pushed hard and Caliban fell over and ripped a handful of silk out of her dress. She covered herself up as best she could and ran away. Caliban's laughter followed her all the way to the door.

PART FOUR

Caliban attacked the wall with bare hands and booted feet. The air was full of pulverized rockplug, but still he hadn't hit the other side. He could hear the Prefects getting closer, their heavy footsteps and angry shouts echoing up the wide spiral stairway that curled around the shaft connecting the pyramid with the caverns below. They had been hunting him for two hours, ever since the Watchmaker had chased him from his shop. Caliban cursed him – he would make him pay for all this trouble one day.

The man had looked up from his work suspiciously as Caliban walked into his workshop.

"What do you want, boy?" he demanded, pushing his loupe back behind his head. "Shouldn't you be in school at this time?"

Caliban coughed into a silk handkerchief. "I've been ill for some day with an ague." The Watchmaker edged back a little. "But, I'm better now and mamma suggested I go for a walk. She's been a wonder looking after me while I was ill, so I though I might buy her a thank you gift, something in silver, perhaps –"

Caliban left the bait dangling, but the Watchmaker was

still suspicious.

"Your mamma?

"Lady Bergthora Baumgard," Caliban said with little in the way of nonchalance.

The Watchmaker's eyes brightened greedily. "Well, yes, maybe I have some small pieces that might interest her, I mean you, My, ahem, young Lordship."

The Watchmaker showed him a range of intricate and expensive timepieces. Caliban turned the watches and small clocks over in his hands, while the man droned on about their mechanisms and cunning complexities. The boy nodded occasionally, but paid no real attention to the craftsman's witterings. He was much more interested in the tiny electric tickling in his fingertips as the Jackotrades bled through his skin. The sensation of control was delicious. Often recently, it had seemed as if the little machines that permeated his flesh were working to a will of their own. But, when he woke up that morning, he knew that this was going to be a good day, a day when he was in charge.

"Well, young Master. I was wondering –" the Watchmaker asked, nervously. He had a slender sandclock in his hands. It was made from tiny twisted ropes of gold and silver, and its pivots had onyx and agate seatings. Despite its relative inaccuracy compared to mechanical clocks and watches, Caliban guessed that it was the most expensive timepiece in the shop.

"I won't be buying," Caliban said.

The Watchmaker's face fell. "May I ask why not?"

"Because your clocks don't work." He pointed to the first timepiece the Watchmaker had showed him. "That one seems to have seized up."

The Watchmaker picked up the clock and looked at it incredulously. He tipped his loupe down in front of his right eye, and opened the back of the clock with a small tool that he carried in his sleeve. His face turned red as he twiddled screws and nudged tiny springs.

"Is it broken?" Caliban asked.

The Watchmaker shook his head. "No, I can fix it. It's nothing."

Caliban patted him on the back. "That's good to hear.

Especially since all your other pieces seem to be broken too – oh except for the sandclock – pity it's so gaudy – not quite right for a Lady's home, I think."

The Watchmaker ran his trembling hands the rest of his ruined timepieces; then he looked at Caliban with a mixture of disbelief and hatred.

"You did this?" he snarled in a tiny, choking voice.

Caliban winked and ran from the shop. After a moment the Watchmaker ran after him. That wouldn't normally have been a problem; Caliban was fast on his feet and knew ever nook and cranny of the Redoubt. However, just as the man burst into the street, flinging curses and shouting for help in a surprisingly loud voice, a squad of Prefects turned the corner.

Caliban took his pursuers on an epic and exhilarating run through the Craftsman's district, in and out of the Shambles and around the Great Arbor. He felt like he was flying over the short red grass, but the Prefects never gave up. In fact, more of them joined the chase. By the time he reached the rarely used tunnels that surrounded the Arbor and led up to the Stress-Master's domain, a dozen Prefects were hunting him. A detour into a ventilation pipe lost them for a while, but they soon caught up with his trail again.

Now they were only minutes away, and he had nowhere left to run to.

Cursing, he backed hard up against the sandstone wall and balled his fists. The hunters were almost upon him. Sweat poured won his face and his breath came in rasps; they had him this time.

Then he took another step backwards.

The workshop was a shambles. Hundreds of jars were broken or spilled, ten-foot high mahogany shelves dripped with viscous fluids, notebooks were sticky with black ooze, and the floor was covered with broken glass. The Moramor prodded a jar of binder Jackotrades. Shattered into a countless fragments, it was held together by its sticky, dead contents.

He gave it a tap, and the jar gave way, slowly slumping down into a glutinous, glass pierced heap. It was the same all over his workshop. The only part of the Jackotrade Master's arsenal that was undamaged was the collection of tinctures and potions used to guide the tiny machines to their tasks. The Moramor leaned forward and sniffed the rows of undamaged jars. They smelled of sharp acids and oils.

"And you found the damage this morning, yes?" the Moramor asked.

"Yes, My Lord. I opened up as usual this morning," Hugh replied. "Well, to be truthful I was a bit early, you see I was going –"

"He doesn't need to know that," Hugh's wife interrupted.

"Yes, he does, he needs to know everything, don't you, Sir?"

"Well, perhaps not everything," the Moramor said, dryly.

"Told you."

"Be still, wife," Hugh said.

Essa folded her arms and fell silent. From the look on her face, the Moramor doubted that she would stay that way for long. He listened politely as Hugh blathered on about his duties. It was becoming an increasingly familiar tale. Mysterious acts of vandalism were happening all over the redoubt – a plague of maggots in the cheese bazaar – Hour-Slip tubes gummed up with cob nut husks – slippery, hard-to-see oil on the shaded paths under the Flying Wood. He knew full well who was responsible, but catching the culprit was easier said than done. Just yesterday, he had led a squad of hunters into the wide spiral stairways that curled around the shaft connecting the pyramid with the caverns below. At first the boy's trail was easy to follow – he had kicked his way through the soft rockplug seals blocking the stairs – but then all trace of him disappeared apart from a pile of thinly shredded clothes.

The Moramor picked up another broken jar. Whatever had happened here, it wasn't the feral boy's handywork. Something subtler was at work here.

Caliban screamed incessantly during the thousands of

years he was entombed in the wall. It made no difference; the rock was indifferent. Blazing agony coursed through every part of his being but, although most of his consciousness was lost to howling, a tiny, rational part calmly analyzed what had happened. Before he abandoned such unnecessary activities, he had been a reasonably attentive student. He remembered being told that he was a coalition of trillions of tiny cells, and inside each cell there were legions of symbiotic organelles, all busy with their own evolutionary agendas while helping him through life. It seemed absurd to him, and at the time he didn't care.

Being dragged into solid rock had sharpened his interest in the nature of life.

He had been squeezed and stretched – each cell separated from its neighbors and spread over the infinity of the rock universe. Despite the diaspora, something was holding him together. After untold ages, he realized that he could will his separate parts to flow. At first his reformation was agonizingly slow, but gradually the pace quickened and he fell from the wall. It was a long time before he stopped screaming. He lay naked on the cold stone floor unable to remember who he was. The puzzle was almost beyond him, but he finally remembered.

He was Caliban, and he was special.

Monstruwacan Lindos wandered through the Great Arbor in something of a trance, his mind filled with cubic splines and partial derivatives. So intent had he been on his books and abaci, that only the emptiness in his stomach told him the best part of the day had passed. Reluctantly, he decided to walk to the Shambles in search of a pasty or sweetmeat. Pleased at his sudden burst of practicality. Lindos stepped into the nearest shop. A woman was berating the Baker. Lindos began to edge out of the shop, but she spotted him.

"A Monstruwacan, ha!" she said. She picked up a loaf and brandished it at him. "Look at this! Every loaf ruined. It's been the same all week. Perhaps is you lot got off your fat backsides and brought your precious Master –"

Lindos pushed the loaf away from his face with his outstretched fingertips. It was covered in a vivid red fungus and smelled of sweet decay. The woman shoved it back. Lindos desperately wanted to get away from her. He turned to leave but found that the door was blocked by several people. They pushed into the shop forcing Lindos back.

"I'm sure the matter is under consideration, Madam. The authorities are – ," Lindos blurted.

"The Authorities – lot of good they are – couldn't find their own asses with both hands!"

The fast growing crowd laughed. Lindos wasn't sure what they found funny. It was so unfair; what had rotting bread to do with him? He knew something was up; anyone who had a glimmering of the Night Hearing could sense the growing irritation and worry throughout the Redoubt. The stability of their world was fraying at the edges, taking many certainties with it. It was only little things really; food corrupting in hours not days, an unexplained fire that left half-a-dozen undercriers nursing burns, a plague of nasty, biting mosquitoes in the public baths, and a dozen other minor irritations. Each incident would have been unremarkable on its own, things go amiss in even the best-regulated societies but, with so many things going wrong at once, tension was growing.

"I am so sorry," Lindos said.

"Sorry isn't good enough!" someone shouted.

Other angry voices joined the complaint. The crowd surged forward, Lindos tried to run, but they were soon upon him.

Four hours later word of the incident had reached the Gallowglass in his Keep.

"A Monstruwacan beaten!" He crushed the report in his hand. "Where were our men when this mob was loose?"

"Our numbers are few, we cannot be everywhere –" the Moramor began.

"I am not interested in excuses, I want the culprits hunted down. I will personally flog every one of them. A Monstruwacan beaten! Never in the annals of the Prefects has such a thing happened. If this spreads we will have anarchy on our hands – or civil war! Never have we fallen so low!"

"The offenders are being sought, My Lord. They will be brought to justice. But –"

The Gallowglass sat down, and spread the crumpled papers on the wooden table in front of him. He looked at the reports lying on jet-black wood. "Our numbers are few, and problems multiply by the day," he said.

"Yes, My Lord. Fouled water in the Eastern terraces, fires in the News Crier's Guild House, the strange behavior of the Jackotrades –"

"What news on that?"

"I am meeting with someone from the Jackotrade Guild later today. Perhaps he can shed some light on the events. Their Guild House must be in ferment. They are being tight-lipped, but I have determined that at least a third of their Masters have lost their stocks in the last month."

"What is the people's mood overall?"

"They are afraid, My Lord. Rumors are spreading like lice."

"Rumors?"

"That the dark forces have found away into our home, that something malign slinks though the gaps behind our walls, working mischief wherever it goes. That Guild system is falling apart, and that –"

"Out with it, man."

"People say that the Master Monstruwacan spends all his days lost in the Vault of Ages, searching desperately for some miraculous way to stop the End of Days."

"That is an . . . exaggeration, nor is this is not the End of Days."

"Maybe not. I have no knowledge of such things. I do know that the Monstruwacan Council has not met for six years, and that they fester at their impotence, and that the Guilds –"

The Gallowglass' voice fell to a whisper. "Enough! You stretch the bounds of our friendship to near breaking point."

"My Lord, I was not speaking to you as one who loves you,

but as your second-in-command," the Moramor said calmly.

The Gallowglass flinched as from a slap, looked into his friend eyes and nodded sadly. "You are right. The public mood is a legitimate matter for concern, and I will raise it the Lord of the Redoubt."

The yellow-blue and red abstract shapes projected onto the curving wall reflected in the vitreous armor of his squad. Whatever way he looked at the images, the Moramor could make nothing of their rough-hewn geometries.

"What am I looking at?" he asked, hoping the girl had not realized how flummoxed he had been when she had turned out not to be the man he had expected.

Theodora looked up from her instruments. She was sitting in front of a tall silver tower festooned with dials, ratchets and eyepieces. Dozens of similar gadgets were scattered on wooden workbenches.

"Ask your men to leave," she said.

"Why?"

"I can hardly tell why they need to leave while they are still here, can I?"

"Your reasoning is impeccable," he said, as he dismissed his men with a hand signal.

Theodora waited as the Prefects spun on their heels and marched quickly from the room, then stood beside the projector.

"This picture is magnified near two thousand times. The large irregular, red-black particles are ferric oxide, rust, if you prefer," she said.

"You mean corrosion? That is impossible. The Jackotrades should repair any damage before it becomes a problem."

"Evidently not," Theodora said. "You see the small yellow objects?"

He nodded.

"They are redundant Jackotrades."

"By redundant you mean dead?"

"Yes."

"My knowledge of such matters is scant. I understand that they live, if that is even the right word, for but a short time, then die after which their essentials are used to fashion subsequent generations."

"All of the samples your men collected in the Long Galleries are filled with dead Jackotrades – and none that are living."

"Oh."

"You have a gift for pithiness, Moramor."

"You find this humorous?"

"The end of our civilization and the Fall of Night? Strangely, I don't find that funny. Look, there is another sample you should look at. This is from the inside of one my Master's jars."

She fiddled with her microscope, opening doors, pushing and pulling slides, peering down optics and twiddling with knobs, working to sharpen the amorphous green blur on the wall. Finally, the image clarified into something that looked like holes in cheese. She reduced the magnification, and the holes began to form a pattern.

"That almost looks like –" the Moramor began.

"The Jackotrades tunneled their way out," she confirmed.

"Why would they do that?"

"That is an interesting question, and the only answers I can imagine terrify me."

Just to the east of the Shine lay the desolate landscape called the Place of Gas. The thin zephyrs that whistled across the Night Land made no impression on the miasma of death that hung about the place. All but the most brutish of Night's inhabitants knew better than to enter the killing zone. The boundary was easy to see: the wretched scrubby vegetation that somehow had found a foothold in the Night stopped at the edge, as if it had run into an invisible wall. Just inside the boundary, there was a ring of bones, bleached and pitted by the corrosive air.

Something was happening in the Shine, and it was drawing

the creatures of the Night towards the deadly zone. Beast men and more unspeakable things stood in a widely spaced line around the Place of Gas. They shook with terror and howled defiance at the vague shapes coalescing amid the blue glow. Creatures with hands or claws grasped rocks or bone clubs; the others bared their teeth or unsheathed claws.

The Master Monstruwacan sat cross-legged at the center of the Vault of Ages, surrounded by dozens of pieces of paper; each one covered in his precise handwriting and tiny drawings. He picked one up, scrutinized it carefully, then put it down and picked up another. He read the entire collection six times before he was satisfied.

After sixteen years fruitless searching, he had finally found the blueprints for a Master-Word machine.

His wiped the rheum from his eyes, and took a draught of stewed Madder root tea. Three days had passed since he had last slept, and he hardly noticed the stimulant's bitter taste and pungent overtones. Twelve hours had passed since the unexpected harvest from Search Engines had dried up, but only now did he dare consider leaving the Vault. He had no idea why the machines had suddenly found the secrets he search for so long and, even when he had finished transcribing the wonderful secrets they had found was reluctant to leave in case they other revelations for him.

In the end the well dried up – but he was satisfied – now he needed to decide what to do next.

Bergthora and the Master were alone in his Audience chamber; even the Prefect honor guard was absent, called away to deal with some trouble nearby. The Master sat on his dais, and listened dispassionately to Theodora's news.

"There is no possibility this is wrong?" he said.

"The facts have been checked, and checked time and again," she said, her voice echoing around the undamped spaces of the Audience chamber. "The native Jackotrade colonies are migrating. At this rate, in ten years, the pyramid will be devoid of them, in two hundred they will have abandoned the Redoubt."

"This is . . . unusual news you bring me."

Exasperated by the Master's strange mood, Bergthora felt a sudden urge to race up the dais steps and slap his face, but before she could the chamber's doors slung open to admit the Gallowglass. His booted footsteps cracked and reverberated around the chamber as he marched towards the dais. A tang of ozone clung to him and a livid bruise covered half of his face. He bowed perfunctorily to the Master, and ignored Bergthora.

"My Lord! Things are coming out of the Shine, the Jackotrades are deserting us, and the people are in ferment. What are we to do?"

The Master stared into the Gallowglass' eyes then, after a long moment, he embraced the soldier, and then pushed him away gently. He nodded gravely. "You are right, Gallowglass. These are unprecedented times. We are assailed on all sides and from within. But there is hope. It is time to make decisions that have been put off for too long."

"Decisions?"

"Yes, in particular there is a final reform I want to put in place – the creation of a new Guild."

Bergthora looked at him with sudden understanding in her eyes. He shook his head, and she kept her peace.

"This new Guild will be given a great task," the Master said. "Trust me, old friend, there is hope that, whatever happens, something true will survive."

"You are talking about the Final Battle," the Gallowglass said.

Bergthora stood beside the Gallowglass. "Tell him everything," she said. "He deserves to know what he may be asked to die for."

The Gallowglass hardly noticed the ice-laden wind whipping his face. Far to the South the blue glow from the Shine was laced with red and silver. Waves of distress pulsed from it and battered the Redoubt. All of the Watchers were cowering below the battlements, but he was pleased to see than none of them had left their stations. They would recover their courage soon enough, until then he and his Prefects would keep the watch. His men were stone-faced and unflinching, but he could sense their inner torment.

Even the truest can be daunted – and can die.

The Master had spent an hour telling him about his enKernelling, and explaining why the children had been brought together. Oddly, the Gallowglass found the end of the Redoubt easier to accept than the idea that a child held the secret to the survival of humankind.

"I am a soldier, show me something I can fight."

One of the Watchers heard his whispered comment and looked up puzzled.

The Gallowglass squeezed the Watcher's shoulder. "Don't worry, my friend. I was just gathering gossamer threads to make a coat of wishes."

The Watcher looked unconvinced, but smiled bravely and, after a deep breath stood up and took his place at a loophole. Soon after, the rest of his Watch joined him in facing down the hurricane of hate howling across the Night Land.

"He goes too far this time!" Cambyses shouted as he burst into the room.

Lanyard looked up from the game of Congkak he was playing with Argus. Cambyses was out of breath and waving a sheaf of Hour-Slips.

"Good day, Master Cambyses." Lanyard said as he scooped up a handful of beads then spilled them smoothly one-by-one into Argus' Southern houses. His opponent pulled a face and rested his chin on his wrinkled hands. Recognizing this as a sign of a lengthy analysis Lanyard turned to face Cambyses. "And what has our esteemed Master Monstruwacan done to annoy you on this day, Master Cambyses?"

Cambyses pushed the Hour-Slip under Lanyard's nose. "Read this! You won't believe what he has done this time. He's only proposing setting up a new Guild House, and filling it with a bunch of children – some of them of peasant and artisan rank."

For all his comical bluster, Cambyses had gained Lanyard's attention. Even Argus looked up for a few seconds before turning his attention back to the game. Lanyard took the Hour-Slips and carefully read them.

"This is unusual," he said eventually.

"Unusual? Unprecedented would be a better word. The Monstruwacan Council should meet to discuss this."

"Well, wouldn't that be a novelty. What is it – seven years – since we last met? Perhaps you would like to petition the Master on this matter, Master Cambyses?"

Cambyses shuffled his feet.

"Precisely," Lanyard said.

"Something must be done," Cambyses hissed, looking around nervously as if expecting the Master to leap out from behind the arras. "He refuses to let us meet or advise him, spends all of his time either with that woman of his or the Gallowglass – and the rest of his days searching in the Vault of Ages – and now this! The people will be unhappy, I can guarantee that."

"Yes," Lanyard said in a chilly voice. "I'm sure you can."

Cambyses' expression flickered angrily for an instant, and then he snatched the Hour-Slip back and stormed out of the room. Lanyard leaned back in his chair and pondered the implications of the news. Cambyses might be a slinker, but he had the ears of the leaders of several Guilds, and was bound to make a bad situation worse. A soft tapping disturbed his concentration, and he looked up in time to see Argus' shaking fingers flick a dozen shells into the diagonal houses, and four into Lanyard's own. The old man grinned happily.

"Game's over," he said.

The Shine was tormented like a volcano chained at the

instant before eruption. Entities trapped for aeons clawed at their bonds and rent the Night with their frustration. But the ancient bounds held fast, and the captives finally admitted defeat and slumped into bitter silence. Outside the Shine, the death zone stretched for tens of miles. Hundreds of beasts lay dead or dying, their souls torn and scattered into the endless Night. The husks of snaggletoothed harpy worms lay everywhere; supremely hardy lichens had been reduced to carbon; rock-burrowing bacteria and slimy, thick-walled protozoa had been consumed from the inside out.

Inside the Redoubt day began after a night tortured by terrible nightmares – even for the majority of who had found no sleep. Bleary-eyed people comforted each other as best they could, although nothing could be said that would take away the terrible memories. When the Redoubt slowly got about its business they began to find the victims. A hundred people had died or taken their own lives during the psychic onslaught. Later, when the initial shock was over, the talk turned to revenge and responsibility – what were their leaders doing to allow such a thing to befall them? With drink inside them, a few bold, if ill-equipped souls demanded to know why the Prefects and the Master Monstruwacan weren't spending more effort devising strategies to fight the Night terrors.

"Surely the Redoubt can defend itself?" they asked resentfully.

Which was somewhat ironic because, lying among and within the dead of the Night Land were countless blasted microscopic metallic husks – unacknowledged fighters from the Lesser Redoubt.

The Guild-House smelled of new paint and wood polish, but the walls were made of strong steel and Prefects guarded the entrances. Naani couldn't decide whether the Prefects were there to keep people out, or keep the children in. She had been one of the first to arrive; an hour later there were nearly sixty of them – all around her age. She knew a few of them, but was surprised at how many of her contemporaries she had never met. A tall blond girl, who spoke with a strong farmer's accent, asked her if she knew what was going on. Naani shook her head, feeling obscurely grateful that the girl did not recognize her.

"Took me away from my work," the girl said. "It's brambling time to – they be plenty of cuts and scrapes to treat, and me stuck here."

"You're a healer?"

"Just a third-ranker so far, and I don't see how coming to this place is going to improve my skills. Oh, by the way, I'm called Arian, and you are –"

A small freckled-faced boy joined them. "Naani, what's going on here? I was practically dragged out of my Guild House – you should have seen the look on my master's face when the Prefects arrived."

"You're the Master's daughter?" Arian asked.

"Someone has to be," Naani said too quickly. Arian's face flushed like she had been slapped, and she turned around and walked away.

"Wait, I'm sorry," Naani called after Arian, but she had disappeared into the crowd.

"She's tetchy," Aldous said. "Anyway, do you know what's going on here?"

Before Naani could answer, a Prefect sounded a short blast on a bugle. "Give your attention to the Master Monstruwacan," he shouted.

The undercurrent of chatter in the room stilled, and everyone looked towards the small stage at the back of the room. The Master walked in accompanied by a red-haired woman, who Naani didn't recognize, and the Gallowglass. Naani sent a brief mental greeting to her father but, if he heard it, it was ignored. Several weeks had passed since she had last met, when she looked carefully at him, it seemed that he had aged ten years since them. His face was drawn and his eyes tired, but when he spoke, his voice had all of its old resonance.

"Greetings – and welcome to your Guild House." A brief hubbub of surprise rose among the children, then their discipline asserted itself and they fell quickly silent as the Master continued. "You have been chosen to found a new

Guild, a Guild to span all the Guilds. Many of you have spent the last two years as apprentices and most of the others have been following special teaching programs designed to make them ready for this new challenge. For too long the people of the Lesser Redoubt have dully followed paths lain down aeons, in some cases millions of years, ago. The old ways will not serve us any longer. There are great problems facing us, problems that have not yet been revealed to the general population. It will be your duty to face these problems head on, and create solutions that would have been unthinkable before."

He paused as if trying to gauge his audience's reaction. They just looked back at him in stunned silence. For an instant his eyes met Naani's and she saw into his heart. Several moments passed before she realized that he had started to speak again.

"I have a special task that will let you to show your mettle," he said. "A task that has been impossible until now. Impossible for two reasons, firstly I only recently discovered the way of doing this thing, secondly the wide range of skills needed do not exist in any single Guild, and the existing Houses are too fractious and divided to come together for this task."

He paused again then, at the perfect moment, continued. "I want you to build a new Master-Word machine."

The room erupted in cheering and amazement. The Master held his hands up for quiet. When that didn't work, the Prefect's bugle was blown long and loud.

"There will be time for questions later," he said. "For now, you should settle into your new home." He gestured to the woman at his side. "Lady Baumgard will describe your domestic arrangements, dormitories and rules and such like. I will speak to you again later."

The Master left without a glance at his daughter. She knew why; she had seen into his soul and knew that, in some fundamental way, he was lying.

PART FIVE

"We are ready to begin, My Lord," Aldous said.

The Master nodded and Aldous called his team of operators together. The redheaded, freckle-faced boy was small for his age, but the Master could easily see him heading a revived Electromechanics Guild. He settled back in his chair, and watched as the instrument was assembled around Naani. He had decided in the earliest days of the work that the children would use the Master Word machine. It was their great achievement, and they deserved the chance.

In any case, he doubted he had the skills and strength needed.

The children decided among themselves who would be first. There was no discussion, and no campaigning. A secret ballot was held and, apart from her own vote for Aldous, Naani was the unanimous choice.

The Master watched while final adjustments were made. The urge to intervene was almost irresistible, and he found himself missing Bergthora's quiet calm. Unfortunately, she was somewhere in the Redoubt, searching for the fifty-ninth child – her ever-elusive son.

"With your permission, My Lord," Aldous said. "Naani is ready."

Naani smiled at her father. She was standing on a glass plate and was surrounded by a horseshoe of stacked white cylinders, each a foot in length and three inches around. The cylinders seemed to be hovering in mid-air, but that was an illusion. They were encased a framework of glass so transparent it was hard to distinguish from empty air. The reason why such an exotic, fiendishly difficult to fabricate, material was needed was mystery. The children joked that it was just for decoration. The Master secretly rather liked that idea; if after millions of years of silence, they discovered they were not alone of the Earth, the instrument would have earned its rich garment.

"Hello," Naani said quietly.

The solemn throb of the Master-Word beat out into the Night. Many of the children fell to their knees, gasping; for the Master it was like being truly alive for first time.

"A voice!" Naani shouted. "I am answered!"

"Call again!" Her friends cried through their tears.

Mirdath – Mirdath – Mirdath

Naani shook her head in disbelief. The instrument fell silent, and the endless river that carried the Master-Word faded away. The children clustered around Naani, bombarding her with questions. They parted as the Master stepped forward and touched his daughter's hand.

"Are you well, my child?" he asked.

Naani smiled broadly "I have never felt better in my life."

The children's questions persisted: "Who is Mirdath? It felt like you knew this woman – it is a woman, isn't it?"

"Yes," Naani said quietly. "I think she is a woman. But I don't know who she is, I think I must have remembered her name from an old book I read once. I'm not sure but I think it was a love story."

She looked wistfully at her father, and he caught her mood.

"It is best if Naani rests now," he said. "She can try again later. What you have achieved here is remarkable, and epoch-making, but it is best to take things slowly."

The children agreed reluctantly, and began disassembling the apparatus. The Master reached out and touched their thoughts; the warm thrill of the Master-Word still beat in their minds. Almost as much as Naani's success, that simple resonance heartened and dismayed him. The children were different – the Master-Word of the Great Redoubt had quickly faded from his thoughts and, after only five minutes, he could hardly recall its shape or sense.

The tavern's doors were closed and locked, but a group of drinkers still clustered around a table in a dimly lit back room. Their flagons of moss beer were full, and the air was thick with the smoke from their bacca pipes. A man whose muscular farmer's build was in marked contrast to his withered right arm, leaned forward and started hard at Caliban.

"Do that thing again," he said in a voice slurred by too much drink.

The boy stared back at him and smiled thinly. Farmer folk were notoriously clannish and distrustful of outsiders but, despite being outnumbered six to one, he didn't seem to be intimidated.

"Why don't you try it?" Caliban said calmly.

The farmer swept his good arm across the table, sending several flagons crashing to the floor.

"Don't mock me, boy. I want proof before I'll sign up for this."

Caliban smiled again, and nodded almost imperceptibly. He held his hand palm-up and fingers spread for a few seconds, then inverted it and pressed down on the table. The watchers crowded close. Caliban noticed that his loud-mouthed friend wasn't looking his hand but his face. He wasn't worried, after a lot of practice he found he could bear the agony without it showing in his expression. The pain was dreadful beyond words, like burning rivulets of acid coursing through his flesh, but he had no intention of letting these peasants see his suffering. He was in control here.

He smiled and looked down. His fingers were buried three inches into the oak table.

"Who are you?" the farmer asked.

"You can call me Harlequin," Caliban said.

"Mother! Will you stand still long enough to listen to me?" Theodora demanded.

Bergthora looked up briefly then continued loading Hour-Slips and bound books into the arms of the young apprentice.

The girl was having trouble balancing her load, which almost reached to her chin. Theodora found room for a last Hour-Slip under her arm then shooed her away. The poor girl tottered out of the hallway but a few moments after she passed from sight there was a subdued crash from outside.

"Jessamy, are you alright?" Theodora shouted.

"Yes, My Lady," came the muffled reply.

Bergthora sat down on a white-painted wooden stool. "Well?"

"Well? What you mean *well?* I'm your daughter!"

Bergthora smoothed away a crease on her dress. "Yes you are. And I will thank you to show the dignity and politeness you were taught."

Speechless with exasperation, Theodora paced in front of her mother, who waited patiently. The sounds of running feet and excited young voices filtered in from outside.

"You must use your influence, mother," Theodora said eventually. "Things are going from bad to worse –"

"The Master is well-aware –"

Theodora knelt down pressed her hands into her mother's. "My Guild is dying," she said. "The Jackotrades have almost deserted us."

"Many old certainties are being challenged."

"You should see Master Hugh. It's terrible what this is doing to him. When it first happened he took to drink. But –"

"There was trouble?"

Theodora shook her head. "I won't say. It was a mistake and everyone involved forgives him. But since then he has been like a walking dead man. I almost wish he would take a drink again, but he swore an oath never to again."

Bergthora touched the tears flowing down her daughter's cheeks, and spoke softly. "I am so sorry." She helped her daughter to her feet. "Be brave, my sweetest and only child –"

Her words jarred Theodora. "So I have no brother now?"

"You never did," Bergthora sighed. "It is best you never think of him again."

"I hardly ever do. It's like the time when I was sister to an innocent baby, who turned into a nasty little boy happened to someone else. What went wrong? I know it was about the time he was Assessed –"

Bergthora ignored her probings. "I don't know. Just fate I suppose. We were not to blame. No one was."

There was a soft knocking from outside and the apprentice girl came in again. She glanced in surprise at Theodora, then curtsied to Bergthora.

"Begging pardon, My Lady, But you are needed in the –"

"Yes. I will be along very soon. You are dismissed."

The girl scurried from the room like a Sand Viper was chasing her.

"She is one of your special children?" Theodora asked with raised eyebrows.

"Jessamy is perhaps not the brightest jewel, but she works hard. Maybe that is enough in these dark days."

"Master Hugh worked hard." Theodora said bitterly. "Is his fate in the hands of such as her?"

Her mother just looked at her. She did not try to speak mind-to-mind nor did she change her neutral expression.

"Tell me there is hope," Theodora said slowly.

Her mother's silence was more expressive than a thousand words.

"How many times has she tried since her first success," Bergthora asked quietly, still mulling over the difficult meeting with her daughter the day before.

The Master scowled. "Six times, and all of the other children have tried – and failed."

"Maybe conditions are wrong . . . somehow."

"Somehow? And if they were what could be do to change them? It has been millions of years since humans attempted a task so complex. The truth is that we are like worker bees. Blindly we built our hive, but we have no idea what it does, or how it works. The machine is beyond our comprehension. We were just lucky the first time – or deluded."

"We can try again tomorrow. Or maybe you should try –"

"I cannot. If this thing is to be done it must be done by

the children. That much is certain."

The Jackotrade colony slid through the interstices of the metal wall, and pooled together on the floor. Attracted by the soft hum of the Earth-Current, and the subtle, metallic tinkling of the Master-Word, it flowed toward the glass and metal mountain standing in the center of the room. The colony touched the glass cliff and exchanged ambassadors with the tribes inhabiting the instrument.

The metal floor was chilly under Naani's bare feet, and the only light came from the machine. The other children were all asleep. The Prefect guards were awake, of course, and had watched quietly as she left the dormitory. One of them had fallen in behind her, but remained outside the room. Unsure of why she was drawn here, she walked slowly around the partly disassembled Master-Word machine. Then she sat down inside the instrument. It hummed softly and was slightly warm to her touch. She closed her eyes, and let her mind fill with thoughts about Mirdath and her bright warrior. Theirs was an ancient story, a tale of love and loss, filled with strange conceptions such as the mystery of the evening, the glamour of night, and the joy of dawn. Feeling guilty, and oddly childish, she allowed herself to imagine that bright warrior of her dreams was the ancient hero, somehow brought back by her love.

The Master-Word enveloped her softly, and suddenly she felt lightheaded. This wasn't the strident, bell-like chiming of her first experience. It was more delicate, yet somehow deeper and more textured. There was no reply, but she sensed that someone was listening. Laughing quietly with joy, she let her thoughts of love and life tumble into the aether.

Behind the instrument, the Jackotrade colony made its chemical and electrical farewells, then slipped through the floor.

Engineers swarmed over the Earth-Current machine, desperately trying to trace the source of the problem. They clamped instruments to the torus and the conduits that snaked away from the twelve turbines. But the changes in the machine's music continued. Dissonant overtones calved from its normal pure note, and there was an almost subliminal grating noise coming from somewhere under the machine. In control rooms set into the walls, supervisors stared in disbelief and fear at the growing fluctuations in the current. They could find nothing wrong with their engine – the fault seemed to lie with the Earth. It was almost as if the orientation and spin of planet's magnetic core were fluctuating, setting up dangerous sympathetic vibrations in the generator. Needles flicked off-scale, and numerals blurred, and the dissonance turned into a shrieking whine that penetrated every cell of every person's body.

The Masters of the Guild conferred. Their discussion was brief – it was obvious that that had no alternative – unless something was done, the Earth-Current generator was going to shake itself to pieces.

The eight highest ranked among them stood at their appointed stations, inserted their sigils into ten small apertures and, when the word was given, turned the Earth Current machine off.

The Gallowglass stared at the bitter, tannic dregs in his wine cup. His stomach was sour, but not from the wine. He had spent a sleepless night pacing the Prefecture halls, endlessly mulling over the Master's bizarre revelations. Now, he sat alone in the Buttery, unable to decide what was worse: the grotesque idea that the Redoubt must be sacrificed to save humanity or the Master's growing fatalism. For decades he had defended the Lord of the Redoubt by word and deed. Now, for the first time he began to see the Master as the people saw him, indecisive and capricious; one moment too fearful to act, the next forcing the pace of change too hard.

It was a sobering vision, and he knew it was unfair. The Master didn't cause the Jackotrades to desert, or fill the Legions of the Night with bitter hatred for humanity. Nor could he be blamed for his fractious people – the Gallowglass blamed himself for that – he should have stamped on the first signs of trouble decades ago. But despite all the great questions facing the Redoubt, he suspected that the Master's biggest problem was his lack of self-belief. Many times over the years he had dropped sour hints about his election. Two decades since he put on the Ruby robes, he was still half a century younger than the next youngest Master in history was at his election. It was obvious that the Monstruwacan Council had elected him precisely because they expected to be able to easily manipulate such an inexperienced man.

They were wrong. For good or ill, whatever really happened during his enKernelling, it had put the Master beyond the reach of mere political machinations.

At that moment the Earth Current failed.

The Gallowglass took an instant to orient himself in the pitch darkness, then strode quickly out of the room, easily avoiding the chairs and tables between him and the door. Outside, a squad of Prefects ran towards him, their spinning Diskos lighting the corridor. He snapped orders at them – wake the Prefecture – assemble everyone on the Parade Ground – find lights.

Fire broke out in a draper's shop in the Shambles district when a hastily improvised oil lamp fell over. The burning oil splashed onto curtains and boles of cotton, and set them alight. In a few minutes the shop was ablaze and burning debris were drifting down the street. People reacted well, waking their neighbors and organizing bucket chains to get water to the seat of the fire. At first they appeared to be gaining ground on the fire then the water supply slowed to a trickle. Cursing their luck – and the Redoubt's government – they fell back to safe ground, and watched the fire destroy their homes.

The Redoubt's ventilation system was convoluted, and linked the entire edifice together in a contiguous system. The smoke billowing from the Shambles was sucked into massive ducts and quickly spread to unaffected areas. Thousands of people woke up choking in the dark, terrified for themselves and their families. Those who stumbled from their homes walked into a living nightmare. Desperate mobs formed, attacking anyone who was foolish enough to show a light.

The Moramor led a platoon of Prefects in a fast run around the circumference of the Great Arbor. Apart from the light from their Diskos, the only other illumination came from a few windows in the Guild Houses they passed. His orders were clear – defend the children – at all costs. Six Prefects already guarded them, but he doubted that would be enough. The squad ran in silence, a little moving island of light in the immense darkness. Suddenly, there was a trace of smoke on the air and, in the distance, another group of flickering lights was racing across the Arbor. The Moramor squinted, but it was too far away from him to see, he needed younger eyes.

"Sergeant, how many men in that crowd?"

"At least two hundred, My Lord."

"Faster!"

The Prefects reached the children's Guild House while the mob were still three hundred yards away. Calmly, the Moramor ordered his men into a skirmish line in front of the house, and waited for the mob to arrive. They were mostly men, although there were a few women in their ranks. They carried flaming, pitch-soaked torches, and hastily improvised clubs and quarterstaffs. Over their heads crude banners flew. Some were red with a white hand whose fingers had been cut off at the knuckles, others were a riot of colored patches like a jester's motley.

The Moramor stepped forward.

"Stop, place your weapons on the floor, and walk slowly

away from this place," he said in a voice that carried easily to every person in front of him.

The crowd halted for an instant, then a burly man with a withered arm walked forward. His good hand held a hefty wooden club. He stood a pace away from the Moramor. "There are only a dozen of you. We are hundreds strong. Let us through, we have business here."

In a blur of electricity the man's head spun away from his body. Before the corpse hit the floor, the Moramor was in his place in the picket line.

"Prefects Avaunt," he ordered.

A ripple of chained lightning swept along the thin line of Prefects as they brought their Diskos to battle-ready. The men at the front of mob quailed for an instant, then were pushed forward by the growing press behind.

Bergthora slipped into her old habits of secrecy and disguise, and had been able to blend into the crowds milling in every open space. The Earth-Current had been restored six hours ago, ending the half day long nightmare, but there was still widespread anarchy. Everywhere she went she heard angry demands for retribution – the higher-ups had failed them, and the people demanded scapegoats. Anyone who looked like a noble was in danger of being set upon but, in her farmer's smock and old boots, she was able to pass safely. Trying not to look like a woman with a purpose, she flitted from place to place, stopping regularly to listen to ranting orators, even adding her own cheers when it seemed sensible to. The speakers railed about scandalous failure of the Redoubt's government, especially the Master Monstruwacan. They wanted the old ways torn apart, but seemed to have little to offer in exchange. Some spoke of an enigmatic man who could walk through walls and had chained the energies of the Night to him. Improvised banners with truncated hands painted in bright red waved, and their owners cheered wildly.

Gradually she closed the distance to the children's house. The other Guild Houses were shut up tight, and most of them had Prefects watching warily from roofs or high windows.

Some where less lucky: the Ancestors' House had been burned to the ground, leaving only cinders and ash to mark the passing of one of the Redoubt's oldest Guilds.

A crowd of hundreds of people surrounded the children's house. Bergthora pushed through them, treading on feet and using her elbows without compunction. A couple of fights broke out in her wake, but she kept going. Strangely, the crowd thinned a little at the front, and the going was suddenly easy. The people were quieter too. It was easy to see why; one look at the carnage in front of the house was enough to silence anyone. Sliced up and burned bodies were piled like a rampart. Most of them were rioters, but she could see the remains of several Prefects among the grisly pile. At first glance the house seemed undamaged, then she noticed the smashed-in doors and broken windows. Setting caution aside, she opened her mind. For a time all she could sense was hatred and fear – mostly fear – so she battled to filter the gross emotions out and tune her mind to search for the children.

The house was empty. If any of the children were inside, they were surely dead. She nearly abandoned herself to grief, and then she noticed a dirty knotted handkerchief hanging from a broken window. Carrying a faint hope in her heart, she made her way slowly back through the crowd.

The tunnel was long, hot and foul smelling, and slimy water dripped from the roof. The Moramor's right arm ached and his tunic was stiff with crusted half-dried blood. When the mob had surged forward, someone has stuck him with a crude spear. An upward slash of his Diskos has disposed of his attacker, but had been left with the broken-off tip of the spear grating against his collarbone. They had been running through the old tunnels for at least two hours, and the children were in desperate need of rest, but he was still afraid of pursuit. His men would have hidden the secret way out, and defended it with their lives, but there was always the chance of discovery.

He had failed once today. He had no intention of failing again.

Someone pulled at his elbow, triggering off a volley of stabbing pains in his shoulder.

"Moramor, we must stop, we need water and rest."

"I'm sorry, Lady Naani, we must keep going on."

She stepped in front of him. "No. We must stop now. We can't go on without water. People are becoming dehydrated."

He saw the exhaustion in her eyes, and the cracks around her lips, and realized she was right. He took of his jerkin and handed it to a boy standing beside Naani. "Knot a sleeve and the wrist, then pour water through it. That will filter any badness out."

Naani watched the boy collecting water in the jerkin, after a few seconds clear droplets began to trickle from its tapered bottom. Cups appeared out of satchels and were used to collect the pure water.

"That is a clever thing," Naani said. "The fabled resourcefulness of the Prefects –"

"Do you mock me child? I left good men to die to save your lives."

Naani put a hand to the Moramor's face. "You are hurt."

"It is nothing. Gather the water, then we must move on."

"Arian, come here. The Moramor is injured."

A tall, fair-haired girl joined Naani. She brushed aside the Moramor's complaints and ordered him to sit down while she examined him. Surprisingly, he obeyed. Arian opened his jerkin and carefully examined the wound, using both eyes and mind. Then she tore a long strip of cloth from her own dress and used it to pack the wound. The Moramor flinched as she tightened his clothes.

"This is a serious injury," she said. "Something is buried inside his shoulder, and I cannot risk cutting it out here, it is close to an artery and the bleeding might prove fatal."

"How far do we have to go?" Naani asked.

"Another two hours, maybe," the Moramor replied. "Then we should reach the one of our hidden forts. There are supplies there, and security. We will have time to plan our next move."

"Good," Naani said. "When everyone had had water, we will move again."

Just before they set off again, Aldous came up to Naani and the Moramor. He held up an index finger. A sliver of quicksilver was curling around it. "Jackotrades," he said. "The walls are saturated with them."

It was late in the day when Bergthora reached the Vault of Ages. Most people had returned to their homes or, if they had no homes to go to, congregated in impromptu camps in the Great Arbor. With the Prefects out of sight and the Guild Houses buttoned up tight, there were no clear targets available. Violence still simmered close to the surface, but the mood seemed to have calmed down a little. She could also sense widespread shock and shame at what had happened when the lights went out.

She took a roundabout path to the Vault of Ages, avoiding the main entrance; guessing that would have been a likely target for rioters. She opened a secret door in the rarely visited Western side of the Vault. A terrified-looking Prefect apprentice immediately challenged her. His only weapon was a short sword, held in a trembling hand.

"Look at me," Bergthora said. "Do you recognize me?"

"I think so."

"I am Lady Bergthora Baumgard, have you heard of me?"

Recognition dawned on the boy's face. Bergthora sensed that he was desperate for anyone familiar. "Yes. I mean yes, My Lady."

"Good." Bergthora spoke quietly and slowly, careful not to frighten the boy. "You have done well, Prefect Apprentice. The Gallowglass will be proud of you."

"You know of the Gallowglass? What news have you of my brothers? I was ordered to guard here when the Earth-Current failed."

"Hush, hush," Bergthora said. "Things are difficult outside. It is hard to get accurate information."

"Then I must return to the Prefecture."

"No! Not yet," Bergthora said quickly. "Do you have food and water?"

"I have field rations for a week."

"Then stay here for a few days. Follow your orders. When you leave remove your uniform and avoid other people."

Realization dawned on the boy's face. "How bad are things?"

"Bad enough that you getting killed won't change anything. Promise me you'll stay here."

"I promise, My Lady."

"Good. I must go now, I have business in the Vault."

The young Prefect nodded. Bergthora could only hope that his old habits of discipline and obedience would keep him safe in his bolt-hole for as long as possible – she feared he would have little chance outside.

The Search Engine rocked from side-to-side, and a thin trickle of smoke escaped from a crack in its casing. Bergthora could hear the faint whining of its internal mechanisms, but it was clear that the machine was dying. Compared to the carnage happening all over the Redoubt, wasting pity on a machine seemed absurd. Nevertheless, her heart ached for it.

"I've smashed them all."

Bergthora spun around, her heart racing. The Master was leaning against a pillar. He was holding a long metal bar. It was bent and battered.

"They will not deceive anyone again," the Master said. He held up the bar, and looked at it strangely, as if seeing it for the first time. He shrugged and let it slip through his fingers. It landed with a dull metallic crack.

"My Lord –"

"I am nothing. Don't call me that."

Bergthora stepped forward and slapped him across the face.

He smiled, and touched the red patch on his cheek. "You have wanted to do that for a long time."

She slapped him on the other cheek. "Pull yourself together! The Redoubt needs you now more than ever – your people need you – the children need you!"

He flinched as if she had slapped him again. "The children's house was ransacked," he said bitterly. "They are all dead."

"Some survived – a secret sign was left on their house – there is hope."

"There is hope," he repeated, then fell to his knees. "I thought the last chance had gone. I though it was too late for my bargain . . . that it was too later for Naani." Tears filled his eyes. "There is hope? I didn't know. I think it's too late now. What time is it?"

Bergthora recoiled from him, realizing that something was terribly wrong.

"What have you done?"

"Do you really want to know?"

"Tell me everything."

He smiled thinly and told her about the forgotten experiment he found hidden in the rock above the Great Arbor: how it too him years to discover the machine's function, and how crushed he was when he realized that it was just another failure. But he never forgot about the hidden room, and when his people fell into anarchy he remembered, and conceived of a use for its mechanisms.

The experiment was a desperate throw of the dice by a people assailed by the forces of the Night, and searching for any hope. The idea was that the immense pressures that existed between the palladium atoms in the cube could be used to crush hydrogen and deuterium atoms together, liberating vast amounts of energy in the process. The experiment had been doomed to fail, even its creators eventually realizing that their early results were phantoms. More seriously, the small-scale prototypes they created had a tendency to explode – killing several people in the process. Had they gone ahead with the full-scale test, the newly-build Redoubt might have been seriously damaged.

Just in time less radical pioneers were able to harness the Earth Current, relegating more exotic approaches to history.

At the last he had to be very careful. It wouldn't have done for a spark of static electricity to start the destruction prematurely. He wore clothes and shoes made of thick cotton, and wrapped gauze around his fingers. He explained that he found the absence of choice comforting. It was like being a Search Engine with a set of instructions to follow – turn that dial, connect this pipe, bring the pressure of hydrogen up to that value. It took a surprisingly short time, then he flicked a switch that began the countdown to the destruction of everything he was sworn to preserve.

The palladium cube saturated with oxygen and hydrogen at the expected rate. After a few days the process would be irreversible.

"You see, I kept my part of the bargain," he said. "The rest is up to the forces of the Night. The damage will be considerable, but nothing we can't repair if we work together again like the Redoubt Builders did. Think of it as a new beginning."

Bergthora knelt down beside him. There didn't seem to be anything worth saying. Then she heard a distant rumbling.

For four days, bone-dry hydrogen and oxygen trickled through the palladium cube. In the normal way of things, the equilibrium saturation of metal with hydrogen would be relatively low, significantly reducing the explosive yeild. However, other forces had been at work. Every crack, crystalline flaw and atomic interstice was saturated with the gases. After four days pumping the critical point had passed. If a spontaneous reaction started inside the cube now it would make little difference to the outcome. The extra day passed, a circuit closed, and electricity began to flow through the cube. The potent cocktail of gases and metal had been teetering on the edge for days – the first few billion electrons were enough to push it over.

Oxygen and hydrogen fell together – and were blasted apart a picosecond later – the palladium cube exploded in a billion places at once – the shock waves met, crashed off each other and imploded – the second wave of explosions happened six nanoseconds after the first – releasing more than mere chemical fury.

Taking the path of least resistance the explosion barreled up the shaft and ripped the granite cap from its mountings. Ten tons of rock smashed into the roof fifty feet above and was blasted into dust and flinders. The flaming wavefront snatched the debris up and added their mass to its fury. Adjoining rooms were flattened; their wooden doors and brick walls swept aside like tissue. Two Prefects were the first to die: crushed as the empty corridors surrounding the ancient research center imploded. An instant later, the walls of the shaft were punched back a dozen feet, vaporized ceramics melding with pulverized sandstone. The concussion sent cracks racing outwards through the bedrock.

The research center was directly under the half-mile diameter collar of molded basalt at the base of the ten-mile long shaft that linked the metal pyramid and the underground regions. Seconds after the first explosion, dust heaved from the mouths of the twelve tunnels leading away from the core. Concussions swept up the shaft and careful balanced beams and arms twisted then teetered past the point of no return. Flung by enormous, uncontrolled energies, the machines tore the shaft and everything in it to pieces. One-by-one airlocks crumpled until there was nothing to hold back the ten-mile column of air above. In macabre symmetry, a katabatic avalanche of air killed at the foot of the shaft, while a sudden vacuum wrought similar havoc ten miles above.

The dying spasm of the Stress Master's machines ripped the lining from the bottom three miles of the shaft, and the debris sealed the breach.

Two hundred feet of bedrock separated the explosion from the roof of the Great Arbor. The explosion's energy propagated through the soft rock at ten times the speed of sound in air, recoiled from the surrounding granite intrusions, and crashed back to its origin. Concentric cracks propagated through the brutalized rock. Cracks bled into fissures, and fissures into fractures.

Monstruwacan Lindos was walking slowly under the Flying Wood. He was using a cane, still not having fully recovered from the incident in the Baker's shop. He tried to ignore the pair of Prefects who dogged his every step. It had taken two hours of closely reasoned arguments before they agreed to escort him to back to his Guild House. Or, maybe he conceded he simply wore them down. So far, the trip had been uneventful.

Then the world shuddered.

Millions of red oak leaves fluttered down as the fold in the Air Plug was overwhelmed. People began to panic as clods of soil and torn branches fell among them. Lindos was pushed over by someone he didn't see; another person trod on his hand. Groggily, he tried to stand but was knocked down by a knee in his face.

A deafening howl of tortured rock silenced the screams.

Lindos lay on his back, his head spinning and his vision blurred. He couldn't fully comprehend what he was seeing but the last rational part of his mind tried to calculate the energy that would be released when the Flying Wood impacted with the floor of the Great Arbor.

He didn't quite have enough time.

The Arborists, clustered in their control rooms halfway up the walls, had the best view. They watched cracks race across the roof and the twisting of the glass ropes that held the forest up. The ropes twisted and stretched then disintegrated into molten shards. The forest held together as it fell the half-mile to the Arbor floor – a tribute to the engineering skills of the Arborists – many of who chose to leap to their deaths as their creation fell past them. After a surreal, silent fall, the wood landed with a soft flop, then disintegrated. A wall of soil and whirling branches swept outwards, crushing hundreds people who had been far enough away to survive the initial impact.

Ears bleeding and heads ringing, the surviving Arborists looked dumbly at the devastation below. A billowing, suffocating, cloud of dust was climbing rapidly towards them. The winding stairways to their control rooms had all been ripped from their anchors – and there was no other way out.

Then the roof fell in.

The Earth Current generator was seated on granite footings cut a half-mile into the crust. Its builders had calculated that only an external event capable of annihilating the metal pyramid would disturb its foundations. They were right, but they had not anticipated a self-inflicted disaster, tearing the Redoubt apart from inside. When ten million tons of rock crashed down three miles above, the generator room rang like cracked bell. Stairways and gantries rippled and tore apart; walls exploded into dust and, fatally, the generator's footings shifted. Turbine coils glowed as they battled with the electromagnetic forces pulling them in every direction. A few turbines slagged into grey lumps, but most exploded, blasting rainstorms of white-hot metal in all directions.

Most of the thousand turbine workers were crushed or incinerated in the first seconds. The few who survived lived long enough to witness a possibility only hinted at in the most secret, most pessimistic annals of their Guild. Inside the Earth Current generator, the perfect, whirling circle of metallic hydrogen tilted by a tenth of a degree. Roaring with energy, the circle slipped passed its failing magnetic shackles and touched the metal walls. The detonation ripped out in a flat plane, annihilating everything it touched, splashing against the walls and burning its way deep into the rock.

As an encore, the air in the chamber exploded.

A last pulse of energy exploded thousands of lights, and then darkness fell forever in the Lesser Redoubt.

In the Vault of Ages, the Master Monstruwacan lay on the

floor beside Bergthora's body. The shattered ceiling tile that had killed her had missed him by a few inches, but he didn't seem to have noticed. He kept saying a single word, over-and-over again.

"Impossible."

PART SIX

"Has he spoken yet?" the Gallowglass asked.

The Perfect shook his head as he unlocked the cell door. "Not a word, My Lord. He eats when we feed him and uses the midden hole when he needs to. The rest of the time he stares at the same spot on the wall. Even when he sleeps, his eyes are turned to the northwest."

"Very well, you are dismissed. You should go to the Buttery, I hear they've found a barrel of almost unspoiled biscuits."

"But, My Lord –"

"I will remain here until you return. Go, get some food inside you while you can."

The Gallowglass closed the cell door and sat down beside the Master. He hardly recognized him. Skin hung from the man's bones like a translucent shroud, and his eyes were lifeless and lorn. He reached inside his jerkin and pulled out a leather pouch. He took a sticky lozenge out and pressed it into the Master's hand.

"Here, My Lord, a peppermint comfit, I recall you liked them."

The Master looked blankly at the lozenge, and then swallowed it without chewing. The Gallowglass was content to sit with his old friend for a while. The four weeks since the disaster had passed like a single exhausting day, each hour indistinguishable from the last.

In the early days, attempts had been made to search for survivors in the in the underground parts of the Redoubt – with some success – a couple of thousand people were rounded up. They were put to work helping search for food and other survivors. The Master was found wandering in the rubble surrounding the Great Arbor, but he didn't seem to know who he was.

Everyone near the old research center, the Arbor and the Earth Current generator died in the first few minutes. Circles of destruction spread from these loci, burning or crushing all in their path. Sixteen Guild Houses were destroyed, including those of the Bee Masters, Mathematicians, Hour Criers, and Silk Masters. The already fire-damaged Shambles had been swept away. Annihilation roared up the shaft to the pyramid, and spread to the fringes of the Underground Country and beyond. It was impossible to know how many had died. Countless tunnels, bridges and caverns had collapsed, slicing the lost home of Mankind into isolated, doomed islands. The metal pyramid was least damaged and, despite the catastrophic decompression caused when the air locks failed, took the fewest casualties. Chill air rushed through cracks in its ancient metal walls, bringing life to the surviving Prefects. Half the order – five hundred men – was lost; either killed outright or missing in the underground regions. The Moramor and the Master's chosen children were among the lost.

Eventually, the people of the Redoubt found a new spirit amid the ruins. Leaders came to the fore, among them a middle-aged woman called Essa, who set aside her grief over her husband and daughter to lead and inspire her people.

This was as well – the Prefecture had other problems.

It took several days for the creatures of the Night to realize that the pyramid was vulnerable. Even when the three great lights flickered out they hesitated. Eventually, the bravest, or most stupid, chanced the limits of the old defenses. Claws scratched tentatively at glassy rock, long hairy noses sniffed cautiously. For the first time in eight million years, electric death wasn't waiting for them. Howling gleefully, they charged towards the pyramid. For two days they attacked the metal walls. Well-built and, until recently, well maintained by the Jackotrades, the task was beyond them. High above, grim-faced Prefects waited and sharpened their weapons. It was almost a relief when the first squirming thing began to crawl towards the open gantries at the apex. For a time the battle was easy; the Prefects waited until the monsters were close enough, then swept them to their deaths with raining metal fragments or burning oil. But the guard was only a handful against inexhaustible legions. The geometry of the pyramid helped, the attackers had to bunch closer as they neared the apex, but at times it seemed like the whole structure was covered in writhing horrors. Twenty Prefects fought shoulder to shoulder for thirty minutes, until the next shift replaced them on the killing floor. Human chains filled the long stairways, ferrying rubble and twisted metal – anything that could be hurled down on the attackers – to the thin line of fighters.

The Gallowglass was in the Master Monstruwacan's Audience Chamber watching the bodies of the fallen being wrapped in their bitumen-soaked cloaks. They were laid on a mound of kindling made from broken furniture. When the worst happened, the penultimate act of the living would be to save their dead from the beasts.

A young Prefect approached him. Barely past his teens, the lad looked beyond the point of exhaustion. His armor was cracked and his Diskos scored with blue streaking. A gaggle of disheveled Monstruwacans trailed behind him.

"My Lord, the Monstruwacans wish audience with you," the Prefect said.

"What do you want, Master Lanyard?" the Gallowglass asked.

Lanyard was quite young for a Monstruwacan, barely out of his seventies, and normally looked almost bright-eyed compared to his fellows. The Gallowglass doubted that he had ever seen a more defeated bunch.

Lanyard gestured at his colleagues. "We have news. For a week, the surviving Lords of the Empathy have listened for traces of the Night Speech, and called out to the survivors trapped below."

"Did you find anyone?"

"Precious few who we did not already know about."

"If nothing has changed why bother me?"

"Because something has changed," a particularly wizened Monstruwacan said. His voice was like sandpaper on softwood. "Two things are new. A clarion voice is calling out the Master-Word, someone is coming, a great hero –"

"With an army?" the young Prefect asked too quickly. He looked at his feet, blushing.

"Ah no, he is on his own," old Monstruwacan said. "He is a lone hero, sallying out from the Great Redoubt his mind on noble deeds. He seems to be preoccupied with searching for his long-lost love. He is obviously quite mad. Wandering in the Night Land will do that to a body."

The aged Monstruwacan's words trailed off into muttering.

"You mentioned two new things," the Gallowglass said.

"I did? Of course I did." His voice fell to a barely audible whisper. "Bitter things are spawning in the Shine, when they are birthed they will make the creatures that assail us now seem like fluttering moths. Their desires are plain, they want the Master Monstruwacan."

"I will not permit that," The Gallowglass said.

The oily river wound slowly through a complex waterscape of ox-bow lakes and little islands. The Moramor and the children had been traveling for a week, hoping to find some way back to the Lesser Redoubt.

Four weeks ago, they were settling down inside the hidden castle when an unknown, but obviously tremendous disaster rocked the Redoubt. They were safe inside the castle's twenty-foot thick walls, but when they opened the door a week later they were met with desolation. The tunnel they had escaped through was crushed. Another tunnel ran away from the castle, but the Moramor was reluctant to risk it, fearing it led into the Night Land. After twenty days with no sign of rescue, he handed the decision over to the children; and they voted to try the dangerous road. After several false starts, and much backtracking, they found the river. The Moramor was immediately suspicious of such an easy path but, in truth, it was the only way open to them.

"Where do you think we are?" Arian asked. They were sat together at the front of the boat, dipping their paddles in the water only when the boat drifted away from the middle of the stream.

"It is difficult to say. The river seems to be following a slow northwestern curve, but with so many twists and turns and false leads I have no idea how far we have traveled. I suspect that we have passed beyond Redoubt Hill and are somewhere near the great cliffs bordering the old sea, but that is only a guess."

Arian smiled at him, her eyes twinkling in the soft phosphorescent light falling from the algae-encrusted walls. "You guesses are worth ten other men's certainties."

There was a quickly stifled giggle from behind, and shushing whispers. It was no secret that Arian had offered to share her sleeping bag with him – and that he had refused.

Suddenly, there was a shout from ahead. "An opening – an opening ahead."

The Moramor checked that his Diskos was at hand. "Paddle steady," he ordered. "I must see where we are."

Torches were lit, but when they crossed the threshold into the Night Land, their feeble light was swallowed by the immense darkness. They paddled in silence, drawing their boats close together. The river wound along a deep-cut valley with steep, unclimbable walls. As their eyes adjusted they realized that the darkness was not complete. The sky was dull red, its dark light reflecting in the world around them. For a long time there was nothing to see, then the landscape began to slowly change. The valley became broader and shallower, and they found that they could look a little way into the Night Land.

A pillar of fire rose to the West, and beyond it lay the cold burning blue of the Shine. The Northern horizon was lit by a dull red glow, and to the South there was a range of black hills. But most of them were looking to the East – towards the Lesser Redoubt. Many miles away, it was only visible as a faint distant glow. The Moramor took a telescope out of his pack and scrutinized the distant light for a couple of minutes, and then handed the instrument to Arian. It took her a moment to focus the telescope, and then the pyramid sprang into view. It was lit with strands of small lights and glowed red at the apex. Gradually, she realized that the strands of light were moving slowly, randomly, and the hill below was covered in a black writing mass.

"They are under siege from the forces of darkness," the Moramor whispered. "The end cannot be far away."

Then someone in another boat started screaming.

"Here they come again lads – steady – let them get on the parapet – steady – wait for the command – now!"

At the Gallowglass' command, a dozen ten-foot long steel pikes drove outwards skewering the wave of attackers. He put his back to one of the pikes, helping it to pivot in its socket hole, lifting the writhing, screaming thing impaled on it above the defender's heads. He didn't look to closely at the creature as the pike fell back sending the dying beast crashing among its fellows. The glimpse he had of it was enough; it had a ring of hands around its neck, and each hand had an eye in its palm.

"Reset the pikes," he shouted as he rushed forward slashing as the head of a beast man poked above the parapet. The creature ducked under his roundhouse swing then leapt towards him. He smashed an armored elbow into its face, then took its head off with a backhand swipe of his sword. Strong hands pulled him back as the pikes crashed forward again. The world turned into a vortex of claws and teeth and tentacles and parts that defined naming. The Gallowglass slashed blindly with his sword and screamed the order to retreat. Somehow he made it inside, then ran to join the line of men forming against the back wall. He was handed a Diskos. He hefted it, running his hands over the incomprehensibly ancient symbols cut into its shining disk.

"Form a skirmish line," he shouted, "spread out and give your mates plenty of killing room."

Tensely the line of men waited. Outside on the parapet, brave men were fighting and dying. They tightened their grip on their weapons and waited their turn.

The riverbank was covered with tens of thousands of crabs. Their carapaces shone blood red. The largest were as wide as man's outstretched arms and the smallest no bigger than a fingernail. The tiny ones swarmed incessantly over their larger brethren. Claws were raised, and clacked continuously – but silently.

But the worst thing was their eyes – little white balls on red stalks that followed every move in the boats. As the party drifted slowly past the growing congregation, thousands of stalked eyes watched. The Moramor turned his head, and it seemed to him that every crab was watching him and him alone. He knew this was an illusion. The knowledge did not help ease his dread. Dully, he remembered his duty.

"Close your eyes," he whispered to Arian.

"I can't."

He tried to close his own eyes, but the crabs wouldn't let him.

"Look behind us!"

A hundred yards behind them a man was running through the crabs. At least it, seemed to be a man, it was hard to tell with hundreds of tiny crabs writhing over his body. He screamed in silent agony and waved his arms beseechingly.

"Headcount!" the Moramor shouted. "Is anyone missing?"

"All here – all here – all here –"

The man stopped, spread his arms wide, and disintegrated in a welter of scarlet gouts. In the gloom it was impossible to tell whether he had been a false man made from crabs, or a real man ripped into tiny gobbets by them.

"Steady there," the Moramor said in a whisper that carried along the line of boats. "They're only beasts, and we'll soon be past them."

With his men nearing their utter limits, the beasts regrouped. In the temporary lull, the last Gallowglass called his Sergeants together and told them his last secret and let them decide how to act. They agreed that the end was near, and their support for his decision was unanimous. The Gallowglass took six men to the hidden room under the Master Monstruwacan's Audience chamber. Monstruwacans Lanyard and Argus were waiting for them, and together the nine unlocked the seals and turned the valves.

Mechanisms, stilled since the time of the Builders, came to life. Eight million years ago, the Builders conceived a defiant, optimistic gesture to commemorate the day when humanity finally retook the Earth. That day never came, and the secret design was forgotten by all but the long line of Master Monstruwacans and Gallowglasses.

Slowly at first, but with quickly increasing speed, mercury began to spill from reservoirs hidden throughout the pyramid. It flowed into narrow pipes twisted into tori around metal cores. Dynamos spun and capacitors filled with electricity, ready to feed power to cables buried in the outer skin of the pyramid. The mercury continued its journey; eventually falling into catchpots cut in the rock surrounding the central shaft. The mercury counterweight removed; huge carefully balanced levers toppled – and the pyramid began to flower.

A shudder passed vibrated the metal walls as the levers fell. High above, warring men and monsters were flung about like rag dolls. A few creatures held on for a few seconds but, when the walls began to open, most slipped and fell, setting off an avalanche of flesh.

An arrow-straight vertical crack appeared in the metal wall of the pyramid, and began steadily widening. The metal was vibrating, and the slab was moving inexorably sideways and outwards. Capacitors discharged, and the surface of the pyramid was bathed in pure white light.

Hundreds of the creatures of the Night lay dead or dying at the foot of Redoubt Hill, thousands more were transfixed, unable to comprehend what they were seeing. Some tried to run away from the bright-lit flower blooming on the hill, but the press of bodies behind them made escape impossible. In the panic hundreds more died under stamping hooves and slashing claws.

After an unending hour they left the crabs behind them, and paddled on for half a day without incident. Suddenly the river began to quicken. Within a few oar strokes they were battling to avoid being swept away by a raging cataract. Crashing waves threatened to capsize their boats, and water poured dangerously over the gunwales. Progress was impossible, so the Moramor ordered them to turn to the riverside. His boat reached the shore first and, after helping beach it he plunged hip-deep into the river to guide the other boats. His strong arms, and a fair measure of luck, allowed all three boats to reach safety.

The Moramor sat down, shucked his boots off and poured a quart of oily water out of each. "We should climb yonder hill before we go on," he said. "We must find as much as can about the lay of the land before we chose a path."

They climbed to the top a small cinder hill. The Lesser Redoubt was about ten miles to the North. At first they through it was on fire, but their telescopes revealed something wondrous – the Redoubt had blossomed – its three sides had opened like petals spilling clean light into the Night. The attacking horde had been pushed back and were holding their distance a mile from the base of Redoubt Hill. The refugees cheered when they saw that the beasts had retreated, but the Moramor kept his own council.

"My father is alive," Naani said quietly. "But he is in pain. He blames himself for the disaster. I wish I could go to him but I can't." She turned to the South and pointed. "Someone is coming. I have to go and meet him."

"Who is coming, Lady Naani?" the Moramor asked.

"Don't call me that," Naani said, and turned her face away from him.

"We should stay together," Arian said. "We are safer if we stay together. The Moramor can only be in one place at once, and we need his strong arm is we are to survive in this place."

The Moramor embraced her. "Ah, sweet healer," he said softly. "Our paths must part soon."

She pushed him back. "You intend to return to the Redoubt?"

"My brothers will be making their final stand soon, and I must join them."

Arian waved at the horde surrounding the Redoubt. "Are you mad? You can't get though the enemy's lines! They would cut you down in an instant."

"Maybe. But I still have some tricks to share with the beasts of the Night. The land to the northeast is thinly populated. I think I can get through."

"You would leave us? You would leave me?"

The Moramor hefted his Diskos. "I sorry," he said. "I love you – I love you all – but that isn't enough." Then he turned on his heels and raced down the hill at a dead run. Distraught at his betrayal, the children watched him for ten minutes until he disappeared in the gloomy, boulder-strewn land.

Arian angrily dismissed Naani's efforts to comfort her, walked a little way off and squatted down on her haunches with her head bowed. The others respected her grief, and let her be while they discussed what to do next. Talk quickly turned to Naani's vision. She opened her mind and told them all she knew about her dream warrior and Mirdath, the love that had lasted aeons, and the urgent sense of destiny she felt. Her friends were skeptical, but in the absence of a better plan, they agreed to follow her South.

They loaded one of the boats with supplies and dragged it like a sled down the scree slope to the seabed. They passed the huge waterfall that they nearly been swept over. The water fell in an iridescent stream that glistened with a thousand oily colors. But when it touched the bone-dry sand at the bottom, it disappeared, shedding not a single drop, or moistening a grain of sand. The place had an air of unrequited want, and they quickly set off South.

The seabed was featureless and soon swallowed them, leaving their long wake of dust as the only mark on the endless gloomy landscape. The going was easy and, after a time, Naani felt she was almost flying over the surface. She knew it would be harder when it was her turn to help with the hauling, but for the moment she was enjoying the exercise. An illusion began to grow in her mind – she was standing still, while the Earth rolled under her feet. She fancied this was how the people of the moving cities must have felt.

"Hello!" someone shouted.

Naani blinked and looked around. Her friends were gone, and the only feature she could see was the arrow-straight line of dust she had raised, and that disappeared in the murk a hundred yards away.

"Hello!"

"I'm over here!" she shouted.

Aldous and another boy – Rauli – ran along her dust trail. They held a short rope between them.

"Don't worry, we'll get you back to the rest," Rauli said.

"But how –" Naani began.

"People are wandering away," Aldous said. "We didn't notice at first, it's like we're all in a trance."

Walking quickly, it took five minutes to reach place where Naani had gone astray, then another ten minutes to reach the caravan. Along the path, other dust trails led away into the darkness. Two other rescue parties joined them. Three people had walked away – and only Naani had been found – the other trails ended for no clear reason and with no one in sight. They waited a little while, but it was obvious there was no hope. Ropes were dug out of storage, and everyone tied themselves to lines fanning out from the boats. The going became harder.

Caliban knew everything and was everywhere. He flowed like a shimmering wave through the soft sedimentary rocks, and touched every facet of the World Soul. He was as big as a mountain and as tiny as the smallest part of a living cell. He knew all the secrets of the Fixed Giants, and the understood the immemorial machinations of the Jackotrades. He itched in sympathy as sweat ran down the back of the man from the Great Redoubt while he battled yet another beast on his road to meet his love. The endless chattering of the Silent Ones amused him, and he would have laughed – had he lungs and a mouth – at the real reason why the Silent Watchers watched. The world's glorious pointlessness both moved him deeply and amused him. His life was like an endless moment – past, past present and future piled higgledy-piggledy together – life, birth and death indistinguishable.

He had no idea much time had passed since the mobs he briefly inspired with his old destructive passion turned on their would-be savior. He didn't care. At the climactic moment of his life, the Jackotrades had protected him.

He was special.

He recalled with glee the astonishment on the faces of his attackers when he fell into the stone floor. His body spread like smoke through the rock, but he could still sense their baffled anger. Seething resentment at their treachery rose in him, and he longed to unleash his new mastery of the elements on them. But the Jackotrades took charge and forced him to migrate away from the central parts of the Redoubt. Despite his helplessness, the sensation was wonderful, and was it was a long time before it dawned on him that that the extraordinary process was quite painless – unlike the coruscating agonies his previous merging with solid objects that provoked. As his vision widened to encompass the whole world, he could not bring himself to hate it for the unnecessary agonies that it had inflicted on him over the years.

It was only when the Jackotrades told him that they had one last task for him, after which he would be free, that he started to hate again.

The Great Door was a hundred feet tall and wide. Cut

from a twenty-foot thick slab of pink veined granite, it was opened once every ten thousand years. Floods of electric fire would scour the hill on which the pyramid stood, sweeping the beasts of the night away. Then in a strange gesture of defiance, a flock of a few hundred butterflies would be released. The reasons for this strange ritual were long forgotten, but obscurity was never enough reason to stop doing something in the Lesser Redoubt.

The door was open, and it would never be closed again.

Three hundred Prefects lined up in four perfect ranks just inside the Great Door. A group of six hundred or so ordinary men and women stood behind them. They had made the difficult climb up from the underground lands. The Gallowglass looked on them with immense admiration; they had no weapons but they were ready for the final battle. Many carried musical instruments – drums and flutes, harps and bells – the rest bore bright flowers or skillfully wrought handicrafts. Among the ordinary people stood a small number of former Monstruwacans, including Lanyard and Argus. They had cast aside their trappings of office, and wore the rough-cut garments of working people.

Behind them the remaining Monstruwacans fretted in their rich gowns, peered over the heads of the Prefects and citizens, and looked fearfully into the Night Land. Suddenly, a man wearing a dirty grey robe pushed through the ranks of the Monstruwacans. "Who is in charge here?" he asked.

The Gallowglass turned, then knelt before the Lord of the Redoubt.

"There is no need to kneel before me, Lord Gallowglass. I have no rank anymore. I am just a man, nothing more or less. Call me Denholm, like you did all those yours ago when you were the sternest of my tutors."

The Gallowglass smiled broadly. "It is a long time since anyone called was permitted to call you that, old friend. It is Law that the Master cannot have a name – do you bring revolution with you?"

"I fear revolution is upon us already," Denholm said quietly. He touched the Gallowglass' battered armor. "I see you have been in battle, old friend."

"The Redoubt has been hard pressed lately . . . Denholm. I don't understand what is stopping them now."

Denholm waved his hand, taking in the Prefects, the loyal Monstruwacans, and ordinary people of the Redoubt, "The Word being flung across the Land by the defiance of people of the Redoubt. The Word is terrible to them. It denies their place in our world – even those who were once human –"

"Blasphemer!"

"Keep that rabble quiet, Sergeant," the Gallowglass ordered. Six Prefects lined up in front of the cowering Monstruwacans, who fell into a resentful silence.

"The Word is in their flesh and minds. Starkly, it shows them how alien they are. How they have lost their own true place more surely than humanity has – at least we had a chance, if only a small one, of reclaiming our world – their home is gone forever. For tens of millions of years they have been denied even the small solace of glimpsing the greater universe from where they came. You see, our ancestor's great gamble paid off, albeit too late to keep the hordes of night out –"

"My Lord, I have no knowledge of that things you speak of," the Gallowglass said.

"I know. Don't worry, I speak for posterity. We may all die this day, but there are things out there than are all-knowing and all-remembering. Now, where was I? Ah yes, the gamble – we had a moon once you know? We destroyed it to try and keep the dark at bay. We failed to do that but we succeeded in sundering two of creations great rivers of consciousness from their homes. Mankind was driven from the surface into dead cities of metal, while the invaders were denied the universe that is their true domain. Little wonder we that we never found common ground."

"A joke?"

"The biggest joke in history, Lord Gallowglass."

"What now then?"

He smiled and kissed the Gallowglass on the cheek. "Now I must go. I have matters to attend in the Night. Be true, old friend."

Denholm walked slowly through the Great Door and into

the Night Land. The beasts made no attempt to attack him and, when he reached their front rank, it parted to let him through. Then they closed ranks and swallowed him up. The Gallowglass' eyes filled with tears, and he could hear weeping among the ordinary people. He hung his head in shame that he had allowed this thing to come to pass.

"It is not your fault, my friend," someone said in a familiar voice.

Disbelieving, the Gallowglass turned to greet the Moramor. His old friend stood beside him, smiling.

"You have seen battle today," the Gallowglass said.

The Moramor ran a finger over the gash that split his face from forehead to jaw, and then turned to look at the Prefects and the people behind them. His voice fell to a whisper. "And we will see it again soon – what a terrible waste."

Naani wanted to run away, and never stop running, but she couldn't leave Nyven and Aldous to die alone. They had been marching for several hours when the two boys walked into a patch of quicksand. Although frightening, the danger did not seem too great – after all, they were all roped together – rescue seemed easy. But this was no ordinary quicksand. The boys had been pulled down to their knees by the time their friends were organized. There still seemed to be plenty of time. The rescuers lent on their ropes. For a moment everything went well, and the boys began to ease out of the morass.

Then they started screaming. Their would-be rescuers dropped their ropes and stared in horror at the petrifaction climbing up the boy's legs. Before their eyes, their friends were being changed into pillars of sandstone. At first, the change was rapid, and quickly reached their chests. Then it slowed down, taking six hours to climb to their necks. Three hours had passed since they stopped screaming or breathing for all it mattered, but somehow they still clung to a semblance of life. In their extremity, the boys had grown strong in the Master-Word, and their agony beat in waves across the world. Naani opened her heart and mind to the hurricane of agony.

In the end she was so soul-whipped she didn't notice her friends die.

Someone helped her stand up and whispered comforting nonsense to her – something about not being able to continue South, about having to retrace their steps, then maybe turn to the West. Naani nodded automatically, she had no real idea what Arian was talking about, but leaving this terrible place seemed a good idea. As they turned their boat around, Naani took one last look back. Aldous and Nyven were gone; replaced by two amorphous humps of gritty yellow rock.

"Prefects Avaunt!"

Three hundred Diskos burst into whirling, fire-spitting life and the front rank gave voice to a thundering cheer.

"Life!"

The cheer mounted as the other ranks joined in.

"Life! Life! Life!"

Behind them the ordinary people of the land raised their own glorious cacophony, filling the air with music and petals.

The Gallowglass and Moramor took their place side-by-side in the Vanguard. They kissed then the Gallowglass raised his Diskos high in the air.

"Shall we walk to meet the enemy?" he asked his men.

"No!"

They were trotting as they passed through the Great Door. They accelerated down Redoubt Hill and, by the time they hit the plain below were running pell-mell. The ground was broken but that made no difference – they raced over it as if on winged feet. The legions of the Night backed away, trampling and gouging each other in their haste to escape the charge. But the army of Night was vast and, the great horde behind prevented escape. Diskos whirling, the Prefect's first rank hit full on like a thunderstorm touching earth, and tore a hundred and fifty yard wide gap into the enemy horde. The next two ranks hit the flanks with almost as much venom and the fourth tore into the breach.

For ten minutes the Prefects held the field, but then the tide began to turn. Their opponents were still terrified but in the crush a panicking beast was almost as dangerous one full of fight. The Prefects never slacked their furious assault but their ranks began to thin – at first slowly – then with sudden quickness. Giant rolling things with no heads and a forest of curved teeth smashed through them, and before they could regroup the horde fell on them.

Lanyard stood just inside the Great Door and watched waves of beasts sweep over the Prefects. Behind him the people of the Redoubt crowded close, their music stilled.

Denholm hesitated at the threshold of the Shine. The boundary was strewn with bloated corpses and the stink from them was hideous, but that was not why he wavered. Nor did the certainty of death hold him back.

He was afraid of being judged. By every normal criterion his life had been a failure; as Master Monstruwacan he held the greatest responsibility – to keep his people safe until he died and the burden passed to his successor. His attempt to shake his people out of their million-years-long lethargy had failed – or had succeeded disastrously, he couldn't decide which. The pain of his survival was like an iron band around his heart. He had failed as a father too – his belief that he could raise a child while carrying the office of Lord of the Redoubt revealed as unbelievable arrogance.

He had failed humanity in the round and the singular. Now he was afraid that the Fixed Giants would judge him a failure too. Steeling himself, he prepared to step into the Place of Gas. He would die, but maybe in his last moments answers would be revealed to him.

Before he could step forward he was engulfed in a blizzard of bees. They battered his body, forcing him to his knees, and then fell back to form a writhing wall. A solitary bee flew close to his face and he realized that it wasn't an insect at all, but a tiny nugget of metal held in the air by spinning, iridescent wings. He looked closely as the machine tore itself apart and the fragments burst into dust and mist. Like a visual fugue, the dissolution spread through the entire swarm leaving Denholm surrounded by a slowly twisting tornado of microscopic entities. He felt something beat on his mind, then slid away before it could be grasped.

"I can't hear you," he shouted. "I can't hear the Master-Word."

The maelstrom paused then flowed away from him. It fell like mist on the ground then rose to form a tapered column of smoke that coalesced into the form of a slim youth. Denholm had never met Bergthora Baumgard's son, but he recognized him. Caliban was changed however and, as Denholm turned his head, splinters of blue light from the Shine fell through the boy's body. When he spoke it was like Denholm's mind was suddenly encased in ice and shards of glass were being dashed against it.

Youhavelostthemasterword

"Please, your voice is strange – it grates."

The boy-thing considered his options for a moment and, when he spoke again it was not the Master-Word, or the Night Hearing. Denholm had no idea how the Jackotrade avatar was communicating with him. This was something new.

You must not enter the Death Lands. Your work is not done.

"I have to know."

There is nothing to know. You have never been in the Shine, either in mind or body. You have never had discourse with the Fixed Giants. You are too small for them to notice.

"But –"

The boy's skin turned into a quicksilver mirror that reflected Denholm's life from the perspective of the multi-billion-generation history of the Jackotrade tribes. They told his life story backwards, starting with the destruction of the Redoubt, an event made all the more cataclysmic by their hidden machinations; hundreds of billions of the machines giving up their tiny lives fuel the explosion with surface-bonded hydrogen and oxygen.

Shaking with barely contained anger, Denholm raged. "I

only wanted to shake them out of their complacency. I couldn't understand why the explosion was so large. Why did you make it so bad? Why kill so many? Why destroy the Redoubt?"

The boy-thing ignored him, then revealed Naani's successful attempt with the Master-Word machine, and how the legions of Jackotrades gave her the strength to contact her Bright Warrior from the Great Redoubt.

Denholm felt crushed, and overwhelmed with guilt. "I didn't know. I though she failed – is she alive?"

Your child is abroad in the Night Land. Soon you must leave this place and go to her. There is a force we cannot influence that will hunt her. You must save her.

"Where is she?" Denholm shouted.

Your life has been a lie.

The words were like a slap, and Denholm flinched because he knew what they were going to say next.

The Kernel was a lie.

They showed how they manipulated his mind, just like they had done with the thirty-seven thousand six hundred and fifteen Masters before him. Memory blocks fell and he remembered hammering on the Kernel's walls, desperate to escape as it filled with seething legions of Jackotrades. Tides of them washed through his skin and flowed into every space in his body; gifting him profound peace and clarity. He was like a blank white canvas, on which they painted their abstractions of reality. Their revelations rung with truth – in his heart he always doubted he had the strength to stand with the Fixed Giants – what human did?

They were merciless, showing how they had manipulated him, and his people, at every turn, and how they were the true agents of change in his little Kingdom. Humanity was, as he had long suspected, a tiny mote caught in the swirling morass of life forces that covered the Earth. It was an epic vision: ants and bees, humans and the beasts of the Night, moss growing on frost-blackened rocks, the things in the Shine, Jackotrades and all the other myriad tribes of this troubled world – each individual a mote of life sharing a minuscule portion of the World Soul.

Gripped by an urgent need to take stock, Denholm stood up and carefully brushed the dirt from his gown. In his heart, he suspected there were lies here.

"Who am I talking to?" Suddenly animated, Denholm paced up-and-down in front of the boy-thing, waving his arms extravagantly and speaking in volleys of words. "The son of Bergthora Baumgard, a trillion Jackotrades, or some unholy amalgam of child and machine?" Denholm drummed his fingers theatrically on his chin. "How to tell? What questions would reveal your true nature? I know, why don't you tell me something – anything – which would prove that the boy is the puppet of the machines, or that he wears them like a cloak, or that a chimera stands before me."

The Caliban-thing remained silent.

"You offer no proof, so I will assume, for the moment, that you are lying. Let us consider an alternative hypothesis, one that was old in this world long before the hands of men crafted your earliest ancestors. Its first tenet can be stated simply – we are fallen spirits chained by irrationality and doubt to an existence far beneath our true place in the universe."

Perhaps that is where you deserve to be.

"We can change. Three million years ago there was a man called Harlequin who taught that our spiritual destiny lies in our own hands, and is influenced only by our characters and deeds."

What happened to Harlequin?

"A question with a snare at its heart. Sadly, I am unable to avoid stepping into it. He was killed aeons ago, and I had the last of his followers executed twenty years ago."

All of them?

The Master smiled, but refused to answer. "Why is my daughter so important?"

Why do you think she is?

Denholm laughed again. "You don't know, do you?" He gestured at the Caliban-thing. "This metal and flesh concoction was your last hope, wasn't it? I don't care how many billions of generations of you there have been, in the end you had to find a way to speak directly to us. Your schemes and eternal wars are beyond human ken, but you can't understand us either, and wedding yourself to this pathetic excuse for a human didn't help, did it?"

No.

The word rang with truth, and Denholm sensed an undercurrent of boiling anger. He knew it wasn't from the Jackotrades – human emotions were foreign to them – this hatred was pouring from the boy. As the torrent of bile grew, Denholm felt sorrow. Caliban had a black heart all of his own, and he must have initiated the symbiosis with Jackotrades, but Denholm was appalled at the tortures he had suffered. But the child-monster was still dangerous, and would become a ranging beast when the Jackotrades left him. He shook his head as if clearing away mental cobwebs. Then he started to laugh – just a chuckle at first, but quickly turned into uproarious, gut-clutching laughter.

We do not understand.

It took Denholm several attempts before he could speak. When he did, he was still barely able to keep his bubbling hilarity in check.

"Of course you don't," he said between sobs of laughter. "Twelve million years ago, a hundred philosophers labored for a hundred years to define Godhead, and the best they could come up with was God was a standing wave in the unified consciousness of humanity."

We do not understand.

"No you don't. You know, we really should have had this conversation before."

We do –

"I want to tell you my credo: I chose to believe in the transcendental nature of all life. I chose to believe that humanity has greatness woven in its genes, as have all other living things – including the machine tribes infesting this tragic child before me. Above all, I chose to believe that our destiny is in our hands and, if I die today, it will be in the knowledge that I have lived my life by this set of beliefs. You – the Fixed Giants – the Silent Ones – the old lady who lives in a bucket on the shore of the Waveless Sea – it doesn't matter who I met in the Kernel. Do you seriously think I would have done the things I did if I hadn't believed in them?"

The Caliban-thing didn't reply. Denholm couldn't be sure but he thought that the fluctuations in its mirror-surface were slowing, or maybe becoming more regular in their nutations.

"I have known all my life that the Lesser Redoubt was doomed. Our population has collapsed to unviable levels over the last three million years. There are maybe fifty thousand of us left, out of the half million who launched the great endeavor eight million years ago – five hundred thousand brave souls defying the Night determined to recover the world for its true inhabitants. At least we tried!"

You failed.

"Did we, or is this just more lies?"

Your conceptions of truth and lies are redundant.

"No they aren't, at least not from my perspective – and that's the only one that matters."

A limited viewpoint.

"Where is my daughter?" Denholm demanded.

The Jackotrades abandoned Caliban, flowing from every organelle and every cell, collecting in the tiny spaces of his body, and then pooling in his veins and arteries, entrails and lungs. He spasmed, vomiting a silver stream of machine life, his skin turned silver, and then dead white as his symbiotes deserted him. A glistening argent pool formed at his feet, then disappeared into the black earth. For a long time he didn't dare breath, so terrified was he that the merest motion would cause his body to slump into a bindless sludge. Finally, a single choking breath told him he was alive, and a cautious step proved that he was still vital. He wrapped his arms around his chest and held his hatred close. The Master's footprints were easy to follow.

The snake women's attacks went on until the last of the

boys was dead. As Rauli slumped over, his face purpled and his tongue bulging and bloodied, his attacker decomposed into a slinking oily ash. For half-a-day, the boys had been singled out one-by-one for attack. The first had happened with blinding suddenness. A fist of viper-tailed women with eyes like burning embers and serrated hooks instead of hands, had burst from behind a rock, and surrounded Paamis. While the others held his friends at bay, one of them embraced him in a quickly tightening embrace, and crushed the life out of him. When her work was done, the snake woman unwound her deadly grip fell into torpor. Her sisters slinked away, leaving the fast putrefying killer behind. The children stuck close together as they climbed the long slope up from the dry seabed and, when the next attack came, they were better prepared. In the end it made little difference; the snake-women were cunning and single-minded. When they fixed on a victim – always a boy – it was only a question of time before one of them broke through and killed him.

With Nyven dead, the attacks ended. Only Naani and three of the girls – Jessamy, Winter and Tigris Tinsley – were alive of the sixteen children who the Moramor had led into the Night Land. The others hugged each other and wailed, but Naani stood apart, her head held high. The Earth was silent, apart from a keening from the northwest.

Jessamy looked up from her grief. "What's that noise?"

"Just the Night Land," Naani said. "Don't upset yourself."

The other girl flinched and buried her face in her hands. Naani ignored her, she had no comforting words for them, they would either have to pull themselves together, or they would die soon.

Just like my father's people.

So far as she could tell, she alone had shared the last moments of the Redoubt's defenders. At first she had through their deaths were waking nightmares but, as dozens, then as hundreds of them had fled their lives she could no longer deny the scale of the tragedy she was witnessing. The end had happened so quickly; it took a handful of minutes while she stood lookout and her friends wept for the lost boys.

"You don't care!" Tigris Tinsley shouted.

Naani listened to the Night Land. She could hear things scurrying among the rocks; things emboldened by the death of the last Lamia. Her awareness encompassed every creature for miles around – from slithering worms to creeping beast men – all of them keen to feast on four lonely girls. There was another voice: in the distance, her Bright Warrior was striding quickly towards her. She sent a wordless cry of love into the Night. She could not grasp his reply, but she was sure that he had heard and would quicken his pace.

There were two other voices that did not belong in the Night Land. She recognized one of them – and it filled her with a sad joy. The other was clouded and shifted like sand in a gale wind, like it was part of the world, yet apart from it. Instinct told her who it was, and that she would have to deal with it soon.

"Come," she said to the others. "My father is in the wilderness with us. He is a good distance away and needs our help – we must hurry."

Caliban had closed to within a hundred paces of his enemy, so close that he could smell him, even if he couldn't sense his thoughts. When the Jackotrades drained from him they took their world-sense with them. Suddenly, the man looked in his direction. Caliban threw himself flat into a low ditch filled with swarming mites. The lice skittered away from him. He slapped his palm down killing a thousand of them, then held up his gore-splattered hand and looked at it for a long time. It wasn't the same, he realized; killing things wasn't as satisfying when you couldn't feel their tiny souls snuffing out.

Wiping his hand on a rock, he found some consolation in the hope that killing his enemy might reawaken a little of his old passion. Repeating that happy thought over-and-over, he stood up cautiously – and was slammed to the ground by a mass of claws and fur. At first Caliban was furious that he had allowed a beast to sneak up on him. Then he was fighting for his life. The beast man knocked the wind from him.

Through his breathless agony, Caliban saw the creature prepare to leap again and, just as it fell, he rolled aside and staggered to his feet. For an instant his attacker seemed baffled by the escape of its prey and Caliban took the opportunity to leap on its back. He two fistfuls of the mat of greasy hair on its head and smashed its face against the rocky ground. Before the beast man could recover, Caliban wrapped his arms around its neck and squeezed as hard as he could.

It was several minutes before Caliban heard the beast man's death rattle. He shoved his face close to its head and listened in vain for its life force taking wings. He kicked the dead creature away, and squatted on his haunches, listening closely for other potential attackers. He was about to restart his pursuit, when another idea occurred to him. Laughing at his cleverness, he found a sharp flint flake in the rubble, and began to skin the beast man. When he was done he threw the mattered pelt over his shoulders like a cloak.

Unsurprisingly, his enemy was gone from sight. He was about to start tracking him when he realized that he was thirsty. There was no water anywhere near, but he squeezed the beast man's pelt, forcing a few drops of blood and fat into his upraised palm. He swallowed the bitter, salty slop. It was awful, but it would give him the strength he needed for his last task.

Naani and her father met on small flat-topped hill. It was capped with a large triangular rock a hundred yards along each side. Neither of them knew that it was the base of one of the prehistoric watchtowers of their people. Unused since the Redoubt was completed; all traces of humanity had long ago been scoured from its face. The underside was covered with eight million-year-old writings, but they were lost to all but the trillions of Jackotrades who had been drawn to this climatic moment – and they did not care about them.

Father and daughter approached each other slowly. The other three girls cowered beside a nearby boulder and watched in disbelief. Naani held her hands out and Denholm softly took them in his. They did not say anything but, for the first time in their lives, looked into each other's eyes. Their mutual understanding had been long coming, but was complete, and all sins and omissions were set aside in a profound act of reconciliation. Naani rested her head on her father's chest and listened to his slow steady heartbeat. The universe was arrested in her perfect moment – the blowing dust stopped in mid-air – the ice-cracked rock flake defined gravity – the cellular processes of the lowliest algae paused in reverence.

Beneath her feet, the Jackotrade tribes waited.

Then something rushed in a blur of stinking hair and pale limbs across the flat rock, screaming and wielding a flint knife. Denholm pushed his daughter aside and stepped into Caliban's path. He slammed into the creature, shattering its bones and tearing its sinews. They crashed to the rocky ground. After a moment, Denholm heaved Caliban aside – Naani rushed up, grabbed a fist-sized rock and finished the boy-monster off. She threw her weapon away, and knelt by her father. His hands covered the flint knife that was buried in his chest. She pressed her head to his body and listened as his heart stopped beating.

I love you.

I know.

It was an hour before Naani let go of her father. The other girls stood around in silence, unsure of what to do or say. Then she stood up and looked towards the southwest. She could hear her Bright Warrior from the Great Redoubt, he was many days away yet, but she knew with absolute certainty that their meeting would not be too long delayed.

"I am going to the west," she said without turning to look at her companions. "My salvation and my love is hurrying North, and I long to join him. You can come with me if you wish. The way will likely be hard, but that is true of all roads in this desolate land and it is time for us to stop being afraid of the dark." She paused and waited for the other to reply. When they didn't she shook her head sadly, and continued.

"First through we must bury my father. I cannot stomach the thought of leaving him naked in this place."

"You should look at this, Naani," Jessamy said in a near-whisper.

Naani looked back at her father's body. It was lying in a smooth shallow depression in the rock. As she watched, the grave slowly deepened and trickles of fine dust started to cover the body.

It took the Jackotrades six hours to bury Denholm, and when they were done his resting-place was covered with an oval slab of smooth, impenetrable granite. Naani offered silent thanks then, after kissing the monument, she set out to meet her destiny.

Seeking Survival

Erin Donahoe

And for a moment, brief though it may be,
they forgot the Night Land, the Silent Ones,
allowed the Northwest Watching Thing to watch
if it would, for this was worth the struggle.

She sought, with fingers no longer soft, and
a body made hard by the world they roamed,
she sought in him a matching hardness, a
physical bond to match their meeting minds.

Uncertain, still, they fumbled their way through
lands as foreign as any they had seen,
led by forgotten ghosts of ages past,
souls' worths of longing their imperfect map.

And when the map proved useless, still they went,
finding in each other heat as sating
as any stolen from the cooling earth,
more fulfilling for being given while
they cried out as one against the darkness.

Awake in the Night

John C. Wright

Years ago, my friend Perithoös went into the Night Lands. His whole company had perished in their flesh, or had been Destroyed in their souls. I am awake in the night, and I hear his voice.

Our law is that no man can go into the Night Lands without the Preparation, and the capsule of release; nor can any man with bride or child to support, nor any man who is a debtor, or who knows the secrets of the Monstruwacans; nor a man of unsound mind or unfit character; nor any man younger than twenty-two years; and no woman, ever.

The last remnant of mankind endures, besieged, in our invulnerable redoubt, a pyramid of gray metal rising seven miles high above the volcano-lit gloom, venom-dripping ice-flows, and the cold mud-deserts of the Night Lands. Our buried grain fields and gardenlands delve another one hundred miles into the bedrock.

Night-Hounds, Dire Worms, and Lumbering Behemoths

are but the visible part of the hosts that afflict us; monsters more cunning than these, such as the Things Which Peer, and Toiling Giants, and Those Who Mock, walk abroad, and build their strange contrivances, and burrow their tunnels. Part of the host besieging us is invisible; part is immaterial; part is we know not what.

There are ulterior beings, forces of unknown and perhaps unimaginable power, which our telescopes can see crouching motionless on cold hillsides to every side of us, moving so slowly that their positions change, if at all, only across the centuries. Silent and terrible they wait and watch, and their eyes are ever upon us.

Through my open window I can hear the roar and murmur of the Night Lands, or the eerie stillness that comes when one of the Silent Ones walks abroad, gliding in silence, shrouded in gray, down ancient highways no longer trod by any man, and the yammering monsters cower and hush.

Before me is a brazen book of antique lore, which speaks of nigh-forgotten times, now myth, when the pyramid was bright and strong, and the Earth-Current flowed without interruption.

Men were braver in those days, and an expedition went north and west, beyond the land of the abhumans, seeking another source of the Earth-Current, fearing the time when the chasm above which our pyramid rests might grow dark. And the book said Usire (for that was the name of the Captain), had his men build a stronghold walled of living metal, atop the fountain-head of this new source of current; and they reared a lofty dome, around was set a great circle charged with spiritual fire; and they drove a shaft into the rock.

One volume lays open before me now, the whispering thought-patterns impregnated into its glistening pages murmuring softly when I touch the letters. In youth, I found this book written in a language dead to everyone but me. It was this book that persuaded the lovely Hellenore (in violation of all law and wisdom) to sneak from the safety of the pyramid into the horror-haunted outer lands.

Perithoös had no choice but to follow. This very book I read slew my boyhood friend . . . if indeed he is dead.

Through the casement above me, the cold air blows. Some fume not entirely blocked by the Air-Clog that surrounds our pyramid stings my nose. Softly, I can hear murmurs and screams as a rout of monsters passes along a line of dark hills and crumbling ruins in the West, following the paths of lava-flows that issue from a dimly-shining tumble of burning mountains.

More softly, I can hear a voice that seems human, begging to be let in. It is not the kind of voice that one hears with the ear. I am not the only thing awake in the night.

Scholars who read of the most ancient records say the world was not always as it is now. They say it was not always night, then; but what it may have been if it were not unending night, the records do not make clear.

Certain dreamers (once or twice a generation, we are born, the great dreamers whose dreams reach beyond the walls of time) tell of aeons older than the scholars tell. The dreamers say there was once a vapor overhead, from which pure water fell, and there was no master of the pump-house to ration it; they say the air was not an inky darkness whence fell voices cry.

In those days, there was in heaven, a brightness like unto a greater and a lesser lamp, and when the greater lamp was hooded, then the upper air was filled with diamonds that twinkled.

Other sources say that the inhabitants of heaven were not diamonds at all, but balls of gas, immeasurably distant, but visible through the transparent air. Still others say they were not gas, but fire. Somehow, despite all these contradictory reports, I have always believed in the days of light.

No proofs can be shown for these strange glimpses of times agone, but, when great dreamers sleep, the instruments of the

Monstruwacans do not register the energies that are believed to accompany malign influence from beyond our walls. If it is madness to have faith in what the ancients knew, it is a madness natural to human kind, not a Sending meant to deceive us.

As I nodded, half-awake, softly there came what seemed to be the voice of Perithoös into my sad and idle thoughts. I was called by my name.

"Telemachos, Telemachos! Undo for me the door as once I did for you; return the good deed you said you would. If vows are nothing, what is anything?"

I did not move or raise my head, but my brain elements sent this message softly out into the night, even though my lips did not move. "Perithoös, closer than a brother, I wept when I heard your company was overwhelmed by the monsters. What became of the maiden you set out to rescue?"

"Maiden no more I found her. Dead, dead, horribly dead, and by my hand. Herself and her child; and I had not the courage to join them."

"How are you alive after all these years?"

"I cannot make the door to open."

"Call to the gate-warden, Perithoös, and he will lower a speaking tube from a Meurtriere and you may whisper the Master-Word into it, and so prove your human soul has not been destroyed, and I will be the first to welcome you."

The Master-Word did not come. Instead, mere words, such as any fell creature of the night could impersonate, now whispered in my brain: *"Telemachos, son of Amphion! I am still human, I still remember life, but I cannot say the Master-Word."*

"You lie. That cannot be."

And yet a felt a tear stinging in my eye, and I knew, somehow, that this voice did not lie: he was still human. But how could he forget the Word?

"Though it has never been before, in the name of the blood we shed together as boys, the gruel in which we bound our silly oath, I call on you to believe and know that a new sorrow has appeared in

this old, sad world, like fresh blood from an old scar; it is possible to forget what it means to be a man, and yet remain one. I have lost the Master-Word; I have my very self. Let me through the door. I am so cold."

I did no longer answer him, but stirred my heavy limbs.

Though my hands and feet felt like lead, I moved and trembled and slid from my desk where I slumbered, and fell to the floor heavily enough to jar myself awake.

How long I lay I do not know. My memory is dark, and perhaps time was not for me then flowing as it should have been. I remember being cold, but not having the strength to rise and shut the window; and this was an old part of the library, so there were no thought-switches I could close just by wishing them closed.

My thoughts drifted with the cold wind from the window.

This wing of the library had been deserted for half a million of years. No one came into this wing, since no one could read the language, or understand the thoughts, of the long-forgotten peoples who had sent Usire out to found a new stronghold. Only I knew the real name of those ancient folk; modern antiquarians called them the Orichalcum people, because they were the only ones who the secret of that metal; and no other trace of them survived.

And so the Air Masters, during the last two hundred years of power-outages, had lowered the ventilation budget in this wing to a minimum. I had needed vasculum of breathing-leaf just to get in here, and would have fainted with the window shut.

Nor were failures of the ventilations rare. Most windows of most of the middle-level cities stood open, these days, no matter what the wise traditions of elder times required.

It was two miles above the Night Land. No monster could cross the White Circle, and nothing has climbed so high since the Incursions of four hundred thousand years ago; and even if they did, this window was too small to admit them.

I remembered wings. In my dreams I see doves, or the machines used by ancient men to impersonate them. But the air is thin, and even the dark and famished things have no wings to mount so high.

I thought there was no danger to have the window open. Stinging insects, vapors, or particles would be surely stopped by the Air Clog. But what if the power losses over the last few centuries were greater than is publicly admitted by the Aediles or the Castellan? But it had not stopped the Mind-Call, as it should have done.

Many Foretellers have dreamt that it is five million years before the final extinction of mankind. Most of the visions agree on certain basic elements, though much is in dispute. Five million years. We are supposed to have that long. I wondered, not for the first time, if those who say that they can see the shape of fate are wrong.

I came awake when there was a movement, a clang, behind me as the hatch swung open. Here was a Master of the Watch, clad from head to toe in full armor, and carrying in hand that terrible weapon called the Diskos.

I knew better than to wonder why a Watchman was here. He came into the chamber, his blade extending before him as he stepped, and his eyes never left me. The shaft was extended. The blade was lit and spinning. The furious noise of the weapon filled the room. Flickering shadows fled up and down the walls and bookshelves as eerie sparks snapped, and I felt the hair on my head, the little hairs on my naked arms, stir and stand up. I smelled ozone.

Without rising, I raised my hands. "I am a man! I am human!"

His voice was very deep, a rumble of gravel. "They all say that, those that talk."

Slowly, loudly, clearly, I said the master-word, both aloud with reverent lips, and by sending it with my brain-elements.

It seemed so dark in the chamber when he doused his blade, but his smile of relief was bright.

My youth had been a solitary one. To hold one's ancestors in honor, and to love the lore of half-forgotten things, has never been in fashion among school-boys. The pride of young men requires that they seem wise, despite their inexperience, and the only way to appear all-knowing without going to the tedium of acquiring knowledge, is to hold all knowledge in weary-seeming contempt. Students and apprentices (and, yes, teachers also) bestowed on me their well-practiced sneers; but when my dreams began, and ghosts of other lives came softly into my brain as I slept, then I was marked as a pariah, and was made the butt of every prank and cruelty boyish imagination could invent.

Perithoös was as popular as I was unpopular. He was an alarming boy to have as a schoolmate, for he had the gift of the Night-Hearing, and he could hear unspoken thoughts. All secrets were open to him; he knew passwords to open locked doors and cabinets, and could avoid orderlies after lights-out. He knew the answers to tests before the schoolmasters gave them, and the plays of the opposing team on the tourney field. He was good at everything, feared nothing, and anarchy and confusion spread from his wake. What was there for a schoolboy not to love?

Once, when the Head Boy and his gang had me locked in the cable-wheel closet, so that I would be absent from the feast-day assembly and gift-giving, Perithoös left the assembly (a thing forbidden by the headmaster's rules), took a practice blade from the arm's-locker and spun the charged blade against the closet door hinges, shattering the panel with a blast of noise.

Not just school proctors, but civic rectors and men of the Corridor Guard arrived. To use one of the Great Weapons while inside the pyramid was a grave offense; and neither one of us would admit who did it, even though they surely knew.

We both were scourged by the headmaster and given triple-duty, and had porridge for our holiday feast, while the other boys dined on viands and candied peaches.

Perithoös and I ate alone in the staff commissary, our shirts off (so that our backs would heal) and shivering the cold of the unheated room. We were not allowed to speak, but I tipped my bowl onto the board and wrote in the porridge letters from the set-speech: *shed blood makes us brothers-I shall return this deed.*

Even at that age, he was taller than the other lads, broad

of shoulder and quick of eye and hand, the victor of every sport and contest, the darling of those who wagered on gymnastics games. He was as well-liked as I was ill-liked. So I expected to see doubt, or, worse, a look of patronizing kindness in his eye.

But he merely nodded, wiped away the porridge-stain with his hand quickly, so that the proctor would not see the message. Under the table, with perfect seriousness, he clasped my hand with his, and we shook on it. Porridge dripped through our fingers, but, nonetheless, that handclasp was sacred, and he and I were friends.

At that time, neither one of us knew Hellenore of High Aerie.

I had been found in the library by proctors of the Watch, whose instruments had detected the aetheric disturbance sent by the voice in the Night.

The Monstruwacans kept me for a time as a guest in their tower, and I drank their potions, and held the sensitive grips of their machines, while they muttered in their white beards and looked doubtful. More than once I slept beneath their oneirometers, or was examined inch by inch by a physician's glass.

I told them many times of my mind-speech with Perithoös, and they did not look pleased; but the physician's glass said my soul was without taint, and my nervous system seemed sound, and besides, both the Archivist (the head of my guild) and the Master of Architects (the head of my father's) sent letters urging my release, or else demanding that an inquest be convened at once.

I spent the remainder of my convalescence in Darklairstead, my father's mansions on level Fourscore-and-Five. Ever since, a generation ago, the power failed along this stretch of corridor (half the country receiving from the sub-station at Bountigrace is dark) it has been a quiet and restful place.

Among my very earliest memories was one dream, repeated so many times in my childhood that I filled a whole diary with scrawled words and clumsy sketches trying to capture what I saw.

When I was seven years, my mother died, and her shining coffin was lowered into the silvery rays of the Great Chasm. My father became strange and cold. He sent my brother Arion to prentice with the Structural Stress Masters. Tmelos (who is younger than I) was sent to the quarters of my Aunt Elegia, in Forecourtshire, for her to raise; Patricia took holy orders, and Phthia stayed with Father to run the house and rule the servants. Me, I was sent to board at a school in Longnorthhall of Floor 601, where the landing of the Boreal Stair reaches for many shining marble acres under lamps of the elder days, and potted Redwoods grow. When I left home for school, the dream left me.

As I recovered at my father's manse, the dream came once again, and it no longer frightened me, for nothing that reminds one of childhood, even ill things, can be utterly without a certain charm.

It was a dream of doors.

I saw tall doors made of a substance that gleamed like bronze and red gold (which I later found to be a metal called *Orichalcum,* an alloy made by a secret only the ancients knew). The doors were carven with many strange scenes of things that had been and things that would be.

In the dream I would be terrified that they would open.

Father and I would dine alone, without servants. The dining chamber is a pillared hall, wide and gloomy. Out of the hatch window, I would often see, across the air shaft from me, little candles dancing in the hatches of some of my neighbors. Once, candles had been used only for the most solemn ceremonies, back when the ancient rules against open flames in the pyramid had been enforced: the sight of candles used as candles always saddened me.

Some nights there was a hint of music from some city far overhead, echoing down the shaft, and, once, the hiss of a bat-winged machine carrying a Currier-boy (only boys are small enough) down the airshaft on some business of the Life Support House, or perhaps the Castellan, too urgent to wait for the lifts.

Our table was made from a tree felled down in the underground country, by a craftsman whose art is the cutting and jointing of living material, an art called Carpentry. Such is Father's prestige he can have such things brought up the lifts for him, but he has never moved the family to better quarters.

My father is a big, tall man, with fierce, penetrating eyes in an otherwise very mild face. He shaves his chin, but has a moustache that bristles, and this gives his penetrating eyes a strange and savage look.

I have dreamed of other lives, and once, in a prehistoric world, a dusky savage who was me, strong and lean of limb, and braver than I ever hoped to me, died beneath the claws of a tiger. The great cat was more bright of hue than anything in our world is, shining orange and black as it slunk through dripping jungles beneath a sun as hot as the muzzle of a culverin. I wonder what became of that species, that lived on some continent long since swallowed by the seas, before the seas dried up, before the sun died. I have always though that extinct beast looked something like my father.

His bald head was growing back in new hair, as sometimes happens to men of his order, for men who work near the Earth-Current, their vitality was greater than normal.

After dinner, we brought out carafes of water and wine, which glistened in the candlelight, and mixed them in our bowls. I am sparing of the wine and he is sparing of the water; but he is sober even when he drinks deep, and shows no levity nor thickwittedness. Perhaps exposure to the Earth-Current helps here too.

He sat with his bowl in his hand, staring out the air-shaft. He spoke without turning his head. "You know the tale of Andros and Naäni. You were raised on it. I am sure I hate it as much as you adore it."

I said, "Andrew Eddins of Kent, and Christina Lynn Mirdath the Beautiful. The tale shows that, even in a world as dark as ours, there is light."

Father shook his head. "False light. Will-o'-Wisp light! I do not blame the hero for his deeds. They were great, and he was a mighty man, high-hearted and without vice. But the hope he brought served us ill. Perithoös was no Andros, go into the Night. And that highborn girl who toyed with your affections; Hellenore. She was no Mirdath the Beautiful. Hellenore the Vain, I should call her."

"Please speak no ill of the dead, father. They cannot answer you."

He raised his bowl with a graceful gesture and took a silent sip, and paused to admire the taste. "Hm. Neither can they hear me, and so they will not flinch. She is not the first of the dead who have served the living poorly. He did us ill, whichever forefather first thought it would be wise to leave us tales and songs that tell young boys to go be brave and die, or to perish for a gesture."

I said, "Keeping a promise counts for more than mere gesture, Father."

"Does keeping a promise count more than preserving flesh or soul?"

I said, "Those who study such matters say that souls are born again in later ages, even if the conscious memories are lost; poets claim that oath-breakers are reborn into lives accursed with turmoil and bitter anguish. If so, then each man in his present life must take care to die spotlessly, his soul still pure."

Father smiled bitterly. He did not read poets. "What point is the punishment, if, in his next life, each criminal has forgotten what crime he did?"

I said, "So that even men who are stoical and hard in this life will fear to break their word; for, in their next, they will be young and green again; and suffering that comes unannounced, for reasons that seem reasonless, are surely the hardest pains of all to bear."

"A pretty tale. Must you die for an idle fiction?"

"Sir, it is not a fiction."

He said: "Must you die, fiction or not?"

"I had no other friend in my school days."

"Perithoös was no true friend!"

"And yet I gave my word to him, friend or not. Now I am called to fulfill it."

"Who calls? There are Powers in the dark who can mock our voices and our thoughts, and deceive even the wisest of us. Only the Master-Word is one the Horrors cannot utter, for it represents a concept that they cannot understand, an essence that does not dwell in them. If what called to you did not call out the Master-Word, you know our law commands you not to heed it."

I answered: "Despite the law, despite all wisdom, still, a hope possesses me that he is alive, and undestroyed, somehow."

He said grimly: "A true man would not call out to you."

I did not know if he meant that a man of honor would die before he let himself be used to lure a friend out into the darkness; or if he meant that what called out to me had not been human at all. Perhaps both.

I said: "What sort of man would I be, if it truly were Perithoös calling, and I did not answer?"

He said: "It is your death calling."

And I had no answer back for that. I knew it was so.

After a space of silence, eventually he spoke again: "Do you see any cause for hope you say has taken possession of you?"

"I see no cause."

"But – ?"

"But hope fills me up, father, nonetheless, and it burns in my heart like a lamp, and makes my limbs light. There are many ugly things we do not see in this dark land that surrounds us, father, horrors unseen. And there are said to be good powers as well, whose strange benevolence works wonders, though never in a way humans can know. And they also are not seen, or only rarely. There are many things, which, although unseen, are real. More real than the imperishable metal of our pyramid, more potent that the living power of the Earth-Current. More real than fire. So, I admit, I see no cause for hope. And yet it fills me."

He was silent for a while, and sipped his wine. He is a

rational man, who solved problems by means of square and chisel, stone and steel, measured currents of energy, knowing the strengths of structures and what load each support can bear. I knew my words meant little to him.

He reached his hand and doused the lantern, so that I could not see the pain in his face. He voice hovered in the dark, and he tried to make his words cold: "I will not forbid you to venture into the Night Lands . . ."

"Thank you, Father."

". . . Since I have other sons to carry on my name."

Visions, pulmenoscopy, and extra-temporal manifestations are not unknown to the people of the Last Redoubt. The greatest among us are known to have the Gift; and at least one of the Lesser Redoubt also was endowed with the Night-Hearing, and memory-dreams.

Mirdath the Beautiful is the only woman known to have crossed the Night Lands, and her nine scrolls of the histories and customs of the Lesser Redoubt are the only record of any kind we have for the history, literature, folkways and sciences of that long-lost race of mankind. All the mathematical theories of Galois we know only from her memory; the plays of Euryphaean, and the music of an instrument called a pianoforte, infinite resistance coil and the sanity glass, and all the inventions that sprang from them, are due to her recollection. Her people were a frugal folk, and the energy-saving circuits they used, the methods of storing battery power, were known to them a million years ago, and greatly conserved our wealth. Much of what she knew of farming and crops we could not use, for the livestock and seed of our buried fields were strange to her.

She knew more of the lost aeons than even Andros, and was able to tell tales from the time of the Cities Ever Moving West, of the Painted Bird, and of the Gardens of the Moon; she knew something of the Failures of the Star-Farers, and of the Sundering of the Earth.

More, she also had the gift of the Foretelling, for some of

the dreams she had were not of the past, but of the future, and she wrote of the things to come, the Darkening, the False Reprieve, the disaster of the Diaspora into the Land of Water and Fire, the collapse of the Gate beneath the paw of the South Watching Thing, the years of misery and the death of man, beyond which is a time from which no dreams return, although there is said to be a screaming in the aether, dimly heard through the doors of time, the time-echo of some event after the destruction of all human life. All these things are set out in the Great Book, and for this reason Mirdath is also called The Predictress.

Mirdath and Andros had fifty sons and daughters, and all the folk of High Aerie claim descent from them, some truly, and some not.

Hellenore of High Aerie was one of those who made that claim truly.

When I was a young man, a time came when my future had disturbed those whose business it is to seek foreknowledge from dreams, and I was summoned to an audience.

For many generations the Foretelling art had fallen in disrepute, and charlatans rose to deceive the common people; but then a girl of the blood of Mirdath was born whose gift was proven by many sad events, the Library of Ages-Yet-To-Be was reopened. The Sibylline Book had more treatises of prophecy added to it, and eschatologists compared dream-journals and revised their estimates. Even I had heard of her: the hour-slips said she was sure to be the next Sibyl.

I don't recall the date. It must have been soon after my Initiation, for I wore my virile robe, and my hair was cropped short as befits a man. The blade that was ever after to be partnered with my life, I had hung over the narrow door to my cell in the journeyman's room of the Librarian's Guildhouse, as only those beyond their fourteenth year are permitted. I remember that the squire to come fetch me called me 'Sir' instead of 'Lad', even though he (to my young eyes) seemed incredibly old.

I remember the Earth-Current was running strong that year. It was my first time at the Great Lift Station for my floor. Invisible forces lifted the platform in a great surge of wind off the deck. Maidens clutched their bonnets and squealed, and many a young gallant (for a strong flow of the Earth Current makes lads more bold and amorous) took the opportunity to put an arm around fair shoulders to steady a maiden making her first voyage away from her level. Some of the more daring boys learned over the rail, and waved their caps at the rapidly dwindling squares and rooftops of the city, before, like an iron sky, the underside of the next deck upwards swallowed the lift platform. I rode the axial express all the way to the utmost level. I remember I had to drink a potion made by the apothecary, because of the thinness of the air.

Fate House that sits atop the highest stories of the highest city; the hanging gardens of High Aerie sit between the shining skylights of West Cupola and the pleasances and airy walks of Minor Penthouse. There are floral gardens here, under glass, as well as pools and lakes amid the rooftop-fields of the long-empty aerodromes built by ancient peoples.

The domes of Fate House are dusky blue, inscribed with gold, and, above the roof-tiles, many a monument of ancient hero or winged genius of the household stood on slender pillars among the minarets. All within was a somber and august as a fane.

Here was Hellenore daughter of Eris. I see again the sheen of her satiny dress, as she sat beneath the rose lamp on a Lector's chair too large for her delicate frame. How like a swan's, her neck, all her mass of ink-black hair was gathered up and held in place with amethyst pins, jewel-drops like the stars the ancients knew, within the clear darkness of their temporary nights. I recall the delicate small hairs, wanton and wild, that had strayed from the strictness of her coiffure, and kissed the nape of her neck.

None of our pyramid has eyes like that, hair like that, save those descended from the strange blood of Mirdath the Beautiful. And none but me remembered the grace of the swan, and so none but me could see it in her.

Her voice was soft music, each word careful and light, like a brushstroke of calligraphy laid in the air. With what delicate tones she spoke of the grim horrors in the night, the grim future she foresaw nightly in her dreams!

We spoke for a time, of the horrors of the Deception two million years hence (slightly less than half way between now and the Extinction), when colonies of man leaving the Great Pyramid would go to dwell in what seemed a fair country to the West, even as certain legends said, not knowing that the House of Silence had already cursed and undermined the whole of that land, and merely held their influence at bay for millennia, waiting for the memory of these prophecies of Hellenore to be forgotten. Whole cities, pyramids and domes as great as ours, would be swallowed and cracked open, and multitudes would die, one entire branch of the human family wiped out; the survivors to be changed into something not human.

Then we spoke of my fate.

"My visions revealed hundreds shall die because of some ill-considered act you set in motion; first one, then many more, will go pelting out into the darkened world to perish amid the ice, or be ripped to bloody rags by Night Hounds, to be sucked clean of their souls and left as husks, grinning mouths and eyes as dry as stones. Heed me! I see many prints of boots across the icy dust of the Night Land, leading outward from our gates; I see but one set coming in."

I asked: "Must these things come to pass?"

"No human power can alter what must be."

"And powers more than human?"

She said softly: "We foreseers behold the structure of time; there are creatures not quite wholly inside of time, powers of the Night Land, whose malice we cannot foretell, since they are above and alien to the rules of time and space that bind all mortal life; there are said to be good powers, too."

"A riddle! Man's fate can be changed, but men cannot change fate." I asked.

Her full lips toyed with a smile, but she did not allow the smile to appear. "We are but drops in a river, young man," she said, "No matter what one drop might wish or do, the river course is set, and all waters glide to the ocean."

These words electrified me. "Ah!" I said, forgetting my manners, jumping up and taking her hand. "Then you have seen them too! Rivers and oceans! In visions, I have seen and heard the waters flowing, ebbing, pulled by tides, crashing by the shore. There is no sound alike it in the world, now."

She was startled and displeased, and favored me with a look of ice as she drew her fair and slender hand from mine. "Strange boy – what is your name again? – I spoke a line from old poetry. My people in the high-most towers are learned in such lore, and know old words like *river* and *sea*; but no one has seen them, except in the decorations of volumes none can read."

I did not say that there was one who could read what others had forgotten. I spoke stiffly, "My apologies, highborn one. Your comment thrilled my heart, for I had thought you meant to say that we would do great deeds in times to come, to defy that ocean that must swallow of human lore and history, so that the watercourse down which the current takes us might be ripped free of its bed, and set to a new path."

"Strange boy! What strange things you say!" She recoiled, one slim hand on her soft bosom, her lovely long-lashed eyes looking at me askance. Even in surprise, even when showing disdain, how elegant her every gesture!

"There was a time when all men spoke thus, and did deeds to match."

"Only men?" But she was not looking at me. Her eyes were turned sideways, and she stared at some spot on the walls of her family's presence chamber. There were many busts, portraits, and engraved tablets along the walls. I don't know which ancestor her gaze was resting on. In hindsight, it surely was Mirdath.

I said, "Can you tell me what this ill-considered act might be?"

Her eyes were elsewhere; she spoke airily, unheeding: "Oh, some chance remark spoken to some girl you fall in love with."

My voice was hollow, and my stomach was empty. "What? Must I vow to be silent, to speak never more to any woman?"

It took me a moment to rally my courage. I drew a breath, and spoke. "If that is my doom, I will learn to welcome it. If I must, I will take the vow, and go to some monastery in the buried basements, forbidden to woman, that I might never meet my love."

Her glittering eyes returned to me, and now a girlish mischief was in them. She said archly: "You will defy the structures of time and destiny, and rip up the pillars of the laws of nature, but you will meekly foreswear love and speech, merely because you are ordered to it? Backward boy! You would challenge what we cannot change, but would submit to what we can!"

That made me smile. "Perithoös says the same thing of me. Always looking backwards! We were walking at the Embrasures, and he joked once that-"

Hellenore sat upright, eyes shining. She said, "You know Perithoös, the athlete? What hour does he stroll upon the balcony, what level, where?"

A glow of joy lived in her face; and then she blushed and my heart ached with pleasure to see her cheek glow; but the thought of meeting Perithoös was such that she could not put away her smile, so she lifted her slender hand to hide it. If you have seen young maidens in the grip of first love, you know the sight; if not, my poor pen cannot mark it.

I told her I would arrange a meeting, and the smile came out again.

Beautiful, was that smile; though not for me.

And yet so lovely!

They met, at first, with chaperones.

At first. One of them could see the future and the other could see thoughts; both were bold, nobly born, and love-drunk. How was a duenna to keep them under watch?

They died swiftly, those who died, when the three hundred suitors set out to rescue Hellenore.

The company had been divided into three columns of one hundred men each. Before five-and-twenty hours of march, the rearguard column had driven off a host of troll-things from the ice hills, and stopped to rest and tend their wounds. From the balconies, and from the viewing tables, we watched them made a camp. It was hard to see, for it was well camouflaged; the tents and palisade were mere shadows among shadows, even under the most powerful magnification; and the sentries at the picket moved without making noise, warily.

But then they did not stir again. Either a sending from the House of Silence, or an invisible fume leaking from the ground, made the sleepers not to wake. Long-range telescopes glimpsed the survivors, perhaps the sentries who did not lay down, trying to carry one or two men to higher ground. The rest were left behind. A pallid slug a thousand feet long oozed into view near the last known position of those men; the Monstruwacan instruments recorded tiny Earth-Current discharges at about that same time, so it was thought that the survivors swung their weapons once or twice before they died.

At about seventy hours, the main column was beset by the Great Gray Hag, mate of the monster slain by Andros, and her fleshy fingers pushed men into the sagging hole that formed her maw, armor and all. The column was routed, and fled into the Deathly Shining Lands to escape her. They did not emerge. The Shine is opaque, and nothing has been seen again of those men. The scouts accompanying the main column were eaten by Night Hounds, one by one.

The vanguard column lasted until the end of the second week, when the Bell of Darkness descended from the cloud, and tolled its dire toll. Only seven out of those hundred had the presence of mind, or strength of will, to bare their forearms and bite down on the Capsule of Release. Those whose nerve failed them, and who did not slay themselves in time, were drawn silently up into the air, their eyes all empty, and strange little vulgar grins upon their lips, and their bodies floated upward into the mouth of the Bell.

We all watched from the balconies. I heard from underfoot, like an ocean, the sound of mothers and wives weeping, men shouting, children crying, and the noise was like the oceans of the ancient world, but all of grief.

The shattering noise of the Home-call echoing from the upper cities interrupted, ordering all the millions to shut their windows; and lesser horns were sounded on the balconies to pass the warning to the lower cities. The watchmen ordered the Blinds raised up on their great pistons to block the windows and embrasures of every city and hamlet dug into the northeastern side of the pyramid; and the towers and dormer windows lowered their armor.

I remember hearing, before the Blinds closed over us, the whispering murmur of the air-clog, straining under double power, raising an unseen curtain to deflect the malice of the tolling bell, lest the sound of it drive mad the multitudes.

Perithoös had been in the vanguard. The Monstruwacans studied blurry prints made from long-range telescopes, and tried to confirm each death, what little comfort that might have been to the grieving families. Not every corpse was accounted-for.

My cousin Thaïs came to see me while I was undergoing Preparation. She is pretty and curt, with a sly sense of humor and a good head for chess and math. Thaïs did not, aloud, try to argue me out of my venture, but she showed me her calculation: The expected average lifespan of men who went forth to save Hellenore worked out to an hour, twelve minutes.

By traditions so ancient that no record now recalls a time when they were not, those who venture into the Night Land do not carry lamps. It is too well known, too long confirmed by experience, that a traveler cannot resist the temptation to light such lamps, when the darkness has starved his eyes for too many fortnights.

And so it is thought, that since the weapons we carry give off light when they are spun, that those who walk in the Night will have light when and only when it is needful: that is, namely, when one of the monstrosities is no further off from us than a yard or two; for then we must strike, we must see to make the stroke.

Our craftsman could make lamps to burn a million years or more. We will not carry them into the Dark. A man who will not trust his soul to warn him of unseen dangers coming silently upon him, is the only kind who needs a lantern in the Night. But would such a man, too unsure to trust his soul, be man enough to beat back all the horrors his lantern would attract?

We carry also a dial of the type that can be read by touch, for to lose track of hours, and proper times for rest and sup, is to court madness.

There is a scrip for toting the tablets, made of solidified vital nutrients, which is the traveler's sole food; for there is nothing wholesome in the Night Lands to eat, and more solid food, even a bite from an apple, might bring too much belly-cheer, and relax the discipline of the Preparation.

Likewise, water is condensed out of the atmosphere in a special cup by a powder made by the Chemist's guild. The new-water is pure and clear, but bitterly cold, and the cup has that virtue that anything placed in it is cleansed of venom or morbific animacules. Some travelers hold the cup over mouth and nose when treading lands were the air is bad.

The mantle is woven of a fiber that, though it is not alive, is wise enough to shed heat more or less as the deadliness of the chill grows more or less, depending on the amount heat escaping from the ground.

The armor is so stern, and made so cunningly, that even monsters many times the strength of a man cannot dint it, and the joints are fitted at a level to fine for the eye to see. A blessing in the metal, an energy not unlike what throbs so purely in the fires of the White Circle, is impregnated into the helm and breastplate, to help slow those particular influences that attack the brain and freeze the heart.

Arms, armor, mantle, are made by craft a million years has perfected; and they are fair to the eye, but grim and without ornament, as befits the sobriety of the undertaking.

At last the torment of the Preparation Chambers ended.

I was oddly clear-headed after the fasting and the injections, and I had endured the test of being forced to view that which still lives, pinning to a slab and sobbing, within the refrigerated cell at the center of the secret museum of the Monstruwacans. I had read the bestiaries of former travelers returned sane from outer voyaging, and learnt what they said of the ways and habits of the night-beasts; and I understood why such journals are not shown to any save those whose quest carries them outside our walls.

The Capsule of Release still ached within the tender flesh of my fore-arm; and the hour of parting was come.

The lamps of the Final Stair were darkened. The watchmen, armed with living blades and armored in imperishable gray metal, stood for a time in silence, composing their thoughts, so that no disturbance in the aether, no stray gleam of thought or metal or sudden noise, would tell the waiting horrors of the night lands that a child of man had strayed among their cold hills.

I stood with my face pressed to the periscope for many minutes, and the escort with me showed no impatience, for they knew it was my life I staked at hazard on my judgment of the ground.

At last I raised my hand.

The Master of the Gatehouse saluted me with his dark Diskos, and the door-tender closed the switch that sent power to the valves. The metals leaves of the inner gate swung shut behind me, and then the outer leaves swung open, very swiftly and silently.

Out I stepped. The ashy soil crunched beneath my boot. The air was as chill as death. The outer valve was already shut behind me, and two layers of armor heavily closed back over it, locking pistons clicking shut almost without noise. If a monster were now to lunge across the Circle from the all-surrounding darkness now, or a Presence to manifest itself, the door wardens were obliged to do nothing but guard the door. I was already beyond rescue.

None within would come out for me, as I was now going out for Perithoös, and he had gone out for his fair Hellenore. Prudent men, they all.

It was but a few minutes walk (no more than half a mile) until I crossed the place where where a hollow tube of transparent metal, charged with holy white energies, makes a circle around the vast base of the pyramid. It is held to be one of the greatest artifacts of ancient times, the one thing that keeps all the malefic pressures, the eerie calls and poisonous clouds and groping fingers of subtle force at bay. The hollow tube is two inches in diameter, hardly higher than my boot-top. It only took a single step to cross it, but I must clear my mind of all distempered thought before the unseen curtain would part for me. My ears popped with the change in pressure.

It is customary not to look back when one steps across the line of light. I was inclined to follow the custom.

My father had not been present to see me off.

We who live within this mountain-sized fortress of a million windows of shining light, we cannot see, where flat high rocky plains lift their faces into our light, the long dark shadows cast by the rocks and hillocks and moss-bushes radiating away from the pyramid; darkness that never moves, straight and level as if drawn by a ruler. Even the smallest rock has a train of shadow trailing away from it, reaching out into the general night, so that, looking left and right, the traveler sees what seem to be a hundred hundred long fingers of gloom, all pointing straight toward the Last Redoubt of Man.

But no traveler is unwise enough to step into such a high plain lit so well. The bottom mile of the pyramid is darkened, her base-level cities long abandoned, and the lower windows covered over with armor plate. A skirt, as it were, of shadow surrounded the base of the pyramid, and one must travel away from the pyramid to expose oneself to the shining of the many windows of the Last Redoubt; even before leaving the protection of the skirt of shadow, there are many places where the ground has been tormented into crooked dells and ragged shapes, dry canyons, or deep scars from the ancient glaciers or the far more ancient weapons of prehistory. Such broken ground I sought.

I entered the canyons to the west within the first two hours of traveling, and encountered no beasts, no forces of horror.

My way was blocked by a river of boiling mud shown on none of our maps. The telescopes and viewing tables of our pyramid had never noted it, despite that it was so close to us, for ash floated in a layer atop the mud-flow, and was the same hue as the ground itself. It was not visible to me until my foot broke the sticky surface and I scalded my foot. Perhaps it was newly-erupted from some fire-hole; or perhaps it had been here for centuries. We know so little.

This mud river drove me south and curving around the side of the pyramid, and I marched thirty hours and three. I ate twice of the tablets, and slept once, finding a warm space behind a tall rock where heat and some uncouth vapor escaped from a rent in the ground.

Before I slept, I probed the sand near the rent with the hilt of my Diskos, and a little serpent, no more than an ell in length, reared up. It was a blind albino worm, of the kind called the amphisbaena, for its tail had a scorpion's stinger. I slew it with a fire-glittering stroke from my roaring weapon, and the heavy blade passed through the worm as it were made of air, and the halves were flung smoking to either side. It was with great contentment I slept, deeming myself to be a mighty hero and a slayer of monsters.

The encampment and stronghold of Usire, I knew from my books, and from my memory-dreams, lay to the north by northwest beyond the shoulders and back of the Northwest Watching Thing. There are other watchers more dreadful, but none is more alert, for the ground to the Northwest is a wide and flat in prospect, and it is lit by the Vale of Red Fire; and there is neither a crown nor eye-beam nor wide dome of light to interfere with the view the monster commands.

To go to the country beyond the creature, my way must go far around, for the North way was too well watched. To my

West was the Pit of Red Smoke itself, a land of boiling chasms and lakes of fire, impassible. To the East of me, I could see the silhouette of the Gray Dunes: and here was a sunken country populated by thin and stilt-legged creatures, much in shape like featherless birds, and they carried iron hooks, and they were very careful never to expose themselves to the windows of the pyramid as they stirred and crawled from pit to pit. The canyon-walls were riddled with black doorways, from whence, now and again, the Wailing which gives the Place of Wailing its name would rise from these doorways, and the bird-things would caper silently and flourish their hooks. To the east I would not go.

I went South.

Each time I rose after snatched sleep, the shapes of two of the Great Watching Things, malign and silent, were closer and clearer to my gaze.

First, to my right, rising, vast and motionless, the Thing of the Southwest was but a dim silhouette, larger than a hill. It was alive, but not as we know life. There was a crack in the ground at its feet, from which a beam of light rose, to illume part of that monster-cheek, and cast shadows across its lowering brow. Its bright left eye hung in the blackness, slit-pupiled and covered with red veins, seemingly as big as the Full Moon that once hung above a world whose nights came and went.

Some say this eye is blinded by the beam, and that the beam was sent by Good Forces to preserve us. Others say the beam assists the eye to cast its baleful influence upon us, for it is noted by those whose business it is to study nightmares, that this great catlike eye appears more often in our dreams than any other image of the Night Lands.

I remember my mother telling me once, how a time came when that great eye, over a period of weeks, was seen to close; and a great celebration was held in the many cities of the pyramid, and they celebrated for a reason they knew not why. They knew only that the eye had never before been known to close. But the lid was not to stay closed forever and aye; in eleven year's time, a crack had appeared between the upper and nether lid, for the monster was only blinking a blink.

Each year the crack widened. By the time I was born, the eye was fully opened, and so it had been all of my life.

Second, to my left was the great Watching Thing of the South, which is larger and younger than the other Watching Things, being only some three million years ago that it emerged from the darkness of the unexplored southern lands, advancing several inches a decade, and it passed over the Road Where the Silent Ones Walk between twenty-five and twenty-four hundred thousand years ago.

Then, suddenly, some twenty-two hundred thousand years ago, before its mighty paws, there opened a rent in the ground, from which a pearl or bubble of pure white light rose into view. Over many centuries the pearl grew to form a great smooth dome some half a mile broad. The Watching Thing of the South placed its paw on the dome, and it rises no further, but neither has the Watching Thing advanced across that mighty dome of light in all these years.

It is known from prophecy that this is the Watcher who will break open the doors of the Pyramid with one stroke of its paw, some four and a half million years from now, but that the death of all mankind will be prevented for another half million years by a pale and slender strand of white light that will emerge from the ground at the very threshold of the great gates. More than this, the dreams of the future do not tell.

Between the Watching Thing of the South and of the Southwest, the Road Where the Silent Ones Walk runs across a dark land. The Road was broad, and could not be crossed except in the full view of the Watching Things to the South and the Southwest. But the ground on the far side of the Road is dim, lit by few fire-pits, and coated with rubble and drifts of black snow, where a man could hide.

In this direction was my only hope. Suppose that the eye-beam does indeed blind the right eye of the Watching Thing of the Southwest, and suppose again that the dome of light troubles the vision of the Great Watcher of the South more than the Monstruwacans have guessed: I could cross the Great Road on the blind-side of the Southwest monster, and sneak between him and his brother, perhaps to hide among the black snow-drifts beyond. I would then follow the road as it wound past the place of the Abhumans, and then leave the road and venture north, into the unknown country called the Place Where the Silent Ones Kill.

Many weeks of terror and hardship passed, and my supplies grew sparse.

Once an party of abhumans came upon me by surprise; I slew two of them with my Diskos, though it was a near thing, and I fled when the others stopped to chew their comrade.

Once a luminous manifestation meant to wrap me in her misty arms; but the fire which spun from my weapon could do hurt to subtle substances even when there was no material substance for the blade to bite; swirled lightning dispelled part of the tension that held her cloudy fingers together, and she flew off, maimed and sobbing.

Once a Night-Hound ran at me suddenly from the darkness, and I chopped him in the neck before he could rend me; the blade of the Diskos shot sparks into the smoldering wound, and the monster's huge limbs jerked and danced as it fell, and it could not control its jaws enough to bite me. A soft voice from the corpse called me by name and spoke words of ill to me, but I fled. I will not write down the words in this place: it is not good to heed things heard in the Night Land.

As I passed through the ab-human lands, they grew aware of me, and hunted me.

I was driven far away from the Road into lands that grew ever colder. Each time I lay down to sleep, the hills between me and the Pyramid were higher. A time came when I passed beyond the sight of the Last Redoubt; even the tallest tower of the Monstruwacans was not tall enough to see into this land where I now found myself. I was beyond all maps, all reckoning.

At first, I walked. Each score of hours my dial counted, I

slept four. Because there were crevasses, I struck the ice before me with the haft of my weapon as I walked. Then I grew aware of how loudly the echo of my metallic taps floated away across the utter darkness of the icy world, and I grew very afraid.

After this, I crawled across the ice in utter blackness. I surely crawled in circles.

After four score more hours, about half a week of crawling, I felt a pressure in the air. It was so malign that I was certain one of the Outer Presences must be standing near. All was utter black, and I saw nothing but ghosts of light starved eyes create.

For about an hour I crouched with my forearm bare, my hand numb without my gauntlet, and the capsule touching my lips; but the pressure against my spirit grew no greater. I heard no sound.

So I crawled away. Over many hours I crawled and slept and crawled again, but whatever stood on the ice behind me, I could sense its power even as a blind man can feel when the door of an oven is opened across the room. I took my bearings from this, and kept the power forever behind me.

A time came when I saw light in the distance. I went toward it, and, over very many hours, I began to sense the downward slope of the ice. The path soon became broken, and I crawled from crag to crag, from high hill to low hill of ice.

The light grew clearer as I trudged down the mighty slope of ice, and I could see the footing well enough to walk. I put my spyglass to my eye, and scanned the horizon.

Here I saw, looming huge and strange, the head and shoulders of the Northwest Watching Thing. The crown of its head was mingled with the clouds and smokes of the Night Land; and to the left and right of his shoulders, like wings, I saw long, streaming shafts of pure and radiant light. This was the reflected glow of the Last Redoubt, bright the dark air of the night world.

I was behind the Watcher; seeing it from an angle no human person had ever seen it. The Last Redoubt was blocked from view; I was in the shadow of the monster.

A cold awe ran through me then, as if a man from the ancient times were to wake to find himself on the side of the moon (back when there was a moon) that forever turned its face away from earth.

I had come into the Place Where the Silent Ones Kill.

When Hellenore's father forbad the courting of Perithoös to go forward, they began to meet by secret, and my father's mansions, the darkened passages of Darklairstead, were used for the rendezvous. I helped Perithoös because he asked it of me, and I felt obligated to do him a good turn, even though it troubled me. As for Hellenore, she was beautiful and I was young. She barely knew I existed, but I could deny her nothing. She many suitors; how I envied them!

Once, not entirely by accident, I came across where Perithoös and Hellenore sat alone in a bower before a fountain in the greenhouse down the corridor not far from the doors of my father's officer's country. The greenhouse was built along the stairs of Waterfall Park, downstream from where a main broke a thousand years ago. Near the top, it is a sloping land of green ferns under bright lamps, and the water bubbles white as it tumbles from stair to stair, with small ponds shining at the landings. Near the bottom, the ceiling is far away, and the lamps were dim. At the bottom landing is a statue of the Founder's Lady, surrounded by naiads, and water poured from their ewers into a pond bright with dappled fish whose fins were fine as moth-wings.

Through the obscuring leaves that half-hid them, I saw Perithoös sitting on the grass, his back resting on the fountain's raised lip, and one arm around Hellenore's bare shoulders. In his other hand, he held a little book of metal, of the kind whose pages turn themselves, and the letters shined like gems; ferns and flowering iris grew to their left and right, half-surrounding the pair in flowery walls. Her head was on his shoulder, and her dark hair was like a waterfall of darkness, clouding his neck and chest.

In this wing of the greenhouse, many of the lamps had died a century ago, and so the air was half as bright here as elsewhere. To me, the view seemed like a cloudy day, or a sunset; but I was the only one in all mankind who knew what twilight was. How strange that, so many millions of years after it could not ever be found again, lovers still sought twilight.

As I approached, I heard Hellenore's soft laugh-but when she spoke, her whisper was cross. "Here he comes, just as I foresaw."

Perithoös whispered back, "The boy is sick for love of you, but too polite to say aloud what is in his mind."

"But not polite enough to stay where he is not welcome!" she scolded.

"Hush! He hears us now."

I pushed aside the leafy mass of fern. Crystal drops, as small as tears, clung to the little leaves, and wetted me when I stepped forward.

Now she was primly kneeling half a yard from him, and her elbows were in the air, for she had pulled her hair up, and, in some fashion I could not fathom, fixed it in place with a swift and single twist of her hands. The same gesture had drawn her silken sleeves (that had been falling halfway to her elbow) back up to cover her shoulders.

Perithoös, one elbow languidly on the fountain lip, waved his book airily at me, the most casual of salutes. "Telemachos! The lad who lived a million lives before! What a surprise this would have been, eh?" And he smiled at Hellenore.

I bowed toward her and nodded toward him. "Milady. Perithoös. Excuse me. I was just . . ."

Hellenore favored me with one cool glance from her exotic, tip-tilted eyes, and turned her head, her slender hands still busy pinning her hair in place. If anything, her profile was more fair than her straight glance, for now she was looking down (I saw that there were amethyst-tipped hair-pins driven point-first in the soil at her knees), and the drop of her lashes gave her an aspect both pensive and demur, achingly lovely.

Seeing himself ignored, Perithoös plucked up a fern-leaf, and reached over to tickle Hellenore's ear. She frowned (though, clearly, she was not displeased) and made as if to stab his hand with one of her jeweled pins.

Perithoös playfully (but swifter than the eye could see) grabbed her slender wrist with his free hand before she could stab him, and perhaps would have done more, but he saw my eyes on him, and casually released her. I wondered how he dared be so rough with a woman so refined and reserved; but she was smothering a smile, and her dark eyes danced when she looked on him.

I said awkwardly in the silence, "I had not expected to find you here."

Perithoös, "By which you mean, you expected us to flee before we let ourselves be found. Come now! There is no need to be polite with me: I see your dark thoughts. You came to gaze on Hellenore. Well, who would not? She knows it as well. How many suitors have you now, golden girl? Three hundred?"

My heartbeat was in my face, for I was blushing. But I said merely, "I hope you see my brighter thoughts as well. Of the three of us, surely one should be polite."

Perithoös laughed loudly, and was about (I could see from his gesture) to tell me to go away; but Hellenore, her calm unruffled, spoke in her voice that I and I alone knew had the cooing of doves in it: "Please sit. We were reading from a new book. There are scholars in South Bay Window, on level 475, who have challenged all the schoolmen, and wish to reform the ways the young are taught."

I did sit, and I thought that Hellenore must have been well-bred indeed, to invite so unwelcome an intruder as I was, to consume the brief time she had to share with her young wooer.

She passed the book to me, but I read nothing. Instead, I was staring at sketches that had been penned into the flyleaves. "Whose hand is this?" I said, my voice hoarse.

Hellenore tilted her head, puzzled, but answered that the drawings were her own, taken from her dreams.

"I know," I said, my head bowed. And by the time I raised my eyes, I had remembered many strange things, things that had happened to me, but not in this life.

They both looked so young, so achingly young, so full of the pompous folly and charming energy of youth. So inexperienced.

Perithoös was looking at me oddly. Though I do not have his gift, I would venture that I knew his thought, then: He saw what I was thinking, but did not know how someone my age could be thinking it.

Perithoös said, "Telemachos will be against it, no matter what the South Bay Window scholars suggest. All new things pucker up his mouth, for they are sour to his taste."

"Only when they are worse than the old things." I said.

Perithoös tossed a leaf at me: "For you, that is each time."

"Almost each time. Mostly, what is called 'new' is nothing more than old mistakes decked out in new garb."

"The New Learning is revolutionary and hopeful. Come! Shake off the old horrors of old dreams! The world is less hideous than we thought. These studies prove that the outside was never meant for man; do you see the implication?"

I shook my head.

He said happily: "It implies that our ancestors did not come from the Night Lands. We are not the last of a defeated people, no, but the first of a race destined to conquer! The Bay scholars claim that we have always dwelt in this pyramid, and deny what the old myths say. Look at the size and shape of the doors and door-handles. It was clear that men first evolved from marmosets and other creatures in the zoological gardens. Our ancestors kept other creatures who bore live young, cats and dogs and homunculi, you see, in special houses, this was back before the Second Age of Starvation. I assume our ancestors ate them to extinction."

I blinked at him, wondering if he had lost his mind, or if I had lost my ability to tell when he was joking.

"'Evolved'?"

"By natural selection. Blind chance. We were the first animals who were of a size and stature to pass easily down these corridors and enter and exist the places here. Other creatures were too large or too small, and these were cast out in the Night Land after many unrecorded wars of prehistory. The New Learning allows us hope to escape from the promise of universal death for our race: We need merely wait for the time when we will evolve to be suited to fit the environment outside; and we will be changed; and those horrors will no longer seem hideous to the changed brains of the creatures we shall become."

I said sternly: "The Old Learning speaks of such a possibility as well. It is hinted that the abhumans were once True Men, before the House of Silence altered them. The tradition of the Capsule of release is not without roots."

"Prejudice! Antique parochialism! The only reason why what we think of as True Men prevailed, is because our hands were best fitted to work the controls of the lifts and valves, our eyes best adapted to the lighting conditions, and we were small enough to enter the crawlspaces if giants chased us. Those giants outside are outside because they were too big for these chambers."

"And if we never dwelt in any place except this pyramid, whence came the ancestress of Hellenore? Whence came Mirdath? Or does your book prove she does not exist as well?"

He opened his mouth, glanced at Hellenore (who gave him an arch look), and closed it again. He dismissed the question with an airy wave of his hand. "Whatever might be the case here, skepticism will break down all the old rules and old ways, and leave us free. To live as we wish and love as we wish! Who could not long for such a thing?"

"Those who know the barren places where such wishful thinking leads," I said heavily, climbing to my feet.

Unexpectedly, Perithoös seemed angry. He shook his finger at me. "And where does thinking like *yours* lead, Telemachos? Are we always to be frozen in place, living the lives our ancestors lived?"

I did not then guess (though I should have) what provoked him. The traditional way of arranging a marriage, and so, by extension, the traditional way of doing anything, could not have had much appeal for him, not just then.

I spoke more sternly than I should have: "We are men born in a land of eternal darkness. We grope where we cannot see clearly. Why mistrust what ancient books say? Why mistrust our souls say? Our forefathers gave us this lamp, and the flame was lit in brighter days, when men saw further. I agree the lamp-light of such far-off lore, is dim for us; but surely that proves it to be folly, not wisdom, to cast the lamp aside: for then we are blind."

He said: "What use is light to us, if all it shows us it images of horror?"

I said, "There are still great deeds to be done; there will be heroes in times to come." And I did not say aloud, but surely Perithoös saw my thought: *unless this generation makes all its children to forget what heroism is.*

"Bah!" said Perithoös. His anger was hidden now, smothered somewhat beneath a show of light-heartedness. He smiled. "Will our writings be published in any other place than within these walls? Why will we do praiseworthy acts, when we know there will be nothing and no one left to sing our praises? Even you, who claims you will be born once more, will have no place left to be born into, when this redoubt falls."

I said, "Do not be jealous. I am not unlike you. This life could be my final one. You both have had others you forget; but this could be the first you will remember next time."

Perithoös looked troubled when I said this; I saw on his face how eerie my words (which seemed so normal to me) must have sounded to him.

Hellenore said eagerly, "What do you remember of us? Were Perithoös and I-" But then she broke off and finished haltingly; "How did the three of us know each other before?"

I said, "You were one of Usire's company, and lived in a strong place, a place of encampment, in a valley our telescopes no longer see, for the Watching Thing of the Northwest moved to block the view, once the House of Silence smothered the area with its influence. You, milady, were an architect, for women studied the liberal arts in those strange times; and you were possessed of the same gift you have now. In those times, you saw these ages now, and you sculpted one of the *orichalcum* doors before the main museum of Usire's stronghold, and wrought the door-panels with images of things to come."

Perithoös smiled sourly. "What Telemachos is not willing to say is. . . ."

I interrupted him. "Madame, I was favored by you then,

though I was of high rank and you were not. I help sculpt the other door with images of things that had been."

Hellenore looked embarrassed. I hoped my face did not show the shame I felt.

I turned to Perithoös, but I continued speaking to Hellenore, though I did not look at her. "Since we are being honest and free with each other's secrets: what Perithoös is not will to say is, he cannot fathom why I am not jealous of your love for him, even though he sees in my mind that I am not. He sees it, but he does not believe it. But that is the answer. Last time, he lost. This time, me. It does not mean we are not friends and always will be."

Hellenore was disquieted: I could see the look in her eye. "So I have not loved the same man in all ages, in every life . . ."

She was no doubt thinking of Mirdath the Beautiful, whose own true love was constant through all time.

I said awkwardly: "You have always loved noble men."

But she was looking doubtfully at Perithoös, and he was looking angrily at me. Odd that he was now angry. Surely I had said no more than what he had been about to say was in my mind. But perhaps he did not expect Hellenore to take seriously the thought that they were not eternal lovers.

Perithoös said: "No doubt if we three are born in some remote age in the future, and find ourselves the very last left living of mankind, you will seek to do the noble deed of poisoning minds against me, and worming your way into to intimacies where you are not wanted! Is this the kind of praiseworthy and noble things you practice, Telemachos?"

Angry answers rose to my lips, but I knew that, even if I did not say them aloud, Perithoös would see them burning in my heart. With no more than a nod, and a muttered apology (how glad I was later to have uttered it, even if they did not hear!) I spun on my heel and marched from the grove, dashing the wet ferns away from my face with awkward gestures. The scattered drops dripped down my cheeks.

Behind me, I heard Hellenore saying, "Don't speak ill of Telemachos!"

Perithoös spoke in a voice of surprise. "What is this?" (which I took to be a sign that she had not had in her mind what to say before she spoke).

She said, "I foresee that my family will bring more pressure to bear against Telemachos, for my father suspects he knows the secret places where we meet. He will bear it manfully, and not betray us, though his family will suffer for it. You have chosen your friend well, Perithoös."

Perithoös said, "Ah. Well, he actually chose me."

She murmured something softly back. By then I was out of ear-shot.

My dial marked sixty hours passing while I descended the icy slope into this land, Place Where the Silent Ones Kill, and I slept twice and ate of the tablets three times. The altimeter built into the dial measured the descent to be twenty-two thousand feet. During the middle part of that time, I passed through an area of cold mists where the air was unhealthy, and left me dazed and sick.

This area of bad mist was a low-hanging layer of cloud. The cloud formed an unseen ceiling over a dark land of ash cones, craters, and dry riverbeds, lit now and again by strange, slow flares of gray light from overhead. The ash cones in this area were tall enough to be decapitated by the low-hanging clouds. I spent another thirty hours wandering at random in this land, hoping to stumble across some feature or landmark I would know from my memory-dreams.

Once, a flickering gray light of particular intensity trembled through the clouds above. I saw the silhouette of what I thought (at first) was yet one more ash cone; but it had a profile; I saw heavy brows, slanting cheeks, the muzzle and mouth-parts of a Behemoth, but huge, far more huge than any of his cousins ever seen near the Last Redoubt. A new breed of them, perhaps? It was as still as a Watching Thing, and a terrible awareness, a sense of sleepless vigilance came from it. It was taller than a Fixed Giant, for the dread face was wrapped partly in the low-hanging clouds, and wisps blew across its burning, horrible eyes. How one of that kind had come to be here, or why, was a mystery before which I am mute.

I looked left and right. In the dim and seething half-light of the cloud overhead, it seemed to me that there were other Behemoths here; two more I saw staring north, their eyes unwinking. I traveled along the bottoms of the dead river-beds after that, hoping to avoid the gaze of the Behemoths: but now I knew the place I sought lay in the direction the giant creatures faced.

The gray light faded, and I walked in darkness for thirty-five hours. A briefer flare of gray light came again; and I saw, in the distance, a great inhuman face gazing toward me, and yet I saw nearer at hand, another Behemoth to my left facing toward him. By these signs, I knew the massive shadow rising between me and that far Behemoth was what I sought.

The colorless light-flare ended, and all was dark as a tomb. But I felt a faint pressure, as of extraterrestrial thought reaching out, and I feared the Behemoth facing me, over all those miles, had seen me.

I crept forward more warily. The ground here was becoming irregular underfoot, sloping downward. I walked and crawled across the jagged slabs of broken rock I found beneath my feet and fingers, ever downward. I could not see enough to confirm whether this was a crater-lip.

After another mile, ground changed under my hands. Here there was ash and sand underfoot, for soft debris, over the aeons, had filled this crater-bottom. I was able to stand and move without much noise, and I waved the haft of my weapon before me in the dark as I walked, the blade unlit, like a blind-man's cane, hoping it would warn me of rocks or sudden pits or the legs of motionless giants.

After an hour's walk or two, under my boot, I felt smooth and hard stones. Stooping, I traced their shape in the dark. They were square, fitted together. Manmade. A road. A few more steps along, I felt something looming the utter dark near me: by touch, I found it was a stele, a mile-stone cut with letters of an ancient language.

I knew the glyphs from former lives: the name spelled USIRE.

One hundred, two hundred paces further on, and my fingers touched the pillars and post of a great gate. I touched a bent shape that had once been a hinge: I touched the broken gate-bars, the shattered cylinders that had once been pistons holding these doors shut against the night.

Beyond the doors, I felt nothing but more sand, and here and there a slab of stone or huge column of bent and rusted metal. I sensed nothing alive here; no Earth-current pulsing through power-lines; no throb of living metal. The place where wholesome men dwell often will carry a sense in the aether, like the perfume of a beautiful woman who has just left the chamber, a hint that something wholesome and fair had once been here: there was nothing like that here.

Instead, I felt a coldness. I felt no horror or fear in my heart, and I realized how strange that must be.

I was surely near the center of where a ring of the Behemoths bent their gazes; even in the dark, I should have felt it as a weight on my heart, a sense of suffocation in my soul. Instead I was at ease.

Or else benumbed.

How very silent it was here!

Slowly at first, and then with greater speed, I backed away from the broken gates that once had housed the stronghold of Usire. Blind in the utter dark, I ran.

I was in still the open when the gray light came again, and slowly trembled from cloud to cloud overhead, lighting the ground below with fits and starts, a dull beam touching here, a momentary curtain of light falling there, allowing colorless images to appear and disappear.

I beheld a mighty ruin where once had been a metropolis; its dome was shattered and rent, and its towers were utterly dark. Here and there among the towers were shapes that were not towers, and their expressionless eyes were turned down; watching the ruins at their feet, waiting with eternal, immortal patience, for some further sign of the life that had been quenched here, countless ages ago.

More than merely giants stood waiting here. The gray light shifted through the clouds, and beams fell near me.

A great company of hooded figures, shrouded in long gray veils, stood without noise or motion facing the broken walls. They were tall as tall men, but more slender. The nearest was not more than twelve feet from me, but its hood was facing away.

There next two of the coven stood perhaps twenty feet from me, near the broken gate; it was a miracle I had not brushed against them in the dark as I crept between them, unknowing of my danger. Even as quiet as I was, how had they not heard the tiny noises I had made, creeping in their very midst?

Then I knew. It was not the noise carried by the air they heeded. It was not with ears they heard. They were spirits mighty, fell, and terrible, and they did never sleep nor pause in their watch. A hundred years, a thousand, a million, meant nothing to them. They had been waiting for some unwise child of man to sneak forth from the Last Redoubt to find the empty house of Usire, dead these many years. They had been waiting for a thought of fear to touch among them: fear like mine.

With one accord, making no sound at all, the dozens of hooded figures turned, and the hoods now faced me.

I felt a coldness enter into my heart, and I knew that I was about to die, for I felt the coldness somehow (and I know not how this could be, and I know not how I knew it) was swallowing the very matter and substance of my heart into an awful silence. My cells, my blood, my nerves, were being robbed of life, or of the properties of matter that allow physical creatures such as man to be alive.

I turned to flee, but I fell, for my legs had turned cold. I made to raise my forearm to my lips and bite down on the capsule, but my arm would not obey. My other arm was numb also, and the great weapon fell from my fingers. Nor could my spirit sense the power in the metal any longer, despite that the shaft and blade were still whole. The Diskos was still alive, but I wondered if its soul had been Destroyed, and feared I was to follow.

Then I could neither move my eyes nor close them. Above me there was only black cloud, lit here and there with a creeping gray half-light. A sharp rock was pushed into the joint between my gorget and the neck-piece of my helm, so that my head was craned back at a painful angle; and yet I could not lift my head.

The Silent Ones made no noise, and I could not see if they approached, but in my soul I felt them drifting near, their empty hoods bent toward me, solemn and quiet.

Then the clouds above me parted.

I saw a star.

Whether all the stars had been extinguished; or whether the zone of radiation that surrounds our world, transparent in former ages, had grown opaque; or whether there was merely a permanent layer of cloud and ash suffocating our world, helping to slow the escape of heat, had been debated for many an age among savants and knowledgeable people. Of these three, I had always inclined to the last opinion, thinking the stars too high and fine to have been reached by the corrupt powers of the Night Land.

That the Night had power to quench the stars was too dread to believe; but that the stars should have the grace to push aside the smog and filth of the earth, and allow one small man one last glimpse of something high and beautiful, was too wondrous to hope.

I cannot tell you how I knew it was a star, and not the eye of some beast leaning down from a cliff impossibly high above, or some enigmatic torch of the Night World suspended and weightless in the upper air, bent on strange and dreadful business.

And yet more than my eye was touched by the silvery ray that descended from that elfin light; I saw it was diamond in heaven, indeed, but somehow also a flame and a burning ball of gas, immensely far away; and how such a thing could have a mind, and be aware of me, and turn and look at me, and come to my aid in my hour of need, I cannot tell you, for diamonds and flames and balls of gas do not have souls; but neither can I tell you how a hill, shaped like unto a grisly inhuman thing, could sit and watch the Last Redoubt of Man, without stirring and flinching for a million years. Is the one more unlikely than the other?

I felt strength burning in me, human strength, and I raised

my head.

The coven of Silent Ones was here, but the blank hoods were lifted and turned toward the one star. The thoughts, the cold thoughts of the Silent Ones were no longer in me.

A fog was rising. As mild and as little as the light from the star might have been, it somehow made little fingers of white mist seep up from the sand.

There may have been a natural, rather than a supernatural explanation for this; but I doubt it. Like a veil, the pure cloud rose to hide me from the enemy; the delicate rays of this one star still shined through these pearly curtains, and illuminated them, and made every bead and hanging breath of the mist all silvery and fair to see.

If this were not supernatural, than the supernatural world should be ashamed that such wonders can be wrought by merely natural means, by star-light, and little water-drops.

While the Silent Ones were closed off behind a wall of fog, I picked up my weapon and crept away. I was blinded, so I followed the star. Here and there about me in the silvery mists, I could see looming shadows of the Silent Ones, terrible and motionless. And yet they did not sense me, or do me hurt, which I attest is starkly impossible, unless but that one of the Good Powers that old tales said sometimes save men from the horrors of the Night had indeed suspended the normal course of time, or relaxed the iron laws of nature out of mercy. No one knows these things.

The star led me to where a little stand of moss-bush spread. Beneath the bush was hid a door, set flat into the rock underfoot; and one of the leaves of the door had been forced inward a little way against its hinges. The crooked opening was large enough perhaps to admit a man, or the small nasty crawling things and vermin of the Night Lands, stinging snakes and centipedes, but too narrow to let any of the larger brutes or monsters pass in.

The star went out, and the mists that hid me began to part. I saw tall shadows slanting through the mists, and feared the Silent Ones were drifting near.

I doffed my helm and breastplate and undid my vambraces, that I might be lithe and small enough to squeeze in through this crack. It might have been wise to drop my armor into the crack before I went in; but wisdom also warned me not to make a clatter, so I pushed the armor plates beneath a moss-bush, where (I hoped) they would not be seen.

The edges of the door scraped and cut me; I was blood-streaked when I fell into the dark place beneath.

Of the wonders of the city of Usire, I have not space to say. Let it suffice that there were many miles of rock that had been mined out to form the fields and farms beneath the dome, and that the dome itself, even broken, was a mighty structure, many miles across, and half a mile high. There were places where the feet and legs of the Behemoths had broken through the roof, and I would peer out across a shattered balcony to see the knees and thighs of rough and leprous hide, knowing that somewhere, far below, were feet; and the palaces and museums, fanes and libraries of Usire, a great civilization of which the folk of the Last Redoubt know nothing, lay trampled underfoot. Many layers of roof and hull had been shattered in the footfalls of the giants, back, ages ago when the giants walked; darkness and cold had entered in.

I found the doors of orichalcum I had seen so often in my dreams.

The images carved into the right-hand leaf of the door were as I had seen them, exactly (now that the memory came back to me) as I had carved them in a former life.

The right-hand door was of the past: here were sculpted images of star-farers landing their winged ships on worlds of bone and skull, horror on their faces as they came to know our earth was the only world remaining in all the universe not yet murdered. The fall of the moon was pictured, and the sundering of the earth-crust. Here were the Road-Makers, greatest of all the ancient peoples; and there were the Cliff-

Dwellers, whose mighty cities and empires clung to endless miles of chasm walls, during the age when the upper surface of earth was ice, but the floor of the great rift was not yet cooled enough for men to walk upon it. Here was an image of the Founder, tracing the boundaries where the Last Redoubt would rise with a plow pulled by a type of beast now long extinct: and this was a legend from the first aeon of the Last Redoubt; and twenty aeons and one have passed since that time.

The left-hand door held images from the end of time: the Breaking of the Gate was pictured here, and the severing of man into two races, those trapped far below ground, and those trapped in the highest towers, when all the middle miles of the Last Redoubt were made the inhabitation of unclean things that wallowed in the darkness. The tragedy of the Last Flight was pictured, millions women and children of the Upper Folk attempting escape by air, in a winged vehicle like those used by our earliest ancestors; the image showed the winged ship, buoyancy lost, falling among the waiting tribes of sardonic abhumans, the loathly gargoyles, and furious Night Hounds.

The time of the Final Thousand was shown, when all living humans would know not just their own lives, but the lives of all who came before, so that each man was a multitude; each woman, all her mothers.

Here was a picture of the Last Child, born by candlelight in her mother's ice-rimmed coffin; there was an icon of the Triage. Three shades, representing all the dead fated to fade from the world's dying aura, were bowing toward the wise-eyed child proffering their ghostly dirks hilt-first. Any shade the Last Child shunned, had no hope of further human vessels for its memories.

The final panel of the furthest future, which formed the highest part of the left-hand door, showed the Archons of High Darkness, Antiseraphim and other almighty powers of the universal night, seated on thrones among the ruins of the Last Redoubt; and while Silent Ones bowed to them; and the Southern Watching thing fawned and licked their dripping hands; all the books and tools and works of man were pictured heaped upon a bonfire around which abhumans cavorted; and the greater servants were shown eating the lesser servants at feast.

These images were fanciful, mere iconography. The Ulterior Beings have no form or substance, no shape that can be drawn with pencil or carved in stone. Nonetheless, the doormaker carved well the nightmare scene, and I knew what she meant to portray.

There was on the right, in the past, at highest part of the door, an image directly opposite the image of the triumphant powers of darkness at feast. Here, golden, was the many-rayed orb which was meant to represent the Last Sunset, which was the earliest legend of the earliest time, and, in the foreground, here was the mother and father of mankind, holding hands sadly and watching the dusk; the man was pictured with one hand raised, as if to salute, or bid farewell, whatever unimaginable age of gladness had ruled the upper air before that time.

I was cheered to think that, even then, my ancient self who made these doors had not considered the days of light tò be a myth to be ashamed of.

I put my shoulder to the cunningly carven panels and pushed.

They were the doors to a museum, of course.

Here I found the dusty and rusted wreckage of broken stalls and looted displays: tarnished machines, broken weapons, dead glasses, and empty bookshelves. But in the ruin was one machine, shaped like a coffin, still bright. Light came from its porthole.

This casket was a type long forgotten in the Last Redoubt, able to suspend the tiny biotic motions we call life, each cell frozen, and carefully thawed again by an alchemy that revives each cell separately. These once had been used in aeons when men ventured into the Void, but those who slept to long in them came out changed, troubled by strange dreams sent to them from minds that roamed the deepest void between the stars, and loyal to things not of earth.

Inside the casket was Perithoös.

I wiped the frost from the porthole to peer inside. He was horribly maimed; scar tissue clotted his empty eyesockets; his left arm was off at the elbow, a mere stump. No wonder he had never attempted to find the Last Redoubt again: blind, maimed, and without the Capsule.

A few minutes search allowed me to find a spirit glass in an alcove; I brought it back and connected it to the physician's socket by means of a thinking-wire cannibalized from an inscription machine. I tilted the glass until I caught an image of Perithoös in it. And there, shining at the bottom of his soul, tangled in a network of associations, dreams, fears, and other dark things, like a last redoubt, besieged by fear yet unafraid, was the thing in us that knows and recognizes the master-word.

I whispered the Master-Word. The shining, timeless fragment in his soul pulsed in glad recognition.

Human. Perithoös was human.

The Master-Word stirred something in him. Even though he was frozen, his blood and nerves all solid, there was sufficient action in his brain to allow his thought to reach through the armor of the coffin and touch my brain:

You came!

"I came."

It was not unexpected that even a frozen man could still send and hear thoughts. If this method of suspending life could have also suspended the spiritual essences of life, and kept them safe, the star-voyages of early man would not have ended in such nightmarish horror, for the space-men would have been deaf to the things that whisper in the dark of the aetheric spaces, and would have returned from the void whole and sane.

Slay me and then slay yourself. We are surrounded by the powers from the House of Silence.

"I came to save you, not to kill you."

I merit death. I slew Mirdath.

"Mirdath? She lived and died many generations ago."

Hellenore. I mean Hellenore. My only love; the fairest maid our pyramid ever knew. She was to be my bride. And I also slew her child. The child in the womb reached out and touched my mind, and told me things I should not have heard.

"Your child?"

No. A creature who carried her off to the Tower-Without-Doors and violated her; things were done to her womb to permit her to conceive a nonhuman.

I winced at the thought. "What creature? An ab-human?"

No, though it answered to them. The bridegroom was a thing bred or made by the arts of the House of Silence, in the centuries since the fall of the Lesser Redoubt.

I knew that when that Redoubt fell, out of all those millions, only Mirdath had been saved. Of the rest, not all of them had been allowed to die without suffering, especially not the women, and most were put to pain of the type death does not ease.

"You call it a bridegroom? She married it?"

The abhumans mock our sacraments. You know why.

I nodded. It is not enough that we die; that will not satisfy them. They must make the things we deem precious seem grotesque and ugly, even to us, so that there is nothing fair left in the world. (I speak of the lesser servants, the ones once human. We are not in the thoughts of the greater ones).

The bridegroom bit my weapon out of my hand, and tore off my arm, but the capsule buried in my forearm broke beneath its iron teeth, and venom filled its mouth.

"It died instantly?"

No. Its unnatural life stayed in its frame long enough to slay the rest of my men.

I killed the child with my thoughts, for its life was weak: but Hellenore, by then, had no soul to slay, and I strangled her one-handed while she clawed out my eyes. Such was my last sight.

Slay me, that I may cease from seeing it ever and again forever.

"Many a weary mile, I have walked to save you, Perithoös, for I will not fail of the promise we made as children. Why did you call out to me, across all miles of the Night-Lands, if you did not wish me to bring you back into the warmth and human comfort of our mighty home?"

I cannot open the door.

"Do you mean the casket lid?"

The door that opens to escape from a life that grows intolerable. The door that honor commands men to use when all other doors are shut. You must open the door for me. You of all men know that there is something beyond that door, and that it opens back into this life again, but with forgetfulness, blessed forgetfulness, to quench the pain of memory. There is much I must forget.

A picture came from his brain-elements into the visual centers of my brain. It was an image of Hellenore, her eyes filled with childish faith in the man she loved. She raised a gauntlet too large for the slender hand that bore it, and tilted back a helmet too large for her, and raised her mouth for one last kiss, before she slid down a rope from a small window in the postern gate.

Away across the black and grainy soil of the Night Land she walked; and there she was, outlined for a moment against the glow of the Electric Circle; then she was gone.

She had not been moving as those who are Prepared are trained to move, skulking from rock to rock, or standing motionless to let one's gray cloak blend with the gray background, avoiding discolored patches of ground. She did not know how to walk.

And she dragged the great weapon behind her, for the weight was more than she could bear, and she wheeled it like a wheel-barrow on its blade; an image that would be comical, were it not so horrifying.

His thoughts were clear as crystal, sharps as knives:

She will not be born anew. The darkness consumed her. I have destroyed her forever. I sent her into the Night without a capsule, without the words and rites, without the exercises of the soul and mind, carrying a weapon she had never swung before, in armor too big for her.

More images. Perithoös had sent her out. He lowered her on a rope from a window in the postern gate and watched her walk away. His gift allowed him to chose a time when the portreve was one who admired his fame too much to turn him in, and the gate-warden he could blackmail with knowledge taken from the man's own guilty mind.

The enormity of the crime was too great for me to take in. I was overcome with emotion at that moment. The strength left my legs, and I sat. My weapon I put down, the first time it had left my grip in weeks. I put my head in my hands.

"Madness!" I said. "Madness. There were simpler ways to die, and ways that do not carry hundreds of dead down with you! Was she so jealous of Mirdath, did the law that forbids women to walk the Night Land offend her so much? Did she so much want to be thought more manly than a man? It was not enough for her that she was more fair than women?"

That was not the reason.

Eventually, I said softly: "Why?"

For love.

"What?"

Love. Surely that emotion excuses us from all limits, all law. We thought we could be together, here. We thought the stronghold of Usire would provide us some sanctuary against the Night, but that we would be far from the Pyramid, free to live as we wished . . .

"Madness! Would she step to the bottom of the sea without a suit, or play with lepers without an immunity? Ah, but you don't know about oceans or lepers, do you? All old things are dead to you, including the wisdom of our laws!"

Some old things I know. I gave her a harquebus from a museum, and brought it to life with the Earth-Current. I rendered it obedient to her with my thought. The piece was able to discharge a streamer over 900 yards, carrying a charge enough to kill a Dun Giant.

"You know why the ancients forbade us to use such weapons. The energy can be sensed from miles away, even of a single shot. Or do you? How little do you know of the world you live in, of what has come before? Why trick her into killing herself in such a foolish fashion? Surely it would have been simpler to throw her from an embrasure, or dash out her brains against a post, or bury her alive. Did you want to feed them? Feed the horrors?"

I was imagining her, surprised by a petty-worm or scorpion, touching off the voltage, and sending a lighting-bolt echoing across the darkened land. I imagined the thing we see shadowed in one of the windows of the House of Silence tilting its dark head toward the source of the energy-noise. I imagined Night Hounds, pack upon pack, swarming down from the Lesser Dome of Far Too Many Doors, baying as they came.

I spoke in a voice made hollow and weak from despair and disgust. How could he overlook what was so plain to see?

"No woman, ever, must travel in the Night Lands. Here are monsters to slay us."

She thought she would foresee them, or that my spirit would warn me ere they came near. And. . . . And. . . .

"And what?"

I had prepared everything for us, a capsule she could carry in her poke, an instrument that would lead us to where the Stronghold of Usire was, by the traces of Earth-Current it still gave off. If the instrument sensed nothing, we would turn and come back home; and so there was no risk-we thought that the monsters would stay clear of any land were the Earth Current was running. And if we found this place, we could reconnect the White Circle to the Current, sanctify the ground, and erect an Air Clog of our own, stronger than that we had left. It would have been, not as safe as Home, but safer!

"You sent her off by herself? By herself?!"

I meant to meet her before the hour was gone! Less! Forty minutes, no more! Time enough for me to descend and escape out of a wicket, carrying the other gear. I had to stay behind to joggle the power, or else the Air Clog would not have parted for us.

From a low window, we had together picked the rock where she was to hide and wait for me; it was less than eighty yards from the gate! Eighty yards! She could not have mistaken the rock; we had studied every feature lovingly. She could not have mistaken the rock! It was cleft like a miter, and one part jutted like my sister Phaegia's nose.

He said more, much more, then; many excuses, much sophistry. I could not make myself heed his thoughts. My own thoughts were too loud: I kept picturing what it must have been for her.

To be trapped in the darkness of the outer lands, being hunted by Night-Hounds, to have the eyes of inhuman beings searching the unending night – and then, after hunger and weariness and nightmares and false hopes – to be found by the Cold Ones, and taken to their secret places, and to have one's nervous system laid open, and all one's intimate thoughts laid bare. And then to be raped by unclean creatures, and then to marry one's rapist. And all this time to wonder why one's own beloved, one's true love, the beloved you trusted and cherished above all others, to have him merely abandon you to this fate . . .

I was walking up and down the aisles of the ruined museum, looking for an axe or heavy bar. It was not something I meant to think, but I was looking for something to smash in the casket lid, and expose the freezing innards to the air. (Even in may anger and turmoil, I note that it never occurred to me to use the Diskos on him: it is something we only ever swing against monsters. I do not know if any human person has ever been struck with one.)

Perithoös broke into my endless circle of thought: *I tried! I was prevented! I wanted to come after her immediately. That was our plan, but –*

I pounded my fist against the portal where his frozen, maimed face was held in ice. The noise was loud, but the glass held, despite the hardness of my gauntlets.

Like water bubbling from a holed jug, my anger left me. Men who have eaten nothing but the tablets for weeks do not have stomach enough to stay angry.

I sat down again.

"But you were arrested by the magistrates, weren't you?"

Yes.

I said: "They granted clemency on your promise that you would venture out after her. Has the world gone mad? You mocked the law that says no woman ever may venture into the Land; they mocked that law that forbids a man of unsound mind or unfit character may go. You were but a callow youth, perhaps that can excuse; but they were judges. Men of the law!"

The judges thought that no punishment the hand of man could mete out would match this.

"And no one else could trace the screaming, her voice you could hear in your head, back to the source: they needed you to find her."

The Silent Ones let her scream so that others would come forth from the Pyramid and be Destroyed. They opened their barrier to let my call reach you for the same reason.

I nodded sadly. And the Silent Ones would have had me, had not one of those Powers that no one can explain intervened.

You know I betrayed you.

"You were afraid the Silent Ones would destroy you unless you called others children of men out from the Last Redoubt. It is an old, old trick. An old fear."

A fear you do not share. What is wrong with your thoughts? Why are you not afraid?

"I was spared."

The Silent Ones will not permit us to leave this place! I am wounded and blind. How can you hope we can cross the Night Land together? Hellenore said she saw many pairs of boot-prints leading out, but only one coming back in. You will live; not me. It is fated.

I said "Fated. I don't understand why Hellenore went forth. Were her visions of the future unclear? Did she have some vision that told her she was to be a wife and mother, but it cruelly deceived her?"

I deceived her. She saw what was to come. I told her not to believe her visions.

"Why did she listen to such a stupid idea?"

Because you deceived her. You convinced her that fate could be changed.

"I said the opposite; that we must endure what could not be changed."

She was convinced of that, too. Even when I talked her into venturing forth, in her mind there was nothing but grim resolve. Women sacrifice much and suffer much to become our wives, to bear our children; nature inclines them to endure great sacrifice.

"A sacrifice for what? For what gain? She knew that bloodshed and destruction would spring from her going-forth. What-"

Something like laughter came from his frozen brain. *She saw far, far into the future. Isn't it obvious? I found the shaft. I reconnect the main leads. I restored the power. As I had planned from the start. But it took me months.*

"What do you mean? What – ?"

Are you an idiot? The casket is powered. The Earth Current is alive here, still strong, but deep, deep beneath the rock. And so the victory of the dark powers here is not complete.

You must return to the Last Redoubt with this news: if they drive a shaft deep enough, and at an angle to find the sources directly beneath this spot, the Last Redoubt will live out its promised span of life five million years hence; otherwise we fail within a few hundred years.

The engineering needed to drive a shaft so many miles to find so small a place might be beyond the powers of the present generation of men; but there would be generations to come. The gardens, and fields, and mines beneath the Great Redoubt were so extensive, that, compared to that work, what Perithoös proposed was not an insurmountable matter.

I cannot explain why I laughed. The laughter was bitter on my tongue. I said, "So all our proud and vain dreams of returning as a heroes will come true, won't they? We will be lauded. I can think of no more just punishment for folly, than to have foolish wish come true."

We?

(I admit the word surprised me as well. It just slipped out; but, once I had said it . . .)

"We."

I am blind and crippled, and wicked besides.

"You are coming with me."

If I return to the pyramid, the magistrates will condemn me to death.

"And so your wish shall be granted! Or perhaps the law that you may not stand twice for the same offense will forbid a new hearing. If judges still uphold our laws, which seems not the fashion among these modern folk. In any case, it is their affair, not mine."

Why do you not bestow the death my acts have merited? Have you no sense of justice?

"Well, obviously, not so much as I should have. A just man would have not answered your plea."

I felt a stirring in the aether, as if he were gathering his brain-elements to send a thought, but the thought was too confused, too full of shame, to send. Had his face not been frozen, I wonder what his expression might have given away.

"You put me on trial, didn't you? You pretended to misplace the Master-Word. If I had been a man of justice, obedient to our laws, I would have been safe, and never answered you. I failed your trial and you condemned me to death and annihilation at the hands of the Silent Ones. Your justice condemned me; but something spared me. I wonder why. Why was I spared?"

You knew *you should not come. Why did you come?*

I came because I am a romantic fool, the kind of fool it is easy to fool. But he had asked the wrong question.

"Don't ask why I came. Ask why had I been *permitted* to come. Ask why the cunning of the House of Silence did not prevail. A miracle was wrought to permit me to be here. My certain destruction and doom was set aside. Why?"

I saw now why the star had parted the clouds to touch me, and to restore my life to me.

It was, at once, a reprieve and a punishment heavier than I could imagine: for my punishment was to stand, in relation to Perithoös, as that star had stood to me, and save him. To be his friend, despite all his crimes, all his foolish pride and boastful madness, to be his friend nonetheless, and save him.

Perhaps the Good Power that had saved me meant to save the Last Redoubt as well, to let the message go though telling where an other vein of the Earth-Current could be found in the shrinking core of the planet. But, somehow, I doubted it. The things that seem great and momentous to men, I am sure are of little matter to the Ulterior Powers who sometimes protect Life.

I knew the words to start the rebirth-cycle for the coffin, and how to adjust the feeds to bring the Earth-Current back into his body, so that uneven thawing would not mar him.

I picked up my weapon again, and leaned on it. The Earth-Current within the haft was aware of the current flowing in the casket: a phenomenon spiritualists call affected resonance. It felt good to have the warlike spirit of my Diskos propping me up at that moment; in a former life, I owned a boarhound, and his loyalty had been the not unlike this.

Perithoös touched his mind to mine again, but weakly. His

spirit was faint, for his aura was being drawn back close to his flesh in preparation for the decanting, he would sleep many hours before the lid would open and he would wake. But I heard him.

I don't understand.

"How can you not understand me? You see my thoughts."

I see your thoughts, but they are senseless.

Strange. My thoughts seemed perfectly clear to me.

The same madness that drove Perithoös into the night was the only thing that might save him from it. The love that binds friends or brothers is no less real than that which binds wooer and beloved. The power that saved me surely knew what a boastful and foolish man I was: But mothers do not strangle their babies if they are born lame; the stars do not cease to shine on us if we men cripple ourselves.

And I should not abandon my friend, whether he was a true friend to me, or not.

Men' souls are crooked and unsound things, not good materials out of which to build friendships, families, households, cities, civilizations. But good or no, these things must be built, and we must craft them with the materials at hand, and make as strong and stubborn redoubt as we can make, lest the horrors of the Night should triumph over us, not in some distant age to come, but now.

We are surrounded by the Silent Ones. We are fated to die. One of us will perish before we regain the pyramid; Hellenore saw only one pair of footprints leading back. How is it possible that we both shall live?

But by then the cycling process was too advanced, and his thoughts lost focus. Many hours must pass before I would open the lid, and answer his question.

As I carried him on my back, out past the golden doors, I lead his blind hand to touch the bas-relief on the left panel of the golden doors.

Here was the panel carven long ago by Hellenore in a former time, was a small depiction of one small event on what, to her, had been the future, now our present. Here was a man without a breastplate or helm, wearing only gauntlets and greaves, carrying a one-armed man on his back; a blindfold (but I knew now it was a bandage) covered his eyes.

The image showed a star shining down on them, and the gates of the Last Redoubt opening to receive them. Only one pair of footprints led in.

Meanwhile, She Dreams

Brett Davidson

Meanwhile, she dreams. She dreams of ochre and gold tiles, diamonds and darts, that rustle in her eyes like autumn leaves and are autumn leaves caught in an eddy of winds, like . . . she has never seen such a thing – but she remembers. There is a flash, so bright, of something blue, and then she wakes. Fragments of the dream that is itself a fragment linger. Blue, gold, the wind against the bare skin of her face and something bright. There is something so very bright that it sears, a light that looks like, is like, liquid metal, droplets falling into her eyes, burning holes in her retina and leaving scars of color that chase themselves across her vision.

She cries in pain and terror and her mother hears her and comes into the room and comforts her, and with gentle hands brushes away all trace of that terrible dream.

This is when she is a child. Too often, to her mother's horror, the dreams are of a longing to be Outside.

There are patterned tiles in her thoughts as she awakes on this day. It is years later and she is a novice Scholar and she does not speak of her dreams.

Her mother married a hero and now she is a widow, thankful that she has successfully guided her daughter into scholarship and that she will never repeat her mistake. While Scholarship it is not a lucrative vocation, it begets and requires an aura of stability and propriety, and she must not speak of her inner life and the unarticulated hopes that it engenders.

Leaving her domus for the gate court of her clan complex this morning, she pauses for a moment at the vine wreathing the portals. She and her girlfriends had raised this vine, this darling-vine, tending it from a mere cutting from the Underground Country until it grew to wreath the doors and columns and became the Fey tree of their cohort. As is her right, she plucks one grape, and its flavor is an explosion of sweetness in her mouth. It tastes of her childhood and the childhoods of all her friends now grown. Perhaps it tastes like liquid sunlight, she thinks and leaves the compound. Perhaps it is a parting kiss from home.

She wears a veil in the passages of the city. Where there is no distance to provide space and privacy and she can never quite shut out the static of the minds around her, concealment and disinterest are the minimum of good civic manners, and no one ever admits to penetrating a disguise.

"Ilde, ex Timarchos," she says to the guardian at the Initiates' Portal of the city library, giving her name and clan affiliation as she always does. She proceeds through the maze of crazy-tiled passages to the office of the Magister of Assignments. There she is given the access codes for the reports compiled by the Monstruwacans that she has been told that she must read and catalogue this week. As she continues deeper into the inner windings and convolutions of the library, she sneaks a look at the titles, and whistles quietly when she discovers that one refers to events outside in the Night Land.

Despite the eternal tension of the siege and the occasional furious moments of battle, life in the Land is slow and any happening is rare and extraordinary. It is however a rule that, over the plains of time, even the most improbable thing becomes a virtual certainty. Seen from the height of the Tower and from the inner coils of the libraries, the hills flow like wax and even the Watchers creep. The marvels of centuries swirl and accumulate in great drifts of information and then become an unstoppable torrent. Inside, safe and quiet, deep within miles of concentric shells of metal and seeing only books and patterns about her, she feels a brief sense of vertigo as the aeons spin around her head. If asked, she would admit to being thrilled.

She finds her favorite view table and calls up the reports. She disposes of the routine ones first in a remarkable display of restraint, but savors the thrill of anticipation as their dull statistics flicker under her fingertips. Finally she comes to the crucial, solitary, one and allows herself to think rather than react.

It is indeed no pedestrian description of a patrol along the inner perimeter of the Air Clog, but of a strange and terrible sighting in the Land of a peculiar beast. She almost licks her lips.

The narrative has a broken, breathless style as if the man who has given his testimony was delivering it with his heart still pounding hard against his ribs, his breath coming in brief and rapid pants making his words mere gasps. Maybe that was the case. She reads hungrily.

The cadet and his company were on one of the rare patrols of the external perimeter of the Air Clog and they came across a new growth just by the path from the Great Gate. This thing, she reads, was like a bush, apparently. A fractal perhaps, probably. Branches branching, making an ambulatory thicket. It appeared first as a shadow against the ground, then rose up and spread its horns, fronds, dendrites. They at first assumed by its structure that it was a pneumavore, but it seemed to be made of recognizably solid matter: black glass perhaps, or maybe its surface was wet. In either case, it was dark and it gleamed. Reflections ran over it as it moved, or that could have been the effect of corpuscles of phosphorescence moving under a transparent skin.

There seemed to be no center to it, rather there were many thicker trunks that connected only to each other instead of a recognizable torso or body. Each limb divided and divided again from masses as thick as the body of a man to the finest of filaments, finer and softer than the antennae of moths. They rippled as if in a breeze, but the air was still.

Ilde shakes her head. If only there had been another survivor, she thinks. Then the tale might have some more coherence in the cross-reference of testimony. Or perhaps not.

Her criticisms are unkind, she knows. It is almost incredible that there was even one survivor, and an inexperienced cadet at that. He straggled behind the others a little. It was his slowness that saved him and he is very grateful for his life. She should be grateful too.

She reads on.

One filament touched the cheek of a Watchman and he screamed and froze. His nearest companion tried to brush it away with his hand. It was a foolish gesture: seeing that the dendrite caused pain at least, the man should have swung his diskos and severed it instantly without touching it even through his gauntlet. Instead, he too was caught.

Things happened quickly from this point. The thing had apparently tasted them and liked their flavor because it flung out stouter whips, ensnaring more men before they could react. The threads spread over their armor, weaving amongst their plates, and through their flesh as well, no doubt. They were soon entirely bound up in the fabric of the thing and drawn within. The plates of their armor came apart, were conveyed towards the edges of the thing and fell with a ringing tones upon the earth.

Within, the witness said still more haltingly, the skins on the men were peeling too, and underneath their skins, amongst the fibers of the muscles and veins and in the pooling blood, the black threads were spreading and seemed to be turning red themselves as if they were becoming like veins and muscles. This thing was a spider's web that was the spider itself, or vice versa, he said. Perhaps the Watchmen were not merely being torn apart, they were being eaten, and perhaps instead of being eaten, they were somehow being incorporated into the body of the creature.

Do not interpret, the interrogating Monstruwacan had said. *Only describe.*

Very well, the cadet had said. There was one last thing before he broke the spell of his terror and was finally able to bolt.

And what was that?

Around one branch and its divisions, he said, he saw rings and a bracelet. They were carried as if they had been worn on a wrist and fingers, as if the branches had once been a wrist and fingers and were now transformed.

Do not interpret, the interrogator repeated. The cadet was dismissed and the report concluded. The Monstruwacan's own interpretations follow, expanding on the cadet's testimony.

As she reads this report now she despairs a little, wishing that she had seen this thing with her own eyes, even if only from a balcony high above, through a telescope. The man of the Watch who saw this thing was still half mad with fear and he frequently contradicted himself within the space of a sentence. She wishes, if she had not observed from above, that she could at least have spoken to him herself, to tease some sense of the real facts from him, but it is not permitted.

Stories themselves evolve in the telling. They are collaborations between teller and listener, and, as she thinks she would tease the story out of him, so she would, she would spin her own tale in listening. He would watch her eyes, losing himself in them, seeking to synchronize his thoughts with hers even as he was sure that he was imparting some objective truth and so they would confabulate.

The Land is so alien that everyone who returns is desperate to heal the breach between their own experience and the ground of their essential humanity in the home realm. The Scholastic archivists are charged to collect and sort and store their reports, but they are forbidden to hope that they could understand for themselves or corrupt the witnesses' tales with reflections of their own imagination. Tentative interpretation is left to the Monstruwacans as their privilege, though they call it a curse, and very likely it is a curse. Together with the Scholars, in smooth concert, they assimilate the events of the Land, as that monster had apparently assimilated the Watchmen.

Around her, Ilde feels the thoughts of her colleagues, observations and impressions spilling out of their minds in a faint, incoherent static of fragmentary and overlapping qualia. *"Monster,"* she says, the word slipping unintended from her own lips. She is an untidy eater of books, always spilling fragments of ideas as she feeds on them. This word in particular is a fossil. It has survived almost as long as there have been words and it means *omen.* The Land is a place of monsters. *"Monster, Monstruwacan,"* she says. Indeed, she thinks. The guild that watches is the one that reads omens. Therefore they are the Monstruwacans, who watch and eat omens.

She sighs, obliquely and ironically reconciled to her task's necessity, if not its significance. Disappointment corrodes her sense of wonder. Even if this witness had seen clearly and spoken clearly to his captain and the Monstruwacan interrogator, to classify this thing would be pointless.

It was a unique wonder, and it existed in a world of myriads of solitary and wondrous and ever-changing things that altered by their own impulse or were changed from without. What appeared to be the case with this beast is known to have happened in the past to other adventurers. They had been recognized only by the fragments of armor that they still wore, those pieces themselves corroded with strange patinas and softened like wax.

Some of these ab-humans seemed to remember their former state still, though they could speak of nothing and only seemed to know that they must return, though the purpose of return had been lost with their identities. Better that they died, and so they had been swiftly killed in every case.

Had this beast been a former comrade of the cadet, a cousin, an ancestor? If it assimilated the men, was it changed by them as it changed them? The perverse idea strikes her that perhaps these transformations are not afflictions at all, but adaptations. She shudders once and again at the unexpected thrill of it. What would it be like to be outside?, she wonders, flirting with the evil thought. She is half-sick of shadows of real darkness. What was it like Out in the Night Land?

As if in response, she hears what could almost be the wind whistling about the walls of the Redoubt, but the outer walls are over a mile away in every direction.

Everyone in the libraries thinks as she does at one time or another, which is why it is forbidden. Novice and even experienced Scholars can risk forgetting themselves and long to see the origins of records instead of caring for the records themselves. Worse still, they might ache to become creators of records and become adventurers. And so some do; they walk from the skirts of their Mother Redoubt and mostly, they die. If they return, if they return safe and sane and as whole as were when they left, they are no longer Scholars but witnesses.

What skill a Scholar has in the exercise of disinterested objectivity, however flawed and partial, is vital for the preservation of records over the millennia, because in such time, like the hills and like the Watchers, truth will creep.

Everything is strange today and everything means too much for Ilde to bear. No more work can be done today, and so she rises and leaves her table. She will be back tomorrow. There is, after all, plenty of time, she tells herself, and instantly feels that she is lying.

Her inarticulate wanting without object troubles her and she visits a hall of clocks, hoping to be calmed by the neater and more abstracted cycles on show there.

The clocks held in the halls of the libraries are not mere

curios. Though some are of quaint and impractical design, they are also the pacemakers of the living Redoubt, setting times in a sunless age. There are several atomic clocks on display, but none of them work now. While they were exceedingly precise and accurate, they were ultimately abandoned because they were abstract contraptions, unable to convince anyone that the digital figures that they displayed had any connection with the real world – or that there was a real world with which they were connected.

Ilde looks at their cases and their blank display windows. They died of rhetorical failure, she thinks.

The mechanical clocks may still only refer ultimately only to themselves, but they do it with some conviction, being open calculating mills wound by hand and with visible pendula and sliding, clicking mechanisms supporting complicated analogue dials and orreries. In their ranked niches along the hall they tick according their various tempos, the sound combining and interfering in waves, like the sound of the breeze in the trees and the massed songs of the crickets she had heard on visits to the Underground Country. She has a pet cricket herself; she likes to hear it sing, and decides therefore that she likes these clocks.

There is another presence, distorting the mental silence of the hall. She looks around and sees him, a man in a uniform of the same deep blue as her own. She has not seen him before and there is something curious about him, as if his garb is a disguise.

She watches from a distance for a while. He is, like her and almost everyone outside of a book illustration, albino-pale, though his eyes are of the common sort, onyx to her carnelian. His body language and her own inner sense tell her that he knows that he is being watched, but he will not risk his dignity by acknowledging this. The two of them stand in their mutual tension for a while. His undefined peculiarity strikes an obscure chord for her as though he were as misplaced here exactly as she feels herself to be. This at least makes him interesting, if only as someone to whom she might talk without the risk of her words circulating unfettered amongst her colleagues.

Should she speak to him?, Ilde asks herself. She almost doesn't dare but decides to gamble on an overture nonetheless. She has no rank beyond novice reader and cannot demand that he perform any assignment for her, so she simply walks up to him. Courage rests largely on appearance in such circumstances, she decides.

"Who are you?," she asks bluntly.

"The custodian horologist of this library, named Oughtred, Respected Lady," he says formally. He pauses a moment, noticing her eyes, making her blush. "Ex Parzsal," he adds.

She nods. She doesn't know of Clan Parzsal, but she can find out easily enough. She gives her name and affiliation too, but cannot think of anything more to say. So much for appearance, so much for courage.

The man comes to her rescue. "I maintain the clocks, I ensure their synchronization and I have even designed a few myself."

"Oh," she says clumsily. He will lose interest in her at any moment; she is just being silly and it shows. "Tell me about this hall, these clocks. How do they last so long? Do you repair them? How can you know about all of them. . . ?" Now she is chattering, so she shuts up.

He smiles, disarming and renewing her embarrassment at once. "The answer to at least one of your questions is yes," he says. "And I do know how each of these clocks is made," he adds, letting her know by his slightly wry smile that he is an actor improvising a role for her. "I have the plans for them all filed away, but if they were to be burned or corrupted, I could still remake them. Each displays its workings, showing every part clearly. There is a great deal of repetition of form and proportion in each design too, so that if some piece were to be corroded or warped beyond recognition, I could probably reconstruct them through deduction alone."

"You are very proud of yourself," she observes, a little critical. He seems somewhat suave, but she has detected a vein of nervousness under his façade.

"Oh no," he says. "I am very respectful of my predecessors. They designed these clocks with every contingency in mind.

I could die without having trained an apprentice and it would make no difference in the long run, because whoever walked into this hall could eventually train themselves in the art of horology."

"So do you train an apprentice?," she asks, raising an eyebrow. She is falling into her own role now.

He grins. "Not yet."

Ilde grants him a warmer inflection to her sardonic expression.

"Come, look at this," he says, gesturing. She bends down, keeping a decent distance, and looks to where he points and peers into the stacked rings of the calculating mill. As she watches, a wave of movement passes around the tiny pins and levers with a fluttering motion and the whole ring rotates by an increment and the dial marks another hour.

"Those pins," the man says, "several of those pins were worn out last year. I replaced them all and I didn't even need to look at the plans." He points higher up, at the dial itself, a magnificent mandala of concentric rings around a gleaming convex plate of dark metal ornamented with pearly white dots in an apparently random pattern. "The star map is two hundred and eighteen years old. The bronze ring indicating the position of the sun in the sky, where it would be if we saw it shining; that ring is ninety-five years old." He points down, indicating the torsional pendulum caged within the base of the mechanism and rotating to and fro gently. "Those weights have been there for nearly three thousand years – but not on the same spokes."

She is impressed. Indeed he is isn't boasting, but he is proud, and she likes the sort of pride that has been earned through study. "So how old is this clock?," she asks. "It's older than its oldest component, is it not?"

He nods. She has asked the right question. "It is, yes, nearly the full ten thousand years of its intended span. But that isn't even an appreciable fraction of the age of the Redoubt itself."

"No, of course not . . ." They walk on, steps falling together, and they pass other clocks, all of essentially the same mechanical heritage, but different in their principles of display. Some have armillary spheres and orreries upheld from their mills like cybernetic bushes. They simulate the now invisible Solar System, or at least extrapolate what its probable configuration would be had the sun not died. She knows that some people visit this hall and cast horoscopes from these machines, thinking that black worlds swinging on imaginary orbits through the houses of dead constellations could still pull the strings of their earthly lives.

Some clocks are visual puns. One tropes the Great Redoubt itself, linking its pyramidal form with that of a metronome. Another is small tetrahedron, quite exquisite and bejeweled; plainly it is a representation of the long-lost Lesser Redoubt. Despite the object's beauty, she feels an instinctive aversion to it and will not ask about its history.

Instead she asks the man about his own history. He is, after all, not of the usual kind that she sees in the library and she is curious.

He used to serve the Watch as an armorer, he tells her, making diskoi for them, and now he makes and remakes clocks for the Colleges. "In a way, it's still the same craft," he says. "A diskos spins quickly and a clock turns slowly, but they must both rotate precisely and they both turn more or less the same number of times before they wear out."

Imagine that, a clock turns like a diskos. Fast or slow, it's all a question of perspective. She is genuinely interested.

"Do you have a diskos?," she asks. She has never seen one.

"It is not permitted that one be held outside of a Watch house," he says. This is not an answer.

The next day she returns to the abandoned report. The memory of the encounter is like a secret and she nurses it as such, warming herself as she works. She briskly appends her own comments in an appropriately clear and neutral tone, conducts a few searches of the library databases in order to make suitable cross-references, creates a catalogue entry and files the report where it will be recalled tomorrow or never. Finally she collects a few reports of similar past manifestations in the Land, composes a brief article on what she perceives to be the essential common elements and forwards the bundle to the Monstruwacans.

She spends the rest of the day reading at random and does not visit the horologist. Instead she visits another place.

Nominally, the floors and ceilings of the thirteen hundred and twenty stacked cities of the Redoubt are separated by an average of just over nine yards. But some halls – museums, auditoria, civic assemblies, the old airship hangars and the like – rise to much greater heights and are shared between cities, their volumes pegging the individual planes and societies together. Circulation and exchange shafts for people, air and freight further complicate the simple stratification of the pyramid, threading its near eight miles of altitude above the Land, and there are shafts that lead a hundred miles or more down into the depths of the Underground Country.

Of these spaces, over a hundred are high-ceilinged Halls of Honor, strung like beads in a vertical necklace down the throat of the pyramid. Ilde passes through one of these by habit every day after work to refresh herself with a few moments of quiet and stillness away from the chattering of minds and voices in the streets. Despite the time spent in travel and the conflicting demands of clan and guild, she would never be permanently domiciled in guild quarters as many Scholars have been.

Today, as she does on many days, she evenly paces the chasm of the hall, down the ranks of the millennial army, their features picked out in dramatic chiaroscuro lighting. In this form of history, humanity comes as close as it can now to a sense of the numinous. The things of the Night Land, such as the pneumavores and the Watchers, whose soul-twisting sight can be felt through miles of concentric shells of metal by the most sensitive, should be proof enough of what used to be called the supernatural, but there is something indelibly corrosive about their power. What is necessary is a sense of the human, and it is rich and warm here in the collective body of the Mother Redoubt and its people.

Some of the statues are of Monstruwacans who never left the Redoubt in their lives, save to climb the finial Tower of Observation. They are memorialized for no more nor less than such things as catching the barest echoes of the hypothetical thoughts of the Watchers or seeing shadows of whispers in the House of Silence. Lesser heroes would have been withered and many of these were indeed permanently scarred by psychosis. Their achievements are great, but inscrutable, and the more popular heroes are Watchmen and romantic youths who ventured directly out into the Land. She sees where their feet have been polished by the passing hands of thousands of passing devotees.

One statue is of a man in broken armor supporting the indistinct huddled shape of a woman in rags. Their features are too conventionally stylized to reveal much in the way of real persona, but she knows their story as well as does everyone in this city, even an hundred millennia after their deaths. He was the apprentice Monstruwacan who alone went to the Lesser Redoubt and brought back she, its last survivor.

Expeditions have been planned since their time but never launched, though there is a persistent rumor that the Monstruwacans have been breeding and training sensitives to scan the far regions with their minds. A physical expedition may be yet be launched, she thinks. Perhaps an airship could be reactivated and fly to distant lands. Perhaps even a spaceship could be reconstructed from old designs to explore the greater cosmos of the sky. She would even like to take part in such an expedition herself, which is a common fantasy of course, especially among those who inhabit the universe of memory that is the College library.

She strokes the feet of the entwined figures, wondering if she feels the communal sense of legendary charisma or something more personal.

Space is but black chaos, she tells herself, reciting a maxim of the guild. *Memory is the true cosmos.*

That night she dreams of the Land.

The dream is lucid and she is detached, knowing that it is a dream, having thoughts about the dream. She thinks at first that it was inspired by the report that she read that day, but it contains imagery that she could not have imagined.

She sees first a hand, slender and feminine, which she knows is her own while also knowing that it is not. The hand grasps at some roots or vines to steady herself. She pulls herself to her feet and looks around. She is outside, in the Land somewhere.

All about her is darkness, but isolated sources of light here and there, living phosphorescence and natural vulcanism, give just enough illumination to paint a landscape for her. It is composed largely of horizontals, making a plain as flat as she supposed a sea bed might be. Hot winds come out of the overall cold carrying the stink of sulfur, which makes her throat raw and her eyes water. Much of her skin is exposed, her flimsy city clothes only rags now, and when she is not almost burned she shivers.

Above all, her hearing is alert, because the blended shadows of this world make one vast cloak of concealment through which sounds give the most urgent hints and clues. Volcanic vents hiss and fume, and somewhere something cries. There are pounding footsteps somewhere and she crouches down to conceal herself, but knows that it will not be by sight that she is found. She probably does not have much time left, she was lucky to have lasted this long.

She turns back and sees, a different shade of darkness, a great metal pyramid. It is entirely unlit by its own energy, but delineated by the light of one of the eruptions behind it.

Is this the Last Redoubt?, she wonders. Has it fallen? Is this a prophecy? No, she decides, it is not. Huge as it is, this is not nearly as vast as she knows the Last Redoubt to be.

She hears in her mind a whisper, but a true voice to her night-hearing nonetheless. One word she hears: *"Mirdath,"* and it wakes her.

Another frustrated day passes. On her way home she walks through an older part of the library which is being renewed. Workers are laying new tiles on the floor in the customary style of the Archives.

The tiles are aperiodic and while patterns are seen to emerge at various scales, they are all incomplete and infinitely variable. This is a lesson, she is told, or a lesson has grown to explain this style, which may have simply begun as a caprice. It shows that simple forms can compel complexity, and that therefore while a Scholar will suppose that time runs in cycles and that all changes blur into one continuum, one can also be reassured that within this continuum there is a refuge for uniqueness and freedom.

There is a contrary interpretation, of course, and that is that all the variation at a distance blends into a warm autumnal unity. This is supposed to reassuring too.

There is another simpler story about the tiles: since the cities are all rigidly square, and roofs and floors and shelves are absolutely parallel, some ancient architect decided that a little skewing of the angles is a healthy thing.

Ilde smiles to herself, her eccentric mood persisting. Reading her own lesson from those tiles, she might be tempted to skew her records. But as every lesson leads to another, they remind her that perhaps ultimately, whatever individual freedom she steals, it will be lost in the greater field of variation. Is this the constancy of the Archives, then? Is it all variation without truth?

She visits Oughtred the horologist again. She cannot pretend that the meeting is an accident this time and it should attract attention and censure for any number of reasons, though the Magister Dean of the College Library is a gentle and understanding old man who would most likely offer a few suggestions about the necessity for a chaperone and the exercise of appropriate discretion. She is not sure if she wants their meetings to be frequent, but certainly the occasional meeting that she chooses to think of as casual seems to suit her needs for the time being. They are, she admits, a distraction from her fruitless doubts and questions.

They talk about matters that are more philosophical than professional, and he laughs at her jokes and she smiles at his.

He is, it turns out, an enthusiast for debate as well as time-keeping, and they play board games of his own devising where allegorical pieces are moved about complicated boards to enact elaborate abstract arguments. This man is not ignorant tradesman, but an elite artisan who has become good at his craft because he has understood why he must be good, and he takes an artist's pleasure in an exercise that has been well-resolved.

Their mutual activity pleases and stimulates her more than adequately after all. Perhaps then a chaperone would be appropriate? She smiles and decides that she will not engage one, at least not yet. She flirted with one sin and now she decides to indulge herself with another. The thought unfolds a question of consequence: is she using him for her amusement? She chews her lip, almost saying something.

The horologist has not yet learned to read her thoughts from her dial, but he knows that something complicated is turning within her and he shows his concern. She blushes and looks away, but she cannot help letting so many pieces of her thoughts slip out and she blurts out her request: "Do you have a diskos, a real one? My mother would never take me to see the Militia shows, I've only seen pictures and statues and I want to see something real." Damn her face and tongue!

"It is not permitted," he tells her for the second time.

"I know that. I know also that you are not answering me," she insists, feeling nonetheless that it is grossly unfair of her to press the point. But it is too late for regrets.

Reluctantly he nods. "Follow me," he says, rising.

She should not do this, she thinks. There are so many stories about what happens to women who follow men into secret rooms. But she tells herself that the two of them are simply members of the guild working side by side, sworn to behave decently with one another. She senses has no cause to fear – at least she no cause to fear what she has been told to fear.

The workshop that he keeps behind the hall is small and not particularly tidy. Plans and components lie about in no order that she can discern, and the documents themselves, she sees, are merely scribbles, prompters for the memory rather than precise construction diagrams. He could be either a casual incompetent or a very conscientious man who has trained his own memory to invisibly permeate and encompass the contents of this shop as thoroughly as a vine. The latter is almost certainly the case, and she is sure that if someone were to tidy someone were to tidy up the place, he would be unable to find anything.

He offers a seat and turns to a particularly cluttered bench, brushing metal shavings aside so that they fall glittering to lie amongst the dust on the floor. He sees her looking downwards and misinterprets her expression. "Don't worry about that," he says. "It'll be swept up. They sweep up everything here."

"Of course," she agrees, knowing libraries and their dust well. Here, even dust is not waste but a resource to be cultivated. If it is not swept up today, it will be swept up in a year, and if it is not swept up in a year, it will be swept up nonetheless eventually and the metal shavings will be mined again one day from great hoppers of dust that has been collected from myriads of trivial sweepings. They will find their way into the foundries, melted and poured into ingots and then they may be milled and made into more clocks and diskoi a thousand years from now. Nothing is ever lost in a closed system.

He shifts a few tools and rags to reveal a long box. He picks it up and sits on a stool with the box across his knees. "Here," he says. It is as stained and scratched and as unremarkable as any of the tool boxes lying about, hardly portentous. "I made it for myself and nobody noticed that I took it when I left the Watch."

His black eyes look into hers and his pale, long-fingered hands lie across the lid like moths. Those are an artist's hands, she thinks, not a soldier's, unless a soldier is an artist.

"Will you open it?," she asks, knowing that he is still reluctant to do so and trying therefore to prise it open herself with a little gentle mockery.

"Oh," he says, as if he had forgotten. "Yes." He opens the latches and raises the lid

Inside, the diskos lies on a bed of velvet, curved and as

placidly beautiful as a sleeping scorpion. It is over a yard long, two spans across its circular serrated blade. The light catches it and sparkles and she sees her own coral eyes reflected, making ornament unnecessary. She reaches forward into the box and touches the mirrored surface of the thing. It is cold and she withdraws as if shocked. One pale smudge of a fingerprint is left behind.

"I don't know if I dare," she says, laughing nervously.

"It's not heavy," he tells her. "It's not live; you won't harm yourself – or me."

This is not what she is thinking.

She reaches in again and grasps the handle, which is wrapped in narrow braided strips of black plastic. They are unworn: this weapon has never seen combat. She lifts it up and it is indeed surprisingly light. Standing and backing away to give herself some space, she lets it swing loosely at first like a pendulum and then raises it, trying to get a sense of its use and trying to imagine the ozone tang and flashing blue nimbus of a live blade. She does not know, despite the reports that she has read, exactly what she should imagine, and so she parodies herself, striking poses that she has seen in children's book illustrations.

It is his turn to laugh now. "Live, the spinning blade has a powerful gyroscopic effect, and has to be swung perpendicular to the axis of rotation, otherwise you will find it resisting you," he explains. "Rather than hacking, you weave it about yourself in a spiral or looping zigzag motion, and then you will find it an advantage. But you have to develop quite powerful arms and shoulders to be fully proficient in its use. Women generally don't have the necessary upper body strength, unfortunately."

She shrugs, concealing her disappointment, but suddenly imaginary afterimages weave colored helixes in her mind's eye as if she remembered the sight of combat after all. "Why aren't you still a Watchman?," she asks.

"I never was. By temperament I was a dancer, not a slicer. I was too much the artist, so I made rather than wielded diskoi."

"Why did you leave?"

He shrugs. “Is there any one reason for such decisions?”

“There often is one that stands above all the reasons for staying.”

“Then I had too much imagination,” he admits. “If I could not see the Land and live long enough to make sense of what I had seen, then I thought that I would see if I can know it by other means in a library. I’m no historian like you, so making clocks is the best that I can do.”

Does he envy her?, Ilde asks herself. She had never thought of that. “You are a good horologist, aren’t you?,” she says, suggesting praise that she doesn’t know how to offer directly.

“I am, yes.”

She nods. Her mother would approve of this man, she thinks; he is not a hero, but that is something she certainly will not say. “Do you have doubts, regrets?”

“Of course. Everyone has doubts.”

No, not everyone has doubts.

“What are yours?,” he asks.

She decides to trust him, though she presents her words as a joke. “Suppose someone mistook everything that they saw, or told a lie, or played a practical joke on me and gave me a children’s tale. Suppose that a word that meant one thing to me meant its opposite years ago or a file had been corrupted? Suppose anyway that ultimately none of it has any cause or pattern at all and our libraries are all filled with nothing but pointless fantasy?”

He laughs. “Suppose indeed,” he says. “Suppose that I had made a sprocket with the wrong number of teeth and that what the clocks called a millennium was really only a week!”

She laughs with him and then is quiet and chews her lip. Why does she swing to seriousness and then hide in her silly jokes? She feels awkward, flustered, and she wants to leave but will not. She often wishes that she could read the emanations of other minds with a useful discrimination, but now of all times, she wishes that she could read her own.

Suddenly, Oughtred is more serious again. “I have heard a rumor,” he says.

“Oh yes?,” she says guardedly. She feels the need to share confidences with him, but she also sworn to confidentiality on many things.

"I have heard . . . it's more of a legend . . . that the experiments that lead to the entry of the pneumavores and all the other things . . . that the catastrophe was not an opening of reality that let them into our world, but one that took us into theirs. Do you ask this question? Do you think of what that may imply?"

He sits back and she is silent herself, wondering about what he has just said. He has knowingly or unknowingly shown something of his own secret needs for confirmation to her, and they are no longer mere philosophical correspondents. The both of them want not truths as such, not bare, dry facts, but a truthfulness that is woven of honest and easy need that is simultaneously a bond of profound trust. Each has decided that the other is the window for their secrets and there has never been anything 'mere' about their relationship at all.

It is almost inconsequential that she has asked this question herself, come up against walls of secrecy and honestly does not know the answer.

He tells her that he wishes to make a clock that counts not from past to future, but sideways, to see how far the Redoubt has diverged from the line of its true history. It is almost a joke, but he has made plans and he shows them to her.

She finally excuses herself and hurries home, grateful that the customary veil hides her face from passers-by. A chaperone should be engaged immediately, she decides. If there is a bond, and there is a bond, it must be tempered and it must be trained to grow like a vine on a trellis like her Fey tree, so that it may be fruitful rather than become a disorderly and choking weed.

This is what she wants, but she has been infected with her habit of secrecy. Suddenly, and she never thought that she would, she envies those who have had arranged marriages, where all has been open from the beginning. She catches herself at this point: the word *marriage* has caught in the delicate turnings of her thoughts and of course it slips from her mouth. She coughs to confuse anyone who might have overheard her.

In a dream that night she is in an airship, looking down on the Land. The vision is brief, but astonishing. Someone is with her, his arm around her, his hand resting in the soft curve that lies between ribs and pelvis. Below her the Land, so often described as parts and pathways, becomes a great pattern, just like a tiled floor, but more random, with no segments like any others at all, yet clear for reading and understanding as any map. It is like the view from one of the balconies that must have been in olden times launching stages for the airships.

She has an acute sense of vertigo because she moves and the view shifts. It is as if the Redoubt were toppling over, and she starts, and indeed she does fall: out of her bed and on to the floor.

She lies motionless for a moment, tangled in the sheets with one leg still awkwardly crooked up over the side of the bed. Only her cricket in its cage will have seen her, but she feels ridiculous, and carefully climbs back into bed. She tries to get back to sleep, not least to dream again, and perhaps see the face of the man who was with her.

Dreams compose themselves not only of happenings, but of knowledge also. In a dream, one is sure of many things that make their contents eminently sensible. In this dream she knows that she and the faceless man are lovers and she knows that it is some time in the distant past. Certainly it was in the very distant past because while the Lesser Redoubt fell an hundred thousand years ago, the last airship flew millennia before even that time.

She hopes, but she does not sleep.

What inspired this? Hangars still exist here and there about the perimeters of various cities, but their outer doors have been welded shut and reinforced and the spaces themselves converted to residential purposes or storage or made into gardens. Her own guild maintains a few as museums, and she has seen the plump delta of an almost intact airship that could have been readied for flight outside should the word come. But the word has not come, of course. She once inspected its cockpit and sat for a while in the pilot's seat, but the sight of the blind instruments staring back at her was too disappointing to be endured for long. She never visits these mechanical tombs now.

Despite what she knows and what she doesn't know, she feels that there is an essential link between the dreams that she has had, that there is something constant about who she is and who he might be. Is it just the fantasy of a lonely girl? It doesn't feel like a fantasy. It is in the nature of illusions that credulity is a part of the perception, as one of the essential maxims of the Scholars' guild has it, but she doesn't believe that in this case. She is sure that the dreams are real and that what she knows is true and she wants to know more.

She stares at the ceiling, hating it for her wakefulness, and lets her hands creep lower under the covers. This warms her for a while.

The next day in her free time, she lets herself be driven by impulse. As she wandered into the hall of clocks and learned new things, perhaps she will wander into another hall and add another unexpected dimension to her knowledge.

She imagines that her choice is random, but the hall where she finds herself is too significant for that charade. In the library adjoining the historical archives and reading halls, there are the offices that contain the records of bloodlines. The population of the Redoubt is vast, but it is also finite and over enough time, as there is always enough time, inbreeding is a risk. Therefore all matings are registered and checked for viability. She has seen more than one couple denied license because it was found that both bore the same gene for some fatal condition.

In the past, genetic engineering might have ameliorated their risk, and indeed in this time it does. But rather than making changes in one generation, the Eugenicists of the

Redoubt conduct their work over centuries, guiding clans and bloodlines together and apart by subtle means; sponsoring some alliances, barring others, taxing and rewarding unions. It seems obscure as a lottery to some and she wonders whether the Eugenicists have the same doubts that she has and whether they too have some equivalent of the lessons of the tiles.

She makes herself busy and finds her own Clan Timarchos records. Her options are unlimited, she finds, though her mother has already told her this – or rather her mother had told her that her genetic options were unlimited, despite the peculiarity of her eyes, for what that was worth. Perhaps it is worth something now.

She puts a hand over her mouth as she smirks, thinking that she is being silly. The records of Clan Parzsal flicker across the view table under her fingertips almost by accident.

A few days later she is back in the horological hall.

Some of the instruments are artworks, Oughtred explains, their function lending itself easily to allegory, like his games. Peculiar automata waltz about in a few of the more whimsical specimens. She closely inspects one which at first looks like a scribble of overlapping and eccentric ring segments crossed with a chess board. It has human figures standing on the rings, like planets on the orreries, and they wear stylized costumes. One has a motley pattern not unlike the library's tiles, but more colorful, and another in is baggy white, ornamented with a tiny black cap and pom-poms. Judging by their tracks, they and others in the mechanism will dance about each other, emerging from hatches and concealing themselves singly or in pairs, seen and unseen by the others.

"This is one of my favorites," Oughtred says. Of course it is, it is just like one of his games. "It has a basic cycle of just a week, but each cycle varies slightly. These figures meet over and over again, but never in quite the same way. It is called the Harlequinade Clock, or the Dancers at the End of Time."

"Harlequin? Is that the name of the designer?"

"Nobody knows."

People carried by cycles, powerless in their compulsions. The thought is unbearable and suddenly she must flee this man. Behind her departing back he is frightened himself, because, of course, he desires too: and in her mind it makes a great, hollow sound.

In another dream, again the landscape moves beneath her, but it is seen from a lower perspective than that of the airship this time. She stands on a balcony that vibrates slightly under her feet. A man touches her arm and whispers in her ear. It is him again, she is sure. She drinks a chilled wine and gazes expectantly at a red glow on the horizon. Downwards, at the base of a great black cliff, she sees churning dust and a cracked paving of some sort that slowly slips underneath and appears to be consumed. She is a passenger in some mobile structure, some lesser redoubt that crawls along a road. Looking up again, the glow beckons and warms her just a little. Is there some immense eruption occurring there beyond the rim of her sight? Should they not avoid it?

Her mood is strange, one of longing and anxiety; not fear of this thing, but fear rather that she will never reach it. The wine is no consolation, though the touch and the voice might be. She feels the warmth of his breath on her cheek and they leave the balcony together and in the half-light she almost sees his face.

A quick and almost unnecessary survey in the library reveals the era of this dream. It is of a time when the sun still shone, albeit dimly, and the earth still turned, though slow as a century. The cities of the earth proceeded on tracks circumnavigating the globe to remain in eternal sunlight and the time was called, plainly, The Age When the Cities Went Westwards. That was over twelve million years ago.

Ilde rests her hand on her chin, thinking. Are these dreams

memories of who I was in past ages?, she asks herself. Are our souls reused over and over like the dust? Has the bloodline of humanity simply assimilated me as those Watchmen were absorbed by that beast? Do they dream within its veins now as I dream my life within the Redoubt?

The lesson of the clocks and the dancers and the blood and the dust is that time is cyclic, but what cycles are being measured? The clocks display the orbits of planets that must surely be imaginary now. She has been told and she tells herself that there is enough time for everything, because there has been already, but the cycles also lead forward along a road to where they will one day end. The earth current winds the Redoubt, but one day it will fail and her home will freeze or a Watcher will breach the wall and it will see them all within directly with its own eyes and its seeing will unwind the springs of their being.

She knows that she did not ever go to the horological hall simply to see some happy demonstration of the certainties of her life. Her secret self drove her there because it wanted her to be further tempted to doubt and to wonder. The clocks are too sad for her, too finite. They are too sad for the horologist too, so he tries to lose himself in his games, his ironies and his eccentric designs. The Masters of the guild should never have assigned a thoughtful man to that position.

The Magister of Assignments feeds more reports to her, inadvertently encouraging her ruminations. There are more sightings of the thicket creature, and the Monstruwacans begin to make requests of a highly specific nature. Has anything like this been seen before? Has something similar in certain precise characteristics been seen? If so, how was it dealt with? The orders are transparent: they are surely considering a hunt. Shortly there will follow equests for personnel records, and candidates will undergo assessment.

Of course, this thing is no Titan and a single limited discharge of the earth current might obliterate it. For that matter, it is speculated that even the Watchers might be wounded if they so chose, but the order is careful, not willing to overplay its hand or upset the balances of the Land. In the millions of years of the Redoubt's history they have seen too many unintended consequences, and the reports will be considered for a time yet before any final decision is made.

The interregnum gives her time and impulse to think. She visits the hall of clocks. Oughtred is in the process of dismantling one particularly complicated mechanism. His deadline is close and he has no time to spare, even for her, and his regret is plain. She does not in any case want to speak to him after all; she only wanted to be reminded of his face.

Returning to her post, she feels as if she is part of a huge calculating mill herself, a sentient pin unable to be anything other than a pin. Eventually she will be bent out of true and dropped into the dust to be replaced by another, better pin. The thought is so bathetic that she laughs out loud at herself, attracting surprised glances from her colleagues. She blushes and bows her head to the view table before her again, but thoughts continue to turn and click. The process is almost unconscious, a cascading wave of insights and decisions that are so absurd that she will not name them.

She wonders if she is going mad and gets up, paces a little, attracting curious looks and stranger thoughts again, but she ignores them. Finally she runs to the office of the Magister of Assignments who hears what she has to say and sends her home with orders to remain there until she is called, in the meantime speaking to no one. That last proviso is a relief, sparing her a further, more stressful, confrontation.

Safe within her clan compound, she plucks a grape from the vine, the kiss of her house, but she does not speak to even her mother. She rushes to her private quarters, where she finally achieves some calm playing with her cricket. Its mind is a minuscule pinprick, almost as light in its touch as its tiny clawed feet upon the skin of her wrist. The creature is blessedly incapable of questions, merely an animated jewel, like a clock. She compels it to sing for her, then puts it away in its cage and retires to bed.

A few days later an expected call comes and she returns to work. Her mother, distressed by her silence, waits before the gate of the compound, but Ilde still does not speak and raises her veil, hiding her tears. Whatever happens, dear Mother, she thinks to herself, you will lose me too, in one way or another; and I am sorry, but what can I do?

Arriving at the library, she is met immediately within the Initiate's Portal by the Magister of Assignments, and he leads her straight to a private room. The space is well furnished and venerable, the walls ornamented with portraits and closed cabinets of a deep, expensive gloss. In the center of the room there is a deep rug and a semicircle of half a dozen chairs. A man sits in one of them, long, louche and elegant in rich, wine-purple clothing with delicate luminous embroidery. This is no uniform or formal robe, but she knows immediately that the man is a senior Monstruwacan.

He rises, smiling, and indicates that she should make herself comfortable. Awkwardly, she falls into one of the vacant chairs. The Magister takes another. While this room is no cell, there is no file to be opened and she is no prisoner, charm is the most insidious of tortures and the man knows this. She does not think for a moment that she will leave this room without something having deeply and permanently changed. Her face burns.

The Monstruwacan steeples his fingers, watching her beneath the blush. "Tell, me," he says, "why this request of yours has been necessary."

"Is it true, then?," she blurts.

"Is what true?," the Magister asks, disingenuously. The Monstruwacan silences him with a wave of his hand.

Slowly at first, she explains her suspicions, thinking of the cadet whose report she first read. Will this session also be pored over by some other junior Scholar? "The beast, the thing . . . you will hunt it?"

The man in purple nods. He does not blink, she notices. "That is a possibility that we are considering," he says.

"Why? Wouldn't you upset some balance in the Land?"

"That is also a possibility that we are considering."

"Why do you even think of doing such a thing? You never do this . . ." She stoops herself, realizing that she is being far too forthright, despite the allowances that have been made.

"Your thoughts are congruent with our own. To kill this thing would be a vital act of mercy for the spirits of those that were once human."

She is silent, never having expected such an open admission.

"Now tell me why you have requested to be considered to recruitment for any possible expedition," he asks. "Do you simply want to see the Night Land with your own eyes? Do you wish to kill? Do you wish to die?"

Strange currents are induced in her thoughts. She thinks that this may be her own reaction, but it is possible that he is stirring her mind himself to see what will float to the surface.

She pleads, pointing out that aside from the Magister she has been the principle nexus of communication on the matter of the beast. The Magister nods reluctantly, admitting that this is the case. He is embarrassed in front of the Monstruwacan and does not want to be seen to have acted rashly. She admits that she has never learned the skill or built the physique to handle a live diskos, but as a de facto specialist on the creature, she might direct the Watchmen or be consulted by them in some way. In her nervousness she almost lets slip the fact that she has handled a diskos nonetheless.

The Monstruwacan shakes his head sadly. "It is not a matter of skill, or intelligence or knowledge," he says. "It is not even because you are a young woman. Survival in the Night Land depends on a thousand subtle skills of awareness that can only be acquired through long training and experience . . . and then we would have lost your true talent." He looks at her sympathetically. "You were chosen properly," he adds, with an offhand glance to the Magister, who is visibly relieved. "Your perceptions were accurate. Your compilations were thorough, elegant and even . . . imaginative. We will need your attention and insight yet."

So she is a perfect pin after all, Ilde thinks bitterly, but not truthfully.

There is a sense of unslaked curiosity about the man, but he is also cautious and patient. She is more than a simple component in the apparatus of the Archives, but he has not yet decided where he shall put her, so he will wait until he sees more.

"I endorse your current assignment," he finishes, trying to be kind, and she is ushered out of his presence.

The Magister radiates satisfaction with himself. Incredibly, it seems that he has taken the Monstruwacan at his word and assumes that the inquiry is concluded and the judgment final. But she knows that he caught none of the underlying discourse. Objectively, things have gone well. She will not be disciplined, and with this positive attention she may well be promoted to a position of oversight or permanent liaison when this matter is finally concluded. But it feels like a humiliation nonetheless. Why did she even suggest such an idiotic thing? Talent is one thing, but poor judgment is another.

Freed for the day, though still sworn to silence, she is standing in the Hall of Honor among statues which will never bear her heroic likeness. Does she love that man, Oughtred ex Parzsal?, she asks herself at the feet of the man in broken armor. Does she love simply the idea of that man? Why did she try to escape from him in this way?

She curses this persistent melancholia. "*You are not he,*" she says, another spillage of thought. She looks around, unable to shake of the feeling that she is being watched, but thankfully she is alone.

The next day Ilde speaks to one of the sweepers in the

library, a woman she knows is of a clan allied to her own and on reduced hours leading soon to retirement. She is a grandmother, surely knowledgeable and forgiving and perhaps a little cynical in human affairs. "I wish to engage your services," she says. "My family is not wealthy, but we can pay nonetheless." The woman nods silently; this is not the first time she has taken such a commission and the two are a little familiar with each other in any case.

Ilde is pleased with herself, confident, and stumbles immediately. She finds herself confessing too much, as if the overfull cabinet of her soul has been unlocked and all its contents spill out. "I have secrets," she says. "I haven't told my mother . . . I, he . . . I think it will be something real, something of Mine Own . . ." and so on. The old woman still says nothing, but holds her, and with the pressure of her arms, she realizes that she is shaking.

That night she dreams too vividly again of past times. Is it poor consolation? Does she wish that she was that woman outside the ruins of the Lesser Redoubt, does she prefer to die as the Monstruwacan suggested? For a moment she hates the choices given to her, as if there were no other alternatives, no subtleties, no possibility of interpretation. She may as well hate the air that she breathes.

Will she then, in future, interpret? Will she now tell the Monstruwacans of her dreams, and apply for admission to their order? Will she watch the Watchers from the Tower? Will she present Oughtred with a grape from her Fey tree?

She might, she will.

Whatever happens, she realizes, and it seems to be for the first time that she knows this, she has been a child, and now that cycle has ended and a new hour will begin for her.

No more will she try to read trite and too familiar lessons from the dust and the tiles. This is the moment in which she will begin to make her choices rather than letting her life run in its old, youthful circles.

Time is running down, but it is not yet run out, and her dreams run backwards, each memory still older than the last.

That night, she dreams that leaves now vine green dance like the library's autumn tiles, and bright molten light drips through the fingers shielding her eyes.

It burns her, but it is beautiful and she realizes then that it is the sun.

Out

Andy Robertson

Nothing came from the Land, nothing showed itself. In most places the vegetation Outside grew thick, up to the margin of the force field: bushes remembering ancient habits of photosynthesis, competing for the trickle of light that the Circle donated. Here and there the thick tangles grew man-high, stopping with geometrical exactness in a curved line six inches from the Wall, as if the Land had created a boundary of its own, one made of dark moss-bush fiber. Other segments were clear, with the naked rock as bare as the trodden area Inside. But here, you saw the two sections were at different levels. The rock strata Inside had been worn down the depth of half a foot by the slow attrition of men from the Redoubt, coming here to check Her outermost defense. And there, just Outside, were the remains of the Beasts: a scattering of unique shapes.

"Are they watching us?"

"Always, something is watching."

The Circle was a thin tube, not made of matter, locked into the fabric of the ground below it. Above it, near the ground, the Air Clog, the Wall it anchored, could actually be sensed, roiling the air and humming very very quietly. The curve of the ring of light, eight miles across, was just perceptible. A little outside the incandescent line were the ancient traces of the other, broken Circles: Circles made of glass, of steel, of electromagnetism, of once-flaming plasma: defenses that had been overrun and reconstructed in the ancient past with apocalyptic labor, yeilding ground to the Land, a span in each Aeon

We paced beside them in order, along the Rim: three, then three, each with his allotted sector to scan. To our right loomed the Redoubt, Her brilliance toned down and controlled by the sentinel filters in our helms, so our eyes remained fully night-adapted. To our left, vista after vista of bleak rock, and rubble, and black haired vegetation, passing slowly.

And from time to time, one or another curious sight, near or far.

– ancient bones. The gigantic phalanges of some Titan that had sought to penetrate the shield, or had fled enemies, or had simply shown curiosity. Scattered and broken.

– a carious beehive structure, each cell half a fathom across, their broken conical open ends directed toward the Redoubt. Inside each cell were what seemed to be tiny tools or mechanisms

– a three-fathom wide scar on the ground just Outside, glass-smooth, iridescent, of unguessable source.

– what seemed almost a tree, a giant moss-bush thrice the size of a man.

– a slowly moving mist that bubbled from the ground, hovered, and swirled without dispersing, rearing high and then humping and flattening against the ground.

– more broken organic matter, shells or cast skins, overlaying each other in a heap. Something alive might, or might not, have been concealed beneath them.

– a pit of shards, slowly shifting, with a trickling tinkling sound that could just be heard through the damping effect of the Wall. Possibly a volcanic effect.

– the tusked skull of something not human, as high as a man. Shreds of skin still adhered. It was set up facing the Redoubt, and flanked by an ordered pattern of stones.

– bones tied together and set up in imitation of three set-speech runes: signaling *mist, dream, fire.*

– a strangely beautiful sculpture, of poised rocks thrice the size of a man's body

Now a long passage of quietness and silence, an hour of bleak, open, rock, the far shine of fire-holes, and drifting mists. Darkness above, darkness below, and only far shadows to glimpse.

Now, an attack: A thing like a writhing cone, four fathoms long, a scythed head followed by a train of legs and blades, rolling madly as it ran. It charged the Wall, directly toward us, but Scyrr watched impassively, not even caring to raise his weapon. An instant before it would have leapt the Circle the flash of the earth-current struck it, as its foremost palps contacted the field. It shriveled like a fly, and burst from internal steam pressure, flinging chunks of metal-hard chitin, some of which in turn hit and skipped off the Wall. All the men but I had shielded their eyes with their hands. Despite the Armorers' boasts, the helms were not quite fast enough, not quite smart enough. I was blinded for half a minute, and they laughed at me.

But we continued, past:

– a circular labyrinth of stones, of curious geometry, two furlongs across

– a structure of ice crystals, very slowly growing on one side and melting on the other, creeping along the ground parallel to the Circle, leaving a trail of frost. In three places it had tried to overlap the Wall, and been repulsed.

– a warping focus of dark-within-dark, hovering in the air.

– more hours of emptiness, and our slow tread.

Two quarters of the Circle had been surveyed when Scyrr raised his hand and signaled a pause. Ahead of us were three shapes. Living, not dead. Half again man height, standing in a quiet order, three abreast, equally spaced, only just Outside. They seemed like statues except for the thin plumes of their breath. Naked. Night-grey figures like men, but larger than men, thick-furred, watching calmly.

I expected horrors, and horrors they were: but as we came closer to them it was we who seemed estranged. They were not hostile. They did not move to attack, nor did they show fear. They were at peace, almost. We passed them, and they did not move. They only stared. Only their eyes shifted as we passed. Each picked one of us and stared into our eyes, and each of us stared back, helplessly, until Scyrr, one at a time, broke the link, taking our helmed heads one at a time in his hands and turning them each by force, chanting quietly. He broke us free of their eyes, and we continued, shying away from their gaze. But I alone strove to look back: and Scyrr struck my head, once, swiftly, a ringing blow that did not hurt.

Unstirring, they had sent us no message except their own being. Unable to look with the eyes of my body, I visited that message again in my memory, and found it haltingly interpreted to me thus: that, compared to them, we were strange and small things. Puzzling. Dwarfed, ugly. Trammeled by metal, soft inside. Stinking sweet, corrupt, filthy, brittle.

How could the Land birth such creatures as these?

*T*he last quarter of the Rim. The land beyond the Circle here was bleak, empty, sloping down to the Deep Valley and the ancient shimmering skeletal Towers. Beyond them loomed the Southwest Watcher, an unviewable segment of the horizon, automatically occluded by our helms, however we turned our heads. Nothing here but rock and bare land, not even a lichen or a bone, for three hours of slow march. But here and there, signs showed:

– a mouth of stone, open in a grin, puckering up from the Land in millennial mockery. An image-cast from one of the Watchers, slowly molding the ground.

– a long rod of black metal, seemingly dropped down without care.

– a network of blue glowing light, held aloft by a widespread scaffold of rock splinters, too far away for its details to be seen.

– broken armor: nightsuits of antique pattern, smashed and splintered, scattered in tens and twenties over a wide field, inhabited not by the vanished skeletons of their wearers but by darting tiny insectile things.

Then more bare bleakness, and the distant red and ulfire glint of fires, for mile after mile.

We completed the circuit. Scyrr turned, and saluted the Land.

We moved back, in order. We came to the Petty Door, now open ajar for us. One at a time, poised between the jaws of guardian energies, we Sent, evoking the Master-Word from our Souls in proof of our enduring humanity.

Spared by the fire, we reentered the last home of Man.

Inside. And the beat of the Earth-current filled my bones. The Petty Chamber was still cold, unpressurized, full of grit, but we were home. Light kindled about us. We unhelmed. And Scyrr smiled.

He extended his hand to me, while quick looks flashed between the others.

"Give it to me."

I gave him the stone. He turned it over and over, smiling.

"Respected Senior, Captain, father . . ."

"Never mind. What did she promise you? Is she pretty? Oh, my son, I am sure she is. But you will have to win her with another present. Not something unholy."

He laughed in his beard, lips red among the white, and spun round on his heel. He took the stone and flung it through the Door, hard, far, Out. The Door closed behind us, shutting Out the Night, and he put one hand on my shoulder.

"Come with me, my son."

"So, shall you to the Rim again?"

"In a fortnight. I have no choice, of course. But I'm not trying to pluck you another stone."

"Ah. Coward."

"It's wrong. Cahaire: I'm not afraid. But this is stupid. Every second tenderfoot tries it, on his first Patrol. Scyrr did not have to see me pick it up to know I'd have it in my cuff. And every man there laughed at me." .

She gave me a turned head.

"Cahaire, I – ah! – listen, I want to tell you what I saw"

"Can you not get comfortable?"

"If I don't let anything touch my back."

"Lie there a minute." She rose, and returned with a wide bowl of water.

"Are you mad?"

"You're hurt, aren't you? So it is quite proper for me to do this. *'My mother won't mind, and my father won't find out'.* If you keep your voice down, at least. Now lie down on your front."

"I got spanked, but I'm hardly a wounded hero"

"Oh, but do *lie down,* Bann: you are stubborn." And she tousled my hair, stroked my head till it lay low, slipped up my vest with a kind hand, and started to wash the stripes on my back. Very wifely-in-practice: and what a change. Daring, I tried to settle a kiss on her hip, from where I lay, and earned myself a ringing slap round the ear.

"I wish you would not do that." But I had to laugh, though laughing hurt too. "Scyrr cuffed me, on Patrol. That's worse. How would you like to have your ear clouted in front of twenty million people?"

"Oh? But there is no-one else here but us, and you can pay me back when we are married."

"Cahaire, I will never!"

"Well. Tell me, then. What is it like, in the Land?"

It is . . . it is not like it is here

If you have lived with any quietness in your life at all, you have heard the voices at the edge of your mind, calling.

Humming. Sighing. Here, Inside, at night, when you are asleep, or lying between sleep and waking, when it is quietest and most peaceful, you can hear the mind-murmur of the Folk, a voice too soft to hear awake, a whisper from half a billion Souls. And at night, when it is most silent and most peaceful, you can feel the blood of the Redoubt flowing through Her bones, through switching systems vaster than hills, along conduits thicker than the height of a man, splitting down to the tiniest wires: the Earth-current in its ancient streams.

Two voices there are, of Life. But in the Land, they are not. There is no life: there is only a void. But if you listen very quietly, very carefully, you will begin to think you can hear sounds in that void. Then cease to listen. If you stare intently, you will see the eyes: then cease to stare.

There are no dangers here, no perils Inside the Circle. The Wall guards us completely. I have seen things thrice the length of this room flash into steam when they brushed it with a limb: I have seen boulders greater than that, flung by Titans, puff into dust. Space is not twisted into other space, here, through the Doorways: the Eaters come not near. There is no danger. Even at the Rim.

There is only the Night. And the things that move, and watch, in the Night.

"What happened then?"

"Nothing, Cahaire. They but stared at us. And we couldn't look away. They were the strangest of all the things there. Stranger than the mouth in the ground. Stranger than the crawling ice castle. Because they were somehow beautiful. I think another eye might have seen them as beautiful. And they simply looked. I would ask one of the others, but . . ."

"Ask them"

"Practical. No. I must not. This is one of those things you learn by not being told. *'Selan, shelan, sim, saret, mavv, essnn, kyrr'*"

"What?"

"That is what he said, Scyrr said, when he made us stop looking at them."

"I . . . Say it for me again, please, Bann, and as clearly as you can remember it."

I recited, twice, and she listened, frowning.

The water in the bowl was tinged faintly pink now. She wrung one cloth out with small strong hands, half turned from me, spread it and soaked it again, continuing to listen; and the while, her feet peeked out, and her hair drifted and swung, and her shoulder blades slid across her back.

"When do you train again?"

"Tomorrow. Four day's rest."

"With your back like that? They can't . . . You cannot bear a nightsuit, armor, like that"

"I can, easily. It hurts at first, but after the first few minutes, it is nothing. It is part of you. It slows you a little, that is all"

I had not been excused ordinary duties or ordinary training: only the ranked combats in full armor, unlimited by any rules or constraints, which were the agon of each second day. Not a place for an unfit man. A nightsuit, composed of hundreds of pieces ribbed and fluted like living bone, weighs less than a tenth of your body mass, and will turn a live dyskos, in theory. That, we never tested on each other, for live weapons were too dangerous for unlimited combat, and the spinning disks were edgeless, buffered. But a blow could still flatten, could still do real damage to flesh and bone, however well protected.

The sweat burned. I had expected the deeper pains, but not that. But, past that initial sting, it was amazingly good to fight again. We matched, saluted, gave the cry, and fell to it, man to man. And once I had proper balance and integration the armor again ceased to be protection, ceased to be clothing, and became part of my flesh, not galling or hobbling me. I leapt, I span, joyfully, and I was only a little slower, only a little less quick, than I would have been naked. In return, the nightsuit glanced away every blow.

And then, something utterly new happened. It came upon me, and was not of my will. I went further Out. I fused completely with my armor and gear, and with the weapon I swung, and became one thing. Each gliding plate of metal, each joint, was as alive, as loved, as much part of me, as my own bones. The Dyskos was a limb of my own being. Distractions vanished. I became unaware of any damage or hurt, and totally aware of the position of my body, my limbs and head. My pain was not pain. It was beside me, not within me. I observed it, but it had no mastery over me at all.

I fought, I fought amazingly well. I scored higher in the mêlée than I ever had: but I did not care for my score, or for anything except the battle. I even challenged Scyrr, and got flattened, of course, but I held up against him a few seconds longer than before, I gave him a real fight, I saw him move and understood him in ways I never could have before, ways I could not explain to you in words. And when I fell, I was neither shamed nor stunned.

For a little while I was in That Place, as the masters name it: all one being. I was life. I was the Earth-current. I was blessed. I had touched on that state before, but never entered it. And without the pain driving me Out, I know, would never have gotten there.

But – when I came down from that plateau – when I unarmed – it hurt, and hurt terribly. As I slipped off the gauntlets and vambrace I felt the first return of indwelling agony. Then my whole back seized up, and it took me half an hour to strip to the undersuit, which I peeled off from my flesh an inch at a time.

Funny, almost. I was so ashamed, crouched there, fearing, trying to move, trying not to groan aloud. But there was no real damage, as I checked later. I suppose it was the reflex of my earlier exhilaration. Some necessary growth and movement within the Soul, a debt of pain, which had been set aside, now being repaid. But for a little while I was afraid to try again. Afraid of what it might feel like, when I fought again.

But you can't yeild to that, for if you do, even once, there is no end to surrender.

"So what will you do now?"

"To please you?"

"No, stupid sweetheart. When will you patrol the Rim again??"

"Soon. I told you. A patrol is every fourteen days. It is our City's duty this year . . . But I'm not getting . . . I meant it, Cahaire. Don't ask again"

"Oh no, I don't mean that. I was wrong to ask for that. I was a little spoilt baby." Other couples moved sedately in the half-dark, each flanked by a chaperone. Jewels and lamps and flowers glowed to each side, and the luminous patterns on the pavements shone and dimmed as human warmth shadowed them. She turned sideways, looked up and down the long Concourse: in this light her eyes were flashing black pools, echoed by her ornaments, while her moth, her white-fured Vhasti, fluttered span-wide wings softly round her, settling from time to time on her shoulder and unrolling a long tongue to lap from the cachet-broach there. We walked peacefully enough for a while.

"But it is this. I have read that spell, those words . . . *'Selan, shelan* . . . ' and so forth . . . and I think I understand what he did. And it is very interesting. We study these things."

"Do you? From where?"

"Everything is in the Library. Somewhere." She laughed. "The problem is interpreting it, and finding the truth in a billion lies and echoes."

"It seems to me you would . . . no, excuse me. I do not mean to be rude, but how can you tell what is true?"

"Perhaps we can't. . . . Oh Vhasti, come back!!!" The night-moth had fled, and was bumbling round one of the statues, trying to make love to a pulsing lit jewel. "Catch him, Bann!!" She laughed while I tried to call the moth with my lure, and then called him back herself. I made some conventional comment about her beauty moving all creatures, which she daffed off. “Boring man! No more of that nonsense. Listen to me!”

“Alright. You are ugly, and I am sorry.”

“That is better. But no, those words are known, I have seen them before, in many forms.”

“I did not know that. But I shall have to remain ignorant of those studies.”

“It would help you”

“No. I don’t wish to insult you. I am very thankful that you did this, but you should not have. You must not intrude here.”

“Why not?”

“How can I explain? You must not. We are Watchmen, not Scholars. I must believe that I am told what I need, and in the way I need to be told, and that I am kept ignorant in the ways I need to be ignorant. And the ignorance is important. There are words, and there is knowledge that does not come by words. Like a negative. A cutout. Black spaces. A pattern made by coloring in everything else. In that realm, words are stumbling-blocks. Don’t tell me.”

“I spent three days, searching. Don’t you want to know what I discovered?”

“Tell me what you did”

“I went to the deepest parts of the Library: half a mile in. I climbed through twenty stacks, unpicked the software of two obsolete search engines, and choked on bookworm dust. I got lost ten times. Old, crumbling books. Beetles running, the size of my hand. I swear there are men and women in that place who never emerge. I think they have passages to the other Libraries, in the Cities above and below us.”

“We know about them”

“Then why don’t you tell the scholars?”

“I was joking. There are no such passages. There may have been, once, but they have long since been closed.”

“You are not funny. You are broken-stupid.”

“Cahaire. Stop. Please. Why do I do this to you? You try to help, and I try to explain. And I anger you, and I think sometimes you cry tears. If I smiled and nodded, or only spoke sweet words and lies to you, would you love me? But I must tell you the truth. You must not tell me this, because if you do, it might kill me."

"Ridiculous. And I do not ever weep"

"Don't tell me. Please, you truly might kill me."

"You trust that Captain yours better than me?"

"In the Land? Yes. Of course I do. Cahaire, don't be so incredibly arrogant! He's been Out – beyond the Wall. It's true."

"But something is certainly happening, and I. . . ."

I turned, and signaled to the chaperone. She glided up, bowed, and moved between us. As etiquette compelled, Cahaire retired a little, stiff with rage, and left me to speak to her, while other strollers delicately avoided seeing us or hearing us.

"The lady is not pleased, sire? And I must conduct her home?"

"Yes."

"Shall we see you again?"

"You must ask her. Wait a day, please. She is angry"

"If I may advise, sire . . ." she moved closer to speak privately.

"Ask, respected lady"

"Sire, why do you anger her so? Again?"

"Respected lady, are you married?"

"Forty-three years in his arms, sire: and I love him as if I were yesterday's bride. That is why I am a matchmaker."

"Is it true?"

"What? As the mystes say? That we all lived before, and loved before? You are young, and in love, and you ask an old woman?"

"You are not old, respected lady. Come here" I bent and kissed her on her shaply lined cheek. She went as red as wine, and laughed.

"What shall I do with that? Give it to my husband?"

"No. Give it to her, please."

"Young man, it had much better wait. You Believe: so we are friends, believers in Love, and I will do my very best for you. Tomorrow I will approach her again, and if her mother consents, you will be able to see her again. But if you don't change, she will not endure this for very much longer. Love must rule you, it must rule you both, and nothing else at all. Sire, it will not do."

I bowed and left, looking behind me as I went, and seeing only her rigid back and turned head. I made my way to the commons and the brightly lit areas. Something strange was abroad, as Cahaire had hinted. In the Agora, in the streets, people noted my dress gorget and started toward me, ready to ask a question of an off-duty Watchman. I saw this again and again, from mere strangers: people to whom I had never been introduced, and who should never have approached me. And indeed they remembered their manners, and did not speak, but paused, held their tongues, and went on. It would have been different if I had been on duty, of course: they would have had the right to ask. But in any case, I would not have been able to tell them anything.

As it was the first question uttered came from a near friend: and I was happy to tell him that I knew nothing about new movements in the Land, nothing about any rumors, and to remind him that he could see a lot farther from his cushioned seat in a viewing gallery than I could, marching round the Rim. He complimented me politely, made smalltalk about Cahaire and my luck in getting her, and asked again: was anything happening among the leaders of the Watch? And what was Scyrr about nowadays? With the smile that seemed to touch everyone's face when they spoke of that great Hero. I remarked that Scyrr had had me flogged a week ago, for playing the fool: and that I had deserved it: and apart from that, I knew nothing. I am sure he did not believe me.

No chance of seeing angry Cahaire again today: no more work to do: I quickly became bored. I viewed the Land: I went and bathed, hearing more chatter among the men there, and went Home. I might have seen or visited other friends, but I wanted her, and as was usual and fitting my own stubbornness and arrogance was my own punishment.

I was alert for real news: I wondered what Scyrr was about, knowing that for all the theoretical humility of his position, he was a Master-spirit, a mover among the great of the Redoubt. But you cannot approach such a one with questions

I remember seeing him the next day, stripped to arm, before training. Above the plates of muscle that covered chest and belly was a crisscross of scars easily born; the marks of indriven, splintered, armor, negatived in his flesh still, seventeen years after his return from the Land; and the burns, and the places where acid or some ungessable poison melted flesh, the deep pits, the blurred shapes of the Surgeons' work. All carried like so much skin paint; all transformed, from wound to ornament, by Will.

Whatever pain he suffered . . . he was beyond noticing. Even when he slept. I might achieve it for a moment, but he was always in That Place.

In the mêlée session that followed I tried to recapture the spirit of what I had felt on my last days' training, and I failed, of course. If you try for it, it leaves you. It is not at command. So I merely fought as hard as I could, sheer slogging, and I did not go so badly. On my last match I lost the dyskos, smashed out of my hand, holdbuckle gone, and my whole forearm numbed: and instead of falling I wrapped up, hands over my ears, elbows before my face, and charged my opponent; felled him, straddled him, and unsnapped and ripped off his helm with my gauntleted hands.

Not conventional, but perfectly legal. I made an enemy, I think, but I heard Scyrr laugh behind me.

Later, he had something else to tell me, something else to say, and I had all the news I could stomach.

"Respected Senior – why me?"

"Because you are the best." he glanced around. By common conspiracy the other cadets had all vanished. Veterans occupied them in errands or chores. "You are fast and good, yes, but I have seen better. But there is this one thing: you obey, you don't question, and this of your own will: not of ignorance or humility or cowardice. Because you know that only one mind may guide a flank of men. All others must be limbs, hands and feet obeying. You do not need to be told this. That is why I select you"

"What is the mission?"

"You will not know that, of course. You will go to fight, not to understand. It is seventeen years since any of us were Out. Anything might pick it from your head."

"I cannot believe it"

"Beyond the Wall: a deep probe. If the Civitas agree. I will go. And each City puts forth one man. From our City, you. From these, thirteen hundred and twenty, two hundreds will be selected. Perhaps, perhaps, you may be among them."

"I don't know why I talk to you. I attempted to warn you, and you would not listen. You never listen. No decent woman, no woman of respect, would allow herself to be treated like this." She strode fast, with an angry face.

"But there is no honor like this one"

"It is death. Destruction. I know what is to be done. The investigations. Oh but it is another one of these things you must not know. Because you'll be 'wiser not knowing'. Stupid man"

"What is it?"

"I can not tell you. I am a girl, remember? Ignorant. These are big men's matters."

"You can't know"

"Not in every part. But every Scholar knows what they want to do. Because they have been talking about it, theorizing, at my level, for a decade and more, all through the colleges of the Redoubt. Since your marvelous Captain came back with nothing but his hide and some stories he like enough made up of his nightmares. And I tried to tell you. A sixty per cent chance of mission success. A thirty per cent chance of individual physical survival. A seventy per cent chance of avoiding terminal pneumasomatic Destruction: if the Eaters don't sniff our intentions out of a Watcher's mind and pith you all the instant they depolarize the Wall. Those are some estimates I have read. But what do I know? What does anyone know? You are mad. And you won't listen to me. You will not have any chance."

"I . . ."

"I can tell you what they want to do Out there. In general matters. I can"

"Don't . . ."

"Why not?"

"Because if you do I won't be able to go. The risk will be too great. I have a low index, but I cannot shield my mind, like an adept. I have to be ignorant. Otherwise I will broadcast the knowledge, all our plans, as surely as I would if I was shouting at the top of my voice. And I don't believe you truly know."

"I am sure I do. But I haven't been told by anyone. It is merely obvious. As obvious as where the last piece in a jigsaw must go."

"Tell me one thing. Does it have to do with Them? The ones who came to the Wall, and looked, and did no harm?

"It does. I am sure it does. Can't I tell you?"

"Please, No. Not here."

"Then I will take you somewhere else, and I will tell you there."

She led me to the Colleges, past four or five sealed great ancient Houses where porters drowsed and robed men went in and out, and to the greatest House of all: the city Library, where I had been an hundred times. But the door she took was not one I had ever passed before, and the room we entered was unknown to me: full of equipment and fuller of old books, though the walls were covered with the aperiodic ochre-and-gold dart-and-diamond tiles you see nowhere else.

The backside of the Library, then, not the vast glittering place I had visited an hundred times. I looked on with mild curiosity, but here Cahaire was obviously at home, known, not a half-child but a respected co-worker. Five or six people here knew her.

"Keep silent, and look impressive"

She muttered and argued: I understood that I was there on some official business (I tried to look official) and that authority was to be granted. And granted it was, rather easily. She marched off towards a door (trying to gesture to me to follow in such a way that she was not seen) and I followed her, (trying to look as if I was leading us both with the authority of the Watch). This little comedy ended at once as the door closed behind us. Now she walked fast down the musty, crammed, corridor, her limbs rigid, and her face almost grim. I expected her to tell me her news the moment we were alone: but she led me a long, long, way, down many dim paths, before she attempted to begin her explanations.

Curled up tight now. Hands locked over her breasts. Thighs pressed together, eyes closed, shaking.

"I do love you, Cahaire. And we can't do this"

"No. So you go into the Land and die. That is how it will be." She started shedding furious tears again, clenching her jaw against them. "Where is my honor? Everyone will know"

"Your honor is safe under your heart, where it always is. Safe under my heart, too. No-one will know. I will never tell."

"*Where is my honor if I let you be Destroyed?* You soft bleeding whipped Fool. You think *this* shames me, do you? I knew you wouldn't tell about this, whatever I did. You are a coward. And you believe all that rubbish about Eternity and Love. Fool. Fool. Oh, please, think. Even if we had lived and met before, what is the chance we could find each other here? Now? Among five hundred Millions? Think, you idiot. I never met you before now. Yes, we have Souls, and they last forever: but they don't conjoin in eternity"

"Why. . . ?"

"Because you are pretty. You look as if you have a nice cock, my darling, if you want to know the real reason why. Because I have to marry someone and you are beautiful, even if you are so stupid. And you are a good person, too. I liked you. I thought I was happy."

"And you don't know about . . . . ?"

"No. I lied. Guesses, and nothing else"

"Get up." I wrapped one of the sheets from the tables round her, gently tucked it under her back. She clutched it tight and rocked back and forth. I stroked her head, arranged her hair. "Cahaire: we are lost here, but someone will come soon"

"You are funny. You are Oh such a prude. Old Maris brings lovers in here all the time. I'm surprised we didn't fall over her on the way here."

"Yes. But I don't need to know all the dark secrets of your Guild. Honey. Be wise now, be kind. Do you want to stay here? Or come back?"

"Come back. What else?."

"So sit up. Put your dress on. Comb your hair: it's full of dust. And you are dirty."

"I am *not.*" She turned her back and clasped the sheet to her throat with one hand, picking up her robe with the other, shaking her hair. "Go away. Give me but a minute to get straight and decent"

I turned and went to the door of the stack. Guttering lamps blurred the open book-lined corridor outside. There was no-one visible: but I wondered just who might have been listening. I heard her doing things, but I didn't quite turn away. I watched her, from of the corner of my eye. I confess I was a little, just a little, afraid that she might come at my back, with a splinter from the old shelves.

"I am done"

"And you look very proper, respected lady."

"I beg your pardon, now, sir, for calling you Fool."

"Never mind it. You are probably right. But are we friends?"

"There is no choice, now"

"Then it didn't happen. Never speak of it more. Learn from a Fool, for once: this is the knowledge that does not come by words. This is one of those times."

"O, yes. But I – Please attend. I should have confessed to you long ago. I am sorry they beat you, Bann. I apologize. Pardon me. It was only because I was vain and stupid, and desired you to flatter me, that you were hurt"

I set my two hands on her shoulders and looked at her. Her downcast eyes widened in surprise, or fear, then she stood straight and looked right back at me. I kissed her mouth; as long and as softly as she would permit.

She let me for a very little while, then she suddenly shook free, struck my hands off her shoulders, and put hers on mine, crying out as the children do in their games.

"Truth! Truth! Tell me all! Bann! Do you *want* to go Out? If you were free, not bound by your guild, would you still go?"

"Truth. Yes. I do. I *must.* How many will ever have this chance? To be Out, even for a short time? There? I think it is the greatest thing any man can imagine: even if I was cut down in the first minute. I am very afraid. But if I was free, yes, I would go."

"You mean this?"

"I hesitated, but now I know. And I have no real choice. What will happen to me if I do what you ask, if they offer and I refuse? You talk to me about Dishonor? I might as well kill myself. In a month, I'd have to flee down to the Dead Cities. I wouldn't die, but I'd be Dead. So I lose you, either way. The truth is, we can do nothing to influence this, one way or another. It is coming, and I must run toward it and fight, not flee away. My only chance is to go Out, and return for you.

"But that is not the real reason. I know now. Truth. I have desired this all my life, of itself. To go Out."

She started to cry again, holding herself back desperately. "Mother Redoubt. You really mean it. All I did was make you sure. Oh, I was wrong to try all this."

"Truth. You were the one who was lying."

"Yes. You have no mercy, do you?" I tried to kiss her again, but she pushed me away, and held me at her left arms length while she tried to compose herself. "Alright. I understand now. But you should know this, Bann. There is one thing I did not lie about. The spell, those words . . ."

"Yes?"

"I did find a reference to it. From five hundred years back. It was used by one who returned from the Land, as Scyrr has."

"And?"

"He learned it there. In the Land. So he said."

That was how I first met her. We were children, neighbors: I ignored her, of course, till one day she came up to me with a giggling gang and grabbed my shoulders. *"Truth! Truth! Tell me all! Am I the prettiest?."* And all ran away before I could answer.

We became enemies because of that. Then friends, as much as boys and girls of that age ever can. And later, time and the matters of our different Families separated us. Years.

And then we met again, I, Bann, and she, Cahaire, both a little old for betrothal, both beginning to wonder if we had missed life's chance. And Bann fell in love. And he thought, poor Fool, that she was his own, his aeon-destined One.

We made our long, slow, way back. The brown and yellow corridors passed slowly, lined with ancient volumes and tottering stacks of cybernetic plaquettes, with a dim lamp every twenty paces. It was utterly quiet, and no one was in sight.

"Listen. It is my turn to explain something."

"No more Truth, please"

"Cahaire, no, it is not that. It is something else."

"What, then?"

"Please. Think back and remember. When you were a child . . ."

"Yes?"

"When you were very young, when you were little, did you ever wonder if the world was real?"

"What? Real? What do you mean?"

"A colored show. An illusion. Subjective only. Other people just moving shapes, not alive or conscious. All pretence, the Redoubt, the Land. And yourself, your real Soul, away somewhere else, in some niche of existence, dreaming it all, making it all up, the only real thing in a world of shades."

"Yes." She paced softly for a while, caught off guard. "Yes. How strange: you felt that too?"

"I did"

"Yes. And when I was a little girl. At night. I did. I wondered what was real. My dreams, or the day-time world. They seemed equal, and how could I tell? But I never knew other people felt that way, like me."

We walked for a while more: the old forgotten stories passed us in their ranked millions, and we were as dim and quiet, as silent and sad, as two ghosts.

"So. Are you *there,* Cahaire?"

"What?"

"Are you there? This is a world of shadows. A Night Land. Are you real? Tell me!!"

"Yes!! I am not a shadow!."

"Are you real? Like me?"

"Yes. Oh, I understand what you mean, Bann! But I am real. And I know you are real."

"I'm *here.*" I touched my temple with one knuckle. "I'm here. I hurt you so much, don't I? Again and again. But it is because I am real. If I was only your dream, I could never give you pain. So are you *there?*" I touched the side of her face, and she slowed and turned to look squarely at me, in the shadowy spaces of the old Library corridors. "You hurt me, terribly, too. So are you there? And as real as me? A whole universe? A Redoubt? A Land? All in there?" I stroked the side of her face.

"Yes"

"So. There are two real things, at least."

"Yes."

"Two realities"

"Yes." Timidly, her soft hand touched my face. "did I hurt you, Bann?"

"And where does reality come from, the other things that are not us?"

"Is this going to be another philosophical lecture?" Her hand fell. "Spare me that. You were saying such strange good sense a moment ago. Stop this or I will weep again, I can not endure it anymore."

"Cahaire. I love you, I love you. Please. It is just this, no more. There are two things that are real. Other things are not real, perhaps, or not as real. But if the two joined? Really joined? Really, truly, became one? What then?

"Our Souls endure for eternity. We know. But *where,* Cahaire? In what reality?"

In the Redoubt, strange rumors. I heard details of political fights and maneuvering, things that normally passed over my head. Alliances were forming and dispersing, and Scyrr would be seen or spoken of time and again, talking with this or that group of the Civitas. With the other Captains of the Watch, of course: but also with the Scholars, with the Magistrates, even with a group of Monstruwacans. I saw him civilly a few times: utterly at his ease, magnificent, and the center of every gathering, even of those who far outranked him: and he never failed to acknowledge me with a look or word, and never granted me more than that, nor did I expect it.

There were stories about disturbances in the Land, and about men preparing to go Out: but these latter are never confirmed or denied publicly. Whispers about me, perhaps, being among them, had somehow spread as well, to which I turned a metal face. My family knew, but they were close-mouthed enough: I can not say how the knowledge spread. Not by me, and most certainly not by Cahaire. My second duty at the Rim approached, as the time of the next Patrol neared. Scyrr told me nothing, absolutely nothing, about ultimately going Out: and I asked nothing. But I knew, I felt, that his plans were becoming more and more certain.

I expected the hard word from Cahaire. The return of my gifts, the polite refusal, the ending of our betrothal. If she had had the least sense, she would have left me long ago, I knew, and obviously if was surely and publicly known I would be going Out, she would have to. But it did not happen yet. After all the conflict, a kindness seemed to fall between us, and we were merciful to each other. In the days left before my next expedition to the Rim, she permitted me to walk her along the Concourse thrice. There were no more arguments. There seemed no cause. She held close to my side, and we talked easily, like old friends, not lovers.

In the darkening chamber, we readied ourselves. The pumps cycled and flushed, our ears popped, the lights dwindled to the merest red and ulfire flicker, as we acclimatized. The first eyeball sight of the Land is always a shock, a raw thing breaking in upon you. Some of the Sensitive literally cannot bear it, as they cannot bear even to glance at a Watcher. For us, shielded by our helms and chosen because our minds were almost dumb and deaf to any such call, it was only like the glaring face of an enemy.

With a tearing shriek of air, finally equalizing pressures, the Petty Door opened. We filed towards it, and as we moved to pass Scyrr rested his helm against mine, for an instant.

"Only to the Rim this time. But we go Out, soon."

I knew there had been disturbances: but the changes shocked me when I saw them close. A fourteen-night ago all had been silence. Now, a swarm of dwarfish things scurried round the edge of the northeast quadrant. Each carried a writhing devil-fire over its head, a single lure or signal that pulsed jale and green. From time to time one would bound high and flash out a great dart: in response to this cry or signal, waves of light swept across the swarm and returned. I watched these waves infocus to a spot where the beasts circled, driven to frenzy, digging. They pulled up something like a branched black root that writhed and spat acid, futilely, as it was devoured. They left its remains and flooded toward us: and Scyrr watched impassively, not moving, as the blind snouts butted and darted towards him, not three feet away behind the humming field. But not one of them touched the Wall, and after a time they all swept to the north, running at thrice a man's best pace.

The whole Land was alive, awake. My previous patrol seemed inconsequential: the sights that had so awed me were nothing now but casual debris. Everywhere we looked, now, things crept or ran, some walking like men, others bounding like beasts or scuttling like insects. The bushes moved with the violence of the struggles within them: below our sight, among the roots, fierce wars. And further from the Circle than we could easily see, eyes glinted and talons flashed, hulking shapes maneuvered, or crashed together and ripped apart.

"What has aroused them?"

"It is a demonstration of power."

By whom? I would have asked. But I knew.

We strode round the circuit of Light, a three-hours walk past cold, mutating, hells. They were there, waiting. The three grey shapes again, somehow unmoved, unthreatened, though they were toys compared to the things that warred and fought in the endless dark spaces behind them. I wondered if they had been standing, untiring, since our last patrol.

Scyrr faced them. We five ranged ourselves behind him. Then began the strangest thing I have seen in my life: for he gazed at the central one and did not move. And nor did they move, though horrors raged and triumphed around them, fang, sting, claw and spine, shock and spew of poison, flash of organic electricity, and the dim scream of stunning ultrasound that the Wall could only partly dull.

They did not move. They merely gazed back, untouched, while the demons of the Land danced attendance.

What did Scyrr see? What did he think?

My own eyes were caught and held. I could not move or blink. Scarcely, could I breath. If they had commanded me to come forward and breast the Air Clog and join them, I would have been lost. Yet their eyes told me nothing I could remember or interpret later.

What did Scyrr see there?

At last, the timeless time was ended by a great sound. The Home-call, issuing from the Tower, tearing through every spell. I awoke.

Behind the three ashen shapes, the nightmares were streaming, fleeing in one direction only, around the Circle. They fled from a looming darkness that jolted northward, multi-legged, multi-jawed, making the Land ring like a drum with each limb it let fall. A thing too vast to seize in one glance, sweeping clean a furlongs-wide swathe with a swarm of branched darting secondary manipulators, scarcely seen, far above the mists and fires, yet turning the wide Land into a pillared hall ceilinged by its belly. Dwarfed by nothing at all, save the Watchers and the Redoubt Herself.

Its course was set to intersect the Circle just where we stood: and it came on relentlessly until its first outlying tendrils touched and crisped against the force field. Then it stopped. Low and high, and higher than belief, the plated whips probed, flashing into ruin at every spot, as the Wall flared into a sheet of lightning with each touch: and Inside the Circle, *Inside*, actual matter, actual debris, fell hissing and stinking.

We stood. After nearly an hour it turned clumsily away, and skirted round the Circle, continuing its long harvest northward.

The Three were untouched, unmoved. Whip and palp came not near them.

Power indeed.

We stumbled back. We did not complete the patrol. Obeying the Home-call, we fled.

And the strangest sight of all, seen when we unhelmed, was Scyrr's face, and his tears.

Off duty at last, exhausted after half a day of debriefing and reports and consternation, I fled further, to the Library.

Everywhere on the way there was disturbance, within the Redoubt as without: I saw crowds, groups talking, panic and fear in some places. The news was not in the hour-sheets, but spread by word of mouth. An undercurrent of horror at that Titan in the Land. And more particular, more single, floating above it, a second rumor: that men would indeed soon be going Out. And this rumor was one I could have confirmed, for the formal announcement could only be hours away.

The place was frantically busy, but the older lady at the desk recognized me and gave me a sly smile I did not like, one which vanished at once when showed her official tokens and demanded a Scholar, the journeywoman Cahaire, and presently. This cheat would have cost me far more than a flogging if it had ever been discovered, but I had no care for that now. She appeared, with her hair bound up and her feet muffled in slippers. I took her arm, ignoring the Senior's curious face, and hurried her away.

"The Watch require your advice, respected Scholar"

"Where are you taking me?"

"Let us just walk. No one will notice us. No, not to the Stacks."

Among the crowds in the streets was privacy. Everyone was talking, no-one was listening. We walked fast, avoiding others. Really, I had had no business to approach her like this, but she was obviously the only person who would understand anything or have anything useful to say.

"Cahaire, help me. What was that thing?"

"Have you recorded what you saw, Bann? In detail? People will read what you wrote an hundred thousand years from now"

"Far too much detail, thank you. And I may see more detail in future. But what was it?"

"One of the enUnique forms, we think. The term does not mean much. They are all different. Not a clade. Non-reproducing, immortal, self modifying, bootstrapping. It might have been neo-human once."

"How can it move when it is that big? Why is not it like a Watcher?"

"I suppose it uses something much stronger than bone and

does not have a conventional circulatory system. The Master Scholars do not know, believe me. They are terrified. The Monitors pulled all the public records for that time segment, but I have traced bootlegs spreading in private use. Its back reached Dead City Fifty."

"Trace all the bootlegs and null them. There is too much panic around already"

"Do *not* instruct me in the duties of my Guild, sir."

"Your pardon."

"Could it have gotten through the Wall, Bann? Surely it tried and failed?"

"It was not trying. Just tapping gently on our door. I stood under it. But it doesn't count, Cahaire, what matters are the Ones who control it."

"It's confirmed, isn't it? Men are going Out?"

"Yes"

"What is Scyrr going to do?"

"To seek alliance, make negotiations, maybe." Or something that might have that meaning, in another world of meaning than we know.

"That is Heresy. Could the Civitas truly have sanctioned that?"

"I did not say it."

"No. But it sounds probable enough. Will they take you, Bann?"

"The chance of my going Out should be two hundred in thirteen hundred and twenty. Chosen by lot. It should be. But Scyrr leads in this. And Scyrr will make the call. And Scyrr picked me in the first place."

She stood very straight, looking at me. "So we have only a little time."

"Yes."

Now the blood thudded in my ears, and my throat was stopped up and aching. Speak, end it.

"Respected lady Cahaire. I release you from our betrothal."

"Do you? Well then, I am free. Now understand me, and listen, for once. For now I am free, and I am going to do what I want."

I have not been here often. No-one gives the Magistrates much honor, despite their legal powers. Any man who gets into a serious conflict is either a discourteous Fool, or is allowing himself to be afflicted by one. Any man who cannot settle that conflict without recourse to the law is a coward. Fight, or if you are not well-matched, take Chance. What need for laws?

Except for this, I suppose.

Here she waits. Her feet bare, and the last hand's-breadth of her dress smirched and dirtied, in memory of the lost, lower, Dead Cities. The last hand's-breadth of her wedding dress, which bells widely, which is perfectly white, which narrows to her throat and face, her own Tower of Observation. And she is the very type and pattern of the Redoubt, shaped of womanhood. No butterflies to attend her, no jewels except a single round of heartwood at her throat. White haired, black eyed. A perfect virgin.

"How brave of her." The whispers.

And her family, here too: a sullen crowd. The women look poison at me. Her father gives me the measured stare of a real enemy. Any one of the younger men would call me to Fight at the least excuse, and I respect them all for it. I am going to marry her and leave her a widow in a month or less, and for all the talk about Honor, for all the fears that rive the Pyramid, they hate me, as they ought to. Good.

I never dreamed she would do it. How she must have fought them for this.

A Hasty Licence, one of many granted recently you may be sure. The under-Captain presiding, a guard of brothers-in-arms, an arch of spinning dyskoses to walk down, death and flame just above us, Cahaire as straight as a stringer beside me, yet flinching just a little, something I felt in her arm that held mine, that no-one else could see.

Speeches at the feast, troubled, dishonest. Yet also, heartfelt good wishes, blessings, gifts from old friends. A hundred proper details skipped with criminal ruthlessness, but a hundred gifts of love and time to fill the gaps. Thank you, my father, my sisters, my cousins, my friends, dear Folk.

We processed to my Home: and it was as if we were two parties setting ourselves up for War, my friends and family against hers, and the only ones truly at peace being us two. Theoretical fellowship, theoretical joy. And even I hardly knew if she was a lover or only an enemy crippled by pity for me.

A strange, confused, wedding.

But afterwards, at last, alone. The candles of the bees were lit. True, chemical, flame, the only time and the only place within the Redoubt that it is ever permitted. She unveiled and stripped, and she was silent. In the mist of that ancient, golden, light, she might have been a complete stranger, a dream of flesh, a dream, returned from the Days she denied.

The real Cahaire was within that stranger. But it was only after I had known her and held her for a long time that we met.

Morning, and a call sounding. A messenger, at a time when no man should expect a messenger. She slept. I went and opened the door. It was a Watchman, in nightsuit, visor down, armed with a live dyskos. For an instant I thought he was going to kill me, but he handed me two packets, and left, impassive.

The first package was orders. I ripped it open, and saw a single character. The set-speech rune HAGALAZ. Which means: constraint; denial; negation; stasis. The traditional sign of refusal-of-service.

And in the second package. Heavy, jagged, uneven, black, rough. A stone from the Land.

"You're not going." She was still weeping and embracing me, and clutching the rune to her breast. "Honey. Love. Husband. I was sure. I thought they would take you."

"No. And they sent me this."

I gave her the stone. She took it and threw it with a scream *"Aahhhh!!,"* hard against the wall, and turned again to me, burying her head against my neck, kissing as if she would never stop, gasping, trembling. I rocked her and stroked her and after a while she quietened.

Our tears and our kisses mingled. I had nothing to say.

Later. Still resting. The Lamps were bright, the day was abroad, but we were not.

"Why?"

"I don't know. May be Scyrr has mercy"

"Why is he going Out?"

"To seek Reality." I rolled over and took her head in my hands, looking down at her. She smiled. I kissed the dear Redoubt between my palms, and She kissed me back, all love. "To look for what is even more Real to him than this. I think. There is the strategy and the safety of the Redoubt, there are the great public things, but that is the core, the drive within him. The Reality he has chosen. The agon. The test. Out, in the Land. He wanted it. To return there, and be Real again. That is why he has made this happen. I am sure."

"Could it be . . ."

"What?"

"That he understands this? That you are not just running away, but . . . I don't know how to say it."

"That I am seeking reality, as he is?"

"Yes. Perhaps he saw that in you."

"I can't easily imagine how. But I would put nothing, nothing, beyond him. And if he understood, he would aid me for the sake of the thing itself, far more than for weak mercy. He is a great man."

Her face turned bitter "You want to go Out, don't you? Still? You want to fight, to be Out there, under his command? Don't lie."

"I did. Yes. I confess. But I speak only in the memory of that desire. No more. On my honor and my oath, now all my heart chooses you."

"Look at your hands and your arms. They are shaping to hold the Dyskos, not to touch me." It was true. "If you had a chance, if he commanded, you'd get out of this bed, now, and go"

"Never. No. This is better, a greater thing"

"You would have thrown me away and gone Out. And even after you told me that, I fought, I wept and begged them. For just one month with you, all I hoped for. And you still long to go."

"Forgive me. I love you, and I repent."

She stared hard, tears coming, then closed her eyes and kissed me. After a while, she relaxed.

Sweat drying, hearts slowing.

"I love you. It's Real. Yes."

"I love you"

"I do. But, its . . ."

"What?"

"It's lovely." She kissed me again, very deeply. "Touch me everywhere. Inside, too. But it's not. . . . I still don't understand."

"What?"

"Almost, what you said makes sense. Almost. But it's not making a new universe."

"What is most like that making, then?"

"O, it is when you talk to me." She snuggled close, and consented, tolerant, drowsy, as I disposed her very carefully and delicately, tangling our legs together, embracing her body, wrapping her arms round my neck, so we pressed together from forehead to instep. Using my right hand to draw her hips against me and my left to hold her body. Stroking her for a little while, then pulling her closer, and then caressing her again. She was drifting into sleep. "Or like that. Yes. When you hold me. I'm here"

"I'm here. Not far away."

"Forever, Bann?"

"Perhaps."

"But it can't be true. It's a myth. It's beautiful, but it's just a story."

"Why not?"

"How could it be true?" She stretched, wakeful again now, and sat up. "That a man remembered his ancient Love, from the days of light: And heard her, reborn, somewhere in the Night Land. And went Out, alone, to rescue her. And bought her back?"

"Why not?"

"You've been to the Rim. How could one man survive Out there alone, even for half an hour?"

"The Land is more terrible with every chiliad that passes. Maybe it was easier in those days."

"And where was this place?"

"Another Redoubt, that fell"

"Nonsense. No. And we never met before. Never."

"There has to be a first meeting. Even in Eternity. Perhaps this is it"

"No. No. No. I love you: I know this means all to you. You think love can be forever, and that those Lovers showed the way for us all. But it's so absurd. It's a dream. We can trace that story back and back and back, but it's just a story. A man's dream of woman, and love. Be realistic."

"It seems real to me."

"No. The Days of Light are a dream. If we came from anywhere, we arose from the Land, and built the Redoubt as a refuge"

"Then how did we survive, before we had the Redoubt?"

"Perhaps it was easier. Or perhaps we became weaker afterwards, living here."

"If that's true, we became more loving. Not weaker. Love is better than strength, and stronger."

"That is true at least, darling idiot."

"In any case, I Believe. More than ever. Truly, completely, now. Utterly. And it was you who taught me, and made me sure."

"Well, it is hopeless. It is hopeless. I give in. You win."

"That is most unlike you, Cahaire darling."

"Yes indeed. And for why? Only because I desire that we should stop talking nonsense, and have some *breakfast.*"

"When do they go Out?"

"Soon. And then I must leave the Watch, Cahaire. That stone was my dismissal. Not officially, but that is what it means"

"Yes." She hugged me again, then turned and went back to coiling her hair. "We will be poor. Never mind."

"Not so poor. And it doesn't matter"

"And there will be explanations to make. My father only permitted this because you were going Out, and he would have been shamed to refuse. Now he will be livid. Do not Fight, please."

"I promise. Whatever he does. I shall earn his forgiveness by pleasing his daughter."

"Be sure you do, then." She preened, looking at herself in the mirror. "Now don't I look nice, with my hair up like a married woman? In a few months it will all be past and forgotten, when he sees me happy."

"We may all be dead by then."

"I think we will live. And whatever happens, I have done with fearing. I am going to fear nothing at all"

"No. I am not afraid."

Now Scyrr is gone into the Land, with his two Hundreds. All is quiet. I doubt they may return.

I thought I had nothing. I thought I had a month. I have forty-three years, perhaps. Or Eternity, perhaps. But we rarely talk of that anymore. We address these matters often and often, in detail, but when we do what passes between us is not mere talk. Not mere words. Oh, my preaching to you, love! But at last I learn. I will live it now, not talk about it.

And the little practical problems that surround me. Life. I

touched on great things. I might have been a Hero. But I am just a man, and I can't live my life by might-have-beens. I am happier than I believed possible.

The lowest, sealed, dead, Cities buzz with industry. Culverins and sakers, ancient weapons being researched and rebuilt. Vital work for the Scholars: and the joy of working at it, beside her. And the Matrosses welcome recruits and Guildless men: especially one who has been to the Rim.

One claims that weapons were made that would break mountains. Another traces their scars, Out in the Land. We will never despair or be downcast: there shall be another, stronger, Circle, and if that Titan comes once more, we shall slay it. Fear us.

Fear us. Do not touch, do not harm, my beloved, my Redoubt.

For you in the Land, starveling things, our love may seem the coupling of worms, trapped under some iron tetter. But it is not. It is the meeting of gods. The gaze of her eye has more power than the gaze of the Watchers; the reaching of her arm could brush aside any Leviathan; her voice holds more potency than the Laughter from the East; and her goodness and beauty can swallow all your horror and all your strength and make it nothing. And it will.

Fear her, for she is greater than you. Fear me, because I love her.

I am a Fool, yes, a very great Fool, but I know this is real. I touch it every day. It is not given to us, but built between us, made by us, with every loving action, by all of us, alive here in the midst of your Night Land. And when you are less than memories, it will still endure, Love, resting in Eternity, not in time.

We never met before, in the Days of Light. Our Eternity begins now.

Eater

Andy Robertson

Eight miles above the Land, Khresten looks out into the night, through one of the Eyes of the tower.

The oval screen before her shows a low hill in the middle of a barren plain. The scale bars indicate that it is about two furlongs in height and two miles wide. Set atop it is a knotted complex of rock strands, from which a twisting, iridescent stream of many-colored radiance fountains upward into the everlasting darkness. Glints of vulcanism drain away to the right, but beyond it and to the left there is no light at all and the enhancement routines of the Eye have sketched the naked surface of the Land in symbolic no-color contours as a random jumble of basalt tesserae in low relief.

There is no vegetation nearby, no physical structures of any sort, and no visible movement of beasts or giants. The lesser entities of the Land do not come near. In the ancient records this many-hued blur, dancing in the eternal night sixty leagues to the southwest of the Redoubt, is named The Rainbow That Dies.

Once more she applies herself. Quietening her breath. Humbling, stilling, and opening her mind. The continual fear is under control, nothing is reaching at her mind from out of the Land, and all thoughts of success or failure, of gaining acceptance in her guild, have been banished to irrelevance. She strives only to be part of the machine that scans the night.

Something touches her, inside her eyes.

She cannot sense into the upper dark, but the lower levels are truly open, and the screen becomes clear, detailed, reflecting her mind. The more subtle sight interfaces with the electronics as easily as it does with the organic nerves, delivering information that the computers of the Tower may glut themselves on or a mindblind co-observer may share if only instrument and operator are in harmony. It is an ancient trick of the Monstruwacans.

The images of six black tubes appear on the screen, drawn from her mind to overlay the barren dark. Their roots are spaced symmetrically about the gush of the Rainbow, and they flow upward, swaying, to open in monstrous flowers of night that fray upwards into nothing. Complex structures writhe within them. Peristaltic narrowings pump plasma skeins up and away from the Land, up to the region where the eyes of her soul refuse to construct more lies to overlay the glass and silicon grid before her with a thousand different shades of black. Each dark Flower is about a mile in height, and above the two-hundred fathom level the stalks show some of the typical dendritic character of the pneumavores, branching and rebranching into hard black points. Some of these points wave free, searching. Others are buried avidly in the central bright stream.

All is stable, and the Eye screen is delivering data at an optimum rate for the machines, but the human Monstruwacans who stand around her also require to know what is passing in the mind of their seer. Khresten begins her verbal subjective log.

"Six shapes, like flowers, grow from the Land. Each is . . . thrice the height of the Rainbow."

Are they rooted? Of long residence?

"An air of permanence surrounds them. A year at least. Yet they are not fixed – they are cyclic – they are growing – they waver and change."

Are they Eaters?

" . . . not of us. Of the Rainbow. That is why it is dying. Now they wait . . ."

What do they wait for?

" . . . for something from above, Senior. They are waiting . . ."

. . . to welcome it, she realizes suddenly and says. That is a knowledge that could never be relayed through the screen, but to her it is obvious, immanent.

Once more she feels the insect-touch on her retinae, and though she knows the danger she opens herself further. *They are not conscious of me.*

The screen is suddenly full of detail. The entities of the night come into a sharper focus. Each stalk is a braded, forking, writhing, column of darkness. Tiny motes of unlight stream up and down, pulsing irregular blobs carrying what might be dissolved shreds of their prey, checking and stumbling as they collide with each other . The Flowers are milking the Rainbow, building and strengthening themselves from its flesh, which they suck in and consume through pores that open and close on the tips of the dark branches. They are Eating it. It writhes from one side to the other, from one scourge to another, pierced, trapped, hooked, bled, and its essence diffuses away into the thorned webs of darkness. It is slowly growing weaker and smaller, though it seems still to try to fight its way upwards as its tormentors continue to grow larger and more extended.

The interface between the distant entities adsorbs Khresten's attention entirely, and a sense of the most awful pain, of the diminishment of that far bright being, overwhelmes her. Her mind opens yet further. Despite all warnings and despite all her discipline she begins to lose touch with her own body as her center shifts towards the radiant agony, and she feels herself flowing out into the Night on a slow tide of nausea.

The glutted Flowers become clearly visible as pulsing fractals of black on black, their faces now tilting inward to form a cup, a web, a tangle or nest. They are connecting to each other, fusing together into a complex of threads that moves and links and breaks, not fully symmetrical, but somehow

. . . wet.

And something new is beginning. The Flowers are not alone.

Something is descending out of the night. Threads of sentience fall from the upper dark, and here and there they touch the Land and dissolve to nothing, each returning a racing pulse of information which, in her heightened state, she feels as if it fled along her own nerves. She cannot sense them until they flash: she cannot follow them back to their source: she knows them only by their echo, by the hollow in the night they leave as they vanish.

The threads fall around her and on her, each bringing a spark of unknowable otherness, and her soul reports each touch.

Again. And again.

Gripping, gripping as hard as she can, she is slipping from her points of anchorage. The Tower is tiny and distant, a complex clutter far behind her atop the vast pyramid of shielded life that is the Redoubt. A deep cold surrounds her, a physical sensation like freezing currents of wind, overlaid by the knowledge of ravenous things awakening and approaching. She has gone too far, been too trusting, made foolish errors lethal for a seer, and her immaterial spirit is losing its connection with her flesh and drifting helplessly, out into the Night Land.

I am lost.

But her body, tiny and far from her as a distant doll, still obeys her. With the faraway puppet-eyes of her flesh she can see that the Rainbow is now totally confined, nearly consumed, a smear of light with a thin pulse of despair echoing out from it. She babbles something as she closes her eyes, closes her mind, and releases the gesture of Guard, brushing against the light beams which interthread her fingers for this very purpose. Instantly the ravening electronic shields of the Tower flash into being round her. The room roars as the primary V-pulse fills the walls, the cybernetic memories are blanked with ruthless overriding authority, the screen glares white, then true black, and she falls back trembling in the chair as her returning soul snaps into union with her body.

Not too late. And from the eyes of the grave men and women who surround her, from their voices and hands, from their mind-touch, their speiking, she knows of nothing but affirmation, love and support.

The recovery, the interrogation, the report, are over. With her chaperone, apprentice Khresten descends towards the Redoubt and her home city within it. But she is still pale and shaken, still unstrung, her knees as melting wax, and the older woman must half support her as they ride down the central well of the tower.

When they are alone and there is no risk of indignity Khresten huddles against her companion. *Let us go down quickly, quickly,* she does not say. She blanks her mind, and thinks of home and her younger sisters. A ghost-ache traces the length of her spinal cord and her major nerve trunks, slowly fading as her errant Spirit knits itself back into her flesh. The tall old woman whispers to her and reminds her to be brave.

They fall two hundred fathoms, past level after level of active and passive observation systems – radar, optical, sonar, mindset – past datastores, libraries and power nodes, administrative clusters and support systems. Most of the levels are temporarily shut up and dead. Some are sealed and Forbidden. Others are in use, brightly lit, filled with tangles of enigmatic equipment and moving figures. Day and night, the Monstruwacans interrogate the Land.

They reach the tower's foundation. Below this is the truncated roof of the pyramidal Redoubt proper, three fathoms thick of imperishable metal, quick with subtle fires. But the Tower and the Redoubt are sealed from each other, and they must descend on their own feet, breathing with the aid of air-bells, past the final blanks that insulate the Tower and deny any infection entry to the Redoubt. No dangerous path is permitted. No communications link, no optical fiber, no microwave beam, no quantum pair, may connect the last refuge of humanity with the observatory of the Monstruwacans that looks outward on the Land. Only human beings and written records ever make the passage.

They descend, wading the horizontal Air Clog. They give up the Word. They enter into the safety and the peace.

A day has passed, a night has begun. Far below the Tower, deep within the Lower Cities of the Redoubt, in her home, in her house, in her bed, Khresten dreams.

Sleep-time in the Four Hundred and Third city breathes round her. Her two younger sisters sigh quietly, sleeping, a fathom or so away from her in the same room where she lies. Their minds brighten and dim in a slow rhythm, moving between REM dream and profound theta passivity. In the next chamber the minds of her mother and father are dim red coals radiating a quiet animal warmth. There is a whisper of fluttering fabric strips in the ventilator. A gentle radiance flickers over the walls, too soft to awaken the inhabitants, for in this age no-one ever utterly darkens a room or sleeps alone unless they must.

Khresten dreams that she wakes, that she dresses and walks out of the room. Obedient to an impulse she refuses to acknowledge she leaves her house and makes her way to the public viewing galleries – never empty at any time. She enters and takes a seat well separated from the others, as is her custom.

Before them, with dream-logic, is her screen from the Tower, now somehow grown to the typical dimensions of a viewing gallery. But all is safe now. The monstrous threats of the Land that press inward upon her with a thousand attentions every instant that she is at her duty are absent from this place. She thinks. *We have disarmed them: we can study them in peace.*

Her screen is once more showing the Flowers tormenting the Rainbow. She strokes the machinery with her mind and tries to interface with it, but there is no engagement. And she understands that all that is past. The Flowers are now just one more of the shows – she thinks with faint scorn – the shows, the bogeys, the harmless pictures from the Land that can be used to entertain the half-blind, half-deaf, other people of the Redoubt.

In the audience that surrounds her stupid pity replaces stupid fear as the Flowers consume their prey. The Rainbow is so clearly in agony, so clearly having its very substance sucked away. Unconscious of their own emotional radiations and yet affected by them, the viewers stir helplessly, and one woman, perhaps an undetected and untrained partial Sensitive, has the bad taste to telepathically spiek her feelings in uncontrolled verbalized form. With practiced patience, Khresten guards her scorn, but behind her she feels another consciousness flick in sympathy with hers . . . as now once more the expected climax arrives. The Rainbow withers, fades, and dies, reducing to a blurred nub of mist. The Flowers join together into a single organism, a single intermeshed cup, opening upward.

In silence the other patrons leave. All except that one behind her.

But she is distracted by the screen. The slow fall out of the Night is beginning, and now she will be able to study it safely beyond the point where she was forced to retreat. The shapes stir in the blackness and then become tense and still. She tries to watch, but the threads falling from the upper dark are scarcely visible. It is hopelessly frustrating: there is no contact, no feedback, no *touch.* And she finds herself straining toward the screen and trying to affect it. Her throat constricts. She can see so little but still she can tell that the threads are falling closer and closer to the Flowers. Something is happening.

And now one thread finds, touches, fuses, with the Flowers and this thread does not break, but connects avidly, thickens, plumps. . . . her hands fall into her lap and her palms press into her flesh as the Flowers and the Thread fuse with astonishing violent rapidity into a single thing; a round solid-seeming mass, fat and satiated, settling in on itself, straddling the shreds of the Rainbow that yet remain.

A shock passes through her. Her breastbone quivers.

She awakens.

As she does it comes to her again that there was someone

near her in the gallery, regarding her and understanding her.

Another Sensitive? Khresten thinks. Then the dream recedes. Half-sleeping she comes to the understanding that it was only a dream, that she is safe in her bed. And it was folly of course: it would be Forbidden to duplicate the more subtle and dangerous achievements of the Tower down here. To prevent the creation of a path the galleries of the Redoubt may amplify only visible light. . . . She lies awake for a short time, then sighs, and thinks of other things, and passes to other and unremembered dreams.

Another day. There is no work for her to do in the times set aside for her recovery. But of course there are the children to care for and to teach.

Watch, little sisters. This is how it is done. She bares her arms and throat, and very carefully and exactly dabs a spot of doped nectar on each pulse point. Then she recaps the vials and sits completely still while the heat of her flesh sends pheromones and molecules of glucose adrift through the room.

Magically, jhenna and jhenni drift out of their open cage door, circle and flutter, and settle to feed, perched on her parallel upturned wrists. Her two sisters laugh with delight as their pet butterflies flirt their wings, showing comical eye-spots like perpetually amazed and outraged faces.

Hush, hush, don't frighten them. There is one drop on the hot artery at the base of each thumb, and she has judged the quantities there exactly right, because the two insects take wing again at almost the same time. They flit round her and then resettle on the smaller traces she has left inside each of her elbows, in the hollow next to the big sinew: a sourer blend of fructose and a little vinegar with a different chemical messenger blended in. Again they sip, and again, almost together, they fly away. Perfect.

She sits even more absolutely still now, chin high, smiling. Even her hair must not move, for the third smear is in the tender groove to each side of her larynx, half-brushed by its fall. But only jhenna wants this: her wings tickle Khresten's throat, while mischievous jhenni flies away to investigate the room.

The little girls chase him. *Don't grab, don't grab.* Mnemmne the elder catches jhenni at last, persuading him to perch on her own much-daubed hand.

"Make him spread his wings again, Khresten. What is he thinking?"

I cannot do that with just my mind. Give him something sweet, sweetheart. Look, how he loves you.

"Why did you send the gold butterflies back to that man? They were lovely, I would have liked to play with them too."

You will understand that when you are older, little sister.

The younger sister waits frustrated, beginning to be angry, so Khresten gives jhenna over to her and sits down quietly. The two little girls coo over feeding their pets for a while and get distracted, as usual. Then they let the butterflies free and huddle up on her lap, two sticky little messes of syrup, squashing her, to the further ruin of her thin housegown.

Three more days left. Then she must return to her duty, in the heights above.

The Tower, again: questions.

"I dreamt of it. Of the Rainbow and the Flowers. That may affect my perception, Senior"

Not when you are linked to the machines. Are you afraid?

"Yes, I am afraid."

Good. You have had seven days rest. Are you ready?

"Yes, Senior."

The Rainbow chokes and dies, again and again. The Flowers Eat it. Why? What comes from above?

"What is the Rainbow, Senior?"

Perhaps one of the allies. It survives cycle after cycle of this. But most likely, another unknown.

Begin now, apprentice.

Khresten bows her head, binds the sensors in position, and carefully takes the required conformations with her hands. Each member of the team checks off in turn. All is ready.

Once more she fuses with the Eye and looks out. Below her the Air Clog, the force field that is the first layer of defense, bells out from the foot of the tower down to its anchorage in the radiant circle which surrounds the Redoubt at ground level, miles below. The minds of the Watchers strike against it like furlong-thick bars of metal, but she slips between those bars and turns her regard outward. Though neither her body nor her soul change position her focus of attention flits swiftly, carried by the machine, away from the ancient knot of forces centered on the Redoubt, past and over the Southwest Watcher, past the Road, over leagues and leagues of blackness, to where the Rainbow writhes and flickers.

The Flowers are present again, but they are tiny. A cool mindpressure from the log-monitoring cyberneticist informs her *changed position* and she sees at once that these are successor entities. They are growing in slightly different positions, more widely spaced and shifted slightly clockwise, though still symmetrically surrounding the Rainbow. And these Flowers are not yet flowers but only unbranched stalks, writhing slowly as they grow, stretching upward for a minute and then shrinking in a slow rhythm. It is early in the cycle. The Rainbow is hardly affected. It still flows smoothly upward.

She watches for two hours while the Flowers continue to grow very slowly. At the end of this period she requests a rest, and the team pause to discuss what they have been seeing. They agree to wait five hours and then resume. They have now recorded the cycle in detail at two points, and the important thing, they concur, is to see what follows the growth of the Flowers to their maximum size and their fusion into a single entity.

When Khresten returns to her duty the Flowers are just opening. They bob and dip grotesquely, each black mouth in turn plunging into the flesh of the Rainbow and absorbing a quantum of its being. A different technique of feeding, which Khresten notes and describes . . . *how quickly I become used to this.* This session is shorter. On a simple extrapolation it will be at least twelve hours before the Flowers reach their full height again. Since there is no point in taking the risk of continuous mental observation, two of the other apprentices monitor the Rainbow using only visible light, while the shields go up on low power and Khresten rests.

They call her back when the Rainbow is again guttering down towards extinction. She bows, embraces the metal, and forms for them again a picture of the avid barbed networks consuming the stream of light. But this time she is more careful. Practiced, prudent, she refuses to be lured forth, but watches safely as the Rainbow dies and the flowers fuse once more into a single mesh.

The tangled Flowers become absolutely still and tense, waiting. Now the fall of the threads from above begins. Confined within the Tower she is only just able to detect them but she successfully resists the dangerous urge to see more. The half-seen threads fall closer and closer to the Rainbow, unseeable till they make contact with the surface of the Land, apparently blind, groping, searching, scattering at random without system or logic, until at last and not perceived until it has already happened one has touched the Flowers.

Something like a dark lightening bolt slides down it. The Flowers quiver, seemingly in shock, and fall together into a single globe. She startles.

Once more the shields cut in and the cybernetics zeroes all data. She apologizes to her team, but what she knows cannot tell them. *It startled me because I dreamt it. I dreamt this happening.*

But surely not.

No, it was not exactly the same.

To reset the shields with a proper delicacy will take almost an hour. As the apprentices go about it she relaxes, falls back in the chair – and becomes aware that someone is looking at her: looking *at* her. She unthinkingly jumps to correct her immodest posture, then stops and casts her eyes and her mind about the room in great anger. *Who?* But it was not the Senior, not any one of the grave older men. And it was not any one of the young men, all apprentices like her but not sensitives, not gifted with the Night-hearing, who are utterly absorbed in the matters of their Technos.

Her flowering rage that Eve-teasing should interfere *here,* of all places, falls away as she scans their minds and sees that there is no-one who it could have been, no-one at all.

She was mistaken.

This is really my home, she thinks. Absurd. But here . . . no polite, suitable young men trying to please, while their parents talk formally in the next room. No little poems about the beauty of instep or wrist. No strangers glancing at her, unconscious that their under-minds are rehearsing a rape. No passers-by reimagining her into a stupid naked popsy and tucking her away to dance behind their eyelids while they milk themselves in the night.

I will never marry. This is the better life.

But such thoughts belong to the Redoubt, not the Tower.

She directs the Eye towards the face of the Southwest Watcher and contemplates It, as calmly as possible, not fighting fear, for twenty minutes. It is a much-practiced penance or exercise though not one usually carried out through such an amplifier. Her coworkers understand and allow their minds to subtlety support hers, without questioning her reasons, until she is satisfied that the gaze of the Monster has burned all the littleness out of her.

Calm again, she confronts the Night.

Her focus of attention moves out from the tower to where the lingering ghost of the Rainbow swirls and then halts, aghast, at the monstrous globe of darkness that now squats above the remaining shred of light. It has grown beyond all proportion. It is rooted on the six stalks that were the Flowers, their tips spreading like trees or veins to form multiple points of attachment or support. Its surface seems hard, rigid, almost opaque, utterly beyond any penetration by her. It does not move.

Something is inside it. There is the merest hint of stirring life.

She watches for two hours more but nothing seems to happen.

At last she retires.

The cycle, they agree, is not finished. From the stalks to

the Flowers, from the Flowers to the tangled cup, and from that, fusing with some influence from the deeps of night, to the globe, nearly a mile wide, multi-rooted, hovering above the Land. If the Rainbow follows the cycle as it has done for seven years it will pour forth again in full power in less than three days more. In the intervening period, therefore, something must happen to the globe.

She is exhausted. It is agreed she will descend to her home and rest for one full day. After that, they hope to witness the final mutation.

Coming home earlier than she had expected, safe again within the gates of her own City, Khresten dismisses her chaperone and walks abroad through the streets. She always dresses as anonymously as possible, affects the veil in public as many women do, and once she has taken off the shoes which one wears only for journeys outcity there is nothing to mark her. Few ever recognize her as a Sensitive and one of the apprentice Monstruwacans.

Busy people move to and fro. The buzzing hive of life surrounds her, and the pad of a million bare feet. Though she was warned years ago that the teaching and the exercises of the Tower would continue to increase her sensitivity beyond bearing, she is shocked again by the *noise.* The uncontrolled mental radiations of the inhabitants overwhelm her and though she screws her mind as tightly shut as possible she cannot go on. Regretfully she modifies her path and avoids the most crowded public areas. *Ten days ago my soul was naked in the Land. And can I not endure the Agora of my own home city?* Apparently, she cannot.

That night she dreams again. She walks though the quiet nighttime streets visiting the scenes of her youth: the school, the places where she would meet her playmates, the library, the playgrounds. All those friends are separated from her now, all gone their separate ways and some married already. She walks slowly. Alone she wanders down the long corridors past the statues, past the open public gardens and malls.

Midnight passes, and forty miles below, deep in the Underground Countries, a continent of spices exhales. The Windmasters bring its breath to the Pyramid, and a cool scented breeze blows from the vents. It is jasmineday.

A few other people are abroad and now she must follow them back to the viewing gallery. The Flowers are there. But she has seen this already.

She speaks to her waiting friend

It is an old story. Really, these shows are for fools . . . I come here because I am one of those who looks out on the Land and discovers these things, I suppose. No, these are not bad people. Very few of them are weak or cruel. But they are so blind, so stupid.

You are a stranger here? On your wanderjahr? *I do not need to see this again. I will return home now, but I will show you what I can of the city, on the way. That is right, to a stranger. You will only have a short time here.*

Let us leave the gallery. No, you must not walk beside me! You, a man and a stranger here! Walk to one side and a little behind me, at a proper distance.

So. Here is the Four-hundredth-third city, named Blaise. *What would you see?*

Every House shows a different face. And they are all different behind their masks as well. Most are tens of thousands of years old, and each holds a clan of many families and an hundred old stories. They are private to their owners. I have visited only a few Houses, the Houses of my friends, and they were very different from my own home and from each other.

In that one lives the magistrate: it is not especially marked out, for the position is not hereditary. He is the magistrate for this year only, they are not well pleased with him.

Our lamps are very beautiful, are they not? We can do a thousand things with light. Harsh light, soft light, warm or cold light, calming or enraging, loving or hating. Our Lampmakers make them, and they are famous for it. Of course their best work illuminates this or that great and important public place, not in the open street. We send some of our best lamps to the other cities.

There is little machinery here in the lower cities: no fires, no furnaces, nothing loud or hot. How would we breath? Our own body heat is enough to strain the lungs of the Redoubt. We make few things, so we must make them to last ten thousand years.

Look at this tile beneath my foot. The glyph marks the spot of a murder two hundred years past. That is a most notable memorial, but you can see that each stone once carried a message, though most of them are worn to nothing. Every stone and every wall plate in this city has a story written on it, they say. The ones that are blank are simply those that have been cleaned by time.

And see how many fountains we have in the streets? And the trees? Come past here. When I was very young, this one, here, was the darling tree of my girl-band. Tllellalu *is his name. We watered him, talleyed his leaves, cleaned him of rust or blackrot, celebrated the first flower that blossomed each year. I see the younger bands are taking good care of him. Goodbye,* Tllellalu.

The great pillars support the core of the upper Cities: no doubt you have the same in your own home. Half the lower pyramid is solid metal by volume, they tell us.

The Library. I spent so much time here when I was young. Dreaming. How I wanted to be a hero, and explore the Land. Half the young people do, I suppose. I read story after story. All that is a fantasy, of course, as you come to understand when you grow up: only the insane go. And anyway it is Forbidden for women. But I had the Night-hearing – strongly enough to be trained – and that decided my future.

So now I explore the Land in a different way. I have been a seer for the Monstruwacans for two years. No-one remains a seer for very long because the strain is so great. In two more years my time will be over and I will have a choice, to stay with the guild, or return here to join another guild, or marry, or do some other thing. But if they will have me, I shall stay with the Monstruwacans, and that shall be my life.

This is a duello ground. It is deserted now but even so it is not polite for us to linger here and gawp.

Here is my home. Our whole clan lives here in the separate houses, all within the wall. My mother and father and my sisters: that is our family. And my parents' male cousins and their wives, and the elders of the previous generation.

I will not be living with my parents much longer, I think. I will live in a separate house, but still within our House.

Goodbye, then.

Khresten wakes sleepy and lazy. For once she feels properly rested and happy. She hums as she stretches, and catches the eyes of her youngest sister as that one tiptoes out of the room.

The girl has been told many times by everyone *Let your sister rest* and told *Do not be noisy while Khresten sleeps in the morning* and now she makes a face of exaggerated virtue and patience, mincing out with her finger to her lips and her hips wigwagging. Obviously someone needs to be taught a lesson.

Khresten leaps on her intending to provide instruction, but is fatally surprised when Mnemmne attacks her from behind: the three of them roll over and over in a tangle. Panting, laughing, she pins both of them down at last and tickles them very soundly while they scream and laugh and struggle.

Wai! Wai! She threatens them. *I am a monster from the Land! I am going to eat you!*

The day of rest is past. The great lift bears Khresten upwards again through the miles, and the armor of her resolve closes round her like a nightsuit. This time, she thinks, they will gain the full understanding. She will pluck it from the Night. She will not flinch whatever happens. She is no longer a girl, she is one of the elite of the Redoubt, one of the few for whom the energy needed for such rapid travel can be carelessly and routinely expended, and she will not be coward.

They rise past city after city, up through the last arcology of man, up through the storied and decorated labyrinths, to the steady beat of gongs. Messengers and notables, scientists and governors, join and leave the lift, and as the great pyramid narrows towards its top and the Tower that stands there more and more of them are Monstruwacans, recognizing her and greeting her silently. It is wine to her spirit. Her chaperone stands behind her and is forgotten.

She remembers when she was new to this task. She used to weep with fear when she went up to her duty. Now the fear still comes, but it is a fear that thrills her even when it loosens her bowels and makes her limbs tremble and her heart pound.

Another day of half-life is over. Soon she will look on the Land again.

The globe is still there. Nothing has changed.

The length of the cycle the Rainbow undergoes has been consistent, plus or minus four percent, for the last seven years. Before the start of the present set of phenomena there was a long, long, period of stability when its stream flowed uninterrupted. There are near-legends of previous mutation, reaching one hundred and sixty thousand years back or more, behind the horizon of record, but these are becoming difficult to understand and interpret because of the creeping historical changes in language and writing that even the customs of the Redoubt can not quite freeze into stasis. The last explorer to reach that region and return died ten thousand years ago and had little to say of the Rainbow except to hint that it was not malignant. The only sure legacy from the distant past is the name.

Some time in the next fourteen hours the cycle will complete.

It is long period of continuous duty for any observer, but a pause in the survey cannot be tolerated at this point. The Senior and one of the other Monstruwacans spell Khresten at the Eye, one hour each, turn and turn about. The older men's' time as seers is long past and their sensitivity has deliberately been trained down so they can endure months of Watch but they can monitor major events like this well enough.

Hours pass. At last the call to her comes. A change is imminent. As the Senior rises and gestures her to take the chair he hesitates: he will co-observe using a secondary link to the Eye and either of them will instantly cut the contact if they see fit. *Take very great care.*

The mind-presence of the Senior guards her back, gazes over her shoulder, like an armored man standing there, but the essential vision is still hers. The picture on the screen comes into the clear focus only a trained seer's mind can provide. She sees that superficially the globe is still the same. But there is a sense of increasing tension, of *thinning*. There are movements within it, refinements of essence. It is coming to a cumulation of development, moving from one cusp of stability to another, and some unbearable climax is approaching. Part of her tries and tries to see more clearly and part of her simply endures the constant strain. Slowly, slowly, it changes.

Now the dark sphere seems to swell minutely, a datum sensed telepathically and translated by her brain as an intolerable visceral pressure, a sense of suffocation and confinement. And now, a pause. More minutes pass while she continues to watch. She does not think of herself at all, she tries to be as much as possible a part of the machine, but the tension grows and grows until the transferred sensations rack her to the point of actual pain.

And now the waiting is over. Intolerably complex forces shift and move. Rigidly controlled panic invades her and she denies to herself that there is any change, but the changes happen and continue to happen and now something inside her shrivels and shrinks away as the black sac of night is visibly and enormously deformed from within. Something is moving, something is about to break free. The vast thing changes with frightening speed and something is Oh so obviously *it is being born.* She cannot watch it and yet she will not retreat, she is reduced to a stone trodden underfoot, the fulcrum of intolerable forces, as the carnivorous Thing emerges, pauses, and vaults clear of the Land, expanding malignantly, filling the Night with a web of sentience.

She cannot coexist with it. Her heart still beats and the mechanisms of her mind and spirit still report but there is an instant when she is not. An Eater, one of the great forces of the Night, has been born and has gone out into the seas of darkness.

It flashes away and vanishes. Almost at once the Rainbow flows again.

Khresten makes her report.

Observation is suspended while the climactic events are analyzed. The Master is there, all the most Senior of the Monstruwacans, where Khresten and her team must come and testify in the high shielded chambers of the Tower. They question her endlessly, repeatedly, study the logs, talk and debate, on and on. They question her, most particularly. The mechanical recordings are open to all, but she was the one who received the faint noisings of Other intelligence that might be interpreted as intention, desire, planning, threat, if such words had any meaning at all when applied to the Eaters. Some fractional essence filtered through to her, and now she tries to express it in words, in mind-pictures, thoughts, movements, not trying to understand but simply to pass on what came from the Land. They watch her and listen to her and hier her with absolute attention.

The consensus, after days of meetings, is that the recent mutations of the Rainbow are probably no threat to the Redoubt. To the watchers of the Land something new must always mean something terrible, but it seems, it seems, that whatever is being birthed in the agonies of that distant fountain of light will at least ignore humanity. That is cause for celebration. Also there is a hint that they have learned something vital and new about the reproductive cycle of the Eaters, or at least of one clade of them. But seers are deliberately kept ignorant of these things to avoid giving them preconceptions of what they might sense in the Land, and Khresten is only allowed to know that perhaps there has been some increment of knowledge, some tiny real gain.

Despite her enforced exclusion from the innermost circle of knowledge there is subtle, measured, profound, praise for her. It does not make her proud or joyful but as she listens to it she knows, at last, that her future is fixed. Not because they have started to ask her questions with a real need to hear her answers and her opinions; not because they defer to her in tiny measure; not because she has finally been told, Yes, a place has been readied for her, she will be welcomed with ceremony and honor; but because she now understands and shares what makes them Monstruwacans.

That Thing, rejoicing in the night. That thing and its myriad peers, who are the true children of the universe. The coming eternities of Darkness belong to them, not to humanity. Light and life only had a brief place during the first beginnings of the cosmos, and the great Redoubt with all its millions is only memory of those days, something that will soon be forgotten, a transient, fragile, hive of dust and insects.

The lash has been laid upon her soul. The scar marks her as a Watcher of Monsters for all her life, married to the Night. When she looks at her peers without speaking to them or touching minds with them she sees the same knowledge in their eyes.

She returns home again. Now she walks the busy streets unafraid. The chatter and shouts of undisciplined minds are just noise: the covert or unconscious looks of lust are as meaningless and automatic as the attraction of the lodestone for a grain of iron. *Of what was I afraid?* she thinks. And she thinks, soon I must leave home, leave and live alone.

But there are problems, when she tells. Her mother argues and argues and then, amazingly, weeps and bawls. Then her sisters start. Khresten submits with a distant patience. She is soon to be of age: there is nothing improper about the move: she will still be within the larger House, the linked series of dwellings where her extended family have dwelt for millennia.

But of course the argument is not about where she will live but about the shape that her future life has now irrevocably taken, as they sense with sure instinct. *It has been decided. It happened to me: I did not do it* she thinks. She refrains from trying to make them understand their own true motives. She is quiet, biddable, patient. She is as kind to them as she possibly can be. The ghosts of childish anger and annoyance stir within her and fall to dust.

Sleep-time comes, still called by custom the night. The argument is still bitter and theoretically unresolved, but they go to their room and prepare for bed. And now the girls huddle and whisper, and now little Mnemmne comes forward, with jhenna and jhenni perched on her wrists. Earnest, and serious, grown-up. This is her final effort.

"See how they love us. You have the Night-hearing, you know they love you. Stay with us, please, Khresten. Don't go away to the Tower forever."

Oh Mnemmne, it is not like that. I have *to go. And yes, I have the Night-hearing, but the butterflies do not love. We imagine they do, because they have grown eyes on their wings that look like funny faces, but they have no minds. There is nothing there: nothing at all. It is all just something we make up.*

"You are lying," says Mnemmne, and hits her, no gentle blow. "I hate you."

It does not matter. Khresten is unmoved. She feels as though she could never be deeply moved or grieved by anything in the Redoubt again. She waits while they talk and they cry and they talk and they cry, and at last it ends. She kisses them both. *No, no; do not talk more. Sleep. This will pass.* Tear-stained, they sleep.

She sleeps, too. Then half-wakes, then sleeps again. The night seems endless. The vents flutter. The gentle moving waves of light on the wall counterfeit the Rainbow: the darker shapes of the furniture seem to writhe. She experiences the ghost or echo of the night-fears she knew as a child, and half-thinking compares it with amusement to the real Fear that visits her as she looks on the Land. But it is bad practice to do that. Half the fight is to stop your mind running away, and even a small indulgence may have to be paid for an hundred times over.

She resettles her thoughts by tallying the night shapes in the room with their day-time reality. The table. The chairs. The butterfly-cage. The long rows of the bookshelves. The tall column of the lamp, now in nighttime mode.

Mnemmne's small fist has left a dark sweet bruise on her hip, which she pets, delicately. She sleeps at last.

She dreams, again, and her mind turns to familiar paths. She dreams yet again that she wakes, and she half-recognizes that she is in the same dream-story, yet a third time.

Will she rise now and go out into the City, and visit the gallery, and look on the Land?

But there is no need for her to go anywhere. What she was going out to find has come to her, and a dark shape bends over her, moving.

It is too real to believe. A man? Here? How? She draws her breath, but before she can cry out, instantly and without movement or transition, it is upon her. *You? Is it you?* She is pinned, she is unable to move, her mind is somehow disconnected from her body. Surely it is a dream. As she is pierced. A touch, a touch, but it is not as it is when she touches herself, not like anything she ever anticipated, not the way she thought it might be at all.

Fuzzy-headed, Khresten awakens.

She hurts, never mind. It is necessary to hurry and there are excuses to make. Where is she going? Up to the Tower of course, but best not to tell them that. There is some fuss now, some nonsense which she forgets at once as she dresses and dons her shoes, walks quickly to the city gate, to the Liftport, limps up the stairs, routinely greets the folk from the cities immediately above and below hers as they gather together.

But modest young Khresten has forgot her veil; a joke! Never mind, she says? And where is her chaperone, ha? And there is some more foolish questioning here too, which she must deflect. But she will not ever need to be accompanied by a chaperone from now on, of course.

A moving town, the lift arrives, and slows so that they may embark. She hastens on board as if she could speed it up that way, and frets and paces as it continues to rise, stopping at every tenth city.

How hungry she is! Starving! She jumps to the refectory, eats pastry and pulses, sips tea. Her heart races. Her mind is full of darting thoughts. She looks around at the moving volumes of the Redoubt's inward parts, the heart and lungs of the pyramid, the passages and airways, as if she had never seen them before.

Her ears pop, the temperature falls slowly, and she dons her hooded coat at a certain height, as she always does. Up and up. Stop after stop, and from time to time need for more foolish words. And now she needs to go to piss. There is only a little blood.

It will not be long now. Yes, soon.

Be patient. I cannot make it go faster by any means.

Be patient.

Here at last is the top, the last stop. Above the last city. Now, past the armed men, up through the long twisting ramps. And here are the guarded Locks that lead up to the Tower and the low-pressure areas.

Now I yeild up the Master-Word to them. Be silent. They will let us pass. Silent.

Do you not need a bell. . . ? Well, never mind. Yes, we will go up quickly.

Now here is the chamber at the root of the Tower, and we call the smaller lift that takes us up the spine of the Tower. No, I will not be challenged, I am an Apprentice, trusted, we can go up safely, there is no rigid schedule for my attendance.

Ten levels more.

Here we are. This way.

Why should anyone stop me? I will show you this as well, that is all. You require to look on the Land. I understand. A brief look will be enough, yes, I understand.

This way.

Here is the chamber we are using. Through that doorway. My team will be within.

And who are these people? Senior Monstruwacans. That one is the Senior of my group.

What?

What?

She starts forward in obedience to the clear instructions. *Kill them. Enter the chamber.* She stops. Her confusion is absolute.

She stands, alone and wild-eyed. The Senior regards her. She has seen the young men's' hands move when they fight, and just so, his mind flashes. She senses his decision to violate courtesy and an instant later his thoughts have invaded hers, irresistibly. The flame of alert that detonates in him washes over her. He cries out words of warning and rushes to seize her, but she too is running, towards the doorway.

She is very fast and very strong. He is far stronger, grappling her with arms like brass, breaking her to her knee, smashing her temple against the door frame, extinguishing her consciousness and blinding what rides it, but he is not quite fast enough.

Through the door she has managed to take another glance at the active, telepathic, screen. Something that had entered her and grown there now joins with another part of itself, coming from elsewhere, and, completed, goes about its own busy purposes.

There is an interval. Then Khresten comes to herself again with broken bloody head. She is lying on the threshold half in and half out of the chamber. The raised edge is sharp pain beneath her.

It is dark. Somewhere an alarm thunders endlessly.

Is this nightmare? Another dream?

If not a dream, then what are these shapes that surround her as she rises to her feet?

What men are so tall, so slim? What men writhe so? What men have so many strange arms or such great dark heads?

The braded columns of darkness rise about her, dancing. They trace the movement of her arms and body, gently touch her back and breast. They glide and dip, kind and gentle towards her alone.

The Master, all the most Senior of her guild, were utterly wrong, it seems. The Flowers are here, come to greet their friend and lover.

They plunge no thorn into her, but all around her is death. The walls have warped and most of the lights are out. Blood spreads. The Senior lies nearby, still, and the rest of the team are scattered among the equipment. Here and there other dark Flowers stir, tapping the still-churning mitochondria of the corpses or the hot energies of the power lines. Some of them are perched horribly, on or somehow inside the heads of the dead men and women, seeming to be rooted, moving very slowly. Compared to the monsters in the Land they are tiny: but mere size, she knows, means little to these beings. And they are growing. They move swiftly and easily. They leave smoothed tracks of altered matter on the floor, where metal and plastic have been invaded by Other life, forced temporarily into new structures, and released back to chaos.

She walks forward and the Flowers permit her to move. They rear up three times and seven times her height. And now six surround her, in a familiar hexagonal pattern. They flutter about her and brush her face, a numbing not-touch, but they do not obstruct her in any way. They seem to regard her as some sort of center to organize themselves around, as they explore this new resource, this new kingdom. She understands now what has been done to her mind, what has lived inside her since that first touch out in the Land, and how she has been deceived in her dreams. Or how she has deceived. Perhaps the Flowers sense her only as some mobile part of the Redoubt, some fertile, receptive, area, some weak spot.

She thinks for an instant of their destruction. She only thinks, only for an instant, because in that instant her mind is compelled to alteration. It is not a threat, but simply the fact, known at a level below communication, that if she has enmity towards them she will cease to exist before she has finished coherently forming the idea. She must remain their friend.

So, she will be a friend. It is a delicate balance: her thoughts flow towards hate, fear, horror, rage, again and again, and each time flinch back as if from a charged rod. But after a few seconds some sort of stability is reached. Now she is able to keep her emotions towards them those of love only. She recites to herself *Do not think hatred. Remember, these are guests.*

She has survived. Perhaps others can. Perhaps she will live for a long time here, above a pyramid of slaves and dancing darkness. And that will be good, of course.

She comes to the screen, still somehow powered up. She picks up on the secondary link with her hands held above the hands of the dead and drained husk that sits there, and she looks out. She regards What hovers there in the night. Then she directs the Eye down and around to observe the radius of the Land just beyond the Circle.

Without surprise she notes what is growing down there. What intends, she supposes, to make of the Redoubt what it has made of the Rainbow, what it has made of her.

Her courage, and her silence, and even her ignorance, are important now.

She knows a little of what is coming. She knows, but will not by any means tell until she must, that lightning gathers and thunder rises in the channels of the ancient machines. Nerved by electronic synapses a million times faster than living flesh or stalking ghost, the Tower has gone into secondary lockdown mode. On the instant of first warning every passage between it and the Redoubt was flooded with incandescent plasmas, and now the corrosive energies that infest its outer shell are being fired to tenfold power. The major structural members are lit, and the vibration spreads from limb to limb. The ancient skeleton is aflame. The decks rock.

It is not simply power that is being mustered. These energies are coded, destructive, cunning, violating, sterilizing. Once confined in any way the pneumavores are surprisingly easy to destroy. The best tools of all are certain subtle subsets of electronic vibratory patterns, but many of the Eaters are delicate enough to be wounded and disrupted by a strong beam of coherent light, and if all else fails enough simple heat will do. The Sharks of the Ether can repattern themselves onto condensed matter and twist it to their will, can pluck out a man's soul by the roots streaming fluid like blood and feast on the delicate, lovely, patterns, but the stones and fires of the early universe are not their proper home. They belong among the seas of electrons, the dust and gas and decaying protons, the delicate streams of plasma, the vacuum, the dying microwave echoes. They belong among the things that are to come, not among the energies of the world's short Youth.

But those energies linger here, burning hot, and the beings bred from them linger too. Bred from those energies and skilled in their use, ten million years of war have not left them defenseless, and they do not have to fully understand their enemies in order to destroy them.

And the Flowers can know nothing of this except what Khresten knows, and, perhaps, allows to slip from her mind to them. This is why the wisdom of the Redoubt selects Khresten and her peers to send their minds out into the Land: why it chooses those like Khresten, who would very freely confess that they are only foolish, ignorant, young men and women.

Now, swiftly, war is declared. The walls of the chamber purl with fire. The floors shake. The doors spark. From every point and edge blooms a ghastly nimbus of light. Khresten's white-ash hair rises with the static charge, where it is not glued down with blood.

The Eye, kept open by some unknowable pressure, is fused, as whatever cunning the Eater was using to keep the path available is checkmated by the ancient simplicity of a six thousand percent overvoltage and a failsafe incendiary. Hissing metal scalds Khresten, and the Flowers dance madly.

She touches the nearest dark web and kisses it, with her mind.

Let me explain, she spieks. *It is very sad for us. But I will tell you what I know.*

The fire is the Tower responding. The cybernetics are fast. The Eye-terminal fused because the alarms have destroyed it. And the shields are up, not only round the Tower, but between the levels as well. The Tower, the machines, are fighting us. Not the men, not yet. It is only the machines we fight.

Can you kill the machines? Can you Eat their souls?

We are confined to this level and soon this level will be split up into tiny parts. Then each part will be burned clean and everything in it will be destroyed. But I will try to help you. I will do everything I can. I am trying to warn you now. It was so brave of you, to change yourselves, to make yourselves tiny and explore here, in this inferno. You only wish to live and grow, as all things do. I understand. I do not blame you. How you must hunger, out in the Land.

But there, at the door.

You see it turn silver-white? You do not like that fire, do you? I see you too can die. Oh, that is sad. That is sad. What can be done? How can we save ourselves?

Be very still. Perhaps the fire will not destroy us all. Retreat to me. I will do everything I can to help you. I understand.

I will protect you. It is only the machines we face. It is not the men yet.

Yes, the machines are terrible. But when the men come, you will know Fear.

Her left hand, unregarded, has been writing something over and over again on the surfaces around her, dipping back to the side of her head to pick up its red ink and then fluttering out again. It is writing over and over again in the darting strokes of the set-speech BEWARE DREAMS SEERS BEWARE YOUR DREAMS, she is right-handed, it is in reversed mirror script. She will not think about her left hand and anyway she cannot see well to that side anymore since she struck her head so hard.

She has left her message. Now there is only one other thing to do.

Far below, the bowels of the Redoubt shunt more and more energy to the defense. Mechanism after mechanism goes offline. The ventilators, the fans, the air and water pumps, are temporarily shut down as valves seat against reflux, and floods of power become available. The lifts cease to move. All industry stills. Throughout the pyramid and the Underground Country the lights dim.

The whole Redoubt braces for combat. In the cities, everywhere, there is the racing of armed men, but the Air Clog is unbreached, the temporary pneumavore activity at ground level outside it fading, and it will not be that kind of fight. Instead, the Earth-current, normally diverted into a hundred quiet streams, is being shaped to flow upward for one single purpose, to be forged and barbed by the instrumentalities of the Tower into a sword of defense.

The outer shell of the Tower is totally sealed. The sensors that were acting as paths have been destroyed, internal barriers have successfully prevented any spread of corruption within the structure, and the passages between it and the Redoubt are incandescent, triply impassable. The defense has held firm, above and below. The surviving Monstruwacans turn to counterattack. It is time to harrow the heart of the invasion.

The energies of the Tower are concentrated on the single infected level, and each segment is sterilized and cleared off in turn. Platoons of shielded and nightsuited Watchmen advance through secured areas in the practiced and ordered succession, setting the touchpoints, channeling and guiding the rivers of light. Before them, plastic burns, flesh burns, metal burns. Planes of lightning crisscross the open spaces as the air burns and then submits to its duty, conducting the patterns of hatred and defense which web the structure, tighter and tighter.

If need be, the entire Tower can be melted like a candle. But that will not be necessary.

Khresten stands amid a shrinking crowd of otherness and weeps to see each of them die and vanish. Ozone and nitrous oxides scorch her lungs. She bleeds, she staggers. Not long, now.

The walls belly and drip fire. The hammering pulses invade the raised metal overfloor to a chorus of lightnings, and half the remaining Flowers wink out of existence. Others cling on to dead flesh, to the few remaining insulated structures, or to Khresten herself, protected by the console. They do not take revenge and do not attempt to communicate with her again. *We do not understand them either,* she thinks. *So must it always be.*

The last of them vanishes. Did they ever really spiek to her? Did her mind translate the unknowable into some sort of likeness of humanity? Was what she rendered to herself as dream speech and touch no more a communication than are the tropisms of a plant's root seeking nourishment? Than the butterfly-lure on her wrists?

It does not matter.

Like a swimmer clawing up out of murdering black water, she is herself again, her mind her own. She can see the armored men approaching between the overlapping curtains of brilliance, but there is no rescue for her there, no touch, no warm community of life ever again. She is the enemy. All that remains of the invasion is the thing inside her, the thing that she now she feels, again, somehow interfering with her thoughts.

But you have not behaved well. She thinks. *Not at all in the way that is proper for a guest.*

I would be quit of you.

And now.

What is the proper, the graceful, way to go about this?

The room is a hell of light and power, brighter and brighter.

She kneels down, lies down, embraces the fire, opens herself to it.

Does one of the watching warriors salute her?

The fire is not hot, but it erases all complexity in matter or energy, reducing it identically to molecular and electronic uniformity, be it flesh or cyber or ghost. There is no pain, only numbness as the nerves are destroyed. It burns through her seeking Otherness. It unpicks each cell. It illuminates, from inside, the delicate bones of her skull and the flakes of her back.

They will seal this level, and when they have examined it they will burn every particle of matter in it to ash and gas, and name it Forbidden. They will read her message in burned blood on the burned metal and they will burn it and burn her, too.

But they will learn from her words and they will praise her, for she was faithful, she made a good end.

www.ingramcontent.com/pod-product-compliance
Lightning Source LLC
Chambersburg PA
CBHW020612310726
48979CB00008B/1448/J
* 9 7 8 1 5 9 2 2 4 6 7 8 6 *